VOICE OF REASON

BY

KERRY BARNES

Acknowledgements

Being dyslexic can prove to be an issue when it comes to editing, so I am thankful that I have an editor that knows the mistakes I could make before even I do. I would like to thank Robert Wood, from Epworth Editing, for all the hard work that has gone into editing this book and for the long hours he has spent getting this one right.

Thank you to all the loyal readers who have supported me so much in my career and who I will always be so grateful to.

Facebook Group Gangland Governor – Thank you so much.

Other books by Kerry Barnes

Ruthless

Ruby's Palace

Raw Justice

***

Cruel Secrets

Wicked Lies

Ugly Truth

Raising a Gangster

***

The Hunted

The Rules

The Choice

***

Deceit

PROLOGUE

July 1980

As the footsteps behind her were gaining momentum, she felt the hairs on the back of her neck stand on end. It was dark, and the only light came from the soft glow of the moon. The gravestones looked creepy, but it was the sound coming from behind her that was putting her on edge. *Christ, pull yourself together.* It's only another person, probably taking the short cut she was. The icy footpath and rambling brambles were making the walk more difficult. With her high heels and tight miniskirt, she was not wearing the ideal outfit to make a run for it. She should have stopped at four gin and tonics; that fifth had pushed her into a place where her legs felt wobbly. And the buzzing sound in her ears irritated her. Still, she wasn't completely drunk; she could make it home in one piece, couldn't she?

She tried to quicken her pace. The heavy footsteps were almost upon her. It was at that point she realised she was actually afraid because she couldn't bring herself to look round. She hoped it was someone she knew, from the party maybe, making their way home. Surely, they would call her name? But there was only silence, with just the sound of those heavy footsteps getting closer and closer.

Ahead, the path looked very dark, hidden by the enormous trees, whose branches were so bent they made a tunnel of blackness. She winced as one of the blackberry brambles, which had grown across the path, became wedged between her toes and the sole of her shoe. The sharp prickles tore at her foot and stopped her dead in her tracks. She had to bend down to unravel the rogue weed before it ripped more of her skin. In a panic, she tried to undo the buckle on the side of her black stiletto sandal, still aware of the looming figure behind her. The footsteps had stopped, and now there was complete silence. The sharp thorns dug into her finger, and yet she was numb with fear. But she had to get away. This place was sinister, and the presence of someone behind her conjured up images from a horror scene.

At last, the bramble was free. But no sooner had she stood up to run than a big, heavy hand covered her mouth. Before she could wriggle or fight, she was being dragged into the darkness. Tightening the grip around her mouth, he yanked her up until her feet were off the ground. Without a word, he threw her down with such force that her head hit the trunk of a tree and stunned her.

She couldn't see his features; the baggy hood that covered his head also cast dark shadows across his face. What shocked her most, though, was his size – compared to her, he was humungous. His reticence made him all the more scary. He didn't have to speak; she could sense his determination. His deep breaths and grating growl, as he inhaled through his mouth, said it all.

.

Too afraid to move, she lay there staring up at the monster, and suddenly the reflection of a sharp object in his hand, glistening in the moonlight, caught her eye.

He dropped to his knees, and, like a wild animal, he ripped the clothes off her, throwing her around like a rag doll, until she was completely naked.

In desperation, her eyes became transfixed on the knife. Of course, he could have killed her with his bare hands, but, for some reason, she just couldn't take her eyes away from the sharp object. All the time it was there on the ground and not in her attacker's hand, she felt she had a chance to survive. Consumed by terror, she didn't struggle or scream, and she couldn't look at the man who she knew was about to abuse her dainty body.

With the alcohol in her system and the overwhelming fear, her assailant became the image of the Devil. Pushing her legs apart and tearing into her, he was a beast, a huge animal, ripping her insides. She didn't feel pain; it was as if she'd left her body and was watching from across the path, and yet she still managed to stare at the knife on the ground, even though it was too far to reach it. The horrendous, vile groans, the savage moans, and the smell of death were embedded in her memory, and they would never leave until the day she would die.

CHAPTER ONE

The Mason brothers were close and had been taught well by Archi, their father. He'd once been a well-known face in the South East, and it was obvious that his boys would no doubt take on some of his ways. Geoff, the biggest and the eldest at twenty-two, could handle himself, although he didn't like to get his hands dirty. His olive skin and dark eyes, with a mop of thick black hair, turned heads, just as Archi had done in his youth. In his suits and freshly ironed shirts, Geoff always looked immaculate; he was far from a two-bit scallywag. He was a charmer who had a knack for turning a penny into a pound. His sleek and discreet ways gave him respect among the older villains, and soon the way was paved for the Mason brothers' business. It started out with a few clients and a decent marijuana supplier, until Geoff got a full handle on the game.

But it was Luke, a year younger than Geoff, who managed to skyrocket their business with an idea he had. He'd designed a fuel tank with a separate compartment inside, so any nosy customs official, who wanted to search the vehicles, would never find the marijuana hidden inside. As the money rolled in, Geoff soon realised that Luke, with his muscle and brains, was really an equal partner. Luke wasn't like Geoff at all. He was a little shorter, thinner, and had fair hair with almond-shaped eyes. His face was always stern and his moves were more calculated compared to Geoff, who always offered generous smiles and who laughed a lot. However, because Luke was by far the stronger of the two, and, although Geoff didn't want to admit it, the cleverer, the brothers gained a serious reputation on the streets. Dean, the youngest brother, at only eighteen, was exactly like Geoff, except he was chubbier and had a more rounded face, but his cheeky charm had no doubt been copied from Geoff.

* * *

It was one evening in July 1998 when the family were sitting at the kitchen table to begin their meal cooked by Miriam, their mother.

The mood was sombre. Luke was upset because his girlfriend, Beverley Childs, had taken a job on a cruise ship. Her decision effectively finished their relationship. But they hadn't ended on bad terms – far from it. Each of them knew that if they were still free agents when or even if she returned, they could pick up where they left off.

Interrupted by the bang at the front door, Miriam tutted. She hated anyone calling at dinner time. And she wasn't expecting it to be Dean because if he didn't have his key he would have used the back door.

'Get that, Archi, will you? I've got me hands full here!' Miriam said, gesticulating with the saucepan in one hand and the gravy ladle in the other.

'If Dean's forgotten his key again, I'll bleedin' make him a necklace, so he can wear the sodding thing around his neck.'

But the second Archi opened the door, Dean fell into his arms. His bloody and swollen face looked shocking. Archi held him up and guided him into the kitchen.

Instantly, Luke jumped up from his chair and helped his brother to a seat and crouched down, lifting Dean's head to see what injuries he'd sustained.

Miriam placed the saucepan down, pushed Luke aside, and began lifting Dean's shirt. She was frantic with worry that her baby may have internal injuries. When she pulled his shirt completely up, she could see to her horror the red marks across his chest, which were so horrifically shown by the clear outline of a boot.

'Get him to the hospital!' she screamed.

Archi took on a different look. It was one only Miriam had seen in their younger days when her husband was pretty much a tough bastard. He wouldn't stand anyone treading on his toes. They would get what-for and with a nasty tool to go with it. His favourite was a hammer, and so he earned the nickname 'Jackhammer'.

Little did he know that sitting at the table was a boy much like himself who was festering with rage. It was Luke, not Geoff, the bigger son, but Luke, the more unassuming, quieter boy. But that night, they really got to know the depth of his anger and retribution.

Geoff was hooting and hollering and threatening to smash whoever it was who had beaten up his little brother.

Miriam was fussing over Dean and looking at the damage to his body, using a dishcloth to wipe away the blood.

Archi stared at Luke, who was as white as a ghost. He held a look that Archi had never seen before but it was one that he easily identified.

Luke, who was staring vacantly, suddenly shouted, 'Shut the fuck up!'

The room fell quiet as everyone stared at him.

In a quick movement, he leaned forward into Dean's ear. 'Who, where, and when, Dean?' His tone was so cold: there was no shouting or screeching but a dark foreboding element to his voice.

Archi may have raised his boys to be tough and to handle themselves, but it was Luke who really had it in him. Because if ever there was someone the dead spit of him, then it was his middle boy, the real fucker in the family. And that was where he recognised the incensed look: it was his own expression.

Dean's head was bobbing up and down as if he were drunk. He turned his battered head to face Luke. But with his eyes almost closed, he could hardly see now.

Miriam snivelled into a tea towel. 'Christ, he is just a baby, only eighteen. Who would do this?'

'Shut it, Mother, please,' said Luke.

They waited in silence until Dean could form any words.

His headache was so severe and his lips were so badly torn that he had great difficulty in focusing on his brother. 'Callum . . . Callum Stracken . . . and his two brothers, Ryan and Curtis. I'm sorry . . . I just wanted to earn money like you two . . . I wanted to show him I'm not too young . . .'

Miriam poured him a glass of water. ''Ere, Son, sip this.'

Luke held his hand up to keep her away; he wanted to hear the facts. 'But why, Dean?'

'They robbed the post office, and I was the lookout. Then they fucked me off. The bastards wouldn't pay me. When I argued, they bashed me up.'

Archi watched as Luke's eyes turned almost black and his breathing intensified. 'Did they use a tool, Dean?'

Dean shook his head. 'No. They just kept kicking me and said they would take off me limbs, one by one, if I ever approached them again.'

Luke grabbed Geoff's arm. 'Come on. I'm gonna show them what taking a limb off actually means.'

Miriam tried to stop them, but Archi pulled her back. 'Leave it, Mir. You get our Dean down to A & E. The boys can't stand back and let this go.'

'But what if they get hurt?'

His expression said it all. 'They won't get hurt, but God help the Strackens, that's all I can say.'

Miriam glanced at her husband's face. He had aged but he was still handsome. He looked very Italian except his hair was now grey and thinner and his brows were heavy. She often wondered where his complexion came from since both his parents were of Irish descent.

* * *

The Abbeyfield Estate in Bermondsey, a mixture of high-rise and low-rise blocks, varied in design from the chequerboard gables to the chunks of bland concrete structures. A depressing place, even on a warm, sunny day, it also had a reputation of its own for drugs, violence, and prostitution.

One of its residents, Callum Stracken, a flash bastard, was working his way to the top as a local face, with his brothers not far behind him. All he needed was a pat on the back from his father. Dressed in his new suit and ready for a night on the town, he headed across the road from his house to his newly polished car. Their family, known for being trouble, were feared by the neighbours. As young kids running around with their red hair and milky skin, they'd invariably caused mayhem. They were bullies, but now, as young men, they ran the estate with an iron fist. Ryan was the eldest, with beady green eyes; he was the ugliest of the three. Then there was Callum, who was a cocky kid. He too wasn't much of a babe magnet. The youngest, who at least had some meat on his arms, was Curtis.

Ryan, with his loud mouth, and a name for violence, took what he wanted: puff, cocaine, and even women who worked the streets. Too ugly to get his own girlfriend, he took freebies from the local brasses.

No one argued because they didn't want to face the whole family. One cross word directed towards the Strackens would have the entire clan on their backs. The Strackens knew no different: it was their manor, and all the goodies circling, from fake trackies to bags of ecstasy tablets, were theirs for the taking.

The day Carmel, a close friend of Tilly Naylor's, was attacked by the Strackens was the day a very clear message was sent around the estate. The brutality shown was to put the fear of God into anyone who was stupid enough to think the Strackens had at least an ounce of moral values.

Carmel was only a young mother at the time. With nothing much more than the clothes she stood in and a baby in a second-hand buggy, she made her way along the piss-smelling walkway of a block of maisonettes. She had to swallow the fact that the council had put her at the very top of the block, and so there would be no lift and three flights of concrete stairs to drag the buggy up and down. But having been in a bedsit for the first few months in a shared home, she grabbed the offer to have her own place with both hands.

The weather was bitterly cold, forcing her to pull her jacket around her thin body, but at least her baby was warm in a snug blanket. Battling against the icy wind, she hurried to get to the doctor's before it closed. Her baby had a chest infection and she needed another course of antibiotics. Not in the best of moods, she marched ahead, with her head down. So she didn't see the three lads walking towards her until she was actually physically pushed aside.

Carmel kept herself to herself, except to visit Tilly, a former schoolmate, so she had no idea what the Strackens looked like. But she'd heard of them. Everyone had in this part of South London. All she knew was that they were scumbags who no one would want to cross.

Carmel was no wimp and was used to sticking up for herself, but, stupidly, she yelled out at the three lads, 'Oi, watch what ya doing, you fucking idiots.'

Callum, Curtis, and Ryan all stopped dead in their tracks. Then Ryan spun round, grabbed Carmel by the throat and ruthlessly punched her in the face. Callum ripped the buggy from Carmel – with the baby still inside – and, in one movement, he hung it over the balcony.

Carmel screamed in horror and almost fainted. Her little baby wasn't fully strapped in. One false move, and her daughter would tumble down three floors. 'I-I'm sorry. Please don't hurt her.'

With a sickly laugh, Callum pulled the buggy back from over the balcony and glared at her. 'You ever talk to me like that again, bitch, and, next time, I'll drop that little rug rat.'

Ryan let go of the woman and gently slapped her face. 'Well, me brother must be in a good fucking mood. This is your lucky day.'

Gasping for breath and with her hands trembling, Carmel snatched the buggy and ran as far away from the three men as she could.

A few neighbours had seen the altercation but had decided it was for the best not to intervene for fear of their flats being burned out.

The Strackens never liked to fight one-on-one. They always ganged together, like a pack of wolves.

* * *

As far as Callum was concerned, Dean had been an easy target, eager to be part of a gang and make money to show his brothers he was worthy, but being a Stracken, Callum had no morals and no intention of paying Dean a penny. Also, Callum wanted any excuse to give Dean a good kicking and hopefully ruin his good looks because secretly he wanted Tilly, Dean's girlfriend, for himself. He suspected she only had eyes for Dean and wouldn't even give the steam of her piss to the likes of him, so this was an opportunity to get even.

Tilly had grown up in Bermondsey along with Dean. But that changed when Archi had enough money to move away and upgrade to a finer house in Greenwich. Miriam and Tilly's mother, June, continued to meet for coffee, and the kids maintained their friendship. Growing into teenagers, they were inseparable, and Dean would often jump on the bus and head back to Bermondsey to hang around with her.

That's how he managed to get in with the Strackens. But after the kicking, he wished he never had.

* * *

Luke became more irate as the traffic began to build up. His silence was a sure sign he was ready to explode.

Geoff accompanied him, knowing that he would have to be the one in control and ensure that Luke didn't go over the top and be had up for murder. Right at that moment, Geoff knew that Luke was ready to smash the life out of the Stracken brothers. Nothing and no one would stand in his way.

They eventually pulled up outside Tilly's two-up two-down where she lived with her mother. Geoff waited in the car, while Luke impatiently banged on the door.

Dressed in a pink velour tracksuit and her hair in a ponytail, Tilly pulled the door open, with a big rosy-cheeked smile. Seeing the seething look on Luke's face, she gasped.

'What is it? What's happened?' she cried, throwing her hands to her mouth.

'Tilly, Dean's been bashed up by the Strackens, and I want you to get in the car and show me where they live.'

Tilly was only eighteen herself and felt nervous. She knew how bad the Strackens were and what they were capable of. She'd seen the marks on Carmel's face, and after hearing what the bastards had done to the baby, it had filled her with pure fear. 'Oh my God, is Dean all right?'

'No, he ain't fucking all right! They've kicked the fucking life out of him. Now, come on, Tilly. We ain't got time for this. I wanna know where these scumbags live.'

At that point, Tilly didn't know who was more dangerous, the Strackens or Luke, since she'd never seen his face contorted with so much hate. But without a second to waste, she followed Luke and hopped into the back seat of his plush new Jaguar. Really, they could have walked, but Tilly didn't think; she was numb with shock. Her Dean kicked near to death by those three ruthless ginger tyrants was just unimaginable.

The Strackens' house was just on the edge of the estate. It was as scummy looking as they were. The front garden was overgrown, and blue graffiti had been daubed on the crumbling garden wall. The ripped net curtains were grey with dust, and the paint was peeling off the front door.

Luke brazenly parked directly outside and waited for a few seconds until he'd got his thoughts together.

Geoff was more nervous than he'd let on because the reputation of the Strackens preceded them. Inside, he was annoyed that his youngest brother had even thought about getting caught up with low life like this family, and he was even more angry that he was about to pick up the pieces.

Suddenly, without a word, Luke leaped from the car and lifted the boot. With a monkey wrench in one hand and a hammer in the other, he marched down the garden path like a lone wolf on his mission. He banged on the door so hard that the hammer nearly took the door off its hinges.

Geoff knew that was a mistake because the likelihood was all three brothers could be in the house, and possibly others as well. He hurried after his brother to find the door opening.

Standing in his shorts and a joint in his mouth was Ryan. Before he even had a chance to breathe or gasp, the hammer came smashing down, cracking Ryan on the head. The impact was so significant that he hit the deck instantly.

Curtis left the living room, to see who was at the door, only to find Luke Mason beating his brother about the head with a hammer. The scene was shocking in itself, but it wasn't just the blood spurting up the wall, but the calm and cruel look on Luke's face, as he brutally attacked Ryan in silence. Curtis turned to run down the hallway, but he was chased by Geoff, who didn't have a weapon in his hand.

Luke left Ryan on the floor and stepped over him, still holding his weapons, with the hammer dripping in blood. As he marched into the living room, he saw Curtis and Geoff throwing punches. But as soon as Luke appeared, they stopped.

Whether it was the complete look of a deranged killer or the fact that Luke was wielding two weapons, who knew? But one thing was for sure: Curtis was cornered.

Luke took over. He grabbed Curtis' arm and threw him to the ground. The silence was more terrifying than anything.

Curtis could handle his assailants shouting abuse at him, but the lingering silence sent an avalanche of disturbing thoughts through his mind. He couldn't take his eyes off the towering silhouette in front of him.

Like something from the movie *The Texas Chainsaw Massacre*, Luke gripped the tools even harder, as the only sounds to be heard were the groans from the injuries sustained by Ryan and his own measured breathing.

Curtis could almost taste the hate in the room and feel Luke's eyes boring into him. It wasn't real, surely? He was just having a nightmare, and the vision would disappear the second he woke up. But it was no dream. He really was staring into the dark, evil eyes of a psychopath.

Even Geoff was unnerved by his brother's vacant expression and towering stance. It was as if the nutter inside him had been released.

Finally, in one fluid movement, Luke swung the hammer. Curtis' shins were the targets as Luke smashed each one mercilessly.

Tilly, who had remained in the car, could hear the blood-curdling screams, even with the windows closed. Her hands trembled, and as the vomit at the back of her throat began to rise, she swallowed hard to keep it down.

Luke stared down at the mangled mess he'd made of Curtis' legs, and a crooked grin lifted his cheek. 'Now then, you are gonna call Callum.' He paused and looked down at the dripping hammer. 'Or, I'll give you the same as I gave Ryan.'

Curtis was crying, his splintered shins causing him to convulse in pain. 'Please God! No, please!' he begged, through snot and tears. 'Please, no more!'

The hammer came up, and this time, Luke smashed it into Curtis' shoulder.

Hearing the sounds of even louder guttural screams coming from the house, Tilly covered her ears in alarm.

'All right, please, please stop. I'll call him.'

Geoff snatched the old dirty landline phone from the side table that was covered in ash and Rizlas. He placed it in front of Curtis and stepped back. His hands shook in shock from watching his brother in action.

With pain shooting down both his legs, Curtis was in agony. His left hand trembled as he dialled the number. He decided he would say whatever was asked because he knew by the psychotic look on Luke's face that the hammer would cave his head in if he didn't do as he was told.

'What?' came the ugly sounding voice down the phone.

With gasps of breath and a terrified voice, Curtis said, 'Callum . . . quick . . . you have to come home.'

Curtis replaced the receiver and looked up nervously at Luke, praying that the hammer would stay by his side and not be lifted in the air again.

Geoff walked back to the hallway and nudged Ryan with his boot to see if he was still alive. The moaning and groaning told him all he needed to know – his brother hadn't murdered him yet, thank God.

Curtis was now puking all over the rotten carpet. The pain was excruciating. He needed the hospital, but, until this was over, he knew he was going nowhere.

*   *   *

In The Windsor, on the Old Kent Road, Callum was enjoying a few pints of London Pride. At least he had been until the phone call a few minutes ago. It had stirred an unsettled feeling in his stomach. Curtis had never sounded so nervous.

Leaving his pint still almost half-full on the counter, he rushed out of the pub and legged it to his nine-year-old Mercedes, before setting off at speed to his home. It didn't take his brain long to work out what had been going on in his absence. That little shit Dean Mason must have returned and brought a brother with him. Callum feared no one and wasn't worried about any of the Masons. After all, who were they? He was the boss in these parts. He had the rep, and he was the face.

He pulled up behind Luke's new Jaguar, and that hit a nerve; he'd always wanted a flash car. Then he saw Tilly in the back. He wanted her too. His annoyance reached an angry pitch, and as reckless as he was, he flipped open his boot and pulled out his metal cosh.

As he rushed up the path, to the opened front door, he spotted the blood up the wall in the entrance, and his eldest brother lying curled up in a ball on the floor. Without thinking, he charged in past Ryan, straight into the lion's den.

Geoff was behind the door, and as soon as Callum entered, he cracked him hard on the side of the head, with the wrench that he'd taken from Luke.

The clout was so harsh that Callum saw stars and barely managed to keep himself upright. Staggering into the living room, his vision cleared. That was when he saw Luke properly, standing like a monster, with blood splattered on his face, and his hands white from gripping a hammer. Callum's eyes then focused on Curtis, who was lying on his side and grasping his legs, his face drenched in pain. It was too much for Callum to take in, and so he aimlessly swung the cosh and hoped it would hit Luke. But the pain from Geoff's blow to his head blurred his vision again.

Luke stepped back from Callum's cosh, and a high-pitched chuckle gave even his own brother the creeps.

The unearthly stare and the sickly grin freaked Callum out. He dropped the cosh and held his hands up. 'Please, mate, I don't want no trouble. What do you want from me?'

Slowly and emphatically, Luke nodded, and with deliberate, clear words he said, 'You threatened to take a limb off my brother.'

Callum's eyes were wide, and his pale skin was almost translucent as the blood drained from his face. 'No, no, I didn't mean it.' His arms fell down by his side as he shot a glance at Geoff, hoping this was some kind of joke.

But Geoff was staring at Luke. The statement was clear enough: even Geoff was just as anxious about what his brother would do.

'Look, please, mate, I wouldn't really take off a limb. Christ, that's sick. I only gave him a kicking. Look.' He held his hands up again. 'I'm sorry. I wouldn't hurt the kid, not like that. I swear to ya.'

Luke stood there menacingly silent, still with that sick, twisted smirk. 'I've never seen what it looks like to cut off a limb. Have you, Geoff?'

Callum shot another glance at Geoff for any form of help, but Geoff's expression was frozen.

Looking at the hammer still dripping with blood, Luke gave an exaggerated sigh. 'Geoff, do you have an axe in the boot?'

Callum felt a trickle down his leg and realised he'd wet himself, but, worse, he could feel his bowels moving of their own accord. The vision of having one of his limbs savagely cut from him made him retch. And the demonic look in Luke's eyes, told him there was no getting away. His only hope was to scream, like a girl. Taking a deep breath, he let out a blood-curdling cry that made Geoff jump.

Out of panic, Geoff hit Callum again with the monkey wrench, knocking him clean off his feet.

That's when Luke raised the hammer, and with a tirade of blows, he smashed Callum's legs until the bones turned to mush. Then he looked up at his traumatised brother, winked, and flicked his head to indicate they should leave.

Geoff had to lean against the car before he could get inside. The contents of his stomach were rising, and he didn't want to mess up Luke's motor.

As he took a few deep breaths, he noticed a remarkably tall man watching from the alley between two houses opposite. He seemed odd in the fact he was wearing a coat with a wide hood covering his head and most of his face – and on this warm evening too. He couldn't be sure, but he thought he'd seen him a long time ago outside their school during a morning break. In fact, he remembered having nightmares about the man. He shuddered and hurried inside the car.

'Luke, do you know who that geezer is? Have you seen him before?'

Luke craned his neck, but he couldn't see anyone.

'Fucking hell, Geoff, there's no one there. Let's just get home, eh.'

Geoff wondered if he was having dark thoughts because Luke had acted like some lunatic and it had made him uneasy. Perhaps the tall dark looming figure had been a figment of his imagination.

*   *   *

That was the day the brothers knew that Luke had proved he was not only the fiercest fighter out of the three of them, but, when pressed, he became unhinged and could easily have had the Devil himself shitting hot bricks.

From then on, anyone else who tried to muscle in or cause trouble would assume that all the brothers had the same reckless mentality, and so the Masons had secured a reputation that would see them okay for the future.

Out of fear of retribution, Tilly moved into Miriam's house. And not long after that, she and Dean were expecting their first child, Lee. She had nursed Dean's wounds while showing the family how much she loved their son, and so Miriam treated her like the daughter she'd never had.

Callum remained in hospital for months. He was unable to regain the full use of his legs and was on crutches permanently. Ryan suffered from his head injuries, never speaking a clear word after that. Curtis wasn't the same either; he suffered nightmares and refused to go out, becoming a mumbling recluse.

Naturally, the Strackens held a serious grudge. They vowed that one day they would get even with the Masons.

CHAPTER TWO

2003

Dressed in an ivory satin camisole and French knickers, Dionne Stuart, with chiselled cheekbones, long legs, and a high and generous bust, looked at herself in the mirror. She smiled as she turned her face side to side admiring the professional make-up and then fingered her thick auburn waves, which bounced off her shoulders. She knew that she would look good in her wedding dress. Not many women could get away with wearing a slim fitted satin fishtail with an open back, but she could, at just twenty-three. She was a size 8 on a bad day. *Heads will turn*, she thought. She smiled again. Her self-appraisal was halted when she heard her mother's voice calling to her from the hallway.

'Dionne, love, Josey's here.'

Dionne looked out of the bedroom window to see her old schoolfriend Josey Ward getting out of her boyfriend's battered black Ford Focus.

Josey, six months younger than Dionne, couldn't compete with her friend's looks, being a mere five foot three, small-breasted, and with her skin covered in acne, although her light-brown hair was cut in a fashionable bob style. Always in Dionne's shadow, she couldn't match her friend's extrovert personality. She looked up and gave Dionne a timid wave.

Dionne snatched herself away from the window and marched down the stairs to find Lillian, her mother, at the foot of the stairs with a ridiculous grin on her ruddy cheeks.

Wearing a printed dress that looked as though it had been bought from a charity shop and high heels worn down to nothing, Lillian, at fifty, could have passed for someone a good twenty years older. She actually felt that old. At just over five foot two but over ten stone, Lillian was clearly showing signs of middle-aged spread, but she couldn't exercise because her bones ached most mornings. Her husband Thomas had described her as a real looker in her younger days. However, her once pretty looks had now been replaced with baggy eyes, permanently florid cheeks, and wispy grey hair that needed plenty of TLC. In fact, she looked like a dog's dinner in comparison to her daughter.

As Dionne walked into the living room, she ignored Josey, who was standing by the fireplace wearing a bridesmaid dress that Dionne knew full well had been hired for the occasion because there was no way Josey would have been able to afford *that* little number.

Seeing the photographer getting out his equipment, Dionne tutted. It was a joke. How could she have her photo taken in this dump, of all places. Standing there in her parents' grubby, well-worn living room, with peeling wallpaper and a frayed carpet, she cringed. *No matter how much the photographer edited those pictures, it still boiled down to the fact that you can't polish a turd*, she thought.

'Don't you dare take any photos in here!' she snapped.

The photographer waved his hand and got up to leave. 'I'll take them when you get into your car, then.'

Dionne shot him a glare. 'And make sure you don't have the house in the background.'

She turned to her mother. 'And why ain't you flaming well dressed? The cars will be here soon!'

Sadness crept over her mother's face as she looked down at her summer dress with pretty blue flowers printed in the fabric. 'Oh, well, I, er, I *am* dressed.' She wanted to tell her daughter that she'd saved up and searched the whole of Bromley High Street to find the right outfit and had managed to buy the dress in Peacocks in their sale. But she realised that her daughter was used to shopping in the designer shops now and would no doubt find her purchase from a high street shop an insult to her wedding.

Dionne, hot and flustered while trying to climb into the tight-fitting dress without creasing it, snapped back, 'For fuck's sake, Mother. It's my *wedding*. Couldn't you at least have had your fucking hair done?'

Lillian looked over at the mirror above the fireplace and sighed. She smoothed down the few wispy curls that had sprung up and then sighed again. She'd *had* her hair washed and set that morning before Dionne had even got out of bed. And she'd purchased Rimmel pink shimmer lipstick specially for the occasion. She knew she couldn't look like the other women who would be there. They all had money. She had bugger all, except for the few pounds she'd hidden in her shoe away from her husband – who would have pinched it for a bottle of rum. Her face took on an over-the-top smile, hoping, at least, to get half a grin back from her daughter.

'There . . . just the moisture in the air, that's all, my darling,' she said, trying to flatten the frizz.

Dionne tutted again – even louder this time.

'Josey, help me with the shoes, will you? I can't fucking do them up in this dress.'

Josey looked at Lillian and gave a sad smile as if to say 'sorry'.

*　*　*

From Dionne's side of the family, only her best friend and mother were invited. Her father wasn't because he liked a good drink and would end up pissing someone off. And her mother was an embarrassment, always fussing over her as if she was still a kid. Nevertheless, if she hadn't invited her, then there would have been questions, and she simply couldn't be bothered to have to explain herself.

She also had no choice but to get ready in her old home – her parents' home – and she hated it.

As Dionne's only friend, Josey agreed to be her bridesmaid, but really she didn't even want to go to the wedding. She wasn't daft; she knew that Dionne was just using her.

When they were both single, Dionne wanted a drinking partner and of course someone just to walk into the clubs with. Initially, Josey, who was habitually shy, found it fun and thoroughly enjoyed their nights out. It started as a game. The thrill of getting all glammed up in pursuit of flirting with a decent fella was all a laugh to begin with. But, then, Dionne became obsessed with it all, and that's when the fun wore off.

Once she'd set her sights on Luke, Josey could see Dionne was like a woman possessed and was all over him like a cheap suit. Watching her parading in front of Luke was embarrassing. Her skirts got shorter, her tops were lower, and her make-up was even heavier. It was as if she had a plan, and like a game of archery, Luke was to be the bullseye. And the day that Dionne secured a date was the day she dropped Josey like a hot brick. Josey felt hurt at the time, but now what pissed her off the most was that the more money Dionne had, the more she looked down her nose at people. They'd both come from nothing, and Josey still had very little, but at least she had her pride, unlike Dionne.

Heath, Josey's much older boyfriend, whom she'd met at the Masons' club The Allure around the same time, was an honest, hard-working man, who could never quite fit in with Dionne's boyfriend and his lot. So, there were no double dates or dinner parties between the four of them, and Josey knew it was because her so-called friend, who had expected her to make an irresponsible comment about their past, didn't want to be shown up. *God forbid she would ever have done that*, Josey thought.

Dionne lapped up the attention, the money, and the status. She was Luke's girl, and that meant she had respect. Long gone were the days when she would finish work at the hairdressers' on a Friday, take her wage packet, and go in search of a cheap outfit for the Saturday night drink with Josey. She didn't have to work now. She was given a credit card to buy whatever the fuck she wanted, and she made sure she rinsed it. Her hair was done every week, and she could have the sunbed tan like the other girlfriends and look brown all year round. Her Luke expected no less. He revelled in the fact that his soon-to-be young wife was a looker, with the perfect figure. Whatever she wore, she looked sleek, and her height gave her a model-like appearance.

Lillian tried to help her daughter by buttoning up the lower back of the dress.

'Mother, will you get your fucking fat fingers off and leave it to Josey, for Christ's sake! And see if you can't sort yourself out. I mean, look at ya . . .' She glared down at her mother's shoes.

Lillian backed away and went off to search in the cupboard under the stairs to see if she had another pair of shoes that with a bit of spit and polish would look better than the ones she had on. Just under the gas meter, she found a pair of new sandals. They had been shoved in there because they'd never fitted, but, today, she would squeeze her feet in and sort out the blisters after the wedding.

Lillian returned to find Josey had buttoned the back of Dionne's dress. She watched from the corner of the room while her daughter admired herself in the mirror. *Was Dionne really in love with Luke? Or was there more to this wedding?* she wondered. Nothing Dionne said or did surprised her anymore.

'That's a bit better, Mother,' said Dionne, glaring at Lillian's shoes, 'but they don't match the dress . . . Oh, never bloody mind. Let's go. I've a man waiting at the altar.'

Josey handed Dionne the huge bouquet and had to force herself to say, 'You look beautiful, Dionne. Luke's a lucky man.'

Dionne scoffed. 'Yeah, but I wish his mother thought the same . . . fucking prenup agreement. What a liberty.'

Coming from nothing herself, Dionne was going to have it all, and she made no bones about it. She knew she was a good-looking girl, from the amount of phone numbers she collected. Her eye for fashion did her a big favour, and she could have given Madonna a run for her money.

Luke was hard to lure in at first. However, she had been warned that he wouldn't be an easy target. Dressed to the nines, and under his nose, she worked on him, until, finally, he asked her out on a date. She did everything sexually possible to have him reeled in hook, line, and sinker, and once he dated her and discovered she was good in bed, he wanted more. A lot more.

Living in Luke's house was something she had carefully manipulated. Slowly but surely, she moved her belongings in, until the nights over became weeks and then months. Finally, she had no reason to go back home, and, furthermore, she wasted no time in planning to get him up the aisle in record time.

Luke's mother was suspicious of Dionne's motives from day one, and she was frank about her disdain for the woman. She even went so far as to pull her aside before the final wedding plans were in place and to give her a word of warning: 'He may have shit in his eyes, but, darling, I ain't, and I can smell a gold-digger a fucking mile off. So, Dionne, understand this: I have employed the best lawyer to draw up a prenup, which you are gonna have to sign if you want to walk down that aisle with my son.'

The wedding plans had gone too far to back out now, and if she had, then it would have appeared as if she was after Luke's money. So she signed the agreement and just hoped that enduring a life with Luke would be worth it in the end. She'd been told that Luke was going places. He had the brains and the muscle, and he would make sure they would have a want-for-nothing way of life.

As soon as the Bentley, embellished with white ribbon, pulled away, Dionne glanced out of the side window. *He was there – partially hidden by an overgrown conifer bush.* She smiled and he nodded approvingly.

Once Dionne arrived at the church, she changed her persona. She was full of coy smiles and acted as if she really was the virgin bride. Cameras flashed and people gathered to see her step out of the vintage motor. Inside, the church was packed, with only standing room left.

Lillian crept quietly to a seat offered to her at the back. Covering her belly with her hands, she shrank into the pew. As she gazed around at all the guests, she felt so self-conscious. The women, in classy colourful hats and pretty chiffon dresses, barely covering their tanned legs, looked so wealthy. The men all looked handsome, whether they were young or old. Every one of them was suited and booted and those sitting close to her smelled of expensive aftershave. Still, she was pleased that she could at least get to see her only child glide like a princess down the aisle to meet her groom.

Dionne smiled sweetly as she approached the vicar and savoured the oohs and aahs.

Dressed in a navy-blue suit and a white shirt, with a silver cravat, stood Luke. His fair hair was swept behind his ears and his grey eyes looked glassy.

For a moment, Dionne thought he looked quite handsome, but then her eyes glanced at his two brothers, who looked dashing in comparison.

Geoff, now twenty-seven, stood out and would have in any crowd. He was taller than Luke and he was also strikingly handsome. The summer had darkened his already olive skin and further accentuated his crystal blue eyes.

Dean, approaching his twenty-third birthday, was almost identical in appearance and height to Geoff, but Luke seemed to pale into insignificance in the looks department compared to his two brothers.

* * *

It was no secret to Dionne that outside the home the three brothers were very dangerous men. She liked the idea that she would be married to someone from a family with a reputation. It would do wonders for her self-esteem.

Luke would normally be seen wearing one of his preferred light-grey suits – more akin to a lawyer or stockbroker, sufficient to fool the average man in the street, but, in their line of work, he was a cruel fucker, so everyone said. Not privy to the details of their business, she was always kept in the dark, and it was made clear before they were married that that was how the family wanted it. Of course, she had some inkling, since she had heard him talking about his business interests on the phone, and if the family were over, she would catch snippets about his 'associates', as he called them. So she fathomed he was into arms deals as well as serious money laundering. However, although the London wine bar *was* a front, anyone would assume the Masons were on big earners from that alone. In fact, that was where she had met him two years previously in 2001. The Allure proved to be a very popular bar/club and catered for the more wealthy clientele.

It was a whisper in her ear that told her that the wine bar owner was up for grabs, and if she were to work on him, she could ditch her current sad life and enjoy one that would suit her needs.

* * *

She looked back at her groom, who smiled. He rarely smiled. His face always wore a look of deep thought. A man of few words, he was self-contained and never wore his heart on his sleeve. Luke was often described as mysterious. To Dionne, though, he was just plain boring. However, she'd never taken the time to peel back the layers to find his true depth of character. She guessed many women found him intriguing; she knew many found him attractive, but she didn't, not really. Not now she'd got to know the real Luke. But, in the grand scheme of things, it didn't matter. *She was told that he was on track to be worth a fortune.* The Allure, was just the start of the business.

As Dionne handed Josey the bouquet, she locked eyes with Miriam and gave her a smug smirk, reinforcing the fact that in a few minutes, she would be her precious son's wife. The livid expression on Miriam's face was a picture and gave Dionne another reason to smile.

CHAPTER THREE

2004

A year of living like a pampered princess came crashing down the day she told Luke that the doctor said she was infertile. Up until then, she'd grown used to the new way of life. In fact, it suited them both. While she spent her days shopping or socialising with her new friends, he went about his business hardly speaking very much at all. It was just his way. Unless it was about their future – with children. Then he had plenty to say. She'd joined in, pretending to be just as enthusiastic, but every month, when she had to inform him that she wasn't pregnant, she saw his patience wearing thin, and although he was never violent towards her, he did have a snappy temper at times. But she could always deflect the tension by talking him around with a sweet voice, a pout, and a good time in bed.

It was Luke who'd made the appointment for her with a specialist. But she didn't need to see one. She already knew what the results would say. Unbeknown to Luke, she'd previously had three abortions and had been told that she would be unlikely to conceive again. However, she hadn't been able to get out of this appointment, and so on the day of their first wedding anniversary, she went back to the consultant to get the official results.

Luke stayed at home that day, anxiously awaiting her return. As soon as she was through the door, he was there in the hallway. 'Well, what did the doctor say?'

She didn't expect him to be on to her so quickly, and she hadn't had the time to put on an act placing her firmly as the victim. Sliding her shoes off and dropping her bag on the hallway table, she made her way up the stairs. She hadn't actually noticed the fear in his eyes and so replied, in a laid-back tone, 'Oh, I can't have kids. It's to do with my tubes. They can't pass an egg, or something like that.'

As soon as she reached the bedroom, he was behind her, grabbing her shoulders to spin her around. She turned to face him, expecting a sigh or a 'never mind'. But what she got was a shock. His eyes narrowed and his lips thinned.

'Fuck me. Look at you. You couldn't give a shit, could ya, eh? I would even go as far as to say you're fucking pleased!'

Dionne realised then that she had been preoccupied. In fact, she had totally forgotten to put on a first-class act. She should have forced tears on the way home, or at least looked like she'd been crying, or, failing that, falling into his arms a blubbering wreck. But she hadn't. Her mind was already on the anniversary party that she was organising for the weekend.

'Luke, I, er . . .'

His face was one of horror. Instead of comforting her, he snarled and slammed the bedroom door, before marching down the stairs.

Never had she expected a response like that. Her Luke was invariably sweet and kind to her. He could get a little stroppy at times and become somewhat moody, but this look of rage told a whole different story. It was the first time she'd seen that expression, and she wondered for a moment if she'd got him all wrong. The quiet, reserved man, although she'd heard he had a vile temper, was clearly capable now of being so callous towards *her*. In a strange way, she found his mean look almost sexy. That was until she heard a muffled sound downstairs.

He was on the phone. As she opened the bedroom door to listen, she heard who he was talking to. It was his mother. Dionne ground her teeth and simmered her anger. She might have known. Why his mother had to be at the centre of every piece of news, every decision, and every plan was beyond her. Her Luke was twenty-seven years old, running a club and serious rackets. He could stick up for himself, and so, really, he didn't need his mother's approval.

She was at least grateful that Luke had put his foot down when he'd proposed, although she knew damn well that Miriam was adamant that he should never have let himself get involved.

She remembered overhearing his mother's words. 'Yeah, okay, Luke. You might want to shag the bird but don't be a fool and marry her. She ain't the wifely kind.'

Why Luke always involved his mother in his personal affairs was a mystery. Everything about Luke was calculated, even down to the way he walked with firm strides. The words he used were so well thought-out, he virtually never faltered. Everything was done with so much precision, he was almost like a computer.

After the phone call, Miriam was over like a shot. The rounded, middle-aged woman, with bleached blonde hair that was short at the sides and longer on the top and dressed in a figure-hugging black dress, which showed every lump and bump, bustled through the front door on heels way too high for her. She never had to knock because Luke had given every family member a key.

When Dionne had questioned it, he snapped at her, 'They're my fucking family, got it? And *my* home will always be open to them!'

He was sharp at times, and although he would give Dionne the earth, occasionally he pulled her back into line, and she knew then that that was the time not to push him.

She was married to the Mason family, not just Luke. It would have been okay except his family never really liked her, especially his mother, with her sly jibes. With a sickly sneer plastered across her face, and a look of sheer satisfaction, Miriam was in her element.

Although quite short at five foot four, and stocky with it, her pull-no-punches personality more than made up for her stature. As soon as she was in the lounge, her mouth opened and out spewed verbal diarrhoea. 'You think we were born bleedin' yesterday! You can't tell me you never knew you couldn't have kids! You flaming well married my boy under false pretences, and if he stays married to you, he won't have the joys of fucking fatherhood. I won't stand by and watch my Luke suffer, all because you can't have kids!'

Wide-eyed in shock, Dionne turned to Luke, with her mouth open, waiting for some kind of protection. But all she got was a blank stare. His lack of loyalty infuriated her, and she lashed back. 'Miriam, I never knew I couldn't get pregnant. Christ, how would I have known? I'm fucking twenty-four, not thirty-four. Children were the last thing on my mind.'

'No, getting your hands on my Luke for his money was on *your* fucking mind!'

'Don't be so fucking ridiculous. I love Luke. Whether he had money or fuck all, I would've married him. So your prenup meant jack shit to me!'

'Good!' she snapped. 'So when you pack all your belongings to fuck off, you won't be in the solicitor's office demanding half, then!'

Dionne was reaching her pitch. 'Why don't *you* fuck off and stop interfering? This marriage only has room for two!'

'Oi!' bellowed Luke. 'Watch ya mouth. That's me mother you're talking to!'

Dionne wanted to slap the arrogant smirk clean off Miriam's face, but that would have fucked things up completely. Needing time to cool off, she left the room and slammed the door behind her. But she didn't walk too far, wanting to remain within earshot.

'Luke, Son, why don't you get rid of her and meet a *nice* girl? That money-grabbing trailer trash, she ain't fit to wipe the shit off your shoes. All her parading around like she owns the fucking place, when, really, she is a leech. By Christ, Son, we can *all* see it! Why don't you wake up and smell the coffee? She's taking you for a right mug. Even ya father can see it, and ya know how he walks around with his head up his arse most of the time.'

'Mum, give her a break. She signed your poxy prenup, didn't she? Now, leave it at that.'

Dionne felt her anger subside just a fraction, but then it rose again. Miriam was laying into him.

'Stop fucking living in ya brothers' shadows. Just 'cos they pulled dolly birds, it don't mean *you* have to. I despair, I really bloody do. Luke, you may be the ruthless fucker out of my three boys, but, for some nonsensical reason, you can't seem to keep your sad excuse for a wife in check. She needs a wake-up call, the way she has you in her back pocket. I've seen her strutting around in designer outfits, and those bags of hers probably cost more than your car. She's taking you for a right mug, Son, and you need to grow a pair before she bleeds you dry.'

'Back off, Mother. I don't hear you slate Geoff's and Dean's misses. You're in with them, ain't ya? So why can't you give Dionne a chance, eh?'

Dionne listened intently. She had to know why Miriam hated her so much.

'Because, Son, I ain't blind, and I ain't fucking stupid. When Geoff married Scarlett, he'd been dating her for three years. She worked hard behind the bar, helping in any way she could.'

She lowered her voice, and Dionne strained to hear. 'She even stashed the cocaine in the boot of her little Mini, to save his arse, and that to me,

Son, says it all. If Scarlett was prepared to put her liberty on the fucking line, then she ain't out to mug him off.'

'But, Mum——' He was cut dead.

'And as for Tilly, she's loved Dean since she was five years old, and she's stood by his side when he went away and she visited him every week. That girl dotes on him and forgave him for his little indiscretions. Now, that's a real wife for ya, not like yours, Son. I wouldn't be surprised if your Dionne wasn't having someone on the side, 'cos, sad as it is, my boy, she don't dote over you. She hardly gives you that loving look. It's more like a look of disgust.'

'Now, that's enough, Mother. Dionne may be many things, but unfaithful, she ain't.'

'Really, Son? Really?' Her voice became louder. 'And she can account for her time, can she? Think on, Luke. She is always out and about. She don't work and she don't clean, 'cos you pay for that luxury. So what does she do all day? Bloody think about it!'

Dionne had heard enough and crept up the stairs. She would never win Miriam over, but, more importantly, her husband had stuck up for her.

The front door slammed shut. It was Dionne's cue to return to her husband and for them to join together against his mother. But she had a rude awakening.

'Hear that, did ya?' he asked, coldly.

She nodded. 'Yep, I did, and I must say, she has some nerve. Really, I don't know where she gets her ideas from, marching in here and—'

'Shut ya mouth, Dionne. I didn't defend you because you are my wife. I had a go back because I'm sick to death of being told what to do by you and her. She is right, though, about one thing. I should be more like me brothers. They don't stand no nonsense from any man or woman, and I don't see their wives with an attitude like yours. So, Dionne, from now on, if you want to be in this house, then things are gonna change.'

That was like a cold slap in the face. Dionne inclined her head and put on her sweetest voice. 'But, Luke, babe, things have been good between us. I mean, I know it was hard hearing the news that I can't have children, but imagine how *I* feel when all I ever wanted out of life was to be a wife and a mum.' She forced a tear, hoping it would work.

However, when he said something, he always meant it, and this time, it showed. 'Dionne, cut the crap, love. I heard what you said. Having kids was the last thing on your mind. You're hardly the maternal type, so stop with the fucking whiny voice. It grates on me.'

Dionne stood with her mouth gaping.

* * *

While Luke was in town on business, Dionne set off to her favourite clothes shop in Chislehurst. She intended to rinse Luke's credit card, which she did whenever she was annoyed with him.

The arguments about having kids had gone on long enough. She didn't want them. End of.

After an hour's shopping, she went into the Côte Brasserie to a table reserved in her name. Josey was meeting with her, to tell her, no, doubt about her own fucking pregnancy. Still, the girl might have her uses at some point in the future.

As soon as Josey left, Dionne saw her phone light up. Her eyes widened as she glanced around the restaurant. *He was there and he looked displeased.* Another text came through.

You have messed it up, Dionne. You didn't listen and now you will have to do as I say.

Her mouth felt dry as she glanced over and nodded.

* * *

After a few weeks of complete silence, Luke finally spoke. 'Right, Dionne, if you can't have kids . . .'

She held her breath assuming he would ask for a divorce.

'We are going to adopt because I want children, as well you know.'

At that moment, Dionne would agree to anything rather than being thrown out and ending up back in her mother's poky, rotten house, with the life being sucked out of her. The sneers and looks her father would throw her way made her cringe. Then there was her mother, the titivator, constantly fussing and brooding, and acting the submissive woman. She hated her shuffling around in her dirty slippers, with a pinafore around her waist, cooking, cleaning, and looking a mess. She was embarrassing, and Dionne was ashamed to be seen in public with her.

She remembered the kids' mothers at the school. They all wore fashionable clothes and make-up, while her mother had bushy eyebrows, heavy jowls, tufts of grey hair, and swollen ankles. Her father wasn't much different, with his grubby trousers and patterned woollen tank tops. He would often just sit slumped in the chair supping on a can of Tennent's Super. Hardly ever leaving the house, he merely stared at the TV, moaned, groaned, and farted.

She just didn't fit in. Looking in the mirror, she could never work out how, with her long, slender arms and legs, along with her slim sculptured face and thick auburn hair, she could have been conceived by them, although her mother's sister who had died years ago, was said to be a long-legged beauty. So, then, perhaps she had taken after her.

Living with Luke was worlds apart from her previous existence, and it was a world in which she felt she was born to be a part of. In fact, she was constantly told she could be part of it as long as she listened to *the voice of reason*. She'd become used to the finer things in life and accepted Luke's overdemanding sexual appetite as part of the deal. But she'd also accomplished the art of switching off and enduring the penetration while exaggerating all the moans and groans. Looking out of the corner of her eye at the luxury bedroom, that was enough. She often wondered if that was what prostitutes did – merely look at the money on the bedside table and just get on with it. Perhaps she wasn't so dissimilar.

CHAPTER FOUR

Two years later, 2006

The adoption agency had no qualms about allowing the Masons to adopt. On paper, they were the perfect family. The fact that they were loaded went a long way, so when the twins were put up for adoption, Luke and Dionne were first in line. Luke agreed to an open adoption; he would have agreed to anything because he was so determined to have a family.

Dionne was gutted and hoped that going through the adoption process would take years so that maybe, by the time they were offered a child, Luke would have ditched the idea and taken up golf or something. But in those two years, he became more and more insistent, even to the point where he had the bedroom designed and decorated in anticipation, with three walls painted in pale lemon and the fourth wall papered with grey bunny rabbits. *The voice of reason urged her to go along with it and maintain the pretence of being just as thrilled*, but, inside, she hated the idea. If she'd wanted children, she would never have undertaken the three abortions, including the termination of her husband's baby just before the wedding.

Never in her wildest dreams did she think he would want to adopt. His brothers had children – two boys each – and they, the fathers, were as proud as punch. She naturally assumed Luke would not settle for anything less than his own bloodline to bring up. So, it was a huge surprise when he dotted the i's and crossed the t's on the adoption forms and allowed the agency almost to invade their life in preparation.

The day they got the news that they could adopt these twins – a boy and girl – was the day she saw her husband fit to burst with excitement, and he gathered the family around for a big celebration.

It was Miriam who had to pour oil on troubled waters. She pulled Dionne aside and glared with contempt in her eyes. 'So, now, the days of swanning around and spending all his hard-earned cash will have to stop because you'll be too busy contending with two babies, and trust me, girl, it ain't fucking easy. Maybe being a mother may do you the world of good, to see what it's like to be a real wife.'

That comment was like a bitter taste in her mouth, and Dionne bit back childishly. 'Well, Miriam, I'm not under any illusion that it will be easy, and I know that most nights I'll be dead beat, so I guess some things will suffer . . . like your son getting his regular oats.'

Miriam gave her a beaming smile and mocked. 'Oh, darlin', you really have no idea, do you? If he wants his oats, he'll get them, either from you, or from a younger, prettier, less washed-out version.'

The backlash was sharper and more cutting, but before she stepped forward to slap Miriam's face, she stopped herself. *What was the point of arguing?* she thought. So, instead, she chuckled and gently patted Miriam's arm. 'You're probably right. Besides, Luke will understand, and I'm sure he'll be a great dad, as I'll also be the perfect mother and ensure the babies are brought up very well . . . Oh, what's wrong, Miriam? Did you not factor in the point that I will be the twins' mother? . . . So, let's be clear. I'm not only his wife but I'll soon be the mother of our children.' Holding up high her glass of champagne, she smiled again. 'Cheers, Granny.'

Miriam looked as though she'd swallowed a wasp. 'Dionne, the twins will call me Nanny. I hate Granny.'

Dionne laughed. 'Yes, I know you do, but I'm their mother, and I'll decide what they call you.'

That statement said it all.

* * *

The trip to the agency had Luke driving fast, with a flushed look on his face and a new expression. It was one that Dionne hadn't seen before – excitement. Unlike his brothers, Luke was so hard to read, it was unbearable. That poker face and intense gaze literally gave nothing away.

Dionne felt as if she was staring into an endless pool of puzzles. The only real flicker of emotion was when they were in bed, and he could put on the charm then. She looked out of the passenger window and sighed.

'I'm finally going to be a dad, and we're having twins as well.' He spoke quickly, excitedly, and so unlike his usual smooth dialogue. 'And you did pack the blankets, and the new outfits, and . . . ?'

'Yes, Luke. I packed everything.'

He didn't notice how deflated she sounded. He was too high with anticipation.

* * *

The staff at the agency were all sickly sweet, as they cooed over the babies.

It made Dionne want to puke. Her eyes widened as she was handed the baby girl. She'd never held a baby before.

Holding her daughter for the first time, Dionne knew she should have felt overwhelmed, and, at the very least, happy, but even the perfect round face with big blue eyes didn't move her. Still, she was learning to become a first-class actress. 'Aw, look, Luke. She is so beautiful.' As she peered over at her husband holding his son, Dionne realised that he was wearing another look that she'd never seen before – it was one of pure love.

He cradled the boy in his left arm and reached across to Dionne for her to pass him the girl. He didn't swap the babies; he wanted them both. Dionne carefully laid the pink bundle in his right arm and gazed down at them. She noticed right away how they appeared so content staring up at their father. A sudden rush of jealousy gripped her. Luke's gentle smile and moist eyes, as he dreamily gazed from one baby to the other, provoked annoyance because he'd never looked at her that way – ever.

The social workers, Jane and Sally, nudged each other and grinned.

Luke was silent, overcome with overwhelming emotion; he was holding the most precious things he'd ever had, and everyone could see he had instantly fallen in love.

'Their natural father has made it quite clear that although this is an open adoption, he doesn't want contact. He apparently just wanted to be assured that his children would go to the right home.'

'What! Their natural father actually chose *us*?' asked Dionne, suspiciously.

'Well, yes, actually, he did. It's the benefit of an open adoption.'

'And the mother? You mentioned before that she died. How did she die?' queried Luke.

Sally sighed. 'Well, we believe it was suicide. The birth father mentioned that she never got over losing her mother, and she suffered with postnatal depression, and, so, sadly, she took her own life.'

'Did she have any other family?'

Sally shook her head. 'No. I'm assuming you would want to know the potential of the twins, what they could look like . . . ?' She paused. 'Er, I mean—'

'No,' interrupted Luke. 'I think they're perfect, and if the father chose us, then that's all I need to know.'

Sally was surprised by Mr Mason's response. Usually, the adoptive parents wanted to have as much information as they could legally have, but, still, if the gentleman was in love with the babies, that was good enough for her. She didn't wait for confirmation from Mrs Mason; it was obvious he was in charge. And she really didn't want to divulge the physical characteristics of the natural father because there were no words that would describe him as attractive unless she lied.

Jane was not at all surprised that Luke didn't want to know more about the three-month-old twins' background because they were so perfect, with the blondest waves and the bluest eyes.

Old enough to focus, the babies responded to any facial expression.

'Hello, my angels,' Luke whispered.

For a couple of seconds, Dionne felt as though she was invisible – on the outside looking in – and she wasn't going to start their new journey always being that way. She scooped the boy up from Luke, interrupting his doting moment, and rocked her son. 'Hello, my little boy.' She tried to sound sweet, but, really, she was making a statement and hoped it would sink into Luke's mind. She wasn't just his wife, she was their mother too.

'Oh, and the good news is, Mrs Mason, they sleep through the night, so no midnight feeds,' said Sally, beaming with pride as if they were her own children.

Luke looked up and grinned. 'That's wonderful. We can cancel the nanny, then.' He chuckled, as he tapped the baby girl on the nose. 'There, little princess, now we can have all the cuddles for ourselves.'

Dionne was fuming; she had her heart set on a nanny, believing she could palm the babies off and carry on as usual. She was also sickened by the way her husband was acting like a soppy tart, cooing over their babies.

She looked down at her son again and noticed he was staring off into space and wouldn't make eye contact with her, like he'd done with Luke. Part of her had thought that maybe once she actually got to hold the babies, she would feel something, but there was nothing. They were two thorns in her side, and, worse, more competition for her husband's affections and money.

'And you're sure that the father wants no contact?' asked Luke, not taking his eyes off his daughter.

'Well, Mr Mason, we cannot be a hundred per cent sure, and he may want a photo or a letter, but I spoke to him personally, and he made it clear then that he didn't want to disrupt their lives in any way.'

Sally shuddered as she recalled the meeting, but she pushed the memory from her mind and hoped the children wouldn't grow up to look anything like their father. In fact, she found the whole set-up really very strange. The mother of the twins had been very attractive, and if Sally was honest with herself, she just couldn't imagine the stunning young woman in the photo being with that man, let alone sleep with him. Still, it wasn't her place to judge, and for all she knew, the natural father may have been a really lovely man.

* * *

The drive home had Luke peering every few seconds in the rear-view mirror at those placed on the headrests of the passenger seats that showed the twins were comfortably asleep in their car seats.

Dionne guessed he was in a good mood because he was humming a baby song. 'So were you serious, Luke, about not employing a nanny?'

Instantly, Luke stopped humming. 'Look, Dionne, I know you like time to yourself. I get it, and you will have. Mum will love to babysit, so you can go to the shops or do whatever it is you do.' He paused. 'But,' he said, his voice sounding stern, 'you and I are parents now to two adorable babies, and they come first. We are a family, Dionne.'

'And what about me, Luke? Where will I come in the pecking order?' she said quietly, although, really, she already knew the answer to that question.

Unexpectedly, he reached across and held her hand. 'Me and you, Dionne, have an understanding. We don't talk about it, but we both know. We're not like Geoff and Scarlett or Dean and Tilly. We're the type that go through life together satisfying our needs. Let's not kid ourselves. We both love each other, but, me, I ain't the kind of bloke that flaunts it all the time. I don't like fuss and any public show of emotion. I think it's weak and pathetic, and you, Dionne, you understand me, and . . . I understand your . . . let's just say less than warm ways.'

She snatched her hand away. 'I'm not cold, I'm just . . .'

'Oh, come on, Dionne. The only affection you really do show is when we're fucking like rabbits. But that's fine. I get what I want, and I like to think as my wife, you do too. Me and you, Dionne, are like two peas in a pod really – equal partners. I'm not complaining. It suits us both. So, let's just leave it at that.'

* * *

The adoption party was another excuse for Luke to have his family gathered around, but this time she would be the one on show, parading her son and daughter. She'd naively assumed that by being the mother, she would now have respect from his family, especially Miriam.

However, she was shocked when they arrived at their six-bedroom mock Tudor home to find cars in the drive that she didn't recognise.

Instantly, she jumped out of the car and pushed open the large oak door only to find her house being decorated and strange people busily organising a party. Pink and blue balloons were being tied to the wooden staircase by two young women who smiled at her as soon as she glared their way.

'What's going on?' she snapped at Luke, who was struggling to get through the door holding two baby seats.

'Hold the door open, will ya,' he bellowed.

Dionne had almost forgotten that he was behind her, grappling with the two babies. She spun around and grabbed the door, holding it back so that he could squeeze through. He didn't answer her but made his way up the stairs in front of them to settle the twins into their new-made cots. The journey home had rocked the babies to sleep.

Dionne was more interested in what was going on in her house than in her new babies. She stormed past the young women and peered inside her lounge. Piles of presents had been placed against the open fireplace and a huge banner that said WELCOME HOME had been hung across the beam separating the lounge from the formal dining area.

Now livid, she continued on into her huge sleek open-plan kitchen that extended into the large dining room, and her eyes widened at what she saw through the bifold doors leading out into the garden. Trestle tables covered in pink-and-blue tablecloths were being laid with food. Their summer garden bar even had a cocktail waiter preparing drinks for the guests. She spun around to find organisers pulling food from her ovens, preparing salads, and dressing crabs.

The staff didn't look her way. In fact, they ignored her, too busy to be distracted. Moments later, in walked a strikingly tall long-legged woman in her mid-twenties. Dressed in a smart fitted suit, her blonde hair tumbled down her back.

'Oh, you must be Dionne. I'm Beverley.' She held out her hand politely but was rudely dismissed by Dionne.

'What's going on?' Dionne asked, curtly.

Beverley Childs smiled and looked out on to the patio. 'We're preparing the party up on the terrace,' she said, as she gestured to the tables set up on the Indian sandstone patio. 'I'm just delighted that the weather's fine.'

Clearly, Luke had failed to tell his wife that he'd organised outside caterers for the big occasion, thought Beverley. He would never have treated *her* that way.

Returning her attention to Dionne, Beverley tilted her head to the side. 'Oh, you look surprised. Didn't Lukey tell you?'

Annoyed that the woman was so familiar with her husband, she looked her up and down, before she replied, '*Lukey?* Do you mean *Luke?*'

Almost sarcastically, Beverley smiled sweetly. 'I've always called Luke *Lukey*. We go way back, long before he met you, in fact.' She would have been friendlier if Dionne's face didn't wear such a tight, bitchy expression. But, she had to admit, she was also a little jealous of her.

Without bothering to respond, Dionne spun on her heels and marched back along the hallway and up the oak quarter-turn staircase, only to find Luke fussing over the babies in the specially designed nursery.

'Luke, what's going on, and who the hell is that blonde bird?'

With his back to her and bending over one of the cots, Luke shot Dionne an over-the-shoulder glance. 'Shush. Can't you see? I'm trying to get them back to sleep.'

Dionne tutted. *Why was he making such a fuss? The bloody babies weren't crying.* She walked over to the cots. The twins just lay there looking up at the ceiling. She would have to take charge, or, again, she would suffer the feeling of being pushed out, and she wasn't having any of it. 'Luke, they are quite content. Don't mollycoddle them, or we'll have two demanding babies on our hands. Let them get used to their surroundings.'

With a quick, jerky move, he stood upright and practically pushed her out of the room, quietly closing the door behind him. 'They ain't fucking pet puppies, you know. Now, what's all the noise about?'

For the first time, Dionne noticed how handsome her husband really was. His hair was longer, and his fringe, which gently flopped just above his brow, framed his face. The summer had left him with a golden glow, highlighting his grey eyes. Maybe the last few years had improved his looks, and his slim frame had certainly gained more muscle. He was looking more like his brothers and less like the weedy pale-faced oddball she'd lumbered herself with. Dressed in a collarless white shirt and Levi's, he actually was a real looker.

'I said, what's going on downstairs, and who's that blonde bird acting like she owns the place?' hissed Dionne, through gritted teeth.

Rolling his eyes, he said, 'I thought you would be too busy with the babies to want to organise a party yourself, so my friend Bev offered to do it for me.'

With her hands on her hips, Dionne gave him a vicious sneer. 'Friend, eh?'

'Aw, for fuck's sake, Dionne, this day is s'posed to be about the babies! Go and get ready. Our guests will be here soon.'

Dionne's vision of their guests fussing over her, while she held her darling babies, was cut short when Miriam's voice travelled up from the hallway.

'Where are my grandchildren!' she shrieked, holding several large Harrods bags.

Dionne rushed down the stairs to give her mother-in-law the usual fake two cheeks air kiss but was dismissed when Miriam shoved the bulging bags down in front of her for them to be put somewhere.

By this time, Luke had also descended the stairs, his face full of excitement. 'Come up here, Mum. You'll love them.'

Excitedly, Miriam hurriedly followed after her son, leaving Dionne at the foot of the stairs with the oversized bags as if she were the maid.

In a fit of anger, Dionne threw the bags into the lounge and headed for the twins' bedroom. However, by the time she joined them, Miriam had already scooped the girl from her cot and was gazing down at her, while Luke was holding the boy.

'Oh, I hope you didn't wake them up,' Dionne said, wanting to show her authority as their mother.

Miriam looked up and frowned. 'Don't be silly, Dionne. This is the first time they get to meet their Nanny, and I'm not waiting until they wake up. There'll be plenty of time for sleep.' She looked down at the baby in her arms, and with a silly voice, she said, 'Won't there, little Harley. You're Nanny's best girl. Yes, you are.'

Dionne was gobsmacked and looked at Luke. They hadn't even decided on a name, and there was her worst nightmare, the mother-in-law from hell, making a clear statement that the girl was called Harley.

'Actually, Miriam, we haven't made a solid decision about the names. I like Paige . . .'

Miriam waved a dismissive hand. 'Well, Luke loves the name, and so do the rest of the family. My Dean said he would have called his daughter "Harley" if he'd had one, but he's blessed with boys.'

With flared nostrils and a bitter taste in her mouth, Dionne reached out to take the baby from Miriam. 'They probably need changing,' she retorted.

Luke laughed. 'Yep, little Hudson has filled his nappy as well. Cor, he stinks.'

Ignoring Dionne's outstretched arms, Miriam laughed along with her son. 'Just like ya farver, then. Well, my boy, where's the changing mat? I'll have to teach you how to change a shitty nappy. Now, I know in my day men never did that sort of stuff, but . . .'

'Mum, I want to do it all. They're mine, and I wanna be a good dad.'

Dionne watched as Miriam rubbed his arm.

'And, my boy, you are gonna be a fine one an' all.'

Witnessing their private moment, Dionne felt so excluded. 'Miriam, will you pass me my baby, please?'

But again, her attempt to take control was foiled when Miriam replied, 'Oh, fetch those bags up. I have the perfect outfit for their first party.' She turned to face her son and grinned. 'I bought a little suit for the boy . . . and had his name "Hudson" embroidered on the lapel. And I bought a matching dress and had the name "Harley" embroidered on it too. Honestly, Son, they'll look like royalty.'

Dionne would have launched into one, but there was no point. Instead, she walked away fuming. *How dare they already decide on a name as if she had no part in the decision. They were her kids.* 'Fucking Hudson. What sort of poxy name is that?' she mumbled, under her breath.

Just as she reached the bottom of the stairs, the doorbell rang. Expecting to see more of Luke's family, she was mortified to find her scruffy mother standing there with a beaming smile and holding a Tesco carrier bag. For a second, she thought she was looking at Mary Poppins, with her soppy-looking hat and a long black skirt.

'You'd better come in,' sighed Dionne, as she peered over her mother's shoulder to see if anyone else was about to come in. She had to blink twice. *Surely, he wasn't here spying from between the two towering conifer trees?* She moved aside for her mother to enter. When she shifted her eyes back to the gap in the trees, she noticed that he had gone.

Lillian wiped her shoes on the mat and shyly eased herself into the lounge. Her eyes gazed around and absorbed all the beautiful decor. 'Aw, Dionne, you have got the place so lovely. It's beautiful.'

In a foul mood, Dionne rolled her eyes. 'Yeah, well, I ain't gonna live in another shithole, am I?' she fired back.

Lillian sat awkwardly on the sofa, still clutching the plastic bag in her hand. 'Oh, 'ere, Dionne, I bought the babies a little something each. Nothing special. I thought maybe you would have loads of things. I'll wait until they get a bit bigger and buy 'em something really nice, eh?'

With a quick move, Dionne snatched the bag and peered inside to find two Babygros, still with the sale tickets on. 'You might as well go upstairs. Miriam's up there making a fucking fuss. I'll put these away.'

'Are they all right, those babies' bits? I got aged three months.'

Impatiently, Dionne nodded. 'Yeah, yeah, they're fine. Go on. Go upstairs.'

Lillian eased herself off the sofa and waddled towards the hallway.

The sight of her mother crippled with arthritis would have pricked some feeling of sorrow in most daughters, but it never crossed Dionne's mind. Instead, she was irritated that her mother was so slow. She waited until she was out of sight before heading to the kitchen.

An interested bystander appeared just as Dionne threw the Tesco bag containing the Babygros into a bin. Beverley winced as she watched Dionne act so coldly and spitefully. She shook her head as soon as Dionne clocked her.

'What are *you* looking at?' Dionne snapped.

'Oh, nothing, Dionne, absolutely nothing,' she replied, before she flicked her long hair over her shoulders and headed back out into the garden, exaggerating her sexy walk.

*   *   *

Lillian had just managed to reach the landing and was wondering which one of the many doors to knock on, when Luke appeared. The look of panic was quickly replaced with a huge flushed grin on his face.

'Hello, Lil. Quick. Go in the bathroom. I just need more baby wipes,' he giggled.

Lillian had never been inside their house before. She'd always been left at the doorstep, come rain or shine. As she marvelled at the grandness of it all, she heard Miriam's voice and followed the sounds in that direction until she found herself in the doorway of the bathroom. Two changing tables were pushed together, and she could just make out two tiny wriggling babies.

'Hello, Miriam,' she said, coyly.

Miriam looked back over her shoulder. 'Hi, Lil. Come on in and meet the little cherubs.'

Slowly, Lillian walked over and peered down. She was still clasping her tatty handbag in front of her.

'Aw, look, ain't they something, eh? The little darlings,' said Lillian, gazing in wonder.

'How ya been, Lil? Are you all right, love?'

'Can't complain, Miriam. And yourself?'

'Yeah, you know, same ol', same ol'. 'Ere, hold him still, will ya? This shitty bum of Hudson's is about to cover us in the stuff.' She laughed.

Lillian placed her handbag on the floor. In one swift movement, she grabbed the last baby wipe, clutched the baby's ankles, lifted his bum from the mat, and wiped clean the sticky yellow mess that was stinking to high heaven.

Very impressed, Miriam laughed. 'Well, girl, you've still got the knack.'

Lillian felt more at ease being included, unlike the reception she'd just received from her daughter.

Luke ran back into the bathroom, holding up the new packet of baby wipes, to find Lillian cradling his son with a clean nappy on.

Miriam chuckled. 'Lil wiped that bubba's arse quicker than I can blink.'

Luke placed his arm around Lillian's shoulders and peered down at his son's heavy eyes. 'Ah, would you look at that? Little Hudson loves his Nanny Lillian.'

With a warmth in her heart, Lillian's eyes filled, and, unexpectedly, a tear trickled down her face.

It didn't go unnoticed by Miriam, who gave her a compassionate smile.

Luke had clocked the situation and guided both women, each holding one of the twins, into the bedroom, where, beside the cots, two rocking chairs were placed by the large window overlooking the garden.

As Luke watched both Miriam and Lillian take the weight off their feet, he thought that somehow it seemed quite fitting to have the two grandmothers in the room cooing over their grandchildren. His intuition told him to leave them to have a moment and a granny natter – probably to put the world to rights.

As soon as the door was closed behind him, Lillian said, 'I s'pose I really should make a move before everyone gets 'ere.'

Immediately, Miriam stopped rocking in her chair. 'What do you mean, Lil?'

Looking down with such deep sadness in her eyes, Lillian replied, 'Oh, you know. I don't want to get in the way. Dionne's posh friends and everyone will be here soon, and I don't want to show her up.'

As tough and as curt as Miriam could be, she still held a sense of morals. She may have put her boys on a pedestal, but she still came from nothing and had once lived in a street much like Lillian's. The only difference was her husband was good at his job, and with two serious heists under his belt, they'd made a better life for themselves. They had come from Bermondsey, and it was sink or swim. Either you turned your hand to crime or you were left behind. Archi was a face back then. He'd worked his way up the criminal ladder, and he knew every bent copper, every sly villain, and he was a genius at spotting a sure heist when he saw one.

'Lil, love, you're as much a part of this family as any of us. These precious little bundles are your grandchildren too, and you have just as much right to spend time with them as anyone.'

Looking up, Lillian gave her a wry smile. 'Thank you, Miriam, but, well, my Dionne, she's living like a queen, and I don't wanna show her up, ya know. I never had anything. Me ol' man drinks away every bleedin' penny these days, and I don't want to get in the way of her happiness. I'm content enough knowing that she don't have to live like me. She's got Luke, a lovely lad, and he apparently thinks the world of her.' She suddenly chuckled. 'Well, who wouldn't be over the moon? I mean, your Luke's such a handsome fella, so polite and kind. Ya must be proud, eh?'

It was the first time that Miriam had felt guilty for always boasting about her boys. 'Lillian, love, things are gonna change. Now the babies are 'ere, they'll need *both* their nannies. When you wanna pop over and see them, call me, and I'll pick you up. You've no need to catch all those poxy buses. Oh, and when this tea party's over, I'll get Archi to drop you off. Wait till you see the bleedin' great cake I've ordered. It should be arriving soon.' She laughed. ''Ere, let's swap so you can have a cuddle with your granddaughter.'

Lillian felt her confidence rising. Dionne may have given her the brush-off over the years, but Miriam, the one woman who she'd least expected to show any fuss towards her, was there ensuring that she should be very much a part of the family gathering. A sudden thought gripped her. Dionne would be spitting feathers. But the feeling soon passed. She was enjoying the fuss and the company, and, of course, holding her granddaughter. 'I love a bit of cake.' She laughed, patting her rounded belly.

Miriam grinned. 'Well, there's enough to feed the whole bleedin' street.'

* * *

As far as Luke was concerned, this was the most important day in his life, and he was determined it would be perfect. Accordingly, he had hired staff to wait on his family and friends hand and foot. The service hostesses, dressed in little black skirts and white blouses, greeted the guests by handing out glasses of champagne and relieving everyone of all the gifts, before showing them to the garden.

Dismissing the fact that Miriam and her mother were in the nursery with her children, Dionne went to her bedroom to get changed to be ready to receive her guests. She checked her phone and there was a new text message.

It simply said Make sure you always look after the twins, Dionne.

Her heart beat fast as she stared at those words and an uneasy feeling crept through her. *Why was he so interested in the babies?* She suddenly gasped as a disturbing thought hit her. After a few deep breaths, she shook the thought from her mind and hurriedly deleted the text before mentally preparing for the party.

Dressed in her new black chiffon sleeve fitted number with diamante buttons, she joined everyone in the garden. She paraded around with her nose in the air, kissing her guests and sucking up all the compliments.

When Scarlett and Geoff arrived, they eagerly made their way over to Luke to congratulate him.

Dionne bit her lip in annoyance.

Scarlett, Geoff's wife, was in her early thirties. Not only was she very pretty but she was a real head-turner. Her long slender legs and swanlike neck gave her a sense of gracefulness. They were accentuated by her blonde hair neatly piled in a bun. But she was attractive in more than just the physical sense. In fact, she was the life and soul of the party. Her warm and friendly nature seemed to attract people and draw them into her company. It was no wonder Miriam liked her. Dionne watched through beady eyes as Scarlett hugged Luke and affectionately smiled back at Geoff. She really wanted to interrupt their fond moment, but, instead, she continued to glare as Scarlett's beaming smile made her face glow while lifting her glass to Geoff's lips for him to taste whatever it was she was drinking.

Geoff laughed as he sipped the concoction. Then Scarlett kissed him on the cheek and draped her arm around his shoulder.

As Scarlett and Geoff tapped Luke's glass, they made a toast to the new babies.

Dionne wondered if she would be able to look so well turned out as Scarlett while running around after twins. *What was Scarlett's secret?* she wondered. But then she knew Scarlett and Geoff's sons were proper boisterous lads. Davey, the eldest at seven years, and Nicki at five, were tough lively boys, spurred on by Geoff, who always enjoyed a bit of play-fighting. That was probably why, Dionne concluded, Scarlett had more time to herself to look pristine because her sons were forever climbing over their father, leaving her to dish out the orders without the need to get her hands dirty. The boys weren't tied to her apron strings, and she hoped her twins would be the same – or at least out of her hair.

Dionne's eyes followed Luke as he strolled over to Dean, who, even though he was holding two pints of beer, still managed to hold his arms out to embrace his brother.

Heading towards them was Dean's wife.

Compared to Scarlett, Tilly was shorter and much curvier, with large breasts and long waves of dark hair. At twenty-six, Tilly was very mumsy, and although she wore the latest fashion, it was mainly sportswear, like the clothes her sons wore. She was the mum in the tracksuit and trainers clapping from the touchlines and waving banners while cheering her boys on. Today, however, she looked surprisingly pretty in a flowy blue summer dress and heels. Nevertheless, Dionne did spot that Tilly wasn't comfortable in a dress; she kept fiddling with the straps and smoothing the material down.

Dionne watched as Tilly relieved Dean of one of the pints, took a big swig, and then leaned forward and kissed Luke on the cheek. Dionne continued to observe the happy family but groaned inwardly. They were supposed to be congratulating her, but, instead, it was all about Luke. Even Kai, Dean and Tilly's youngest son, stretched out his hand to shake his uncle's, but Luke just laughed and scooped the six-year-old up in his arms and tickled him until he wriggled free and ran off to join Lee, his eight-year-old brother, who was playing football at the far end of the garden with Geoff's boys. It was unusual because Kai, the shyer boy, had, in the past, tended to be always pulling on his mother's skirt or sitting himself on Miriam's lap. Now they all looked and behaved so much alike, the four boys could have been brothers.

Dionne wondered what her twins would end up like but instantly dismissed the thought. She was here to celebrate being a mother, or, more importantly, to gain status in the Mason household.

Dionne continued to watch from a distance with a deep furrowed frown. The brothers were all now gathered together, patting each other on the back, and her sisters-in-law were clinking glasses. 'Fuck em,' she mumbled, under her breath.

Then she caught Geoff's eye, and her heart was in her mouth, as always. He was the most handsome of the Mason brothers, with a sleekness about him. His darker complexion and softer features were so far removed from those of her Luke. She gave him a half-smile and coyly tilted her head, but he looked away.

Once all the guests had arrived, Luke hurried away to introduce his pride and joy. He didn't wait for Dionne, which, of course, pissed her off even more.

* * *

Miriam and Lillian were still in the rocking chairs in the upstairs nursery and enjoying the peaceful time gassing about the old ways. How times had changed compared to their day. They'd had to wash out the terry towelling nappies and have them looking pure white on the washing line, so the neighbours didn't talk.

'It's time to introduce the new additions,' said Luke, with a huge grin, as he entered the room, eagerly rubbing his hands together.

Lillian eased herself off the rocking chair to hand over the baby girl, but he smiled sweetly. 'Oh no, Lillian, you can hold her.'

She looked down at the baby, and with moist eyes, she looked back up at Luke. 'Oh, I couldn't. I mean, Dionne wouldn't like it.'

Feeling a sharp dig of guilt towards his mother-in-law, he waved his hands. 'I insist. Besides, she is my daughter too and your granddaughter.'

Miriam held her head high, proud that her son was putting his wife in check by going against her wishes.

* * *

Half an hour later, the party had well and truly started. Everyone was now outside. Most were drinking the expensive champagne as if it was going out of fashion.

Dionne knocked back the tall glass of bubbly and snatched another from the young waitress who was handing them around. With her temper rising, Dionne wouldn't make eye contact with anyone. She had decided to take control and be the one they fussed over. After all, she was the mother, for God's sake. Then her eyes nearly popped out of her head when everyone in unison went 'ahh', all rushing over to take a look. Dionne was mortified. There in pink frills and a bonnet was her new daughter. She was being held by her slovenly mother, no less.

Just as Dionne hurried past everyone, wanting to snatch the baby from Lillian but being careful enough not to make too much of a scene, Beverley stopped the music and announced that the cake had arrived.

Dionne was looking daggers at Lillian when Beverley, holding up the bag that Dionne had thoughtlessly tossed away, piped up, 'Dionne, I think you may have thrown this Tesco bag in the bin by mistake. It has two Babygros inside and a card.'

Lillian handed the baby over to her daughter, and with her head down, she said, 'I'm sorry, Dionne. It was all I could afford, love. Never mind. I'll make a move, eh?'

All eyes were on Dionne. The family may all be well off, but they still had high moral values, and right now, they were disgusted with Dionne because they all knew full well that what she had done was no mistake.

Miriam handed over the baby boy to Luke and followed Lillian to the front door. 'Er, wait up, love. Where are you going?'

With tears streaming down her chubby red cheeks, Lillian tried to wipe her face before she could turn around and face Miriam, but it was too late.

Miriam clocked the complete look of despair on the woman's face.

'I'll not have you getting on all those buses. If you want to go, at least let me get you a cab.'

Lillian knew she only had the bus fare and could never afford the cab. 'Oh no, honestly, I am fine. I'm used to bus rides. I get to see the world.' She sniffed back another tear.

Saddened by the look on Lillian's face, Miriam put her arm around the woman's shoulders. 'Listen to me. I know your Dionne is the apple of your eye, much like my boys are to me, but I have to tell ya, she can be a prize prat at times.'

Lillian nodded. 'Yeah, I know, but it's my fault, really. I never had much to give her as a child. I suppose with her father always nine sheets to the wind, and no decent home to bring her friends back to, she holds some resentment. Anyway, she has a nice life now, and I can see why I ain't part of it. I don't fit in.'

Miriam swallowed hard, and a bitter taste gripped the back of her throat. She'd known for years that there was a cold-hearted streak that ran through Dionne. In fact, she'd never liked the girl. From day one, she'd despised her.

Beverley came into the hallway with a massive piece of cake wrapped in a silver napkin. 'Oh, sorry. I didn't mean to interrupt. I thought you might like a slice of cake.'

Miriam gave Beverley a grateful smile. 'Thanks, Bev. You're a darling,' she said, as she took the offering and handed it to Lillian. Secretly, she'd hoped that her Luke would have taken up with Beverley, but that notion had been well and truly dashed. She watched as the tall, sophisticated woman swanned off before she turned to Lillian, who couldn't have looked unhappier if she'd tried.

'Okay, Lil. Wait in the lounge, love. I'll get Archi to run you home. He hates parties, anyway.'

'No, please, Miriam. You've been lovely to me, and I don't want to be a pain. Honestly, I'm happy to hop on the bus.'

Yet Miriam, being the way she was, insisted. She went onto the patio and called her husband, who was sitting away from the cooing crowd and slumped in a high-backed garden chair supping on a pint of Guinness. 'Archi!' She flicked her head for him to come inside the house.

With a face like thunder, he mumbled under his breath, 'What now?'

Looking at her husband, she could see why she'd fallen for him. Archi Mason, a well-built man and now in his prime at fifty-seven, was nearly as tall as his three sons. He still had a good head of hair, although the former dark locks were now becoming grey with age. In his former youth, she had basked in the knowledge that her husband was a face. And he had provided for her family . . . and some. *But the bastard was getting lazy*, she thought. His boys were doing all the work. And now all he cared about was finding the next winner in *Racing Post*.

Once he'd appeared inside, Miriam dragged him into the kitchen and took the pint glass out of his hand.

'Listen, Archi. That poor woman, Lillian, is only gonna get on three buses to get herself home, and the poor cow has arthritis.'

Archi shrugged his shoulders. 'Well, what do you want *me* to do about it?'

Miriam rolled her eyes. 'Take her home, of course.'

'*What?* I've only just got 'ere. I ain't even swallowed me pint.'

'Aw, for fuck's sake, you're one selfish bastard at times, Archi Mason. Why I ever married your lazy arse, I'll never know.'

Leaning against the kitchen worktop, he grinned. ''Cos you were expecting our Geoff, that's why, ya cheeky fucking mare. Right, Mir. Call a cab and put it on my account. Besides, she might feel awkward, me driving her home.'

Miriam hurried back to the entrance hall to find Lillian sitting on the edge of a chair and clenching her 1950s handbag with a hurt expression on her face. It was at that point Miriam detested Dionne, and it would be when hell freezes over that she would ever feel any warmth for the woman . . . Luke's wife or not.

As soon as the cab arrived, Miriam gave Lillian a hug and helped her into the car. She was still waving goodbye when another car pulled up.

A flustered-looking photographer hopped out of a beat-up old banger with the camera around his neck. 'Oh . . . Er . . . Sorry, I'm late. Are the new additions inside?'

Miriam smiled at the thought that her Luke had organised a photographer as well. 'Go straight through to the back garden. You'll find them there.'

Slowly, Miriam made her way back to the garden to find the photographer snapping away at the twins. She watched as Dionne put on such a fake smile and a forced laugh as she looked up at Luke. Miriam knew that Dionne's expression was so put on. Her heart ached for her son. *Why couldn't he see it?* Then she caught sight of Beverley, who was holding a glass and gazing at Luke from afar. And she recognised the fondness in her eyes. If only Luke was as ruthless with Dionne as he was outside the home, then maybe she would bugger off and leave her son to find a woman who truly loved him – Beverley Childs.

CHAPTER FIVE

Five years later, 2011

Lillian looked at the black skies and decided that she wouldn't make the journey over to Dionne's again, not now. In the past, Dionne had never let her stay too long. A quick cup of tea and she was almost pushed out of the door. But last year, when she'd traipsed all the way to her daughter's home, she had got caught in an unexpected downpour, which soaked her to the skin, only to have Dionne snatch the kids' fourth birthday presents from her hands and have the front door shut in her face. She would have knocked again, but she heard Dionne shout out, 'Oh, it was just a delivery. It was no one important.' It had broken her heart, sending a clear message that she wasn't welcome at all. No doubt, Dionne had all her posh friends over and didn't want her there lowering the tone.

The trip home had been worse since she'd not had enough money for the third bus and had to walk the rest of the way home. By the time she'd reached her door, she was feeling rough, her feet were sore, her hips ached, she was shivering constantly, and as for her head – it was pounding something rotten.

To make matters so much worse, when she opened the bedroom door, she found her husband had died. She knew he was on his last legs but he'd refused to go into a hospice. As much as she'd disliked him at times, she had still loved him very much. She collapsed in the chair beside his bed and cried, 'Oh, Thomas, what have I done? Why didn't I just do what I should have done years ago?'

The following week she was in hospital with pneumonia.

* * *

The first day at school was always an edgy time for most parents, not knowing if their dearest children would cope in their new world, with a class full of children and a stranger telling them what to do. However, Dionne was in her element. She almost rushed the twins out of the door, eager to get them into the school so that she could go off and do some serious well-earned shopping.

Luke did all the worrying for both of them, and after taking twenty pictures of the children in their school uniforms, with Dionne waiting impatiently, it was time to go. The twins ran to their father and gave him their usual hug. With annoyance, she tapped her fingers on the kitchen worktop.

Dionne had hoped after five years that there would be some bond between her and the children – whatever that looked like. Not because she loved them. She didn't. She couldn't feel anything for them, and it was a real bind having to work hard at the pretence. The countless times her husband looked at her with obvious disdain wore her down, and no matter what she did for the children, she just couldn't convince him that she loved them too.

Their relationship was so cold that she wondered if he was having an affair – maybe with that Beverley Childs. Or perhaps he now saw her as unimportant to him and his children. She could have been his secretary or cleaner, or even the hairdresser, for all the affection he showed her.

She watched his face come alive with pride as he fussed over the kids. Tinges of jealousy ran through her like burning hot pokers. She did miss him, the old Luke, who, once upon a time, had shown her she was beautiful, with his meaningful remarks. He still caressed her in the bedroom, and he randomly bought her very special gifts, but that was largely then, and this was now. Perhaps that was all he'd actually wanted a wife for – to have his children. It was as if he'd taken every ounce of affection for her – if indeed he had any – added bundles more and had then given it all to the twins.

She inwardly sighed because today was the day she was to begin motherhood alone without the help of the nanny she'd forced Luke to employ. The deal had been to hire one until the kids started school. It had been a real blessing for her. At least she'd never had to change a soiled nappy, or get up in the night, or even get the twins bathed or dressed. If she'd had her way, she would have sent them to boarding school as soon as they were old enough, but Luke would have probably thrown her out on her ear, if she'd even suggested it.

* * *

Once Dionne parked up close to Crofton Infant School in Petts Wood, the twins got out and glanced across to the school playground where there was a hive of activity and excitement. Unlike the other new starters, Hudson and Harley didn't cling to their mum or run to join the other children; they just stood there, with their dark eyes and furrowed brows, holding each other's hand and glaring.

'Why don't you run over and meet the other new children?' asked Dionne, bending down.

Both the twins looked at her and snarled as if she'd asked them to stick their heads in the oven.

'Oh, well,' she said, scornfully, 'I am afraid, kids, you'll have no choice. You're at school now. You'll probably be put into separate classes, so deal with it.' Her tone remained spiteful, and yet she made sure her voice was low enough, so no mothers overheard.

The glare from Harley was like piercing lasers. 'I am *not* going into a separate class,' she hollered, which caught the attention of the cliquey mothers' group, who were huddled together. Clearly, these women had older children at the school because they acted like they knew the ropes. Dionne wasn't a part of them. She wasn't the type to join in a mothers' meeting, although she could imagine Tilly being one of them – talking Clarks shoes and healthy packed lunches.

Hudson pulled Harley away, and, like her, he shot his mother a death stare. He whispered something in Harley's ear that prompted her to turn and smirk.

Dionne swallowed nervously. Although her children were only five years old, she always felt uneasy in their presence. It was probably for that reason she was continually wishing their lives away.

The evil look was interrupted when their new teacher approached. A soft, open-faced woman in her early thirties, Libby Reeves, was very well-liked, not only by the pupils but also by the parents. Dressed in a colourful spotted blouse and grey trousers, she appeared unassuming. Her short dark hair framed her fresh face, showing her natural beauty. She smiled at the twins and held out her two hands for both of them to hold. She hoped to encourage them gently to join the other children, who were all obediently lined up in front of their new class teachers. Yet, even she got a shock when she saw Hudson grip his sister's hand tightly, not allowing her to move away from him.

Not wanting to upset the children on their first day, Mrs Reeves walked forward, holding only Hudson's hand with Harley tagging along. Ignoring the theatrics, she calmly and very sweetly explained that Hudson would be in one class and Harley would be in another and that they would soon make friends with the other children. However, as soon as she let go of Hudson's hand and held Harley's, there was an almighty scream. Instantly, she let go and crouched down to face the distraught child. 'Hey, what on earth's the matter, Harley?'

Staring at her brother, Harley wouldn't even look at the teacher.

Mrs Reeves held Harley by the waist to turn her gently so that she could make eye contact. 'Hey, it's okay, Harley. You will be in the classroom right next door to Hudson's, and you will see him at break time.'

The soft words made not one bit of difference. Harley coldly removed the teacher's hands and stood by Hudson, thereby making a clear statement.

By now, the other teachers were watching, along with some of the mothers.

Dionne swallowed hard once more. She hated being embarrassed by the brats, and right now, she was holding her breath for the explosion. Only she'd hoped that once her kids were at school in among other children and teachers, they would feel overwhelmed and fall into line, and not be so bizarrely close to each other. It was the bond they shared that bothered her the most. She felt as though they were always watching her as if she were in a goldfish bowl.

'Now come on, Harley. Let's meet your teacher.'

Harley didn't move.

Miss Dune, a tall, thin teacher with beady eyes and mousy brown hair tightly pulled back, made her way over. At forty-five and head of reception at this school of five hundred plus pupils, Miss Dune had an air of authority about her.

Mrs Reeves hated Miss Dune. She had been treated like a child herself – on more than one occasion – by the snotty-nosed woman.

'I'll deal with this, Mrs Reeves. You start getting your class inside.' Her acid tone nettled Mrs Reeves, but it wasn't worth arguing with her. Miss Dune was the head of year, and so that was that.

As the children began making their way inside the building, Hudson and Harley remained rooted to the spot. They turned their evil glares towards Miss Dune.

'Hudson, follow your class inside, please.'

His blank expression was a clear demonstration of defiance.

'Now, come along, Hudson. We cannot hold up all the other children. There's a good boy. You will see Harley in an hour or so at breaktime.'

Irritated by the lack of action, Miss Dune looked up at Mrs Mason. 'Will you escort Hudson inside, please? I will take Harley with me. Perhaps it's just first-day nerves.'

Dionne knew it wasn't just nerves; it was so much more. But she had a shopping trip planned and wanted to get away as soon as possible. Roughly, she snatched Hudson's hand and tried to march him away. 'Now come on, Hudson. Don't be a silly boy. You're not a baby.'

Hudson tried with all his might to peel her fingers off him, but she was determined to have him in that classroom, and the stronger of the two won.

Dionne expected to hear deafening screams from the twins; yet for some reason, they were silent. Eventually, she managed to get Hudson inside the classroom with all the other children.

Mrs Reeves then took over and ushered Hudson over to his chair. She nodded to Mrs Mason. 'It's always tough on the first day, but it will get easier.'

For a second, Dionne scanned the classroom to look at the other pupils and noticed how sweet they all appeared, until her gaze eventually landed on Hudson, with his black hair and dark eyes. He wasn't friendly at all. Behind those eyes, she knew intuitively there were plans and schemes at work.

Yet, right now, though, they were the school's problem. She was free for the day to buy herself a new outfit and have lunch with her fake snotty friends. As soon as Dionne walked out of the school gates, she felt her shoulders relax, as if the tension the twins had caused had snapped like a rubber band. With a spring in her step and a smile on her face, she headed to her new Range Rover.

'Let the school deal with the little weirdos,' she mumbled to herself, as she climbed into the driver's seat. But as soon as she glanced in the rear-view mirror, she almost jumped. Parked behind her was a dark Audi. She pretended she hadn't seen the man in the car and swiftly pulled away. *She couldn't understand why he had followed her to the twins' new school.* She looked again but there was no sign of him.

* * *

The first two hours were spent getting the children to mix with each other. It was a fun session painting and sharing. However, Mrs Reeves' concern for Hudson was mounting, and by the time break had arrived, she was relieved he was out of her sight. He refused to talk or join in, and he sat with so much contempt on his face, it caused an atmosphere, that, strangely, affected the others.

As soon as she announced that they could go to the playground, Hudson was the first out of the door, and being one of the biggest in the class, he managed to barge his way through.

Harley did exactly the same, and once the children spilled out onto the playground, Hudson snatched his sister's hand and pulled her over to the fence, away from the others.

Mrs Reeves watched them whispering to each other and called Miss Dune over. 'How did you find Harley?' she asked.

Not wanting to come across as weak, Miss Dune replied, 'Oh, it's probably just first-day nerves, nothing more. She will adjust, soon enough.'

But Mrs Reeves wanted to know more. 'Was she quiet and unsociable?'

Miss Dune shifted her feet and shot Mrs Reeves an icy glare. 'Yes, like I said. It's just first-day nerves.'

But Mrs Reeves could see the face behind the mask: Miss Dune was very disconcerted.

After the break, the children returned to their classrooms, all except for Hudson and Harley. They remained against the wire fence, adamant they were not going back inside.

But as both of their teachers joined forces to coax them inside, Hudson and Harley suddenly launched an attack, and as little as they were, their bites and scratches were harsh and aggressive.

Mrs Reeves backed off when Hudson sank his teeth into her hand, but Miss Dune wouldn't back down, and forcefully snatched Harley's wrist, yanking it up and away from the child's mouth, so that she wouldn't get bitten. But to her horror, Hudson jumped into the air and clawed her arm so deeply that Miss Dune let out a yelp, instantly releasing Harley's wrist. Both children managed to escape the teachers' clutches and ran towards the entrance gate, only to find it locked.

From a safe distance, Mrs Reeves tried to calm the children down. She could see their little chests heaving up and down in a temper. Nevertheless, she wasn't stupid enough to touch them.

'Please, listen, it's okay. I won't hurt you. Just come inside and sit in the office with me, both of you, together.' Her soothing words were wasted as the children's expressions remained angry.

Miss Dune had already left the playground. She'd hurried to the sick bay to get her claw marks seen to before she caught some harmful disease. She hated dirt, and the thought that one of the twins had sunk their teeth into her made her feel quite sick.

Finally, the head teacher, a portly middle-aged man, dressed in a three-piece suit, arrived to assess the situation. But his firm words made not a jot of difference. He decided the children must go home.

* * *

Dionne was browsing the racks of the new boutique just off Chislehurst High Street when the phone rang. She looked at the number and thought about switching her mobile off, irritated by the interruption. When the caller rang off, she put the phone back into her pocket.

Chantelle, the owner, was a young woman who'd taken a big risk opening a shop for the high-end clientele. Chislehurst was an upmarket area. She hoped the return on the investment would be worth it.

She'd seen a woman get out of a new car that had been parked directly in front of the boutique, and Chantelle had also clocked all the bags in the back of the lady's vehicle.

As Dionne entered the shop, Chantelle, not wanting to appear too eager, asked, 'Can I help you with anything? I have more sizes at the back of the shop.'

Dionne glanced around before shaking her head. 'No. I've a good idea of what I like to wear.'

Chantelle got a sense of the customer. She wore an arrogant expression and just the way she spoke to her put her ill at ease.

Dionne went straight to a section where the most expensive dresses were displayed and picked out an Alexander McQueen number in monochrome.

Chantelle didn't warm to the woman, but she admired her taste. With excitement, she couldn't help herself. 'Are you going somewhere special? Because that dress would look stunning on you. Not many women can pull that off, but with your figure . . .'

Dionne turned slowly to face the shop owner. She loved lording it over people like her. 'I am not at a market. I know what suits me, and I like to shop in peace. Flattery bores me.'

Chantelle's flushed cheeks said it all, and she looked away. The woman was rude but she was also rich, so she said no more and just hoped the customer would at least buy the expensive dress she was eyeing up.

Dionne went from rack to rack, loading her arms with new outfits as presents to herself. The shop owner was right. The black dress was a beautiful cut. The back of it was open and the shoestring straps were covered in crystals. It would indeed enhance her sexual presence. She thought of Luke and looked at the dress. What was she really doing? She didn't have to impress him. He got his passionless oats when he wanted them. There was no need to flaunt herself in front of him, and besides that, she had no desire to get him aroused. Her heart began to thump as she suddenly visualised Geoff's hands running down her bare back. The vision ended when her phone rang again. Furious, she slammed the items on the counter, ripped her credit card from her bag, and slapped it into the woman's hand. 'Bag these up as quick as you can.' Again, she ignored the call.

Chantelle was about to make conversation, but as their eyes met, she guessed it wasn't such a good idea. She really wanted to add tissue paper and fold the items neatly into the new boxes she'd had delivered, but she didn't have time and certainly didn't want to lose the sale.

* * *

In a relatively quiet corner of the Rose & Crown, a pub in Green Street Green, Luke was having a late breakfast meeting with his two brothers, and the tension was racking up.

'I reckon we should knock the cocaine on the head for a while. Stevie was fucking adamant that he was followed, and it wasn't the Ol' Bill either. I'll tell ya this for nothing. Some firm is after taking us over,' said Geoff, in his deep, husky voice.

Luke shook his head. 'Stevie is a big fucking tart, probably smoking too much wacky baccy and getting paranoid,' he replied, in his usual serious tone.

Dean was sitting with his hands steepled as if he was praying. It was a habit of his when in deep thought. 'I wouldn't be so flippant, Luke, because that black Audi Stevie reckons was following him was parked up the road from The Allure. I only clocked it myself because I'm after getting the same model. If it's there tonight, I'll take the registration number down.'

Luke sat up straight and glared at Dean. 'You'll do more than that. I want the owner dragged in here by his bollocks, if need be, and I'll smash the life outta him. I'm not gonna have some fucking goon scheming to take me down.'

Geoff held his hands up. 'Easy, Luke. It might all be a coincidence, and we don't want to cause a scene and have the filth sniffing around, do we?'

Jumping up from his chair and tipping it over, Luke banged his hands on the table. 'I swear to God, if there's some bastard out there trying to muscle in, I'll rip their fucking arms off. I ain't worked this hard to have anyone, and I *mean* anyone, take over!'

Geoff and Dean were well aware of Luke's temper. They may have been more significant in size with added muscles on their arms, but Luke had always been the reckless lunatic when it came to fighting.

Luke's mobile rang, and the distraction was a welcome relief to his brothers, who were concerned by some of the customers glancing over at them. Snatching his phone from the table, he told his brothers to hush. 'Hello.'

Head teacher Peter Major, in his best authoritative voice, said, 'Mr Mason, I have tried twice to contact your wife but with no answer. I had to call you. Please would you collect the children immediately? I will discuss the situation when you arrive.'

'Yes, I'll be there in fifteen minutes. Are they okay?'

'Er . . . yes, they're fine, but please hurry, will you?'

Geoff frowned. 'What was *that* all about?'

Heading for the door, Luke called over his shoulder, 'I've got to pick the kids up. Something's happened at school.'

As soon as he'd left the pub, Dean turned to Geoff. 'I bet that Hudson's been rucking.' He chuckled. 'First day, an' all.'

Deep in thought, Geoff ignored the comment.

'What is it, Geoff? You look miles away, mate.'

'I dunno. They worry me, those twins. I know they're only five, and my Davey and Nicki enjoyed a bit of rough and tumble and were a handful at that age. But Davey, he's twelve now, and even he's wary of Hudson. My boys don't like to spend too much time together with him and Harley, not like they do with your Lee and Kai.'

Dean chewed the inside of his mouth. 'Well, I didn't like to say too much. I mean, he's our brother, and they're our niece and nephew, but, I have to admit, I don't feel close to them like I do your boys. But what can ya say? He loves them kids, and God help anyone who even mentions that they're weird.'

Geoff held his hands up to stop Dean from carrying on. ''Ere, hold on, Dean. I never said they were weird.'

Dean chuckled. 'Nah, ya never, but I bet you thought it.'

Geoff smiled. Dean was the baby and still had his boyish, cheeky grin. He could get away with most things, so getting cross with him was hard. They'd always been close. Not that they'd intentionally pushed Luke out. They just had more in common: sports, their sons, and their ideas for the future. Geoff found it hard to connect with Luke at times, and it was often a battle for pack leader. Luke, with his quiet manner and yet forceful voice, came across to any stranger as the eldest brother. So, for the sake of peace, Geoff allowed him enough latitude to get away with it – but only up to a point.

'Yeah, s'pose I did, but listen, Dean. He is our brother, and they're his kids, so let's just leave it, eh?'

With a look of guilt, Dean faced Geoff. 'I know we shouldn't talk about him behind his back, but it does affect us all, ya know. I mean, they *are* different. That Hudson can add up figures better than my Kai, and he's crafty as well. But it's not just that. He's cleverly crafty. Harley's the same. She's a sly little madam. I know they're just outta nappies, but, sometimes, I forget that because of the way they talk and act. They give me the fucking heebie-jeebies.'

Geoff nodded in agreement. 'Well, my Scarlett won't go near them, if she can help it.'

Dean raised his eyebrows. 'Really?'

'Yeah, she said that Harley puts the fucking wind up her, and she did something pretty sick, actually.'

Sitting up straighter, Dean pulled his thick eyebrows together in surprise. 'What did she do?' he asked, as an avalanche of crazy thoughts shot through his mind.

Geoff rolled his neck to de-stress and took a deep breath. 'We were all having lunch in Luke's back garden. The kids were playing in the tree house. Dionne called them over to help themselves to the food she'd laid out . . . That Harley gave Davey a peanut butter sandwich. I don't think it was a mistake either. It was the look on her face, and then both Hudson and Harley appeared to smirk when Davey started having fits. Jesus, it was so fucking lucky that Scarlett had Davey's EpiPen with her or . . . fuck, I would hate to think what could have happened. Every one of us knows he's allergic to peanuts. Me boy could have died.'

'Did you say anything to Luke?' queried Dean.

Geoff nodded, but with a resigned look on his face. 'Yep, and all he said was that it was an accident. See, this is the thing. He can't see any wrong in them.'

'I ain't shocked, ya know. Hudson had one of those poxy BB guns and fired it at my Kai. He caught him right in the corner of his eye. And you know our kids. Anything like that and they would have been sorry and making up. I mean, I know they're into play-fighting all the bleeding time, but if anyone gets hurt, they stop and hug like brothers do. Hudson is different. He wasn't sorry at all, but Luke just took the gun away and said, "Boys will be boys." I swear to God, that has to be the first time I wanted to fucking slap me own brother.'

* * *

Dead on fifteen minutes, Luke arrived at the school and wasted no time in marching towards the head teacher's office. Banging hard on the door, he entered before he was even invited in.

'What's happened? Are my kids all right?' Luke asked, with concern on his face.

Peter Major had been the head of the school for twenty years. He prided himself on the above-average test results and openly bragged about how they were all his doing. He would never admit that most of the children came from wealthy parents who engaged tutors from outside. The school had a good reputation because it was in the middle of an affluent area. He was in a comfortable position and very rarely had to contend with irate parents. Never in his time as head, though, had he ever had any parent burst through the door. However, he could see that Mr Mason did look flustered, and he thought perhaps he should have explained things properly over the phone, instead of leaving the man to worry.

'Yes, yes, they are fine. Please, Mr Mason, take a seat.' He gestured with his hand to the small chair opposite his desk.

Nervously, Major fiddled with his pencils that had been sharpened and neatly lined up. 'Mr Mason, we have a problem. Hudson and Harley have demonstrated very aggressive behaviour, and, sadly, they have left dreadful marks on both Mrs Reeves, who is Hudson's teacher, and Miss Dune, Harley's teacher, and—'

Before he could finish, Luke jumped in. 'Er, what do you mean? Are you telling me they are in *separate classes?*'

Major swallowed hard and tilted his head to the side. 'Why, yes. Your wife insisted upon it. We would gladly have kept them together, and perhaps in the next year placed them apart, but she was adamant that they needed to be taught separately so as not to disturb the class with their naughty antics.'

Major could see Mr Mason was fuming: his face said it all. He felt uneasy, concerned that anytime soon the twins' father would erupt. It was the violence behind the eyes that unnerved him. He didn't like confrontation or anything messy. His own flat was almost bare and clinical, much like his office. He kept himself to himself and had little time for anything out of place.

'Look, might I suggest you take them home today? We will rearrange the class, so tomorrow, they can be together.' He felt he had to appease the parent because he didn't want an irate father who he'd summed up in seconds. The large donation given was enough to build the outside cabins for storage of equipment, and, so, naturally, he'd assumed that Mr Mason was of high standing. And the address in Chislehurst seemed to confirm this was the case. The Masons lived on a well-known private road, where the residents were stonking rich. What was strange, though, was that Mr Mason didn't sound posh. Despite the expensive suit and the confident stance, he didn't think Mr Mason was a stockbroker, doctor, or a lawyer – a criminal maybe.

'Where are my kids now?' demanded Luke, in a tone that suggested he'd completely dismissed the crucial fact that his two children had just attacked their teachers.

'They are together in our library with the assistant teacher. They are fine, Mr Mason. I will take you there myself.'

Hudson and Harley were sitting in a corner of the library, each reading a book, while being closely overseen by the teaching assistant. They looked like butter wouldn't melt.

As Luke saw them, they were his little dark-haired angels. They were very different in appearance from when they had first arrived, with the blondest of waves and pale blue eyes, but, to him, they were perfect and as sweet as they could be.

With open arms, he kneeled down and waited for his children to fall into them.

Major thought the father's reaction was a bit over the top, but he kept that to himself. As he watched them leave and head to their car, he noticed Harley glance back and give him a full-on sneer. For a second, he shuddered. They were only five years old, for God's sake.

*   *   *

Once they were in the car, Harley opened up the conversation. 'Daddy, I didn't like it there. The teacher pulled my arm to stop me holding Hudson's hand, and you always say "Hold hands."'

'It's okay, my princess. Daddy will sort it all out, and tomorrow, you will be in the same class.'

Harley and Hudson turned to one another with huge smiles of approval.

'Daddy, can we get something to eat? We didn't have our breaktime snack like the other children,' stated Hudson, much to the horror of their father.

'Didn't Mummy pack you a lunch box with goodies for your breaks?'

'No!' they both replied in unison.

Luke was now really fuming. He was ready to let rip into Dionne, once he got his hands on her. 'Listen, my angels, I'm going to take you to Nannie's. I have to go back to work, so I'll pick you up later.' He didn't want to have a full-blown argument with his wife in front of them. And he had to collect some money from one of his gunrunners. He wouldn't do that with his precious children in tow.

'Can we order pizza, then?' asked Harley, in her sweetest voice.

'Yes, of course, you can. I'll do it when I drop you off,' he said, as they drove into his parents' drive.

Miriam was in her new pink tracksuit when she opened the door. She held her hands up. 'Let me get changed before I hug you two little rascals.'

Miriam watched the twins giggle. They were as nice to her as they were to their father. She never saw anything strange about them, but, then again, she'd raised three partly unruly boys herself, so any naughty antics were just part and parcel of having lively kids around.

Once the children were in the garden playing, Luke approached his mother. 'I want you to keep them here until tonight because I am fucking *livid* with Dionne. I swear to God, if she even thinks of worming her way out of this, I'll bash the frigging life out of her.'

Holding her hands to her face, Miriam asked, 'What's she gone and done, Son?'

'She told the school she wanted the twins to be in separate classes when I said they must stay together. Now the little ones nearly got themselves expelled because they kicked off.'

Miriam's eyes narrowed with spite. 'I tell ya, Son, she doesn't have the right feeling for those two babies. She ain't the mothering kind, and, well, if she's nasty to those innocent kiddies, then, in my book, she deserves a slap, 'cos, Son, sooner or later, if you don't pull her into line, I fucking will, and, mark my words, I won't hold back.'

Luke looked out of sorts. His tie was loose and his hair was all over the place. 'Right, I'm off.' He kissed his mother on the cheek and was on the point of leaving when he remembered something. 'Aw, Mum, can ya order in pizza? I promised them.'

Almost pushing him out of the door, she replied, 'You know I'll spoil them. Poor little monkeys.'

Collecting the money had gone out of Luke's head; he was too intent on getting home and fronting it out with Dionne. It wasn't just the fact that she'd asked the school to keep the twins separated from each other, but her whole attitude lately vexed him. He'd watched her cold stares and jibes towards the twins. She wasn't unkind or abusive; she was just detached and distant. He couldn't understand why she wasn't affectionate towards them because in his eyes they were adorable, but enough was enough. No one was allowed to upset his kids – no one.

So much had changed since their wedding that he often found himself regretting his decision to marry her. She'd lost her enthusiasm and acted as if he was just a shagging machine. The only affection he received was in bed. There were no more sweet words, and she certainly never offered to do anything for him, not even cook a decent meal. However, he simply couldn't let on that his mother was right and Dionne had sucked him in, and, more importantly, he couldn't risk a court battle over the twins in case he lost. Nevertheless, he wasn't going to stand by and let Dionne mistreat the kids.

Parking haphazardly in their huge drive, he steamed up to the door, unlocked it, and pushed it so hard, it smashed against the wall. He knew she was in because her car was there in the drive.

Dionne heard the front door bang but gave it little thought; she was busy hanging up all her newly purchased clothes and admiring her new designer handbag.

'Dionne, get your fucking self down here, right now!' he hollered, in a deep, gravelly voice.

With the long black evening dress in her hand, she froze. Luke never screamed at her like that; he might occasionally raise his voice, but he'd never bellowed at her.

Allowing the dress to drop onto the bed, she quickly gathered up all the empty shopping bags and shoved them in the bottom of her wardrobe, before making her way downstairs. He was there with his hands on his hips and giving her a sharp, bitter glare. She knew then he was angry: his lips tightened, his eyes narrowed, and his nostrils flared, as he breathed. She paused two steps away from the bottom, wary of his demeanour.

'Get here!' He launched forward and snatched her by her bare arm, pulling her down the final two steps. 'Get your sorry arse in the lounge, because, bitch, me and you are going to have a talk.'

She shook him off. 'What are you doing? Don't you dare manhandle me like that!' she spat back.

'*Manhandle* you? I'll fucking smash your head in.'

Dionne stepped back, realising he was wearing a look of anger on a level she'd never seen before.

'What's going on?'

Luke was out of breath with a temper he only reserved for outside the home. 'You told the fucking school to separate the kids, you didn't give them their lunch boxes, and you didn't even answer the calls from the head teacher. Either of the twins could have been fucking ill, or anything, but you, ya fucking nasty cow, ignored the calls. Shagging around, were ya, eh?' His voice was getting louder and more aggressive, the more he shouted.

Dionne took another step back, trying to think quickly, but all she could say was, 'The school didn't call me. And, by the way, you're wrong about the lunch boxes.'

'Where's ya bag?'

Dionne's eyes were wide. 'I, er . . . I dunno. Why? What do you want it for?'

In a flash, he headed out of the lounge, jumped the stairs two at a time, and rushed into the bedroom. There on the bed was her bag. Tipping out the contents, he snatched her phone, and, sure enough, there was not just one but two missed calls from the school. Almost spitting with fury, he flew down the stairs and launched the phone at Dionne's head, cracking her hard on the side.

Instantly, she gripped her ear and bellowed back, 'What the fuck was *that* for?'

'Because you had my kids put in fucking separate classes, and you ignored the calls from the school.'

'Luke, you have to listen to me. The twins are strange. They ain't right.'

No sooner had she got the words out of her mouth than he lunged forward, grabbed her by her hair, pulled his fist back, and punched her hard, giving her a black eye and practically crushing her cheekbone.

'You ever call my kids strange and I'll kill you.'

Letting her go, he could only watch as she backed away, clutching her face.

He knew he should have felt guilty because he made it a rule never to hit a woman. But he was maddened because he wanted to pulverise her face and leave her unrecognisable. 'You ever mistreat my kids, and I'll fucking make sure you never walk again. Now, get your gear and fuck off. I want you out of this house now. Do you fucking hear me?' In that moment of anger, the concern about her leaving for good and taking the kids with her went out of his head. Once again, his rage had ruled his brain.

Before Dionne fled the room, she retorted angrily, 'I suppose you'll want to move in Beverley fucking Childs.'

Luke's eyes widened. 'You don't know what you're talking about. Now, get your coat and bag and fuck off!'

CHAPTER SIX

Libby Reeves had her back to her husband as she peeled the potatoes, ready to make his favourite – shepherd's pie. She stared out of the window across the vast garden, trying to see if there were any apples left on the trees to make an apple crumble. She enjoyed cooking, especially in their inviting farmhouse kitchen.

Dr Guy Reeves, a specialist psychiatrist, was tired from his work because his new research programme was proving to be a lot tougher to recruit new subjects than he'd anticipated. He sat at the kitchen table with a pile of notes and removed his glasses to wipe his sore eyes. Usually, he would work in his office upstairs, but he had become aware that he'd been neglecting his sweet wife – his pride and joy.

'How was your day, my darling, with the new intake?'

Holding up her hand, she showed him where she had been bitten.

Guy squinted to see properly. 'Oooh, *that* looks nasty.'

'Yes, two new pupils, twins in fact, didn't want to be apart, and Miss Dune and I got the brunt of it.' Grabbing the bottle of red wine, she poured two glasses and passed her husband one before she sat at the table and joined him.

'I don't know, Guy,' she continued, 'they were so vicious – like two wild animals – yet Belinda, the teaching assistant, took them for reading, and she was astonished at how well they could read. She said they each have the ability of a twelve-year-old, so that was the highlight of my day. Other than that, everything was pretty good.' She gulped back a large mouthful of the expensive red that Guy had bought on the way home.

'Er, honey, you should savour that one. It's not cheap plonk, you know.'

She giggled. 'Oops! Sorry. An unsettled day, I guess.'

She could see he'd also endured a tough day. His soft, round face appeared tighter than usual. Well aware he had been an older catch, she hadn't gone for his looks or his money. He had charmed her with his brain and his sunny disposition. She was never one for an obviously handsome man, although Guy was far from ugly. He had a thick mop of silver hair and kind eyes, as she would describe them, and his body, although not popping with muscles, wasn't fat either. She'd seen photos of him in his younger days, when he was extremely good looking, but, still, he just wasn't the type of man who based anything on looks.

Guy peered down at his notes and then stared off into space, only to return his gaze to meet hers. 'Sweetheart, keep an eye on them. They may need some help.'

Libby leaned back on her chair and gave him an inquisitive look. 'I suppose as a psychiatrist, you think they may have mental issues. Don't worry. I will keep a careful check on them. But it may be nothing, and, hopefully, they will settle down. It's just I've never experienced behaviour like it. Anyway, how are you? You seem a little out of sorts.'

Guy looked at his wife's round youthful eyes and pixie cropped brown hair, and his heart melted. Her slim figure and gentle nature added so much to her appeal. She was everything he'd ever wanted, and although there was a significant fifteen-year age gap and he wasn't as fit and toned as men her age, he knew she loved him.

'The Gemini Gene study is proving to be more difficult that I had anticipated.' He held his hands up before she interrupted him. 'I know you and many others believe it's a myth, but we have been looking at certain characteristics of people who would typically fall within the Gemini Gene profile. It's not that we are saying there is such a thing, but, in all likelihood, we think there is a good chance such a gene exists if the characteristics in certain groups of subjects do tick all the right boxes.'

Libby laughed. 'I never said I think it's a myth. In fact, I'd never heard of it. I only googled it to show an interest in your work, but, to be honest, I was confused when I read the word "myth", that's all. And what would I know anyway? So what's the problem?'

'The same study was stopped many moons ago, but we have advanced in technology, so we are re-evaluating again. However, it's not that simple. We have to recruit enough subjects or the study will not be valid. It's difficult because most of our ideal patients are either in prison or on a psychiatric ward on multiple drugs.'

Libby hung on to his every word. She loved to hear him talk about his work. He always sounded so intelligent and interesting, and although he lost her sometimes when it came to the detail, she admired him immensely. Luckily for her, he was kind enough to treat her as the thirty-year-old she was and not talk down to her, or mock her, for that matter.

She looked at the teeth marks on her hand. 'I wouldn't be surprised if these twins end up in a psychiatric ward or prison . . . Oh, sorry. That was cruel. Just ignore me.'

Guy inclined his head. 'Libby, they really have worried you, haven't they?'

She let out a jaded sigh. 'Yes, I keep thinking about them. It was just the looks on their faces and . . . Oh, I can't explain it. They seemed so focused, like no one could distract them, and you know what five-year-olds are like. They can easily be persuaded to behave, but these two, well, it's just different.' She looked at her husband's expression of interest. 'Oh, come on, Guy. Surely, you can't be thinking of enrolling them into the study, are you?'

Guy smiled. 'Perhaps the wine is going to my head. I am just getting carried away with the study. But one of the traits, and I have to say one of the main ones, is hyperfocus.'

'Guy!'

'Ignore me, Libby. I know, it's stupid.'

'Well, look, they'll be in my class tomorrow, so, as their teacher, obviously I will keep notes, if it helps. Not sure if the parents would agree. Apparently, the father was quite aggressive with the head teacher. I think Mr Mason put the wind up him.'

Guy raised his eyebrow. 'So the father is aggressive, is he?'

'I can't confirm that for sure because old Peter is a bit of a girl at times. Anyway, about this Gemini Gene. Isn't it to do with serial killers?'

'Um, well, yes and no. Ninety-nine per cent of serial killers are psychopaths, but not all psychopaths are serial killers. Psychopathic tendencies are found in people who lack empathy, who, in fact, live a normal life, like bank managers and people in high positions.'

Libby raised her brow. 'Really?'

'Yes, but we believe that psychopaths who may have the Gemini Gene are different in so much as their level of intelligence is far superior. They appear to function at a higher level and are far more dangerous.'

Libby took a sip of her wine and digested his words. 'Hmm, I'm not sure I quite understand. So it's not the same gene as a sociopath, then?'

Guy smiled. 'Sorry, Libby, it is a bit confusing, isn't it? We can only really establish a sociopath or a psychopath through a list of traits. There is no biological test, like testing for heart disease. But what we are looking for is a gene that we believe is found in psychopaths but not necessarily in serial killers. Psychopaths are very different from sociopaths. Psychopaths are born, and sociopaths are made. If we can isolate the Gemini Gene and associate it with certain behaviours, then we will have made a huge advancement in mental health.'

Libby soaked up the words and her mind went back to the Mason twins. 'About Harley and Hudson, the Mason children, do you think they could possess this trait?'

Guy smiled. 'Oh, that is impossible to say from what you have told me, but if they do possess any of these traits, they would make ideal candidates for the study. Especially since they are twins. A long shot, I know, and they were probably just showing anxiety to being in a new environment alone, and, again, that is pretty normal.'

Intrigued, Libby asked, 'So, what do I look out for?'

Guy leaned forward, now having her complete attention. 'Well, they are very young to show a clear demonstration of psychopathic tendencies, but watch to see if they don't show empathy, if they are socially awkward, for example, and if they have obsessive thoughts which they may verbalise.'

Libby laughed. 'Well, at my last school, nearly half the class would fit that description.'

He nodded. 'Yes, it is hard when they are so young. That's why we can never diagnose psychosis at such a young age. Yet, it's the level of intelligence and lack of wanting to conform that may be the precursor. Anyway, I am sure you have procedures in place for monitoring children who are proving difficult for one reason or another.'

Swirling her glass, Libby's face became serious. 'Guy, they are just little children. Actually, I am not sure I want to look for these traits. It doesn't seem right to me.'

He reached across and clutched her wrist. 'I am sorry, Libby. Of course, you are right about that. I think I need a break. This research has me grabbing at straws. No, you just go about your work and ignore me.'

Once again, Libby noticed how tired his eyes were. She worried that this research was perhaps not such a good idea. She'd been told about the programme a few years ago, and although many of the details went over her head, it still gave her an uneasy feeling. However, her husband was a well-respected professor, and so who was she to question him? The only issue that did concern her was why he had continued to look for the Holy Grail. Clearly, it was something that must have begun to crystallise in his mind when he was a junior, and he'd never been able to see it through. If that was the case, then, was this project more for a personal reason rather than for determining outcomes that would benefit psychiatry?

* * *

After paying the taxi driver, Dionne hurried into the toilets of the Côte Brasserie to check the marks on her face. She stared in the mirror and sighed. The fresh bruise around her left eye would be a real shiner before tomorrow. She pulled a good foundation coverage from her make-up bag to hide the bruise before anyone in the restaurant saw it. As she dabbed away, she thought back to Luke. He'd had the fucking audacity to kick her out of the marital home. Just like that.

It was absurd. *She* was the one who was supposed to be controlling this relationship. She saw herself actually as the stronger of the two of them – mentally, at least. She should have realised that ignoring the calls from the school would have been like a red rag to a bull, so far as Luke was concerned. As for mentioning the idea that the kids were strange, that was the biggest mistake, and she had the black eye to prove it. The little bastards had set her up because she *had* made up their lunch boxes; in fact, if Luke hadn't been so preoccupied with taking all those photos of the kids, he would have seen them for himself.

She left the ladies' room and took a seat in her regular place, tucked around the corner away from the main area. The waitress brought her over her usual caffe latte and gave her a sympathetic smile.

'Will anyone be joining you today?'

Dionne shook her head and slapped her credit card on the table to pay for her coffee. She would have to make a call and hope *the voice of reason* would tell her what to do because she sure as hell was never going to go back to her mother's house.

Idly, she looked at the screen, and suddenly it pinged, making her jump.

Luke! She read the text and her heart rate plummeted with relief.

Hi, Dionne. Look, sometimes my temper gets the better of me. I may have gone over the top but in future never ignore calls from the school. I found the sandwich boxes in the car. I brought the kids home and had serious words with them about telling lies. So I'm sorry for not believing you. Come home and we can put this behind us.

Luke X

As she sipped her latte, she smiled ruefully. That had been one hell of a close shave. No way was she going to get into trouble like *that* again.

* * *

Entering the house and walking through into the kitchen, Dionne saw Luke playing with the children in the rear garden. The twins couldn't look more angelic. It was obvious they had a great bond with their father.

As soon as she went outside to greet them, Luke turned and looked at his wife. Taking a deep breath, he cast a glance at the mess he'd made of her face and dipped his gaze. He hadn't meant to lash out, but his children's ordeal had angered him beyond any reason. But, to be fair, after she'd left the house, he had thought back to breakfast time, and, yes, she had told him the truth: he did see her making the snacks and sandwiches, and he'd actually found the lunch boxes under the front seats of her car. He should have listened before thumping her one, but her calling the children 'strange' had hit a nerve.

That evening, after a long soak in the bath, Dionne removed her make-up, so she looked ten times worse. She hoped to play on his heartstrings. Wrapped in a dressing gown, she sat and watched the TV.

From time to time, Luke looked over at her, and she was pleased to see his expression of genuine concern.

But that wasn't the case with her darling son.

Hudson looked at her and screwed his button nose up.

'Mummy, why is your face like that?'

She imagined if he were her biological son he would be running to her now and giving her a hug and wearing a look of compassion, but he didn't. And his voice sounded cold and was inquisitive rather than concerned.

Luke answered for her. 'Mummy fell over.'

Dionne felt an urge to correct him. *Mummy was punched around the head and nearly knocked fucking senseless because of you two horrible bastards.* But, instead, she remained silent. And if Hudson's false expression of interest in her wasn't enough to cause her grief, Harley was his equal.

It was her daughter's look of smugness that got to her the most. She should have a bond with her. They should be able to enjoy girlie things like having their hair done, painting their fingernails, and shopping for pretty dresses, but none of those delights applied to her daughter. She wasn't the sort of girl who could be paraded around and shown off. She was more like a tomboy, and as for having her hair cut or curled, it would be like she was trying to drown her; instead, Harley allowed Miriam to trim the ends, and that was it.

Harley had beautiful hair, with long black waves, and although Dionne hated her daughter's eyes because they looked so blank and held a sinister stare, they were very striking, with the deep blue colouring enhanced by their thick black lashes. They could capture the heart of anyone if they just had a sweetness about them, but they were not sweet or adorable; they were cold and calculated, especially when she gave that trademark smirk of hers instead of an innocent smile.

As she turned off the lights to go up to their master bedroom suite, she wondered how things had gone so horribly wrong. Early in their marriage, Luke used to dote on her, but, bit by bit, his affections were dwindling away; maybe he really was having an affair. *Could it be with that Beverley Childs bitch?* she wondered. Because perhaps he was looking for an excuse to kick her out in order to move Beverley in. Well, she would stand her ground from now on and do whatever it took to stay in her beautiful home.

Luke slept in one of the guest bedrooms and was up long before she was – well, so he thought.

But she'd been awake well before the phone rang. She waited for him to answer it in the kitchen before she picked up the receiver to the phone in the bedroom, carefully holding her hand over the mouthpiece, so he couldn't hear her. She listened, thinking perhaps it was Beverley, but it was Dean.

'Luke, you didn't collect the money yesterday. Your man was pissed off. I can't meet him. I'm over in North London. The architect's going over the plans with me and Geoff at the club. So, can you deal with him? And, oh yeah, he wants another two bricks.'

Dionne had sussed out years ago that their secret code for a gun was 'brick'.

She heard her husband's reply. 'Aw, for fuck's sake, I need to take the kids to school. Tell him I'll meet him at The Allure. I'll have to go to the lock-up, then, before that. But I ain't happy about getting me hands dirty, not with this mystery fucking black Audi hovering about. I mean, we don't know if it's the filth.'

'Well, look, just go the club, then. Collect the money, and I'll organise someone to deliver the bricks later. And, Bro, you'd better be vigilant. I feel uneasy about this an' all, Luke.'

'No, it's all right. Tell him just to meet me at the club in two hours' time. I haven't got time to fuck around. I'll take the bricks meself. Why didn't you ring my mobile?'

'I did, but you didn't answer. Sorry, Bro. I had no choice but to call the house phone.'

'No worries. Leave it to me.'

When she heard the click of the receiver, she replaced hers. She could hear Luke climbing the stairs and hoped he would pop into their room and say he was sorry, but, instead, she heard him go into the children's bedroom. His upbeat voice when he woke the twins peeved her. She could hear them all giggling; he was probably tickling them.

Swinging her legs around, she sat up ready to ease herself out of bed. Her head was banging, and her eyes felt even puffier than yesterday. Once he saw the damage he'd inflicted, she thought there was a good chance he would organise an exotic holiday for just the pair of them away from the kids or he would at least treat her to something very special like the latest BMW or Mercedes.

Wrapping the satin dressing gown around her, she made her way to the kitchen where the twins were sitting upright waiting for their breakfast. They ignored her as if she wasn't even in the room.

Luke was cooking scrambled eggs. He glanced over his shoulder to see his wife looking like the bride of Frankenstein. Giving her a wan smile, he said, 'I'm taking the kids to school today.'

'Okay. Do you want a cup of coffee?' She wanted to get his attention.

'I've had one,' he said.

'What time will you be back?'

'No idea. I've some business in town to sort out.'

She deliberately looked over at the twins, who were rosy-cheeked and alert. She narrowed her eyes, warning them that she was not impressed with their attitude, but they didn't cower or show the slightest bit of concern. They merely smiled back as if she meant nothing. Then they did what they often did and looked at each other with menacing grins as though they were plotting something sinister. Sick to death of being an outsider in her own home, she walked away and left them to it. She had her own business to attend to, but she intended to wait until they were out of the house before she got busy.

*   *   *

It was now 3.30 p.m., and Libby was anxious because she was still at school with the twins when all the other children had been collected by their parents fifteen minutes ago. Yet she was sure that Mr Mason would have been there on the dot. He had arrived ten minutes early that morning to settle his children in the classroom and to ensure they were happy to be left. Libby assumed, with his overpowering protective nature, he wouldn't be late in picking them up. After failing to get hold of Mr Mason, Peter called Mrs Mason to collect the children but the phone was engaged.

Libby felt particularly conscious not to upset the children because they had a strange way of showing their distaste. In a room full of other children, their intense demeanours were less noticeable with all the hive of activity, but now, alone with them, it was more apparent than ever that something might kick off.

'I am sure your father has just got caught up in traffic. He will be here soon,' she said, hoping for a smile at least.

They wouldn't look at her; instead, they looked at each other or at the floor. Libby had found them exhausting. Try as she might to get them to interact nicely with the other children, they just wouldn't, and they were not kind about it either.

Little Jake Roberts got the brunt of Hudson's anger when he tried to coax Harley away to finish adding glitter to the new mural.

It had been an idea of Libby's to help the class to bond. They could all add their own characters to the mural that was based on an underwater sea creatures theme.

Jake, a sweet child, with glasses and a cute lisp, had kindly offered to share his pot of glitter to add to the mermaid he'd so proudly painted.

She'd watched him, with his beaming face full of pride, approach Harley and grab her hand.

'Come on, Harley, let's add the glitter together.' He tugged her up from her seat to join him.

From nowhere, Hudson appeared and pushed Jake so hard that he fell onto the floor and covered himself in glitter.

Libby would have dismissed it as a touch of jealousy, but when Harley then stamped on Jake's spectacles, which had come off in the fall, she felt a sickening feeling. It wasn't normal for a five-year-old child to do something so cruel. Perhaps a teenager might but not a child so young. She noticed that Harley wasn't even angry; she was sadistic.

Libby had to stop 'watching' the children. She knew the conversations she'd had about the Mason twins with her husband were beginning to make her paranoid. Subconsciously, she was looking for these psychopathic traits. She sighed and tried to get the images out of her head.

Unexpectedly, Hudson began to speak. *'Il ya quelque chose de mal parce que papa ne voulait pas nous quitter.'*

Libby was taken aback. He was speaking French and with perfect pronunciation. He'd said, more or less, that there was something wrong because their father wouldn't just leave them here.

Libby was well versed in French and replied, *'Ne vous inquirtez pas.'* She told them not to worry, but, really, the subtext of her reply was to let them know she understood what they had said, and so if they thought they could get one over on her, they would be disappointed.

Hudson curled his lip, and Harley just gave her teacher the death stare.

Dionne was on the phone to Josey, on the landline, when she suddenly saw a call on her mobile. The caller was not identified.

'Josey, I'll call you another time, okay?'

Dionne picked up her mobile and answered the call.

An unfamiliar voice said, 'Hello? Is that Dionne Mason?'

'Yes, it is. Can I help you?'

'Mrs Mason, this is Lyle Harris, your husband's solicitor. I don't think we've met. I am calling to tell you that your husband won't be able to collect your children from school.'

'Oh! Right, er, why can't he pick the children up?'

'That was the other reason for calling you. Your husband has been arrested. I am with him now. I cannot tell you any more at the moment, but I am sure Miriam will fill you in soon enough. Luke just wanted to make sure you knew he couldn't pick the children up.'

Dionne hurriedly put her phone in her bag, picked up her car key, and left the house.

* * *

The relief was almost tangible on Mr Major's face as he escorted Mrs Mason into the twins' classroom.

Libby almost gasped at the state of the woman's face; she had clearly been in a fight.

Major nodded for Libby to take over while he made a swift exit.

Exaggerating her look of despair, Dionne pretended she was unsteady and had to sit down.

Libby hurried over and helped her to a chair.

'Are you okay? Shall I get you a glass of water?'

Slowly, Dionne shook her head. 'No, I'll be fine. I just need to sit for a second. I'm sorry for the delay. I think my husband and I got our wires crossed. Anyway, how have they been today?' She looked over, giving her children a compassionate smile.

Still disturbed by the twins' behaviour, Libby wanted to air her concerns, but looking at Mrs Mason's face, she decided what she had to say could wait. 'Yes, I think having them together for the moment is probably in their best interests. Oh, and I didn't realise they could speak French – very impressively, I might add. Are you or your husband from France?'

Dionne shook her head. 'No, and we don't speak French either. Those two watched a French programme and asked to learn the language, so we bought the DVDs to keep them occupied.'

Dionne had no idea that her children were fluent. She assumed they could just pop out a few odd words and the rest was probably made-up gobbledygook.

Libby's fascination was mounting, and probably unhealthily so because she'd also noticed that the twins, with their striking features, did not resemble in any way either their mother or father. While he was tall and fair with sharp features, Mrs Mason had pale skin and auburn hair, with light green eyes. If she wasn't mistaken, the children looked Mediterranean.

'Mrs Mason, it is obvious that you are not – shall I say – feeling well, but, perhaps next week, could we have a talk?'

Dionne knew the kids had been naughty. They always were in one way or another, so it was no surprise to learn that the teacher wanted to focus on her children's behavioural issues. 'Yes, of course, Mrs Reeves. Anything that will help those two monkeys.'

Tilting her head to the side, Libby said, 'Help? What do you mean, Mrs Mason?'

Dionne paused. She looked at Hudson and then at Harley, and slowly, she returned to face Mrs Reeves. 'Perhaps we should have our discussion in private.'

'Oh, yes, quite, of course, um . . . Shall we say next Monday after school? There is a creative after-school club Hudson and Harley could attend while you and I share a coffee.'

Dionne gave Mrs Reeves her best sad smile and rose to leave. 'Perfect,' she replied, holding her hands out for her children to take.

Hudson grabbed Harley – ignoring his mother completely – and together they almost pushed her out of the way.

Again, the twins' behaviour didn't go unnoticed by Libby.

Dionne checked her phone as she left the school building. A message had been sent and she had to read it twice.

Dionne, now that Luke is out of the way, you must protect the children.

She huffed, rolled her eyes, and almost ripped the car door off its hinges.

'Who was that, Mummy?'

'That's for me to know and you to find out, Harley. Get into the car quickly, please.'

Once the children were in the back of the car, Harley spoke up. 'Where's our daddy?' she demanded.

Dionne started up the engine, ignoring her daughter's question.

'Where's Daddy?' demanded Hudson.

Dionne replied, 'You, my son, need to change the tone of your voice, if you want any sort of answer from me.'

Looking in her rear-view mirror, she noticed the twins were both teary-eyed and silent; finally, she'd witnessed a normal reaction.

As soon as they arrived home, Dionne rolled her eyes. Parked in the drive was Miriam's car and next to it was Geoff's.

Hudson and Harley were in the house before Dionne had time to unclip her seat belt.

Dionne smiled. Let the fun begin.

It was obvious to Dionne that Miriam had been crying.

Miriam hugged the twins as if she hadn't seen them in months. Then, she looked up, and her eyes met Dionne's. She should have been mortified at the state of her daughter-in-law's face, but, instead, she glared with contempt.

'Where's Daddy, Nanny?' asked Hudson, in his sweetest voice.

Dionne knew that voice was put on.

'Oh, my little angels, Daddy has had to go away for a while, but don't you two go worrying your little heads, 'cos Nanny's here, and I'm gonna sort it all out.'

Geoff came tearing down the stairs with no time for pleasantries. 'Where's the key to the garage?' he demanded.

Dionne said nothing but handed over her bunch. He snatched them and hurried away. Dionne felt sick. There she was, like she'd just gone a few rounds with Mike Tyson, and no one seemed bothered. But, even more disconcerting, Geoff hadn't even acknowledged her bruised face. Her heart felt like a lead brick. And to top it all, Miriam gave her a look that suggested 'I know what you're up to.'

She should have known. Miriam would always be suspicious of her motives in the marriage. What did she have to do before the family would ever accept her? She and Luke had been married long enough now, and with two children, Dionne could justifiably have expected at least some respect from her mother-in-law.

'What's going on, Miriam? I had a call from Luke's solicitor saying Luke was detained by . . .' She looked down at the children. 'Er, Hudson, Harley, go upstairs and get changed out of your uniform, please.'

Instead of doing as they were asked, they looked up at Miriam for approval. She patted their backsides and asked them to run along.

'Lyle Harris said the police had nicked Luke and would I pick up the kids, so I've no idea what's been happening. Do you?'

Miriam ran her hands through her hair and took a deep breath.

'He's been fucking nicked for . . .' She paused.

'For what, Miriam? This is my fucking husband we're talking about. I'm no stranger. What's he been nicked for?'

'A hundred grand in cash and two guns.' Her eyes narrowed as she carried on. 'So, dear daughter-in-law, it looks like you'll be on your own for the foreseeable.'

Those words should have cut her deeply, but they didn't. What had just happened was the answer to all her prayers. Now she was in control of the family affairs, she would bring up the children exactly the way *she* wanted to. She wouldn't be dictated to by *him* anymore.

'Christ, how long will he go down for?'

Irritated by her line of questioning, Miriam spat back, 'He won't go down, if I can help it. Not that it bothers you, really. Let's be honest, you couldn't give a shit, could ya? The bloody truth be known, Dionne, all you really care about is this house and your credit card. Well, he's instructed Lyle to advise me.' Her face took on a smug grin. 'So, firstly, you can hand over your credit and debit cards because Luke wants me to take over the running of this house.'

'What?' gasped Dionne. 'Don't be ridiculous! I'm his fucking wife. This is *my* home, and they're *my* children. And I won't be handing over control of the finances to *you*.'

Miriam stepped forward and growled between gritted teeth, 'You, lady, don't own this house, and the bank account is not in your name, so that will be closed down, because all his money is tied up right now, not for you to squander. If he gets a long stretch, who's gonna pay the fucking bills, unless you get off your lazy arse and get a job?'

With her hands on her hips, Dionne was well ready for a row because Luke wasn't there to stick up for his mother. 'Miriam, you may have had me sign the prenup, but this is no fucking divorce case. I'm still here, and in case it has escaped your bleedin' notice, I have his two kids to bring up. So you can cut the crap. I ain't blind, deaf, or bloody stupid. The Allure is his business, and I know damn well that it practically runs itself and brings in enough for me and the kids to live comfortably.' She narrowed her eyes. 'And when Luke regains his senses, I'm sure he would want our lives to be disrupted as little as possible, don't you think?'

Miriam looked Dionne and up and down. All her pleas years ago to Luke for him to think again about going ahead with the engagement, though, had fallen on deaf ears. She knew that if it had been Scarlett or Tilly, they would have been in floods of tears and dying to get down to the police station and see that their husbands were okay. The possibility of being skint would never have been high on their agenda. But here was Dionne, with her conniving thoughts around what she was entitled to. Miriam wasn't going to have it, and in her most aggressive tongue she shouted back, 'You fucking gold-digger. Well, Miss Know-It-All, The Allure ain't in just Luke's name, and all the fucking money you've had slapped in your hand for nothing was from illegal shit. So if you think all that cash was from a legitimate business, well, then, take your head from outta ya arse and start planning how you can make a pound stretch to a tenner.'

Before Dionne had a chance to launch an attack, Geoff appeared, handing her back the bunch of keys. 'It's all right, Mum. The garage is clear.' He turned to Dionne. 'Right, Mum will take the kids. You stay here because the police could turn up with a warrant to search the house. You say nothing and do nothing. Got it?'

Shocked by his orders, Dionne was silent. Didn't her in-laws find it strange that she was standing there with a face looking like a medicine ball?

Miriam disappeared up the stairs and was gone for a few minutes while Geoff had one last search downstairs.

'What are you looking for, Geoff?'

He stopped what he was doing, closed a drawer, and tapped the side of his nose.

She heard the kids hurtling down the stairs and just clocked their small holdalls; she knew then that Miriam was keeping them for a while.

Dionne decided to take back control. 'Miriam, if you are keeping them for the weekend, then I will pick them up from school on Monday. I have a meeting with the teacher.'

Miriam ushered the children outside to her car before returning to speak to Dionne again. 'You really are something else. My Luke is locked up in a poxy cell, and all you want to do is to carry on like he never existed. By Christ, girl, I'm glad he walloped you one because you fucking deserved it.'

Entering the hall from the kitchen, Geoff overheard his mother's stern words. He pulled her away, but not before he gave Dionne a look of spite.

The door slammed shut, and the house was at peace. Dionne looked in the mirror. Her in-laws, her husband, and her children all had that same revulsion written in their eyes for her. She let a tear trickle down her cheek to see what she looked like.

CHAPTER SEVEN

The sequence of events that day had left Libby with a lot on her mind. She felt perhaps she should talk with her husband. After all, what did she have to lose? Guy was in his office when she arrived home. After pouring them both a glass of wine, she headed upstairs, gripping the oak banister while carefully ensuring the two glasses didn't slip off the tray. She loved the grand house and its original character. The property had been brought back to life after a complete overhaul two years ago. It was Guy's home initially, until they married, and a far cry from her bedsit in Bromley. Luckily, she wasn't stepping into an ex-wife's cast-offs, as Guy had never been married before, too busy being married to his job.

He looked up at her with a beaming smile. Sliding back on his office chair to give himself enough room to escape the desk, he greeted his wife. 'Well, that's just what the doctor ordered.' He smiled again, taking the glass of wine from her.

'Guy, I know I said I wouldn't watch the twins but their behaviour today was alarming . . . Oh, I don't know. Maybe I am considering too much, since you put the thought out there.'

Guy sat back down and scratched his bristly chin. 'Uh, yes, sorry, my darling. I shouldn't have even mentioned it. Besides, it breaks all the rules of ethics, but, anyway, please do tell me what concerns you.'

For a minute, she felt like a child again. He could be so formal, but, paradoxically, that was one of his most endearing features.

'Well, it's hard to describe, really. The Mason twins are so strange. They don't mix at all with the other children. They won't join in, and they will only speak if they have to. Harley bothers me the most.' She paused, trying to think of the right words to explain herself.

Guy clasped his hands in front of him and swayed gently on his captain's chair, listening as if she were a patient. 'Okay, let's start with how she interacts with the other children. Is it shyness or a total lack of interest?'

'She acts as though there are only Hudson and herself in the room. But here's the thing . . . when Jake, another little boy, pulled her arm to help him paint the mural, Hudson lunged forward and knocked him to the ground, but, as his glasses toppled to the floor, Harley stepped over Jake and stamped her foot on them. It was the look on her face that made me shudder.'

'Well, that is the action of a much older child. It's unusual for a five-year-old. They tend to be less premeditated. I wouldn't worry about it for now. These twins may never have socialised with other children, and we don't know their past. They may have issues witnessing violence. There could be so many reasons for their behaviour.'

Libby placed her glass down and took a deep breath. 'Well, that's it, then, because their mother came to pick them up, and she had bruises on her face. She could be the victim of domestic violence.'

Guy nodded. 'Yes, children pick up on these things and can demonstrate aggression. That's why domestic abusers often come from a family of domestic violence.'

When Libby smiled, she demonstrated two deep dimples, giving her a childlike appearance.

'Right, I will switch off from all these thoughts of sociopaths and psychopaths and the Gemini Gene. Hudson and Harley are just two very clever children with perhaps some home issues.'

Her dimples faded, and she slurped a large mouthful of her wine, leaving a red tinge in the corners of her mouth.

'And they speak French. Apparently, they learned it from language DVDs.' She was just about to get up to leave her husband in peace and start on the dinner, when he sat bolt upright.

'Sorry, what did you say?'

She chuckled. 'Yes, we have two brainboxes on our hands. They speak pretty fluent French, but, apparently, neither parent can. Amazing, huh?'

'Yes,' he said, lost in his own thoughts.

* * *

While the children were at Miriam's, Dionne decided to make some changes.

Hudson and Harley were too old to be still sharing a bedroom, and so she removed all of Harley's things, including her bedding, and took them to another bedroom, where she arranged it as her daughter would have done.

Luckily, the spare bedroom was pink, and so by the time she'd finished, it looked perfect. The shelves were laden with dolls and teddies, and the books were neatly lined up along the double cabinets.

She returned to Hudson's room and pushed the two single beds together, so he now had one big bed, and she rearranged his toys so that the shelves didn't look so empty. The one thing she was pleased about was the fact that her children always kept their room immaculate, with neither a book nor a toy out of place. Maybe with their father gone for a while, she could get a relationship going with her children. *Well*, she thought, *it's been a long time coming*.

* * *

On the Monday morning, the school rang to inform Dionne that Mrs Reeves needed to leave early from her class that afternoon because her dental practice had rung to give her the emergency appointment she desperately needed. So Dionne's appointment with the twins' teacher would take place on the following Tuesday afternoon instead, and the twins would attend the chess club until the meeting concluded.

The journey home from the school was once again quiet, with the children just staring out of the window, but as soon as she pulled into the drive and spotted Miriam's car there, her heart sank.

Hudson hurried in front, eager to see his grandmother. She was inside, of course, because she still had a key.

While the children greeted Miriam, Dionne went into the kitchen and put the kettle on. She was ready to call a truce and talk with her mother-in-law about the future.

'Would you like a coffee, Miriam?' she called out.

There was no reply. All she heard was the sound of the children running up the stairs. Dionne had her back to the door and was about to call out again, but Miriam was there in the doorway, looking like she was chewing a wasp.

'Hi, Mir, do you fancy a coffee or a tea?'

A heavy sigh left Miriam's lips, and Dionne noticed that she was looking the worse for wear, with no make-up and her hair not in its usual neat style. 'Go on. I'll have a tea, no sugar. I need to talk to you about Luke. I met with Lyle—'

Before she had the chance to finish, they both heard a scream from upstairs. Instantly, they hurried through the hallway and began running up the stairs.

Harley was on the landing and being comforted by Hudson.

'What on earth's happened?' hollered Miriam, holding out her arms for the children to run to.

Hudson stared at his mother, and with black eyes and a look of pure hate, he pointed.

Miriam shot a glare at Dionne and demanded to know what the hell was going on.

Holding a tea towel in her hand, Dionne looked as shocked as her and shrugged her shoulders.

'You tried to separate us again!' he spat, with pure venom.

Dionne curled her lip. 'What are you talking about, Hudson?'

He turned to Miriam. 'She moved Harley out of our room and put her in there away from me, to punish us.'

'*What?* No, Hudson, I never did anything of the sort. There was no intention to punish either of you. I just thought that now you are older you might like your own rooms. I thought it would be a nice surprise. For goodness' sake, Hudson, if it's so bad then you can both go back to sleeping in the same room.'

Miriam opened the door opposite and put her hand to her chest in relief. The bedroom was very carefully done, and, in her opinion, it did look sweet and thoughtfully arranged. 'Oh, Harley, the room looks lovely, and your mother is right, you know. Perhaps it's time you had your own rooms.'

Dionne tentatively smiled. Finally, it seemed as though she was gaining Miriam's trust.

'You did it to be nasty, not to be nice!' growled Hudson, before he stormed off with Harley.

Waving her hands in the air, Miriam rolled her eyes. 'They're probably overreacting because Luke's not here.' Her acid tone had gone, and, for the first time, Dionne sensed she was on her side.

They returned to the kitchen and sat at the table drinking tea. 'So, what did Lyle say? Is Luke all right? Does he need anything?' She had learned from the last conversation that she'd better ask after Miriam's precious son.

With a look of pain and despair, she replied, 'They have charged him with intent to sell firearms *and* possession of firearms.'

With an overexaggerated gasp, Dionne put her hands to her mouth. 'Oh my God! How long will he get if he's found guilty?'

Taken in by her little act, Miriam shook her head. 'We don't know yet, but he could get fourteen years. However, his brief reckons he could do seven, with good behaviour.'

'The twins will be twelve years old by then. That's terrible. Does the lawyer reckon he could get a not-guilty verdict or what?'

With a gentle shake of her head, she replied, 'No. The police captured him with two guns and a holdall containing a hundred grand. Geoff reckons the Old Bill have been following them all for a couple of weeks now. And a black Audi was mentioned.'

A black Audi, eh? thought Dionne.

Just as she was about to force out a tear, Hudson and Harley appeared in the kitchen. Dionne could just make out what she had in her hand. It was the doll she'd bought for her daughter. The doll was wearing a yellow dress and yellow bows in its hair, although the toy didn't look as if it was in one piece.

Miriam was taking no notice until Harley placed the remnants of the doll on the table.

'Harley, why did you do that? I bought that today, a present for your new room,' Dionne said, in her softest voice.

The appearance of the doll with its arms and legs dismembered made Miriam shudder, and her reaction was swift.

'You naughty little girl. Why would you do such a terrible thing?' Her tone was not as gentle as it usually was.

Harley didn't answer.

Hudson spoke up. 'She knows Harley hates yellow. We don't have yellow toys.'

The stress of Luke possibly serving years inside, and now this, was the final straw, and she laid into the children. 'Hudson, don't you be so rude, and as for you, Harley, you can say "sorry" to your mother, right this instance.'

But both the children ignored her and stormed out.

'I am sorry, Miriam. They can be cheeky at times.'

'*Cheeky?* They were downright mean and rude.'

With her head lowered, Dionne sighed. 'I just wish they would be kinder and then they would be little angels. Sometimes I think they hate me.'

'What do you mean? Are they often like that, then?'

Dionne realised she would never get a better chance to tell Miriam what her kids were really like.

'They are so good for Luke and you, but when I'm alone with them, they do stuff like this, and I try so hard.' A tear trickled down her cheek. 'I try to hug them, but they push me away. I buy them nice things, but, as you can see, they destroy them . . . Anyway, we have other things on our minds, with Luke being arrested.' She knew that little snippet would have Miriam wanting to know more, and then she wouldn't sound like the moaning mother.

'What else do they do?' asked Miriam, with concern written all over her face.

'It's nothing, Miriam. I think I'm just tired, what with the fight with Luke and now him being locked up. He blamed me, you know, for the kids being separated at school, but it wasn't like that. The teacher had said to me that she thought it would be a good idea, as twins tend to do better in separate classrooms, so I agreed. Did Luke tell you he found the lunch boxes hidden under the front seats of my car?'

'Yes, as a matter of fact, he did mention it. I must say, I'm beginning to get a very different impression of the children. I do wonder if all this behaviour goes back to their birth parents. We don't know much about them, do we?'

Dionne could hardly believe her luck. Somehow she'd managed to get Miriam on her side for the very first time in their relationship. *Strike while the iron is hot*, she thought.

She pressed on. 'The reason I didn't answer the phone when the school rang was because it had fallen out of my bag in the car when I went to the shops, and I had no idea. So we had a terrible row, and he got distraught with me. I, er . . . I did mention to him that I had concerns about the kids, and that's when he went nuts on me. But, Miriam, I do worry about the twins. I fear that I may have gone wrong somewhere along the line because of their behaviour.' She wiped away the tears that had tumbled and gave Miriam her most vulnerable expression.

Watching the troubled look on Dionne's face, Miriam sighed. 'Kids are hard work. I should know. I've raised three boys, but you have to be firm. There's nothing wrong with telling them off, you know. I used to belt my boys to keep them in check. Archi was like a fart in a trance and never pulled them into line. I suppose Luke is the same. He just sees no wrong in them, but, the truth is, it's the mums that get the raw end of the deal.'

It's time to go for it, thought Dionne. Playing what she hoped was her ace to get the relationship properly cemented in her favour, she replied, 'I'm so glad we had this conversation because I have no one, Miriam. I have absolutely no one to talk to, and, right now, with Luke in trouble, I could do with a friend.'

Taken aback, Miriam raised her eyebrow and her face softened. 'Well, my girl, you're still family, and that means we stick together, eh?'

Miriam often got mistaken for a hard-nosed cow, but when push comes to shove, she wasn't so bad, or perhaps she was mellowing in her old age.

* * *

When Tuesday afternoon arrived, Dionne's face was almost back to normal except for some yellow bruises, which she was able to hide with her new make-up. She dressed in jeans, a white T-shirt, and a blue blazer. The Spice Girls were blaring out of the radio as she headed to the school.

Libby was eager to meet Mrs Mason and discuss the twins' behaviour. If they continued to spiral out of control, the school would be looking to expel them.

With the children in an after-school club, Libby waited anxiously for Mrs Mason in the deputy head's office. As she walked in, Libby could see that underneath the swelling and bruises there was a very attractive face.

With a confident handshake and a beaming smile, Dionne sat down, opposite Mrs Reeves.

Libby was somewhat surprised by her manner, since it was only a few days ago when they'd met that Mrs Mason had looked a complete wreck.

'Sorry about the cancelled meeting yesterday. I am glad to see you are looking so much better. Can I get you a coffee?'

Dionne waved her hand. 'Not for me, thank you. I have reached my limit of two cups a day.'

'Right, okay. So, firstly, I want you to know we have kept Hudson and Harley together, hoping they would settle in more easily. I have been very patient, but I also have to be honest, if I am to help them. You see, I've a class of twenty-five, and I have to consider their education and also—'

Dionne sat back on her chair and rolled her eyes. 'What have they been up to?' She had cut Mrs Reeves short but not rudely. She needed her to be frank, and not to beat about the bush.

'I am supposed to add a positive with a negative. It's a teacher thing,' Libby said, sensing that she could be open with Mrs Mason. 'But here's the thing. From an educational point of view, whilst both children are brilliant, I cannot ascertain their level because they will do only what they want to do. So, if I asked them to count, they would clam up, but when I left a numbers game on the table, they completed it quicker than a teenager would. However, on a behavioural level, they score well below average. They refuse to mingle and work with any other pupil. They are very aggressive and will explode at the slightest thing, and when one starts, the other joins in, and we've had some fierce fights since the start of term.'

Poker-faced, Dionne was nodding and taking it all in. *Tell me something I don't know*, she thought. She wasn't going to defend these little shits, even though she knew other parents probably would.

Libby continued. 'They show violence beyond the capability of a typical five-year-old. What I mean is most pupils at this age may lash out in a temper and push, shove, and sometimes punch – that's normal. It's not acceptable, I know, but normal, as they are just not yet used to self-control. However, Hudson and Harley are more premeditated. Harley, for instance, deliberately crushed a child's pair of glasses and Hudson poured a whole bottle of paint over a little girl's head just because she'd accidentally dropped paint on his picture. He wouldn't stop until the paint pot was empty, but it was Harley who held the girl down while he did it, and what was even worse, they both smirked. I couldn't get to them quickly enough, and the poor girl was terrified because it was in her eyes and in her hair. When I asked them to apologise, they refused point-blank. They weren't bothered that they had to stand in the time-out corner.'

She stopped to gauge Mrs Mason's reaction, hoping to prise her from her inscrutable mask.

Dionne quickly cottoned on that she had better express some emotion, at least. 'Mrs Reeves, I am so sorry. I wish I knew what to do. I have the same issues at home, and, to be perfectly honest, I believe there *is* something wrong. I'm afraid I'm a bad parent, and I'm the one to blame.'

Hesitantly, Libby asked a question. 'Look, you may not want to tell me, but I have to ask. Have the children witnessed any domestic abuse? I mean, your face . . .'

Dionne shook her head adamantly. She had expected this question. Over the weekend, she had thought long and hard whether to tell the twins' teacher that she had been struck by Luke. Would it be to her advantage? It was all about strategy. In the end, she came to the conclusion that she would leave Luke out of this. She had gained a great deal over the past few days:

Luke was now out of the equation, and she'd managed to get Miriam on her side. She didn't want Social Services involved. That could get messy.

'No, definitely not. My husband is never violent, and he is not even strict with the kids. I am the one always reciting the rules, but we never smack the kids either . . .' Dionne could see puzzlement on Mrs Reeves' face and changed tack. 'Oh my face? Yes, well, that was an irate neighbour, but even that didn't happen in view of the children.'

'Have you thought about some kind of psychologist, perhaps to ascertain why the children have behavioural problems?' It was a question that could provoke a harsh rebuke, but Libby felt comfortable talking honestly.

'You mean a psychiatrist? Because I have never told anyone before, but I feel they need to see someone. And I do believe they need help – professional help – because I have tried everything, from changing their diets, cutting out all the E-number drinks, teaching them to share with other children, their cousins – even taking them swimming to burn off their energy, but nothing seems to work.'

The door was slightly ajar, and Libby wanted to ensure no one could hear because she knew she was breaking all the rules by her line of questioning. She got up and shut the door. After returning to her seat, she leaned forward and said, 'It's not my place, Mrs Mason, but if I were you, I probably would take them to someone . . . Er, what I mean is, it would be a good idea just to get them checked over, perhaps to unravel their antisocial behaviour. I am by no means suggesting they are mentally unstable, or they have any serious mental conditions. It may be that they have an issue that could easily be remedied to make your life and theirs easier.'

The continual nodding of Mrs Mason's head indicated to Libby that she wasn't talking to a blank wall, and Mrs Mason was listening and approving.

'I agree, Mrs Reeves.'

'Oh, look, please call me Libby. I feel like this conversation is more about a personal problem rather than a parent-teacher scenario, if you know what I mean.'

'Thank you, Libby, and please call me Dionne. Do you know of anyone who could help? I mean, have you seen this problem before?'

'The answers are yes and yes. But please, Dionne, this is outside the school rules.' She winked. 'If you get my drift?'

Dionne nodded. She would take all the help she could get because, secretly, she was beginning to fear her own two children, not fear for them. She knew just how clever they really were. But she also knew she had age, guile, and experience on her side. Those brats wouldn't get the better of her.

Libby pulled out a business card from her back pocket. 'Here, call this doctor. He has a waiting list, but if you tell him the situation, he may bump you up the queue.'

Dionne looked at the card and stared for a second at the words. She shuddered. 'Er, this says "Milo Clinic and Research Institute".' Nervously, she chewed the inside of her lip.

'Yes, but it has the best psychiatrists and psychologists in the world. I guess, if anyone can help, they can.'

'Okay, Libby, I'll call them. I'm desperate to get the twins sorted out before I have them sectioned myself.'

The harsh tone didn't go unnoticed by Libby.

'They don't need sectioning. Perhaps just understanding.'

Dionne may not have known what went on in their heads, but she understood them all right. In her eyes they were not just enigmatic. She knew only too well that the older they would get, the more dangerous they would be.

CHAPTER EIGHT

The anxiety in the house had reached its peak. Miriam was in and out – like a lost lamb – and unable to cope with the fact that her son could end up serving years in prison. Geoff was feeling just as bad. He'd discovered that the Irish had put a block on buying the firearms since Luke was inside.

Luke was a risk, but, not surprisingly, the Irish were on tenterhooks. The deals had gone smoothly for years, but the one thing they didn't know about Luke was could he cope under pressure. Of the three brothers, only Luke had ever escaped a prison sentence. So, the worrying question was this: would he cross that line and do a deal with the Crown Prosecution Service to reduce his sentence? Geoff may be the eldest brother and the brains behind the outfit, but the man they all feared was Luke. On the streets, he had a lethal reputation, and even his business methods were harsh. He simply took no prisoners. Archi always said that if he weren't such a cunning villain he would have been a corporate lawyer because, in the end, it amounted to the same thing.

The fact that Luke's family were scared was not lost on Dionne, and it had her a little on edge. She'd heard snippets, but little did she know the extent of her husband's clout or even his past. There was one story she'd been privy to, regarding the fight with the Strackens, but, even then, she wondered if the details were exaggerated.

With the twins upstairs getting ready for bed, Dionne made her way into the lounge and began channel-surfing. She'd hardly started when she heard a heavy knock at the front door.

It was Geoff, looking somewhat flustered.

Dionne led him into the lounge.

'Dionne, I've got a fella coming over tomorrow. He's gonna set up CCTV all around the house and the outside. So make sure you're in at four o'clock. Is that okay?'

Dionne screwed her nose up. 'Geoff, what exactly is going on? I mean, your mother is a nervous wreck, and you keep searching the house. Why?'

He did look uneasy, and she noticed that his thick wavy hair, which was always neatly combed behind his ears, was now dishevelled and dull; even the glint in his blue eyes had gone.

'Luke's inside, right? And you're here alone with the kids. It's just for protection. Anyone could break in. I mean, it's a fucking big house and tempting for any thief and . . .' He was rambling on.

'No, Geoff. I'm sorry, but I'm not buying your bullshit. I wanna know exactly what's going on here. I know you and your brothers are up to more than you care to say. But I've never been included in the family businesses.'

Blurting those words out made her feel angry; it was a reminder that she was still considered as an outsider. 'Well, Geoff, I think it's time I knew. I've been in this fucking family for long enough now, so don't I deserve to be treated the same as Tilly and Scarlett?'

With a deep sigh, Geoff almost fell onto the deep sofa. Dionne could see the anxiety written all over his face; the whole family seemed to have lost their self-control.

'Yes, I suppose you do,' he replied, in a resigned tone.

Sitting opposite, Dionne got herself comfortable and ready to listen because by the tired look on Geoff's face, this would be a long and exhausting conversation.

'It wasn't intentional to keep you out; it just kinda happened that way. Tilly's been part of the family since she could walk. Her and Dean married young and were always joined at the hip, so I guess she became just a natural part of the business. Scarlett may come across as classy and from a wealthy family but she's . . .' He paused and laughed. 'But she's clever and quick-thinking. She helped a lot when we were struggling. So, really, by the time Luke married you, the club and business were already established, and so there was no need for you to be in—'

Rudely, Dionne interrupted. 'Geoff, cut the crap, right? I wanna know what businesses you're all in, so stop treating me like a child, because, Geoff, I *am* involved whether you, Dean, or your mother like it or not.'

Geoff nodded his head in agreement. He knew her sharp words were said out of frustration. They were in over their heads, and so perhaps it would be safer for her to understand the seriousness of their line of work.

'We supply guns to an Irish firm, a *dangerous* Irish firm. Luke being nicked has made them uneasy because they know that the Crown will try to bargain. They'll see Luke as the middleman, so either side are the real targets – the suppliers and the buyers. The CPS will offer him a deal to grass, give them their names, and there's where the problem lies. This Irish firm, they may feel it necessary to make a statement regarding the consequences, if he was to even think about giving out names. *Now*, do you get what I mean?'

Taking a deep breath, she nodded. She felt calmer now. 'Well, I can pack up and go away until the court case is over, if that's gonna help.'

'No, that's the worst thing you can do because then they'll think Luke has plans to grass, and they'll get someone on the inside to kill him, and I *mean* kill him. These nutters will stop at nothing.'

Dionne watched him carefully. His face looked drained. She knew then that Geoff was shitting himself.

Suddenly, he glanced over her shoulder, and she turned to see what he was looking at. Hudson and Harley were there in their pyjamas, side by side, with a cold stare.

Their demeanour – and the way they stood almost robotically, with their heads tilted down but their eyes looking forward – gave him the shivers. 'You two shouldn't be earwigging,' he snapped.

Annoyed that they had interrupted Geoff's serious conversation, Dionne shouted at them, 'For fuck's sake, will you two stop standing there like something from *The Twilight Zone* and go and play upstairs like normal kids.' No sooner were those words out than she could have kicked herself. And to make matters worse, she held the twins' spiteful gaze longer than was necessary because she didn't want to see the look on Geoff's face.

She'd crossed the line, but it was too late. 'Go on, kids, go and play, and I will order in pizza. How about that?' She lowered her tone to sound more mumsy, hoping the previous comment hadn't raised concerns.

The children left, and she turned back to Geoff with a rueful smile on her face. 'Sorry, Geoff. They do this thing where they try to look angry, but I guess it's cute, really.' She giggled.

But Geoff was still in shock because what she said was right. Hearing it from Dionne's mouth confirmed his own thoughts.

'But *are* they all right, Dionne? Really? I mean, do they know that their dad will be put away and could be for a long time?'

'No, and I won't tell them until the court case. I can't have them worrying unnecessarily. Anyway, you were saying something about Luke.'

Geoff was still distracted by those dead looks behind the children's eyes. If he hadn't known for sure that the kids were adopted, he would actually have believed they were Luke's because he'd seen the same lifeless eyes in him before. It was the day his brother had taken out the Strackens.

'Geoff, what else do I need to know?'

Snapping out of his musing, he said, 'Er . . . Yes, sorry, um, so we need to be sure that the Irish mob don't come here making threats, or worse.'

Dionne jumped up. 'CCTV doesn't wield a gun. How am I gonna protect myself?' She paused and realised she'd said the wrong thing. 'I mean, what about the twins? How will I protect them?'

Running his hands through his hair in deep thought, he replied, 'Do you think you really need a gun?'

'Well, if those Irish lot are as dangerous as you say they are, don't you think I need one?'

He rolled his eyes. 'Jesus, Dionne, this is one big mess.'

Tears welled up in his eyes, and, for a second, he appeared so vulnerable that she sat down beside him and put her arm around his shoulders.

She liked the feel and warmth of his body. Living with Luke had been very much cold and hostile. And, if she were honest, she missed the early days before they adopted the children, when he'd shown her affection. And although the sex was boring it was still sex.

He leaned into her and allowed her to embrace him.

The last few days had left him anxious and exhausted; he needed an escape from a world where the fears of retribution from the Irish gunning down his family could fade into the distance. Slowly, he looked up, and his eyes met hers. She was nothing like his wife; she was shapelier, and, in some ways, sexier. Scarlett was soft and funny; she was tall, slim, and naturally attractive, but Dionne had a hardened look, and he imagined she would like rough sex. She wouldn't be into rose petals laid on a bed. For her, it would be dirty sex up the wall. He swallowed hard. It was wrong. Dionne was his brother's wife, but he couldn't take his eyes off her. She was like a magnet drawing him in. Their gaze lingered for a few seconds, and then he brushed his lips against hers. She didn't move but closed her eyes. He held the back of her head and pulled her closer, almost bruising her mouth with his hungry kiss. She didn't pull away; instead, she climbed on top of him. Her lips briefly touched his face before she began to stroke and bite his neck, which was a new experience for him. Now fully aroused, he pushed her down onto the sofa and began pulling at her top to reveal her breasts. She helped him, tugging him closer, as he sucked her nipples hard enough to make her wince. Not the least bit shy, she pushed him away to strip down to nothing, displaying her smooth naked skin. Then she got to her knees, and with the strength of a man, she tugged his jeans away and began massaging his manhood.

He sat back and looked up to the ceiling, groaning in pleasure. When she placed her mouth over his penis and began to suck it, he felt he'd just entered paradise. Scarlett would never do that.

Writhing in ecstasy, Dionne climbed on top and began to ride him, while simultaneously rubbing his chest and kissing his neck. Wanting more, she rode up and down, feeling his penis deep inside.

In that moment, he didn't care that she was his brother's wife or that he was even married; he was in another place, far away from reality.

Then he came, and after a few seconds, reality came crashing around him, as they both heard movement in the doorway.

Dionne leaped up and stood totally naked, but, shockingly, Hudson and Harley stood there gawping at them both.

Geoff scrambled to his feet, frantically trying to zip up his jeans. As he glanced across the room, the cold stares from the twins infuriated him, and the sudden rush of guilt made him shout, 'Go upstairs!'

Dionne didn't bother to get dressed; instead, she marched over to the children and pushed them out of the room. 'Go away,' she hissed.

Geoff was dressed in record time and sat back down, feeling awkward and dirty.

But Dionne returned, still naked, and sat beside him, 'It's all right, Geoff. They won't say anything. They never do. I hardly get two words out of them, anyway.'

But Geoff wasn't so sure. He'd definitely crossed a line now. One word from the kids to his mum, or, worse, to Luke, could really set the cat among the pigeons. With the whole situation now utterly surreal, Geoff decided it was high time he got up and left.

But Dionne sparked up a cigarette.

Geoff had never seen her smoke.

'Would you like a drink? Perhaps a Scotch or a brandy?' she asked, casually.

He looked at her smoking. *Was this a dream? Had he actually been fucked by her?* he wondered. He shook his head. 'I have to go.'

'Geoff, listen. It's okay. No one will know. It'll be our little secret.' She winked.

'Don't be too sure of that, Dionne. Those kids of yours do. Who knows what they might say? I must go.'

'Geoff, about the gun. I think I need one . . . just in case, eh?'

He nodded and headed for the front door, but as he was about to open it, he could sense two pairs of eyes staring at him, boring into his back, and when he turned around, there they were, standing at the top of the stairs. He slammed the door behind him.

Once outside, he glanced up at a clear, moonlit sky and took a relieved deep breath to calm his nerves. *What have I done?* he thought.

As he started up his Range Rover, he simultaneously lowered his driving window, hoping the cold night air would blow the cobwebs away, but, instead, he found himself driving home with a weird sensation in the pit of his stomach. Those children were so strange. His boys would have screamed blue murder. Not only would they have had a lot to say to him, but the news would have spread like wildfire, through to the whole family. But maybe Dionne was right, though. Perhaps there wouldn't be any comeback since Hudson and Harley were disturbingly quiet.

He thought about them, and then he concluded that he never actually knew them. They simply didn't have any personality – not that he'd noticed, anyway. His own boys and Dean's were verbal, funny, and cheeky. They would talk and laugh and show affection. Hudson was nothing like their boys. And it wasn't because he was adopted – he was just totally different from other children.

CHAPTER NINE

The next morning, as soon as Dionne wandered down into the kitchen, she almost jumped when she saw Harley and Hudson sitting at the breakfast table already dressed and ready for school.

'I'm glad to see you two are up. That's good. Now, would you like some cereal?' she asked, deliberately not making eye contact with the children.

'What were you doing with Uncle Geoff last night?' asked Harley, in a curt tone.

Taking her time to answer, Dionne flicked the kettle switch on and retrieved a cup from the cupboard above her head. She'd known this question would be shot at her, but she needed to get some caffeine inside her first.

'Poor Uncle Geoff was very upset about something, Harley, so I was comforting him. Grown-ups do that, like when Daddy hugs you when you're upset.'

'Liar!' snapped Harley.

Dionne spun around and glared at her daughter. 'Now, Harley, you can stop this attitude. Why you have to be so hateful to me, I don't know, but know this. I *am* your mother, and you must learn to respect me.' She lowered her voice. 'Sweetheart, sometimes it's hard for children to understand grown-up stuff, but when we get frightened and upset, like you do, we need a hug as well. Your Daddy wasn't here to help Uncle Geoff, so I had to. That's what families do.'

'You didn't have your clothes on,' Hudson stated, as he screwed his nose up.

Dionne waved her hands. 'Oh, yes, well, I was just about to get in the bath.'

Harley shook her head. 'No you *weren't*, and I'm going to tell Daddy.'

'Well, of course you can tell Daddy . . . If you want to have him concerned about Uncle Geoff, that is.'

Harley narrowed her eyes and questioningly tilted her head.

Sighing heavily, Dionne ran her hands through her hair. 'Harley, darling, your Daddy has a few problems that he's worrying about at the moment. And I just don't want him to worry about his brother as well. Do you understand what I mean?'

For a long moment, Harley locked eyes with her mother. Then she slumped back in her chair and nodded.

'Good girl. Now, then, who wants some cereal?'

* * *

Once Dionne had dropped the children off at school and returned home, Geoff arrived. Nervous and on edge, he looked worse than yesterday, with a two-day stubble.

'Dionne, about yesterday. I'm sorry, love. I shouldn't have taken advantage of you like that.'

Dionne was surprised that he'd seen it that way.

'Here.' He handed her a box. 'It's a gun, and it's loaded, but only use it if you really have to. Jesus, I don't even know why I'm doing this.'

She gently gripped his arm and whispered, 'Because, Geoff, we both know that if these bastards come for us, I'll need some kind of protection, and CCTV won't stop them. Cancel the appointment this afternoon. There's no need. I'll get a pretend one put on the wall.'

Geoff looked her up and down, noticing the low-cut top and her nipples poking through. Once again, his manly urges came to the fore. He felt a stirring in his groin and the urge to explore her body again. She was looking hot, and as she breathed, her breasts heaved up and down, enticing him in.

Putting the box on the kitchen table, Dionne had the same hungry look of last evening. In three seconds flat, they were all over each other, as they made their way into the lounge.

Unlike before, they were like ravenous animals, pulling and ripping at each other's clothes. But, this time, he took control by gripping her wrists and pinning her down. She felt alive and reacted to his forceful jerks and passionate bites.

Once they'd finished, he got dressed and left. Again, he felt sick with guilt, but there was something there that had drawn him to her.

As soon as Dionne heard his car leave the drive, she clutched the box and lifted the lid. The gun looked brand new. A small weapon and perfect if an intruder broke in, she knew she could protect herself and the kids as she'd been asked to by *the voice of reason*. She lifted the gun, a Glock 42 pistol, from the box and was surprised how light it was. She then wondered if it was even real, since it looked like a toy. She checked the magazine and pulled back the safety catch, admiring its simplicity. She was about to place it back into the box and put it somewhere safe when the phone rang. Leaving the gun on the cabinet in the lounge, she answered the call.

It was the school. The twins had to be collected because they'd destroyed the mural and clawed the stand-in teacher's face.

Dionne was annoyed that her day was being interrupted again by the twins. Why couldn't they just behave like the other kids? She felt at a loss to know what to do with them.

The idea of the psychiatrist jumped to the forefront of her mind. Once this unsettling time was over, she would call the number on the card, and, hopefully, a shrink would be able to prescribe something that would miraculously turn them into regular children.

* * *

Ella Morley, the supply teacher, was barely out of school herself. A stocky woman, with thick black glasses and a mop of black hair, she was wearing a yellow boiler suit pinched in at the waist with a wide white belt and a string of chunky plastic beads hanging around her neck.

When Dionne saw Miss Morley in the school office, she thought the young woman's outfit looked crass – certainly not very professional. However her attention was quickly drawn to the woman stuttering while trying to explain what had happened. Apparently, Miss Morley had unassumingly placed Hudson in group A and Harley in group B. When they'd left their seats to join each other, she'd tried to coax them back to where she'd initially placed them. But they didn't reason with her; instead, they ripped down the mural and began tearing it up. When she tried to calm them down, she was viciously assaulted.

Through a shaky voice, Miss Morley mumbled, 'Team A were to add all the shells and team B were to glue the cotton clouds. I didn't realise the twins weren't supposed to be separated. With Mrs Reeves off sick, no one warned me.'

The tear-stained face of the young teacher had Peter Major riled up.

She was right, he thought. *It was the school's fault for this outburst. The young supply teacher should have been informed about the children's preference to stay together.* But he couldn't deal with these children. He'd already had two vocal parents into his office recently who'd complained quite vociferously about the Mason twins.

Pulling Dionne aside, he said, 'I am afraid that this cannot go on. I think you need to keep the children at home for a few days, perhaps for two weeks. I can't have my staff physically attacked like that.'

'What!' gasped Dionne.

'I'm sorry, Mrs Mason, but until I can think of another option, they will be suspended for now.' Without waiting for a response, Major marched away to the safety of his office. He hated confrontation, and yet he had to make a stand.

That was it: she'd had enough. Her children would have to see a professional, whether they liked it or not, and sooner rather than later.

Once they arrived home, Dionne sat them down at the dining room table. She looked at their flawless faces, their button noses, and their heart-shaped lips and thought they looked perfect. But they were not. The hideous expression in their eyes told her all she needed to know. There was something very wrong with them.

'Now, tell me, why did you hurt the teacher? You know that it's wrong, and you know you've been punished, don't you?' She tried to speak with a soft tone, in the hope that it would get them to open up.

'I don't care!' snapped Harley. 'She should not have moved us. I liked it where I was. I like our table with Hudson, Tommy, and Abbey.'

Dionne's ears pricked up. 'Do you have friends then, Harley?'

She nodded and turned to Hudson, saying something in French.

'Now, then I will help you, but, first, you have to speak English in front of me, and you have to be nice.'

Hudson gave a deep frown, making him look older. 'We *are* nice.'

Dionne inclined her head. 'No, you are *not* nice, Hudson, and I think I would like you to meet someone who can perhaps teach you to be nice.'

The twins threw each other a glance and then babbled away again in French.

'Stop it! You must listen to me. You're not to keep doing this. You cannot teach each other. You have to learn from adults! From me . . . I'm your mother.'

'I want to see *Daddy*!' demanded Harley.

Dionne leaned across to stroke her daughter's hair, but she was shrugged off. 'Harley, I'm not stopping you. He's away at the moment, but as soon as you can see him, I'll take you both there.'

'I hate you!' snapped Hudson. 'You've never liked our father, and you won't let us see him. I know you won't.'

Slamming her hands on the table, she cried, 'For God's sake, you two, will you ever give up? I've tried so damned hard to be nice and fair to you both, but all you ever do is run to your father. You're bloody five years old, but you talk like you're twenty-five. So if this is how it's going to be, then so be it. I cannot make you want to like me, no matter how hard I try. I don't even know why you hate me, but know this: your father is away. It's not my fault, and there's nothing I can do about it. And just so you know, I've no idea how long he'll be away for either.' She paused and sighed as she watched her children's eyes fill up. 'I'm sorry. I understand it's hard. It's hard for me too, but I would never stop you seeing him. I promise you that.'

Hudson comforted his sister when he saw her bottom lip drop and her eyes begin to well up. She never made a noise when she cried, but she looked so sad, his heart went out to her. They sloped off to their bedroom, away from their mother.

Determined to find the psychiatrist's business card, Dionne searched every drawer, until, finally, she had the information in her hand.

Quickly, she dialled the number and waited until a woman's voice answered. She'd stupidly expected the doctor himself.

'Oh, hello. I want to book an appointment for my twins to meet with Dr Reeves. I was given this number and told I should mention their names . . . Hudson and Harley Mason.'

The secretary kept her on the line waiting for the best part of five minutes.

Eventually, she said, 'Yes, can you bring them in next Wednesday at four o'clock? Just come to the reception, and I will escort you to his office.'

Dionne noted the day and time on the kitchen calendar and replaced the receiver. That was it. There was no point in getting Luke's permission for the twins to see a psychiatrist – as he wouldn't be around – and she knew he would go ballistic anyway because, as he saw it, his precious babies were perfectly healthy. But she couldn't carry on with their antics and retain her sanity.

After the children had silently finished their evening meal, they miraculously took their plates to the dishwasher and got themselves ready for bed. When their lights were turned off, Dionne poured herself a large glass of wine and settled down for the evening to watch one of the *Friday the 13th* horror movies.

After her third glass, and once the credits had disappeared from the screen, she walked up the stairs to run a hot bath. She checked on the children. They had moved back into the same room. Gazing around, she could see it was immaculate. All the books were lined up in order of size, the dolls were sitting an inch apart, and the puzzles were stacked in alphabetical order. Then she looked at the two children's faces and their sleepy rosy cheeks. They seemed so small and angelic in the large beds with their eyes closed. How perfect they appeared. If only they looked the same awake.

She ran the hot water and sipped her wine. Adding her expensive oils, she watched the bubbles grow and decided to light the candles to create her own spa. The radio on the windowsill was tuned to Classic FM, and she turned it on, low enough not to wake the kids and spoil her moment of peace. Slipping out of her dressing gown, she eased herself into the warm water and instantly felt her muscles relax. Half-asleep and dreaming of the future, she could hear muffled noises in the distance. Assuming one of the children had popped down to make a drink, she closed her eyes and sighed. She decided to ignore the intrusion.

CHAPTER TEN

It was late, and Geoff had just tucked Davey and Nicki into bed. They had drunk too much Coke and were overexcited. But, for some reason, Scarlett was in a mood and insisted he put the children to bed. Geoff didn't argue; he could see she was ready to explode, and he assumed the boys had been playing up. Once he returned to the lounge, he found her pacing the floor.

'Right, Scarlett, what the fuck's the matter with you? Ya never scream at the boys like that.'

She threw him an evil glare. 'What's going on, Geoff? I'm not good enough anymore, eh? Found yaself a younger model, have ya?'

Geoff felt his heart rate rising and tried to swallow back the guilt. 'What do ya mean?'

Her eyes squinted to a spiteful glare. 'You dirty fucking bastard!'

'You what!' he snapped back.

'I have put up with your bollocks for years. I have given you two beautiful boys and cooked, cleaned, and put up with your snoring, but for what, eh?' Her bottom lip quivered, and her eyes filled with tears. 'For you to go dipping your dirty wick elsewhere . . . How could you, Geoff? How could you?' she screamed, and the tears tumbled down her face. Her face was a mix of pain and anger as she placed her hands over her face and began to sob.

He grabbed her hands away to look at her face. 'I haven't been with any bird.'

'Get off me. Don't fucking *touch* me. I know you have. I do your stinking washing. I wash your pants, remember.'

Geoff's eyes widened. So his wife was acting like a fucking detective now, was she? How the hell was he going to worm his way out of this?

Suddenly, the phone rang, and he stared at the number that flashed on his mobile.

'Is that your fucking girlfriend? Well, is it? Who calls here after ten o'clock, eh? Answer me, Geoff!'

He glared at his wife, and, silently, he left the room.

Following him, Scarlett yelled, 'Who is it?' She tried to snatch the phone from him, but Geoff pushed her hands away and answered the call.

The blood drained from his face when he heard Dionne's hysterical voice.

'Geoff, you have to come over. The kids have found the gun, and . . . Oh my God,' she wailed, before the phone went dead.

Scarlett knew by the look on his face that the call was not from his fancy piece. It was clearly serious business. She'd got it all wrong. Embarrassed, she walked back into the lounge and watched from the window. He was obviously seriously concerned about something, merely by the way he was charging out of the house, while putting on his black leather jacket.

* * *

Geoff arrived at Dionne's home in record time, but he hesitated as soon as he put the key in the door. Something told him that if he entered the home, things would never be the same from this point onwards. But, in any case, it didn't seem right having a set of keys when Luke was no longer there. However, everyone in the family had keys to each other's homes; it was just the way it had always been. Another feeling of unease swept over him. He was going into the unknown; crazy notions ran through his mind. Had Hudson shot Harley, or had Harley shot Hudson, or had one of them even shot Dionne? The kids shooting someone? It was too hard to believe.

As he stood in the doorway, he saw the twins standing at the top of the stairs dressed in pyjamas and holding each other's hands.

Dionne, however, was another story. Her eyes were wide and her movements quick. Wearing her dressing gown, and with her hair wet, she grabbed his arm, pulled him further inside, and shut the door.

He glanced up at the children again. They still remained immobile, their gaze transfixed on him.

'Where's the gun? What happened?' His whispered words tumbled over themselves, but Dionne was silent as she guided him into the kitchen.

He stopped dead as if he were about to fall off a cliff edge.

'Jesus fucking wept!' he said, his words delivered in a deliberate staccato.

'Oh my God, Geoff. What are we gonna do?'

He looked at the fear on her face and then back at the man lying in a pool of blood, which was now congealing into a thick and gory mess. The claret was up the wall and all over the units and looked stark in comparison to the whiteness of the gleaming new kitchen.

Geoff felt bile rising in his throat. Carefully, he stepped forward to see who the man was. As he peered down at his face, he gasped. 'Shit! That's *Curtis Stracken.*'

Geoff could see that the man's face was intact, but the blood had already seeped from his chest and covered his neck and cheekbones. He noticed blood was also on Stracken's hands and guessed that he hadn't died immediately. The marks on the floor clearly showed he'd moved around. 'What the fuck's happened?'

Dionne was gripping Geoff's arm and peering over his shoulder. 'I honestly don't know, Geoff. I really don't know. I was in the bath and I fell asleep. Then I heard a bang. I thought the boiler had blown up or something, so I hurried downstairs. I found him here.'

Geoff swallowed back the bile and tried to slow his rapid heartbeat.

'Who shot him?'

Her eyes first gazed at him, and then, deliberately, she whispered, 'I think it must have been one or both of the twins.'

'*What!* Are you *sure* one of the kids did this?'

A tear fell down her face, and she almost choked, saying, 'Yes, it must have been.'

'There was no one else in the house?' he questioned.

'*No,* just us. I came out of the bathroom and found the kids at the bottom of the stairs. Oh my God. What have they done?'

Unable to understand how two little five-year-old kids could have killed a grown man, Geoff pulled Dionne away from the monstrous scene and took her into the lounge.

'Dionne, don't fuck with me. They are little *children.* How would they even know how to use a gun? I'm not buying that. I know it's a lightweight gun, and if it's set up, it's ready to fire, but a little kid firing it? That's stretching things too far. Look, if you killed him, just say. I mean, it was self-defence, right? I can sort this mess out.'

She sat heavily on a chair. 'Geoff, I swear it wasn't me. If I'd killed him, of course I would tell you. And, to be honest, if I had come down and found a strange man in my house, I probably would have shot him. I mean, I have two kids to protect, but I didn't shoot him.'

Geoff's eyes were wide with shock. 'But surely it wasn't one of them? They are too young. It makes no sense, unless, of course, someone else did it.'

Dionne shook her head. 'Geoff, they may only be young, but, trust me, they are so strong and clever.'

'So you really believe it was them?'

Looking up through her eyelashes Dionne nodded, while nervously biting her nails.

'What am I going to do, Geoff? I can't call the police. The gun will have Hudson's or Harley's prints all over it, and the police will take my babies away.' She buried her head in her hands and sobbed her heart out.

'Listen, Dionne. You make the twins a drink, and we'll go and talk to them. I want to hear what they have to say.'

Watching Dionne shake, in between the sobbing, he stroked her head. 'It's okay. Listen to me. Where's the gun?'

She lifted her head and wiped the snot from her nose. 'I put it in the bottom drawer over there.' She pointed to the lounge cabinet. 'It was on the kitchen table when I came downstairs.'

Thank God, he thought. He sighed with relief. He didn't see why a stranger would come to Dionne's house and kill Stracken. The idea was ludicrous. So he was beginning to believe Dionne that it actually was the kids who'd shot Stracken. But at least they couldn't come back down and take out their mother and him as well.

He then shook his head. *Get your brain in gear, Geoff. There was no way those kids would have known how to handle a gun and actually shoot Stracken. No way.*

Luckily, the mess was only at one end of the kitchen, allowing Dionne to make the children a drink without having to go near the dead body.

Dionne and Geoff walked into the children's bedroom to find them sitting up on their beds and babbling away again in French.

As they saw their mum and uncle arrive, their conversation stopped.

Harley looked up at Geoff fearfully.

But Hudson gave Geoff a long stare and smirked.

Once Dionne handed a drink each to her children, both she and Geoff waited until they'd finished.

With a deferential glance at Dionne, who gave him a slight nod, Geoff sat on the end of Harley's bed, and in a gentle voice, he spoke to the twins.

'Can I talk to you about what has happened this evening?'

It was Harley who spoke first. Urgently, she said, 'We don't really know, Uncle Geoff. There was a loud bang. We came out of our bedroom and went to the bottom of the stairs. Mummy came out of the bathroom, ran downstairs, and went into the kitchen, and that's when she told us to go to our room. Didn't she, Hudson?'

Hudson didn't speak but he nodded.

Geoff decided that it would be best if he and Dionne left the children where they were for the moment. They stepped out of the bedroom, partially closing the door.

'Dionne, are you sure they didn't say anything earlier?'

Dionne gave him a puzzled look. 'What do you mean?'

'Well, if you believe the kids killed him, they must have said something. For Christ's sake, Dionne, there's a fucking grown man on your kitchen floor covered in claret . . . Surely, they would have said something . . . anything?'

Dionne bit her lip. 'I asked them what had happened, but they just ignored me and headed back to their bedroom. As soon as I saw the mess in the kitchen, I assumed it could only have been them. I called you right away. I didn't know what else to do.'

'Maybe I should have another talk with them in the morning and find out exactly what happened.'

'Geoff, don't do that. I'm afraid for them. They may get very scared if you do that. I'll take them away for a few days and see if I can get them to talk. I don't want to frighten them. Christ, they are only very young. Perhaps it was an accident, or perhaps this Stracken man scared them. One of them might then have fired the gun, not really understanding what they were doing.'

'How the hell would they do that? You didn't leave the gun in a place where they could see it, did you, for Christ's sake?'

She knew damn well that not only had she left the gun on the cabinet, having been distracted by the phone call from the school, but she'd also left it with the magazine already engaged and the weapon ready to fire. She'd totally forgotten to put it away.

Not wanting to look a complete idiot, she replied, 'Look, Geoff, I'll be honest. My mind is all over the place at the moment. I can't be sure if I actually put the gun in the cabinet drawer or if those kids watched me set the gun up and clocked me putting it away. They are really clever and fucking devious. They don't miss a trick.'

'Yeah, I'm beginning to get an awful feeling about this, and by that, I mean the kids. When we went into their room, Hudson gave me that smirk of his, and Harley seemed too eager to tell us her version of events. So, perhaps you're right and one of them actually shot him. Thinking about it, that particular gun is fairly easy to fire. Look, Scarlett's parents have a cottage down in Winchelsea. They live in Spain, so it never gets used. Not even Scarlett likes the place, but it's okay. Get the kids dressed and take them away from here. I need to get this mess cleaned up. If Hudson did shoot Stracken – probably by mistake – they mustn't see this.'

'Right, leave it to me.'

'Okay. I never thought that fucker Curtis Stracken would ever turn up here after the bashing he took from Luke years ago.'

Dionne huffed. 'Well, I guess, it was an ideal time to take revenge on me when Luke's inside.'

'Dionne, how would the Strackens even know he was in prison? We've not broadcast it. It's not good for business, you see, and it's not been in the papers either. No, he was here to exact revenge on Luke. Now then, babe, there's a pit in the garage for working under the car. Did Luke ever get around to filling it?'

'His car's parked over it. No, it's still there. Why?'

Geoff shook his head and bit his lip. 'I just wondered . . . Look, take this key. The address is on the label. Head off to the cottage with the twins. Leave this to me, eh?'

Dionne nodded and gave Geoff a hug. It was nothing sexual, just a warm, heartfelt embrace.

He watched as she walked away, her movements slow, and he sighed. She looked to have the world on her shoulders right now. She was worn down by everything, and he knew it. Poor Dionne. She'd been dealt a bad hand. His mother and Scarlett had never really befriended her; Luke, too, could be very difficult, with his spiteful sneer and cold ways; and now, to be left with two kids who were apparently more dangerous than Bonnie and Clyde, she probably felt that her situation couldn't get much worse.

He waited until she had the children strapped in the rear of the car and the bags loaded before he called her back into the house. Clasping her shoulders, he looked at her sad eyes and noticed just how beautiful they were without make-up. With her hair tied in a ponytail and dressed in a simple loose jumper and jeans, she really was a stunner. 'Hey, it's gonna be all right. You stay away, and I'll come and join you in a few days. We'll sort this mess out together, okay?'

She lowered her eyes and allowed another tear to fall. 'Oh, Geoff, what would I do without you?'

After a passionate kiss, he closed the front door, went into the kitchen, and stripped off his clothes, folding them neatly in a pile on a chair.

A door led from the kitchen directly into the garage. He sized up the gap in the doorway against the body on the floor. He knew he could drag Stracken through without marking the doorframe. Carefully, he unravelled the roll of bin liners that he'd found under the sink. Stepping over the body, he entered the garage in search of tape to bind the bags.

Above the workbench he saw hammers, screwdrivers, and tape.

Geoff looked at Luke's car and decided to move it out of the garage first. Luckily, the key was still in the ignition.

It was pitch-black now, the house was far enough away from prying neighbours, and the large bent beech tree obscured the view of the garage from the entrance to the drive. The garage door slid up and over, and Geoff reversed the Porsche out. In a second, he was back inside, and he hastily closed the door behind him. Then he turned on the lights. With a deep breath, he pulled himself together and got to work using all the tape and bin liners to cover the corpse. But when he got to the head, his stomach churned, and he was unable to hold back the vomit. Stracken was staring at him, in a sick, twisted way that made him jump back.

His phone rang, which startled him even more. He looked at the caller; it was Scarlett. Too busy to speak to her right now, he shoved the phone back in his pocket. His priority was to get the body taped and buried and the kitchen cleaned up. Wiping his mouth, he took a deep breath. *Come on, Geoff. Get a fucking grip.* Finally, he managed to secure a black bag over Stracken's head and drag him to the pit.

The body flopped and landed awkwardly; it was all twisted at an odd angle. For a second, Geoff wanted to hop down into the pit and straighten it up, but then he took another deep breath and muttered, 'Christ, Geoff, pull yaself together. He's dead, so what does it matter?'

He stood back and pondered whether to fill the pit first or clean up the kitchen. His nerves were all over the place. Stacked up in a corner of the garage, he noticed a few bags of sand and cement that had been bought to fill the pit when Luke had the time to do it, but, clearly, the lazy sod had never quite got around to it.

Really, to fill a hole that size, he would need to use the cement mixer, and that was noisy. Still, he had no choice; it had to be done. The mix needn't be perfect. As long as it was sufficient to fill the hole, he could level off the entire floor tomorrow. Coughing back the dust from the powdered cement, he poured the bags into the mixer and inserted the hosepipe. It took less time than he expected, and an hour later, the pit was filled.

He returned to the kitchen and looked at the mess; this was a woman's job. Taking out the bottles of cleaning products from under the sink, he poured them all into a bucket of hot water and then began mopping and scrubbing until the kitchen floor was gleaming white again. Although his throat was sore from the bleach and ammonia, at least there was no sign of a murder scene. One word hit him like a brick: murder. From what he could gather from Dionne, those kids, his little niece and nephew, were murderers, probably the youngest in history. And even he found them distinctly odd and somewhat startling.

Suddenly, he wanted to get home and see his children, his dear little boys, with their bright, innocent eyes, goofy teeth ready for braces, oversized knees, and the twinkle in their eyes that was enhanced by their thick dark lashes.

Before he set off, he decided to take a quick shower and wash away any smell off him from this gruesome night. Rarely would he venture upstairs; he would use the downstairs bathroom. And even when he'd done that search for any other weapons, after his brother's arrest, in case the police checked over the house, he'd only gone into Dionne and Luke's bedroom.

His mind wouldn't leave the garage. The vision of the dead guy kept plaguing him with the image of him buried in the garage pit.

He shuddered and headed for the bathroom. Along the way, he passed the children's bedroom. Something made him go inside; maybe it was the fact that he saw them now as plausible killers, and he was still baffled by what he'd seen, which led him naturally into their bedroom. Perhaps he might learn more about his brother's adopted children. He had to think of them like that because the thought of them being in any way, shape, or form his blood relatives really sickened him. At least his own family had the excuse that they didn't share the same DNA.

It wasn't like his own boys' rooms where the clothes would be strewn on the floor, and the toys would be thrown in toy boxes. This room was oddly perfect. Then his eyes were drawn to the two desks and the kids' paintings. He took a closer look and felt strangely terrified. There on their desks were almost identical paintings of four people – two children and two adults. One painting showed a woman with her throat cut. The other picture was almost the same, but here, a man had a knife protruding from his chest. It made no sense, and the fact that the pictures were so mature for five-year-olds worried him even more. His fascination held him in the room longer than it should have. He clocked the puzzles and realised they were for children aged ten and over. Glancing further around the room, his attention turned to the books, which were for older readers aged twelve plus. And then he saw a notebook. With his curiosity piqued, he looked inside to find a story written by Harley, the words being clearly written and punctuated. His own children at ten and twelve were not that neat.

His thoughts returned to Dionne, and he wondered if she would be safe. 'Pull yourself together, man,' he said, aloud. They were only five. Smart kids, maybe, but, still, they were not far off from being babies.

Hastily, he ran the shower and washed away the cement, which had settled like a layer of dust, and the smell, which was probably psychological. He dried himself on the white towel and noticed a small smudge. He checked himself for any cuts but there weren't any, so he concluded some blood had perhaps stuck to his arm and he hadn't washed it off properly. As he pulled his jeans up over his hips, he stopped, frozen to the spot. A sound from downstairs had his heart thumping. Was there someone in the house? Poised for a moment, he strained to listen, but there was nothing – just a cold silence. Taking a deep breath, he tried to relax his shoulders. The events of this evening had well and truly spooked him out.

CHAPTER ELEVEN

The drive to Winchelsea was long and tiring. Even though it was late September, the night was very dark; the moon was out, and the constant movement rocked the children to sleep. Peering in the rear-view mirror, Dionne sighed. Her children looked so sweet with their heads touching. Her perfect little babies. *Hmm, if only they really were*, she thought.

Her mind went to Geoff and how for years she'd watched him from a distance. He was the really handsome brother, the one with the confidence, the muscle, and those eyes that sucked her in. Luke was the one she'd made a play for. But there was no comparison, really. Geoff had the looks and the charm, while Luke had his sour face and awkward ways. He would never have thrown her around the bedroom, too polite for hard sex. She sighed and began daydreaming. If Geoff left Scarlett, they could be a family . . . Her train of thought was interrupted when Hudson coughed. She peered back in the mirror to see his eyes glaring at her. Her thoughts returned to Geoff; he would never take her on with the kids. But when Luke was released, she would be free to go. Luke adored the children, and they adored him. They hated her, that was abundantly clear. Why they despised her was a mystery to Luke but not so much to her. But as for Geoff, would he be prepared to leave Scarlett?

* * *

Scarlett was still up and pacing the floor. It was now 4 a.m., and she couldn't sleep, imagining her husband shagging another woman.

Hearing a key turning in the lock of the front door, she was there, almost ripping it off its hinges.

'Where the fuck have you been, ya dirty bastard?'

'Aw, leave off, Scar. I'm too tired to argue with you. I'm going to my room.'

With a sturdy grip, she pulled him back off the first step of the staircase. 'Oh no, you don't. I wanna know what the fuck's going on.'

His eyes now red from exhaustion, he threw her an evil glare. 'I've been to work. Now I need to fucking sleep, so get out of my face and leave off.'

She tugged at his arm again. 'Been to work, have you? And now they have showers at the club, do they?'

Shaking her off him, he raised his hand. 'Keep on, woman, and I *will* fucking lose it. Now, as I've just said, I've been to work, so, Scarlett, that means I've been to *work*.'

'You liar! You fucking liar. You've been with another woman. I can smell her on you. You left here with ya hair dirty, and you've now come back with it clean. I ain't stupid, Geoff. Who is she, eh?'

He shook his head. 'Shut up, you idiot. I've *not* been with another woman, but if you keep on, I just might fuck off!'

With her mouth wide open, she watched him disappear upstairs. Never in all their years had he ever spoken to her like that. At that moment, she truly believed he *was* having an affair.

* * *

A few days had passed and Dionne was fretting. She hadn't heard from Geoff, and the twins wanted to go home. They couldn't settle in the cottage and were now making her life unbearable. Having waited long enough, she decided to call him. He answered right away.

'Yes.'

'Geoff, love, is it all right to come home? The kids are restless.'

Geoff was in the garden with the boys, and Scarlett was still moping around the house, continually giving him evil looks. 'Yes, sorry, I was gonna come down, but, well, I just couldn't. Everything's fine, though.'

* * *

He replaced the phone in his pocket and took a deep breath. It was so surreal; there he was playing football in the garden, while back at his brother's house, a dead body lay under the garage floor. He'd been back and finished off the work, ensuring it was immaculate, yet he was still troubled by the noise he'd heard. Questions circled his mind. *Had there been someone else in that house when he'd been taking a shower? And if so, who?*

'Dad, it's your turn to be in goal!' shouted Davey.

For a moment, Geoff was dragged from his paranoia. He looked up to see his eldest son, with a big smile that lit up his eyes.

'Yes, my boy, and no soft kicks, not if you wanna be a striker.'

* * *

As Dionne parked her car outside her garage, she gave a huge sigh of relief. She was so pleased to be back at home. Geoff had assured her that the mess was all cleared up. She now wanted to see it for herself because she hated anything being untidy or dirty.

While the twins ran up the stairs with their bags, she headed hesitantly to the kitchen. Her hands flew to her mouth in surprise. Geoff had played a blinder. The kitchen floor was actually gleaming. As hard as she searched for any signs of blood, she found nothing. Nothing at all. Then she ventured into the garage. Under Luke's car the pit was completely covered over. It was so clean that she realised Geoff had screeded the whole floor.

With the house now back to normal, she settled the children in and ordered pizza. While they all waited for the food, she brought down puzzles into the lounge and asked them if she could take part.

Although they viewed her with suspicion at first, it was Harley who nodded for her mother to join in.

Dionne noticed Hudson watching her, but his eyes weren't dark and foreboding; instead, they looked sad.

'Are you okay, Hudson?'

He held a piece of the puzzle in his hand, and she noticed his eyes were welling up.

'What is it?' She attempted a soothing tone.

He bit his bottom lip and looked up. And then a fat tear trickled down his face.

Harley stopped what she was doing and stared at him.

'I miss my Daddy. He liked to play with us. When will he be home, Mummy?'

Looking from one pair of identical eyes to another, she sighed. 'I know you miss him, but I do too.'

'No, you don't, Mummy. You miss *Uncle Geoff*,' said Harley, in a cold, calculated way.

'No, Harley, Uncle Geoff has been kind to us while Daddy is . . .'

'Where is he? And when will he be home? He isn't dead, is he?' asked Hudson.

'Goodness, no! No, he isn't dead. Look, okay, I know you're both young, but I should tell you this. Daddy was arrested and is in prison. We are waiting for the judge to tell us if he'll be able to come home or if he'll have to stay for a while. But I promise you, once the judge decides, I'll tell you.'

'And what about the man who was here? Is he dead?' asked Harley.

Totally stunned, Dionne jolted upright. 'What man?'

Harley gave her a knowing grin. 'The man I heard you and Uncle Geoff talking about.'

'Now listen, both of you. That's a very serious thing to say, and it will end up with you two being carted away and locked up.'

'But why? *We* didn't do anything wrong,' said Hudson.

Scrutinising her children's faces, Dionne felt uneasy. *Jesus, are these kids blaming me?* She shuffled in her chair.

With her heart beating fast, Dionne tried to calm her breathing. 'Okay, okay . . . So tell me exactly what you heard Uncle Geoff say.'

Panic had set in. She'd assumed while they'd been at the cottage the kids had kept quiet about the incident because they knew they were guilty, and she'd hoped it would have stayed that way. Now, she was faced with a worrying problem. If the kids told anyone, how could she explain it away?

'He said, "How did a grown man end up on your kitchen floor covered . . ."' She paused in thought. 'Covered in red or something. I guess, he meant blood.'

Not to be outsmarted by two young children, she laughed. 'Oh goodness gracious me, you hear a snippet like that and then you think there's a dead man in the kitchen. No, no, someone must have tried to break in, if, as you say, you didn't do anything wrong. So that must have been what the bang was all about. And the burglar had cut his arm. But clever Uncle Geoff cleaned the mess up, that's all. So don't worry yourselves because while we were away, Uncle Geoff made sure no burglars could break in again.'

Watching the twins in turn, she could barely believe it. Strangely, both children began working on the puzzle as if she'd never even spoken. She smiled inwardly. She knew she was good but not *that* good. She would use the time now to think of how she would polish up the story of the burglar. However, right now, she did wonder if at some point they would call her bluff. She knew her kids were unusual and had high IQs, along with considerable cunning.

Suddenly, she remembered the psychiatrist's appointment. It was scheduled for tomorrow. She needed to ease the children into the idea, instead of springing it on them. They hated change and didn't take too well to strangers either.

'Tomorrow, we're going to see a man called Mr Reeves. He's a nice man, and he wants to meet with you two because you are both very clever.'

She struggled to think of what else to say. She hoped that would do.

Hudson placed the last piece of the puzzle into position and screwed his button nose up. 'Why?'

'Well, like I've just said, you are very clever.' She smiled at Hudson. 'Look how quickly you finished that puzzle. Mr Reeves is a very nice man. A very important man. He wants to see how clever you really are, that's all. Wouldn't you like to know that as well?'

Ever the arch manipulator, Dionne knew she had won this particular round. Harley gave her a beady stare, and it was at that moment Dionne knew she could pull the wool over her eyes. But she left it like that and went into the kitchen to get them all some drinks.

When she returned to the lounge, they watched a James Bond classic. She'd tried in the past to coax her children to watch films more appropriate for their age, but it had been a complete waste of time. For an hour or so, Dionne felt like she was making headway. And with Luke out of the picture, she hoped eventually she could connect in some way with them and perhaps their future may look brighter, especially if the psychiatrist could sort them out.

* * *

Wednesday afternoon arrived, and Dionne felt uneasy. She hoped that the kids wouldn't kick off and end the session before it had even started. Their school track record was appalling; it clearly demonstrated that they simply had no fear of authority and no respect for anyone other than each other, and, of course, their father.

The clinic itself was set away from the road. The perimeter consisted of high metal railings, and the entrance was gated. She had to stop and look at the address again because she had formed a picture in her head – of a doctor's surgery or a unit in a hospital wing.

The gates opened, and she drove up to the building. The facade consisted of mirrored windows, so it was impossible to see inside. The front entrance comprised huge glass doors, but there was no signage visible referring to mental health or psychiatry; a visitor could have been walking into a classy business centre.

Dionne held Hudson's and Harley's hands, and as they entered the building, they found themselves standing in front of the receptionist's sleek desk.

The secretary, whose name badge showed her as 'Samantha', was dressed in a very smart, tailored navy-blue suit. Her soft features glowed from the application of moisturiser rather than any make-up, and her hair was neatly pulled back in a bun.

Dionne felt awkward; she wondered if the children would settle in this somewhat sanitised building. It had the look and feel of an expensive private hospital.

Samantha walked around her desk and gave the family a warm smile. 'You must be Harley and Hudson,' she said, as she bent down to shake the children's hands. The twins smiled back.

That was a first, thought Dionne. Then the receptionist stood up and shook hands with Dionne.

As the family followed Samantha along the corridor, Dionne noticed that the ambience of the building was not as inhuman as she'd thought. Everywhere they walked had substantial colourful paintings, and, in one corridor, there were fish tanks built into the wall.

Hudson and Harley gripped each other's hands and stopped a few feet behind their mother to stare at the fish.

The last door on the right was Dr Reeves' room. Samantha opened the door and gestured for the family to go in.

Dionne looked behind at the children, and, impatiently, said, 'Come on, both of you.'

Samantha was surprised by the mother's tone. It seemed harsh for young children who were visiting a strange place for the first time.

But Dionne was eager to get the little sods inside before they scarpered.

Surprisingly, they did as they were told and hurriedly caught up with her.

Taken aback by the size of the room and how bright it was, Dionne was distracted for a moment.

'Come in, come in,' said Dr Reeves, in a jolly tone. Jumping up from his chair, he held out his hands to greet them. Like Samantha, he shook hands with the children and then finally with Dionne.

Harley and Hudson both smiled and reciprocated, much to the astonishment of their mother.

'Please, all of you, do take a seat.'

The unfamiliarity of it all and the sleek, high-end furniture made Dionne feel almost like a child herself.

'So, thank you for coming, and here we have our special people.' He gave a generous smile to the two children. 'I hear, Hudson and Harley, that you are very, very smart.'

His deep voice, rosy cheeks, and sunny disposition put the twins instantly at ease; however, Dionne felt like she was in a goldfish bowl.

'So, Mrs Mason, would you mind if I get to know your children? We have a small lounge with magazines and a television, all quite comfortable for you while I talk with these guys.' He pointed to the twins and beamed.

'Oh, er . . . Yes, I mean, er, should I not stay and watch, or something?'

He laughed and waved his hands. 'Oh no, Mrs Mason, they are not under the microscope! I just want to get to know them first, and it's always better when the parents are not in the room.'

'Oh . . . I, er, I see. I didn't think it would be like this.'

Dr Reeves inclined his head. 'No, most people think I will pull out smudged ink pictures and ask them what they see.' He chuckled again. 'No, no, it's nothing like that.'

Samantha stood in the doorway, ready to escort Dionne to the lounge.

But Dionne insisted on waiting just outside to hear if the twins were going to kick off.

Samantha placed an arm around her shoulders. 'They are in good hands. Dr Reeves is the best there is. Come with me. I am sure you will feel so much more comfortable in the guest lounge, as we call it.'

'But if they start to . . . I mean, if they get upset or . . .'

Samantha looked warmly at Mrs Mason and gave her a genuine smile. 'If they show any signs of discomfort, I will fetch you immediately. I promise.'

Dionne reluctantly followed the receptionist to an airy room, which had a touch of indulgence about it. She sat in one of the high-backed chairs and took a copy of *Vogue* magazine to pass the time away. Just as she turned the first page, her phone pinged. She grappled inside her bag to retrieve it, hoping it was a message from Geoff to say that he was coming over, but it wasn't. She read the text and frowned.

I see you have taken the twins to a psychiatric clinic.

Quickly, Dionne jumped up from her seat and tried to peer through the window, but her field of vision was blocked by a delivery van. Nervously, she sat back down and tried to calm herself by looking through the magazine.

* * *

Reeves observed how the twins leaned into each other. 'So, how about I tell you about me?'

Hudson nodded. He was sussing out the doctor just as much as he was sussing out him.

'Well, I am married, and I live in a house with my wife and my little dog called Jimmy.' He pulled a photo from off the desk. 'There, that's him.'

Hudson grinned and nudged his sister.

'My favourite food is pizza, and I like to go fishing.'

Hudson chuckled. 'We like pizza.'

'What else do you like?' Reeves was cracking the ice.

'Um, I like puzzles, and I like books.'

Reeves looked at Harley. 'And what do you like?'

'The same,' she replied.

'Now, isn't that wonderful. You both like exactly the same thing. That must mean you love to play games together. Well, we have a lot in common because I love puzzles, and I love to read. Would you like to show me how good you are at puzzles?' He pointed to the small table and chairs.

Eagerly, they scrambled from their chairs and raced over to the shelves filled with boxes, puzzles, games, and books.

Reeves pulled a very complicated 3D puzzle for adults from the top shelf. It was so taxing that not even he could do it. Placing it on the table, he removed the lid and sighed loudly. 'Oh dear, I think this one is far too hard for you two. Perhaps I'll find an easier one for you both.'

In an instant, Hudson had his little hands firmly over the box. 'No!' he snapped.

Reeves waited for him to apologise or look awkward for being too sharp, but he didn't; he was too engrossed in what was inside the box.

'I still think we should start with another puzzle.'

Harley glared at him in annoyance. 'No!' She copied her brother.

He smiled. 'Okay, you carry on, and I will just watch because I am interested to see how you do it.'

The twins worked like they were one person, both having a job to do and getting it done in record time. Not once did they look at Dr Reeves. Their minds were totally focused on the puzzle, and as this took shape, they gave each other an encouraging grin whenever they managed to concur about a problematic piece.

When the puzzle was complete, Reeves praised them, letting them know how well they'd worked together and how pleased he was with them.

Samantha brought in a selection of fruit juices for the children to choose from, and both picked the purple drinks. Everything was being mentally noted.

An hour had passed, and it was time to go.

Dionne was brought back into the room; she eagerly looked at Dr Reeves for feedback.

'Come in, come in. Please take a seat.'

She'd half-expected the doctor to look worn out with possible teeth or scratch marks. Inexplicably, she found herself seeing her children sitting upright and drinking their juices and contentedly swinging their legs.

'So how do you find them?'

Reeves frowned and shook his head. It was clear he didn't want to discuss anything at this time and not in front of the children.

Hudson glared at his mother with contempt, which didn't go unnoticed.

'So, Hudson and Harley are great company. I have enjoyed our games and conversation. They are very bright children.' He paused and looked at the twins. 'Would you like to see me again?' he asked them, dismissing their mother.

They both nodded, and Harley spoke up first. 'I can show you my drawings and my writing, if you like.'

'Yes, and I have made a boat. I have made it out of matchsticks, so I can show you it,' said Hudson.

'Good. So shall we say I see you again at the same time and the same place next week, then?'

Now giggling, they replied in unison, 'Yes, please.'

He clapped his hands and stood up to see them to the door.

Dionne held back from leaving. She wanted feedback, now concerned that she wasn't being consulted.

As the children skipped on ahead, she turned to Dr Reeves. 'So what do you think? Are they. . . ? I mean, do they have problems?'

Reeves smiled. 'Mrs Mason, it is far too early to make an assumption at this stage, but please bring them in next week, and I will continue to monitor them.'

'Yes, but did you see anything like . . . abnormal?'

With a deep furrowed brow, Reeves shook his head. 'We prefer to use inoffensive terminology, but I will discuss the children with you alone, in probably a month or so.'

'A month!' she gasped.

'Yes, Mrs Mason. A month, if not longer. They are five years old, not twenty-five. It's not easy to diagnose a five-year-old, even if there is an issue.'

Dionne wasn't happy – it was plastered across her face.

'Right, I will bring them next week.' With that, she marched along the corridor to catch up with the children. Her hopes of some quick fix were dashed.

The children seemed happy, though; they were giggling and pointing at the fish. Harley was so mesmerised, Dionne had to prise her away.

CHAPTER TWELVE

Six months later

The morning of the trial brought renewed anxiety. It was the first time in months that Dionne had laid eyes on her husband. He'd refused to see anyone except Miriam and Archi. It suited Dionne because the thought of going all the way to HMP Brixton to wait in queues, and then to sit opposite his miserable face when he had no interest in her, wasn't her idea of a cream cake.

Everything in the home had settled down now. She was able to do whatever she wanted and go wherever she had the desire to go, and the children were coping better at school.

Libby Reeves had managed to ensure the children were kept together and in a regular routine whereby they felt secure, and she was able to build trust with them.

The frequent visits with Guy Reeves were doing something positive because the twins seemed happier at least. Dionne was astonished at how eager they were to get to the clinic and do whatever it was they did. The one-hour visits became two hours, and so Dionne embraced the change, which allowed her to go off and spend an hour or so with an old friend.

The only fly in the ointment was Luke. If he was sent down for a long time, then the house and the lifestyle may well go out of the window, unless she could win over Geoff completely. She needed a plan B, and so she ensured that their little indiscretions continued – but only when the children were in school. Knowing precisely what Geoff was missing at home, Dionne worked her damnedest to fulfil his needs. With Geoff, the hot, passionate sex wasn't a chore – it was an enjoyable pastime, and the more they both had, the more they wanted.

When they all met at Luke's parents' house on the morning of the trial, Dionne recognised just how much the court case had taken its toll on Miriam. She appeared fragile, her shoulders were stooped, and her hair was dull. Archi was the same; he struggled to get out of his chair, and then he staggered as he walked. Whilst it looked to Dionne that Miriam had tried her best to look smart, Dionne noticed her mother-in-law's unkempt nails and the creases in her skirt.

Glancing over at Tilly, who was the same as always, dressed in a modest outfit and wearing very little make-up, although her nails were manicured, Dionne flicked her head for Tilly to join her in the lounge, away from the kitchen, so that she could have a private word. Tilly got up from her chair, and with a puzzled expression, she followed.

'Tilly, what's going on with Miriam? She looks washed out. I've never seen her like that, and it worries me.'

Looking behind her, ensuring they were still alone, Tilly whispered, 'She is worried to fucking death that Luke will get a long bird and . . .' She paused, flicking her eyes from side to side.

'And what, Tilly? Tell me.'

'It's not really for me to say, but I think she hasn't said anything to you because you've enough on your plate, but Scarlett has been here nearly every day, bending her ear about Geoff having an affair. Cor, Jesus, Dionne, I nearly told her to fuck off meself. I tell ya, she's like a bleedin' leech, sucking the life out of Mir.' She looked behind her again. 'I know Mir's worried about Luke. It goes without saying, but she don't need Scarlett going on and on with her paranoia. I tell ya, the girl is losing the plot. She's so fucking convinced he's 'aving it away with some bird. After the trial, I'm gonna have a word with her. 'Cos Mir's like me own mum, and I hate to see her dragged down like this, ya know.'

Dionne's eyes widened. 'I wondered why Geoff looked dead beat. She must be driving him insane, then, if she's whinging to Miriam.'

'If Scarlett carries on, he'll either lump her one or fuck her off. Mir says it's affecting the boys and that's not right, Dionne, is it? They're at that age when they can go off the rails, and if she's making everyone's life a bleedin' misery, she could send Davey and Nicki down the wrong path. And she thought it was me at one point. When he brought the kids over and stayed for coffee, she followed him, convinced it was me. Well, my Dean went mental and threatened to have it out with her, but I told him to leave it.'

'She *follows* him?' asked Dionne, wanting to know more.

'Yep. She'd give any fucking detective a run for their money. Oh yeah, and she thought he was seeing *you*. Apparently, he fixed your sink or something. I dunno, but she followed him, and, by all accounts, he did lose the plot and said if he caught her spying on him ever again he would file for divorce. I don't talk to her anymore 'cos she's pissed on her chips with me. Shame, really, 'cos we were good mates, ya know.'

Their chat was interrupted when the front door opened and in walked Geoff, followed by Scarlett, who looked a shell of a woman she was before.

'State of her,' whispered Tilly, who had a gripe of her own. Usually Tilly would have been the first to go over, pleased to be in her sister-in-law's company, but the tables had well and truly turned. Tilly remained with Dionne and just nodded in Scarlett's direction, merely out of politeness.

In fact, Scarlett did look the worse for wear. Her usual animated and comical personality was so diluted, she was now quiet, and if she stood in the corner, she could have passed for an ornament. Even her graceful and serene look was marred by anxiety. Her hair was flat and in need of recolouring, and her skin seemed sallow. She nodded in their direction but followed Geoff into the kitchen like a lost lamb.

Miriam had heard enough moans and groans from Scarlett and wasn't about to lend an ear to them today. This day was not about Scarlett but her own son Luke.

'Archi, pour me a brandy, will ya, love?'

Archi would have bantered with Miriam, but not today. He got up from the kitchen table and did as he was told.

Miriam gulped the liquor back and shuddered. Placing the glass in the sink, she stared out of the window and fought to hold back the tears. It was like a funeral, except it wasn't: it was the day they'd find out if Luke would be set free or go down. However, they didn't hold out much hope: the solicitor had already told them to be prepared for the worst.

By 10 a.m., there were lots of anxious faces looking at their watches. The time was ticking, literally, as they realised that there was very little left before the trial itself.

While the women were inside drinking copious cups of tea and coffee, Geoff and Dean could be seen walking outside in the beautiful garden.

Archi had decided to steer clear of everyone and had gone down to the furthest part of his garden where he could talk to his roses.

The muddiest part of the lawn, where the boys had played endless games of football, was now returfed, and the kiddies' swings had been taken down. It had saddened Miriam at the time, thinking that even her grandchildren were growing up. The twins, though, never played on the swings anyway; they were more interested in the insects and bugs.

Dionne and Tilly rejoined Miriam in the kitchen. 'Shall I make some more tea and coffee, Mir?' offered Tilly.

With a compassionate smile, but looking as though she had the world on her shoulders, Miriam replied, 'If I drink any more tea, I'll look like a poxy teabag.'

'I know what you mean, Miriam. I have drunk so much tea with all this worry about Geoff and his fucking fancy piece, I swear, if I find—'

That was it: Miriam had taken all she could. 'Shut up, Scarlett. Just shut your bloody mouth, before I fucking shut it for you. My Luke could go down for a long time, and here's you, still going on and fucking on about some mad notion that my son's having an affair. You selfish woman, can't you think of anyone other than yourself? Look at Dionne. You *have* your husband, but she could be on her own for a long time. Now, if you're gonna mention this one more time, then get your bag and get off home.'

All three women were gobsmacked; they knew damn well that Miriam had a curt tongue, but never with Scarlett – until today.

Miriam's words went around in Scarlett's head, but she was so consumed with her own woes, she stupidly lashed back. 'It's no mad notion. And I wouldn't be fucking surprised if you're all in on it. You'd love to see me out of the picture, Miriam, so that you could take over my kids and turn them into saddos like ya own sons.'

No sooner had the words left Scarlett's mouth than Miriam gave her a hard slap across the face.

Instantly, Scarlett lashed back and pushed Miriam into the Aga. She lost her balance and toppled over.

Dionne rushed to help her mother-in-law to her feet, but Tilly was enraged and launched a vicious attack. Snatching Scarlett's hair, she dragged her to the floor, jumped on top of her, and punched her senseless. Luckily, Miriam was only shaken, and there were no bones broken.

Hearing a fiasco, Geoff and Dean rushed back inside, only to find Dionne trying to pull Tilly off Scarlett.

Dean managed it. He dragged Tilly into the lounge and tried to calm her down. 'Jesus, what the fuck, Til?'

Tilly tried to straighten herself, in between angry deep breaths. 'That cow.' She gasped for breath. 'That fucking 'orrible bitch pushed ya muvver over.'

Geoff didn't help his wife to her feet. He just stared at her in disgust as she struggled to pull herself up and wipe the blood from her nose.

There were no tears from Scarlett. She was still angry herself and glared at Miriam, who was now being comforted by Dionne.

Dean was pacing the floor. 'Geoff, you'd better take your missus home. I swear to God, mate, she's nuts and either needs help or a good slap.'

Tilly was still reeling and ready for round two. She was a 'rucker', having been brought up in Bermondsey, where it was dog eat dog, so she could handle herself, unlike Scarlett, who was born in Blackheath and had come from a more well-to-do family. Tilly could smash the life out of any woman, if need be. Her life before Dean had been no bed of roses, and she'd had to fight hard to survive.

With her hair a matted mess, her face red and bruised, and now looking like a scarecrow, Scarlett was ready to give Geoff a piece of her mind. 'You are all snakes, and you, Geoff, will never see the boys again. I will fucking make sure of it. I'm leaving you and taking the boys with me. You lot can rot in hell, and I fucking hope karma comes around to bite you all on the arse.'

With anger rising from the pit of Geoff's stomach, he strode towards her, his hand raised, but before he could strike her, he was pulled back by Dean.

'No, Geoff, let her go. We don't want you nicked as well.'

Scarlett gave them all an acid glare before she left and slammed the door behind her.

Miriam was now in tears. She felt very vulnerable. Gone were the days of her being the strong matriarch of the family. The business with Luke had aged her, and she was now weak with worry.

Dionne patted her shoulder as she sat in the chair. 'Here, ya go, Mir. Sip this brandy or you might go into shock.'

'Go into shock? I might get done for fucking murder, if she ever steps foot in my house again.'

Miriam swallowed the raw spirit and winced. 'Ah, Dionne, love. I'm sorry. I mean, I did give you a rough deal, but I was wrong, and I'm woman enough to admit it. You have been a rock to those kiddies while all this has been going on. My Geoff said you've been handling it well for their sakes. I got you all wrong, girl, and I'm truly sorry, love.'

Dionne chuckled. 'Nah, Mir, I was a bit of a cocky cow. I s'pose I did have me nose in the air. Well, you didn't get rid of me that easily, did you?'

With a heavy sigh, Miriam patted Dionne's hand that was resting on her shoulder. 'No, and I'm glad I didn't scare you off. You're a gem, and my Luke should have been more understanding as far as the kids go. I know they're a handful. I've seen it for meself. Anyway, once he's home again, I'm sure things will get easier.'

* * *

It was time to go to the courthouse and face what the law had in store for them.

The gallery was almost full. Quite a few men were present, dressed in suits.

Geoff was uneasy because he knew they were the dangerous Irish mobsters who had supplied them with the guns. Knowing not to acknowledge them, Geoff sat next to his mother in the front row. He watched Dean gripping Tilly's hand. He was the emotional brother and would shed a tear at the drop of a hat; and seeing his Luke standing in the dock, he knew Dean would be a blubbering wreck.

Luke had insisted he had no visitors, except his parents, during his stay on remand; he didn't want anyone to know what his wife or kids looked like, in case the Irish decided to give him a taste of what was to come if he turned Queen's evidence and grassed up the lot of them.

Dionne sat next to Geoff but made no contact with him. She could see he was on edge, and she wouldn't make things any more difficult for him. It would only take a small indiscretion for Miriam to clock any affection, and she would be like a rat up a drainpipe. Her eye for detail was impeccable, and she could sniff out any wrongdoing in a flash.

The formalities dragged on, and by the afternoon, Dionne was bored shitless. There seemed to be no end to the statements being read out as various police officers took to the stand. Then, finally, at 2.30 p.m., Luke was led to the witness stand.

Miriam waved to let him know she was there, but she had to choke back the sobs waiting to leave her throat.

Dionne felt a twinge of some emotion, but in what way, she couldn't say. She didn't know what to expect, having not seen him for a few months now. But then she noticed his eyes were scanning the gallery, and she guessed he was hoping to see someone else's face. *Perhaps Beverley Childs*, she thought.

Luke wore a white shirt, a blue tie, and a grey suit, all sent in by Miriam. With his long hair now tied back in a ponytail, his face looked more chiselled and different from Geoff's and Dean's, whose faces were rounder and more colourful. His sharp expression did him no favours, though, and with his hair pulled back, he looked even more fierce.

'Aw, bless him. Look, he's lost weight, and he looks so nervous,' whispered Miriam, snivelling.

'He looks all right, Mir. He ain't lost weight, and he don't look shit-scared either,' replied Archi, now annoyed that his wife was once again babying his son.

'He does. Look at his face.'

Archi growled under his breath, 'That's 'cos he's got his hair tied in some poncy ponytail.'

'It's all the rage at the moment.'

Archi shook his head. 'Well, Mir, it won't do him any favours in jail, now will it? Jesus, woman, you worry me. He'll be a right target with long hair.'

Miriam shot him a worried glare. 'What do you mean?'

Fed up with waiting and now hearing his wife talking shit, he waved his hand. 'Nothing, Mir. Just be quiet. I wanna hear what his barrister's saying.'

In a raised voice, she asked, 'Archi, what do you mean?'

The court seemed to stop its business and eyes below turned to look up to the gallery. One of the court ushers hurried upstairs to where Miriam and Archi were sitting and demanded she be quiet.

Miriam, who was now livid, hissed in Archi's ear. 'See what you did? Ya nearly got us kicked out.'

* * *

The jury was out, and before Luke was led away, he looked over at Dionne and winked.

As they all left the courtroom to get a coffee before the verdict, one of the Irishmen, who had occupied the back row, tapped Geoff on the shoulder and nodded his approval. Luke had taken the nicking on the chin and not turned Queen's evidence. Now it was a waiting game.

* * *

The court was back in session. The Mason family all held hands and almost prayed that he wasn't found guilty.

Dionne could feel Miriam shaking as the foreman of the jury stood up to read the verdict. She held her breath and closed her eyes.

'Guilty!'

As Miriam screamed out, 'No!' Archi tried to calm her down. Everyone wanted to hear the sentence.

The judge nodded for the jury members to remain seated, and he reeled off his summing up. The family weren't listening; they only wanted to know one thing. Eventually, after the judge had finished rambling on and on, he said, 'Luke Harry Mason, you are hereby sentenced to twelve years in prison.'

The gallery was shocked into silence; the words 'twelve years' bounced around in Dionne's head.

Luke looked over and smiled to show he was okay.

But it was Dean who was inconsolable. He'd always looked up to Luke. Geoff may have been the eldest, but Dean treated Luke as if he was. When the shit had hit the fan, and Dean had found himself in hot water, it had always been Luke who had turned up and either given someone else a good kicking or bailed him out of the nick. There was only the one time when Luke couldn't get him out of a mess; it had happened when he'd been caught red-handed with a pouch of cocaine on him by a copper, no less. So, he'd had to serve a year inside. Knowing full well what it was really like inside Wormwood Scrubs, he felt sick to his stomach to contemplate that his brother was going to serve a severe lump of bird possibly in a place like that.

Tilly held her husband close, rubbing his back, which heaved up and down in between sobs.

Archi pulled his wife into him to hug her.

Dionne gave Luke a kind smile and nodded as if to say 'We'll be all right.'

Luke was taken away.

The family slowly eased themselves along the seats in the gallery, out of the courtroom, and then they made their way onto the street. It was surreal not knowing what to do now; it was over. Luke would be away for many years, and now they were faced with what to do next.

'Fucking twelve years, Archi. I might not even be alive when he comes home,' Miriam cried.

'Gawd, gal, sometimes I think you're going senile. Our brief's already told us he'll only serve half. He'll do just six years.'

Miriam pushed herself away. 'Archi, six years is still a bleedin' long time. How will my poor boy cope?'

Archi shook his head and rolled his eyes. 'Your blue-eyed baby ain't no fucking pushover. He can handle himself, and, believe me, that lad can do his time standing on his head. Now then, let's go and get ourselves a drink down the pub, eh?'

'Aw, for fuck's sake, Archi. That's all you bleedin' think about.'

'And you didn't bloody moan about necking half that bottle o' brandy this morning, did ya?'

Miriam gave her husband a soft smile and wiped her watery eyes. 'He'll be all right though, Archi, won't he?'

Archi squeezed her shoulder. 'Yeah, my gal. Don't you fret, but his missus might not be.'

Miriam looked over to see Dionne's face a picture of pure shock.

It was Archi who placed his arm around Dionne. 'Listen to me, gal. We'll all pull together, so you won't be alone. We're a family, and that means you're part of us. I know my Luke won't serve time well if he thinks we've neglected you, so you've no need to worry.'

Dionne hugged him and smiled, her eyes moist with tears. 'I know, Archi, and I'm just thankful I have all of you to help me, 'cos it's gonna be hard not to have the love of my life around.'

A fat tear slid down her nose, and Archi squeezed her arm. 'There, gal, let it out, babe. We're 'ere for you.'

As Dionne looked over her father-in-law's shoulder, she noticed how Geoff's head hung in sadness, like a broken man.

Geoff couldn't look at her. He felt overwhelming guilt mixed with sadness. His brother's eyes said he was okay, but what actually lay behind them was probably fear and grief. He would miss out on six years of his children's lives.

*　*　*

While Dionne attended the court case, Hudson and Harley stayed behind in the afternoon club run by Mrs Reeves. They enjoyed the club because it was quieter and they could get more involved in their own work, with less distraction. Harley was proving to be an ace student when it came to design, particularly sculpting, and Hudson could read Shakespeare. Their intelligence was on a whole other level, so what they lacked in social skills they made up for in grades.

Gradually, over the past few weeks, a greater understanding of the twins had led to a more productive time and a calmer atmosphere in the classroom. The other children understood that they mustn't encroach on Harley when she was working, and they must never pull one twin away from the other. The twins would be allowed to mingle separately when they wanted to, and the safe environment was slowly bringing them out of their comfort zone and into the space of the other children.

That was until a new girl joined the class. She was a little madam and not very good when it came to being told what to do. Alice Montgomery-Blythe was almost six years old and was spoiled rotten by her very wealthy father, a commercial haulage director. Her mother, Clara, was a ditzy blonde and paraded Alice as if she were a china doll – a child who was not used to the word 'no', who acted defiantly, and who was out to push her luck.

Alice was livid that her parents were in London, shopping, and would be late, so she had to attend the after-school class. Whinging and whining, she sat begrudgingly next to Harley, in defiance of the fact that the teacher had asked her to sit one chair along.

Hudson was across the room, making a papier mâché dog, while Harley was creating a card for her father.

She'd already framed the card with heart-shaped buttons and was about to fetch more glue to complete an amazing piece of creative art.

But Alice took the card, held it up, and laughed. 'This is for a *girl*, not a *boy*.'

Libby's heart was in her mouth because she knew that ridiculing Harley was a big mistake. She suspected the neatly groomed blonde-haired child was about to take the brunt of Harley's temper.

But, to her surprise, Harley returned to the table, carefully removed the card from Alice's hand, and walked over to Hudson. She whispered something in his ear and handed him her work.

Libby held her breath and edged her way forward before there was any eruption.

But Harley sat back down and began creating another card. This time, she drew a picture of a blonde girl with pink bows in her hair and a pink jacket, obviously representing Alice.

Libby looked at the picture and noticed how every detail was clearly drawn and coloured in.

Alice was still acting loudly and disruptively. 'Miss, can I have a drink, please?' And then she whined, 'Miss, I need more crayons.'

The sickly pitch of the child was getting on Libby's nerves, and she knew it would no doubt wind Harley up.

'Alice, please keep your voice down. There is no need to be so loud, and please move over to this table. Harley is trying to work.'

'Miss! This isn't work time. It's playtime because it's an after-school club.' The prissy tone and rudeness were beyond irritation.

'Alice, don't be so selfish. There are others here. You're not the only one.'

While Libby turned her attention to Harley, ignoring the irritating demands of the petulant Alice, she'd forgotten to check that this pupil had moved to another table, as directed.

'Harley, that's very good. I love the way you've made the jacket look as though it has creases. Very clever. And who's the girl in the picture?'

Harley didn't answer but flicked her eyes to the left, indicating it was Alice.

'Yes, I can see it is, now. You've really drawn a good likeness of Alice.'

In a strop, Alice glared at the drawing, enraged that Harley was getting praised for drawing a picture of her. She then flicked the plastic cup of crayons over, which then rolled across the table and all over Harley's picture.

Hudson had seen the incident, along with Tommy, who knew exactly what the twins would do.

But instead of Harley throwing a complete fit, she picked up the red pen, drew a line, and began colouring in a shape on her drawing.

When Libby took another look, she almost gasped. The perfect picture of the girl in the pink coat now looked as though her throat had been slit, and there was Harley, still colouring in what looked like a pool of blood.

Alice peered down at the drawing and screamed like a banshee. Jumping up from her seat, she snatched the picture and then threw it onto the floor before backing away, while Harley glared with her dark eyes and gave her a twisted grin.

'You're creepy, Harley Mason. I hate you!'

Libby had to intervene and quickly. She pulled Alice away to the other side of the room. But when she turned around to check on the other pupils, both Hudson and Harley were side by side, and even Tommy was with them. They looked like zombies ready to go in for the kill.

'Hudson, go back to your work, and, Harley, fetch the card you were making for your dad. Tommy, get back to your painting.'

But the children didn't move, and Libby could hear Alice behind her, whimpering.

'Hudson, go back to your work!' Libby repeated, her voice now much firmer.

That was when she saw him drop his demonic gaze and relax his shoulders. But when she looked at Harley, the pupil was fixated on Alice. The expression on Harley's face was clear . . . If looks could kill.

'Harley, sit down . . . Harley!' Libby knew she had to break that intense stare to get through to her. 'Harley!'

With the tension remaining high, Hudson tapped Harley's shoulder and made her sit back down.

The distraction worked, much to Libby's relief. Harley did as she was asked, enabling Libby to breathe more easily.

Meanwhile, Chloe, the other little girl in the after-school class, rose from her chair, collected Harley's card from Hudson's table, and placed it in front of her. 'There, Harley. It looks beautiful. Your dad will love it.'

Libby was watching the dynamics. It was clear that the children who had started in the class with the Mason twins on the very first day were understanding their strange behaviour much better; in fact, they were almost joining them, like a pack.

Libby shuddered, thankful that Clara had arrived early to collect her daughter.

When Dionne Mason arrived, nothing was said because Libby found the whole situation inexplicable, and she knew she would sound absurd should she try to rationalise it to the twins' mother. The distant expression on

Dionne's face also told Libby that the woman must have a lot on her mind, so she made a decision to let the incident go, for now. However, she would discuss it with Guy when she got home.

*   *   *

The traffic was unusually heavy, and Libby found herself thinking more and more about the twins. If she was honest with herself, she did have a soft spot for them, or maybe she was just intrigued; but, either way, they played on her mind.

As soon as she arrived home, she stepped out of her little Mini Clubman, took a deep breath, and continued on along the drive and in through the front door. She didn't call out to Guy, still too deep in thought. She needed to take her mind off the Mason children, so, eagerly, she decided to go for the simpler option of making spaghetti bolognaise.

Jimmy, their dog, was not by her ankles, which told her that Guy was upstairs in his office. While the mincemeat and onions were simmering, she pulled Harley's picture out of her bag – the one that Alice had thrown on the classroom floor – and studied it again. Harley really was particularly good at art. The detail of the caricature – the oversized eyes and hair against the fabulous detail of the coat – was mind-blowing and drew her in. Not that she knew too much about art, but because this was so unusual, she thought that perhaps Harley was actually gifted. However, the impression of the throat being cut was so authentic, it was not only disturbing but deeply concerning, and, more than that, the idea that the child was just shy of being six years old made her tremble.

The sudden hissing and spitting as the spaghetti spilled over made Libby jump. She put the drawing back into her bag and continued with the dinner. She needed a glass of wine, and that was not a good thing because her motto was that if teaching ever drove her to drink then she would find a new vocation in life. Dribbling the sauce over the pasta, she sighed heavily.

Guy could smell the aroma of tomatoes and Italian spices wafting upstairs and smiled. His dear Libby was cooking dinner, allowing him to continue working. He admired her so much, and secretly, he'd planned a trip to Venice for the following weekend.

Entering the kitchen, he positively glowed in appreciation. 'Ah, my sweetheart. It smells divine.'

She chuckled. 'Then you must be starving.'

As they tucked in, Guy noticed she was unusually quiet. 'What's on your mind?'

'I'll show you.'

She placed her cutlery down, stood up, and then retrieved her bag that was hanging over the doorknob. 'I know, Guy, that now Hudson and Harley are your patients you cannot discuss them, but I'm really concerned.' She sat back down and handed him the drawing. Sipping her glass of wine, she watched his expression, hoping to find some clue as to his thoughts, but he just stared at the drawing, poker-faced.

'Well?' she asked, impatiently.

'This was Harley's, I take it?'

'How did you know?'

He scratched his stubble. 'Because she draws like this.'

Her pale face took on a look of annoyance. 'Guy, I don't want to know what they do or say in your sessions, but, surely, this is not normal? I have never in all my years of teaching seen anything like it, nor met any child like her.'

He could feel her frustration rising and felt guilt whip out its rousing spoon.

'You were right to send them to me, well, indirectly, anyway. I would be breaking every code under the flipping moon if I discussed them with you . . . But I guess we both have a vested interest in the children, and I'm sure, as my wife, you would never put me in an awkward position.'

She furiously shook her head. 'No, never.'

'Okay, yes, the twins tick many boxes . . . ninety per cent, in fact. They're perfect for the study.'

Libby screwed up her nose. 'Like what?'

He coughed to clear his throat. 'I have watched their behaviour and carried out numerous tests, of course, in the form of games and through drawings. They display fearless emotion. For example, if I show them a picture that should disturb them, they remain unresponsive. So Harley's drawing doesn't surprise me. Harley, in particular, has minimal feeling. She responds to me, now that she trusts me, but she mainly responds to Hudson.'

Libby visibly shuddered. 'My God. I feel like this is some kind of horror film.'

Guy shook his head. 'No, not at all. The one thing that is concerning is that they do lack empathy, so if they were to hurt a person, they wouldn't feel guilty or sorry.'

Libby nodded. 'I know. They never apologise. I remember when Tommy, who is supposed to be their friend, fell over and hurt his chin, they never went over to help him. But if either twin even moans, the other one is there in a flash to help.'

Guy sipped his wine and got up to retrieve another bottle from the wine rack. 'That's explainable. They act as hosts for each other – one cannot exist without the other.'

Libby gasped. 'Jesus! *Hosts?* This really does sound disturbing.'

'Sweetheart, they are still children, and they may grow into productive adults, but, right now, they do not fit into *all* the boxes. There is something else going on. You see, we think that maybe their higher level of intelligence has also allowed them to react to the way *we* expect of them. If they were real sociopaths – and we like to call it an antisocial disorder in younger people even though it amounts to the same thing – they would demonstrate impulsive behaviour, manipulation, and erratic responses. I don't think they show these traits, or, if they do have them, their level of intelligence teaches them to hide it, well, more like a psychopath would.'

Libby raised her eyebrows. 'Aren't sociopath and psychopath more or less the same thing but just different words?'

Slowly, Guy shook his head. 'No, a psychopath is more premeditated and calculated. They lack impulse and use their intelligence to plan. They are unable to bond with people. They tend to view them as objects and will use them as such. They do, however, act very charmingly. Sociopaths are reckless, but they can bond with people, and although they will break the law or any rules, they will do so without prior planning, and they can form bonds with, say, family members.'

'So are you saying these two little five-year-olds are psychopaths? Does that mean their parents could be also?'

'I am not saying they are psychopaths or they will grow into sociopaths, but they do show antisocial behaviour, and the more we look into them, the better picture we will have. That picture, for example, may lead to nothing. Harley may just be demonstrating her hate towards the child. But, much more seriously, if she were older, and the drawings became fixated on the one child, and other things began to happen, then all of that really would be a cause for concern because psychopaths fantasise about harming a victim.'

'Jesus, Guy, I have goosebumps. This is so scary.'

He nodded. 'Well, my sweetheart, I'm afraid psychopaths and sociopaths can be just like that. However, in the case of the Mason twins, they are so young, and it may be they won't conform to the type I've described. So, Dr Renee and Dr Black are interested in the children being placed in the Gemini Gene study. The next step is to discuss it with the mother.'

Libby smiled. 'Good luck with that! Who would want their child in a study like that one? It's almost admitting your kid has a chance of being a dangerous serial killer.'

Guy laughed. 'Libs, that's not what this is about at all, and Mrs Mason will not be told any such thing either. The study is called the Higher Functioning Level Gene Study or HFLGS. It's totally non-invasive, well, apart from the initial blood test, and Mrs Mason will get paid every month for the next ten years.'

'Ten years?'

'Yes,' replied Guy. 'We've had a number of patients, but, for obvious reasons, we can only recruit those who are not institutionalised. The study itself has been recruiting for many years, and we need to fill more places before we can meet our primary end point. For years, we have studied how psychopaths cannot demonstrate between right and wrong, but, more importantly, how they cannot process their emotions to make moral judgements and distinguish between conventional and moral choices when it comes to dilemmas. Hudson and Harley will fit very nicely into our subset of patients who demonstrate traits that do not fit in with the perfect make-up of a psychopath. Now, it may be that they are yet to develop and are guided by their elders – their parents, teachers, and so on. But there will come a time when we see them either make good moral judgements or regress.'

'Gosh, this all sounds very complicated, but if it helps the children in the future, then it has to be done, I guess.'

Nodding slowly, he smiled. 'Libby, if we can isolate the gene then we may have light at the end of the tunnel.'

'It still sounds like a scary movie.' She found her husband so interesting; it was probably the reason she married him.

'Well, it could be the future, if the Gemini Gene actually exists. And if so, then instead of just locking these people away from society, we may be able to utilise them.'

Libby tilted her head to the side and screwed up her nose.

He loved that innocent yet questioning expression on her face.

'Yes, it sounds as though we would create machines. It's not that at all. If we can find a way to use their hyperfocus to benefit them and society, then it will be about brain training. Take Harley, for example. When she concentrates, you can almost see the cogs turning, and whatever she seems to put her mind to, she achieves it. It's that focus that is key.'

With a soft smile, Libby replied, 'I can see where you're coming from. I find I do that with the twins in the classroom. Once I've set them a task, they put their heart and soul into it.'

Guy laughed. 'Let's not get carried away because they may not have the gene we are looking for. It will take many years, even after the blood test, to know if they will have these typical characteristics.'

Libby raised her eyebrow. 'You do have a good idea, though, don't you?'

Without answering, Guy winked.

CHAPTER THIRTEEN

Five years on

Dionne was spray tanning her legs in the bathroom when the doorbell sounded. 'Hudson, get the door!' she yelled.

Hudson was at a loose end. Harley was in the garage making some huge sculpture, and he was done with reading *War and Peace*.

As he pulled the door open, Nicki smiled at him. Now fifteen and looking every bit like his handsome father, Geoff, his soft blue eyes would melt any woman's heart.

'All right, Hudson? Is me dad here?'

'Who is it?' yelled Dionne.

Looking past his cousin, Nicki called up the stairs. 'It's me, Auntie Dionne. Have you seen me ol' man?'

Curious as to why he was at her door, she covered herself in a bathrobe and made her way down to meet him.

'No, Nicki. Is everything all right?'

'Me muvver reckons I ain't getting any pocket money because he ain't paid her maintenance. I reckon she's probably spent it on vodka.'

Dionne looked him up and down; he was growing into a really stunning young man and would probably end up taller than his father. 'I can lend you some. What's it for?'

Nicki looked at his feet and then out of the corner of his eye he squinted at her. 'Nuffin much, really. I was gonna go into town and see what's happening.'

He glanced at Hudson, who was staring as per usual. 'Wanna come too, Hudson?' He'd no sooner let the words out of his mouth than he could have kicked himself. If he bumped into his mates, they would no doubt take the piss. His cousins were weird, and there was no disputing the fact.

'Yes, please,' replied Hudson, politely.

Dionne was shocked. Hudson never went anywhere without Harley, and, just shy of eleven years old, they were usually accompanied.

'Oh, okay. I'll get me purse. Keep an eye out for him though, will you? He . . . well, he needs looking after, that's all.'

With a fifty-pound note in his hand, Nicki headed down the drive with his cousin on his heels. He waited for the door to close before he turned to face Hudson. 'No showing me up, Hudson. Do you hear? I want you to just act . . . What I mean is, don't stare at anyone or talk. If someone says "hello", you reply. *Don't* look like a gormless git, yeah?' He waited for an answer, hoping he wouldn't regret having his cousin tagging along.

'Okay.'

'Good,' replied Nicki, feeling uncomfortable. He hated that dark, brooding look in Hudson's eyes. It always seemed to put the wind up him.

Hudson was silent and just followed his cousin close behind. He hadn't a clue what a 'gormless git' looked like; but, anyway, as far as he was concerned, he was pretty much normal.

They hopped on a bus and headed into town. Bromley High Street was a hang-out for Nicki's mates and the few select shops in which he liked to spend his money. However, as soon as they got off the bus, he received a call from Jack Farley telling him that their arch-enemy Toby Dyer was in The Glades and shouting his mouth off about his mother.

Nicki felt uneasy having Hudson along, but it was too late to turn back. Nicki was no mug; he could handle himself, and when the four of them, his brother Davey and two cousins, Lee and Kai, were together, they were given a wide berth. Not that they were bullies, but they stuck together. Both of their dads had instilled into them that they take no shit and always look out for each other. Davey was on his way, and Kai was somewhere in the shopping centre already.

Nicki looked at his cousin and grinned. 'Listen, Hudson, there may be a bit of trouble, so if there is, you just stand back, all right?'

Hudson nodded, looking wide-eyed and troubled.

'It's okay, Hudson. They won't hurt you. It's just some prick slagging me muvver off.'

Nicki was beginning to think that inviting Hudson along may ruin his street cred. After all, the boy did look a tent short of a full-blown circus. But when he glanced at the serious expression on Hudson's face, he thought there was a good chance the youngster would scare the shit out of Toby.

'Hudson, do you ever smile?'

To Nicki's surprise, a huge grin spread across Hudson's face. 'Yes, but only if I need to.'

Nicki frowned. That was an odd thing to say, but, then, he and his brothers had grown up with the twins being peculiar.

The Glades Shopping Centre was heaving, probably due to a radio show in the centre that was attracting people from all over.

Just as they were going down the escalator, Nicki spotted Jack, his best mate, and putting two fingers in his mouth, he whistled to catch his attention.

Meeting at the foot of the escalator, Nicki and Jack gave each other a fist bump, and then Nicki's friend turned to Hudson with a quizzical expression.

'This is Hudson, me little cousin.'

Jack laughed. 'Little?'

'He's nearly eleven, but, yeah, he's big for his age.'

Jack looked at the solid structure of the boy and mentally compared him to his own brother of the same age; Hudson was way bigger.

'Right, Jack, where's this mouthy little fucker? I'm gonna bust his nose for him, calling me muvver a whore.'

Jack looked at Hudson and then replied, 'He's got some mates with him, from Lewisham. Where's ya cousins? 'Cos, Nicki, you can't go and meet Toby and his crew alone. That lot are nutters.'

Before Nicki had a chance to phone his brother, Toby appeared with his sidekicks.

'I hear you want a word? Taken offence to me calling ya muvver a slag, 'ave ya?' said the smug and scruffy eighteen-year-old.

Dressed in designer ripped jeans, a white T-shirt, and leather jacket, Nicki looked like a model in comparison to Toby, who favoured one for Oxfam. Nicki had a take-no-shit attitude about him and stood with a confident posture. And, unknown to the others, he had a tool shoved up his sleeve.

Nicki sized Toby's gang up. As tough as he was, he didn't fancy taking on four lads who were obviously up for a ruck. Jack was as much help as a cement life jacket, and Hudson was just a kid.

Jack moved a few feet away from Nicki, and after failing to get hold of Lee, he quickly dialled Davey's number. They needed to even the score; he and Nicki were outnumbered and about to face the pasting of their lives.

'Need a firm, do ya, Toby?' jeered Nicki, as he glanced at the Lewisham lot. 'I thought with all your mouth, you could handle yaself. I guess I was wrong.'

Toby was fuming; no way would he be shown up by the likes of any of the Masons. 'Nah, pretty boy. How about you and me have a straightener, outside Belgo's?' The Glades had security guards patrolling, and they would get nicked if they started a fight inside.

On the phone to Davey, Jack still had one ear to the conversation. 'Davey, meet us by Belgo's. Nicki's gonna fight Toby, but, Davey, I reckon the others will all put the boot in. There's fucking four of 'em.'

Davey was up on the top floor at the other end of the centre with Kai. They ran as fast as they could towards the glass lifts – pushing people out of the way in the process – but these were full going up and down, so they tore down the escalator and through the exit door.

Out of breath from running through the shopping centre, Davey had a sudden surge of adrenaline when he saw his brother being attacked by Toby and another lad. A tall guy with red hair, known as Suggs, was dragging Nicki around by his leather jacket and punching him in the face, while Toby was kicking him in the chest.

Enraged, Davey, a good two stone heavier than Nicki, sprinted across the grass and threw himself on top of Toby and began to smash him in the neck.

Kai, the youngest of the four cousins, pulled Suggs away from the fight, but he was then headbutted and kicked to the ground by another teenager – a heavily built mixed-race lad called Tory.

The fight was bloody and relentless.

Hudson stood by and watched, not moving an inch. Nicki had told him not to move.

But another one of the Lewisham firm, a small guy called Blaze, roughly fourteen, thought he would join in, and his target was Hudson. He looked his age, and he wanted in on the action. He saw this as an opportunity to earn his rep by initiating himself into the gang.

Jack hollered as Blaze hurled himself into the attack.

Kai was staggering with blood dripping down his forehead and trying to get to Hudson, but Tory kicked him again.

Davey managed to break free, and just as he was about to pull Blaze off his young cousin, Blaze staggered back, clutching his neck. Davey grabbed Hudson and dragged him away and then looked over his shoulder to see Blaze holding his neck with blood pouring between his fingers.

Now on his knees, Blaze was seriously injured and struggled to breathe.

'Jesus!' screamed Jack.

Toby was now on the ground as Nicki kicked him hard in the ribs. 'Take that, you wanker!' he screamed. But there was a sudden quiet.

Tory stared at Davey. 'Fuck, Blaze has been stabbed.'

He turned to face Hudson who was just staring into space.

The fight stopped as quickly as it had started, and the boys were now staring at Blaze who was covered in blood.

Davey bent down to take a closer look. Sure enough, the blood was pumping out of Blaze's neck, and he looked deathly white.

Glancing at Jack, Davey said, 'Call an ambulance quick.' Taking his jacket and T-shirt off, he held it tight against the wound, hoping to slow the bleeding.

Passers-by hurried over to see what was going on, and one man, a retired doctor, got down on his knees and took over.

Relieved to see the man at work, Davey rose to his feet and took a deep breath before he surveyed the battle scene. The others were all battered and bruised, and they panted heavily from the brawl, but they were not dying, unlike Blaze.

Pointing rudely at Hudson, Toby said, 'That boy, he stabbed him.'

Noticing Hudson was still staring off into space, Nicki knew they were in serious shit. He looked at Davey and Kai as if to say 'What do we do now?'

Suddenly, Kai took the lead and shouted, 'Nah, he never. You did. I saw you!'

'What!' screamed Toby.

'Yeah, I saw you do it. He didn't. He's only fucking ten years old.'

By now a crowd of onlookers had arrived, and Toby, Suggs, and Tory seized the moment to run away like terrified dogs.

The doctor asked everyone to clear the area so that Blaze could breathe. Hearing sirens in the distance and steadily getting closer, the doctor said, 'It's all right, son. The ambulance is almost here. You'll be fine. Just take slow breaths.' The doctor knew that unless the lad got help soon, he would bleed out.

Davey nodded for Nicki to remove Hudson before the police arrived.

Jack sidled up to Davey. 'What do we do now?'

'Fuck off home. Jack, you saw nothing, all right?'

While Jack slyly slid away and left Davey and Kai to deal with the repercussions, Nicki dragged Hudson out of sight and jumped on the first bus that came along. Luckily, it was heading for Chislehurst.

Hudson was still quiet and acting very strange as if he was on a bus going to school.

But he wasn't: if he only knew it, he was possibly heading for a psychiatric unit or prison if Blaze died.

Nicki was sweating; he would have to tell Dionne and his father. He shouldn't have taken Hudson with him, but it was too late now, and he would have to face the consequences. Then it dawned on him what Hudson had actually done.

'Hudson, what did you stab him with?' He kept his voice low, so as not to be overheard by the two old ladies three rows down.

Hudson pulled a Parker pen from his pocket. His hand still had blood on it, and he was still gripping the weapon.

Unsure if Hudson was scared to death or away with the fairies, Nicki put his arm around his shoulders. 'It will be all right, Hudson. Let's just get you home.'

Nicki saw an ambulance pass the bus, closely followed by a police vehicle. He craned his neck to see who was in the back of the cop car, but he couldn't see properly.

As soon as they reached their stop, Nicki guided Hudson off the bus and along the road to Dionne's house. Shaking with shock, Nicki knocked at the door.

Dionne opened it, and, without a hello, Nicki barged past. 'Auntie Dionne, ya better get Dad over here *now*.'

Dionne looked from Hudson to Nicki and back to Hudson again. 'What's happened now?'

Shaking his head, and covered in a layer of sweat, Nicki was hard-pressed to string a sentence together.

Dionne knew it was serious. She snatched the phone from the table and dialled Geoff. Anxiously waiting for Geoff to pick up the phone, Dionne looked over at her son in bewilderment.

Geoff eventually picked up, but he was prevented from even saying 'Hi' before Dionne demanded he get over to her house asap.

Slamming the receiver down and noticing for the first time the terror written all over Nicki's face, she said, 'Now, would you mind telling me exactly what's been going on?'

Nicki flicked his head towards Hudson. 'Tell ya mother, Hudson.'

'Jesus, what's he done *now?*'

Impatiently, Nicki raised his voice. 'Tell ya mother what you did, Hudson.'

Slowly, Hudson pulled the pen, which was still covered in blood, from his pocket, his knuckles white from the grip. He put it on the hall table, next to the phone.

'Oh my God. What the fuck!' She stared in disbelief.

'It's not his fault. Me and Davey were in a fight, and some kid started on Hudson, and the next minute, this kid, Blaze, I think his name was, was on Hudson's back . . .'

He paused as he visualised the sight.

'Then what? Are you hurt, Hudson?' Dionne panicked.

'No, he's fine, but, Jesus, the boy, Blaze, he ain't all right. I think . . . I mean, he's more than likely dead. Hudson stabbed him with a pen.'

Dionne threw her hands to her face in horror. 'No! For Christ's sake. Are you *sure* the kid's dead?'

Nicki shrugged his shoulders. 'Pretty much, I guess. The others scarpered, and Davey and Kai stayed behind. I brought Hudson home. Didn't know what else to do.'

Dionne watched her son's eyes glaze over as his face turned a shade of grey.

She ushered them into the kitchen and put the kettle on. 'You both need a sweet tea.'

Eyeing up Hudson, she concluded that he really had no idea what he'd done or the seriousness of it all.

After both boys had drunk their tea, Dionne's attention turned to Hudson again.

'Go and get me the pen!'

Hudson went back into the hallway. Picking up the pen up from the table, he returned to the kitchen.

Dionne took the pen from him. 'Go and get in the bath.'

Hudson frowned. 'But it's too early. I don't have a bath until six o'clock.'

His voice, thick and husky, sounded manlier than Nicki's.

'Do as you're told. Get in the fucking bath, this instance.'

Hudson gave her a spiteful glare and walked away.

Nicki let out a lungful of air as if he was relieved that Hudson had left the room. He slid himself onto a kitchen chair and ran his hands through his hair, looking so much like his father.

His anxious eyes peered up at Dionne. 'I'm so sorry, Auntie Dionne. I had no idea.'

The bruises and cuts on Nicki's face clearly established he'd been in a vicious fight.

'Here.' She handed him a damp tea cloth. 'You'd better wash your face before your father gets here. He's gonna go mental when he finds out you've taken Hudson to a fight. Jesus, he will lose the plot.'

* * *

Since Luke's imprisonment, Geoff and Dionne had continued with their relationship, although they had done so mainly due to their thirst for animalistic sex. No one in the family had any suspicions: they all assumed that he was taking care of Luke's house while Dionne waited for her husband to come home. Dionne was in her element. She could go out, either shopping or visiting her friends, and not be answerable to anyone. Geoff was kind and gentlemanly and gave her the attention that she yearned for.

Luke, however, had stopped all visits with the twins after a fiasco when they came to see him. Harley and Hudson were a month off their sixth birthday and keen as always to visit their father.

Knowing how the twins were with crowds and queues, she found herself on tenterhooks when she noticed the extra-long line. The prison that day was short-staffed, so going through the search area was taking longer than usual with everyone getting heated because it would cut into their visiting time. As they were ushered through first one metal door and then another, the tension rose, such that by the time they entered the visiting room, the pressure cooker was ready to blow. And blow it did.

Harley and Hudson ran to their dad as soon as he appeared, and the pair of them hugged him full of excitement, a sight that Dionne had rarely seen herself. But when it was time to go, they clung on to his trousers.

At first, the officers gave Luke a wide berth.

Dionne knew then that inside the prison her husband was a handful. The other inmates all nodded politely – as a mark of respect.

When Dionne tried to prise her children away, they turned on her, and that's when, stupidly, the officers assumed they could intervene.

One officer, a new recruit, put his hands around Harley's waist to pull her away, but she let out a scream that was like a deafening siren.

The noise startled Luke, who was now raging, and with two savage blows, he knocked the officer clean off his feet. The second officer, for the children's sakes, attempted to remove them, but instead of Luke lashing out, it was Hudson and Harley who went into a rage.

Even Luke was shocked. So much so, he stood for a moment rooted to the spot.

His two little children were fast and violent, making unearthly growling noises, as they kicked, bit, and clawed like two feral cats.

The other inmates found it all highly amusing and cheered the children on.

Yet Luke was mortified. How could his sweet children turn into wild animals at the switch of a button? He'd never seen anything like it and never wanted to again. They were consequently banned from visits indefinitely, and Luke was sent down the block. He stopped all visits with his children, for everyone's peace of mind. He phoned every other day but only allowed Dionne to come once every other month.

But Dionne, for her part, knew there was no real affection between them. She often wondered if he had fallen out of love with her or if he'd ever loved her at all. He never asked for a divorce or even mentioned breaking up, but he was in prison, so what sort of relationship could they really have anyway? That day in court, when he'd thrown her the little wink, she thought perhaps they had a chance, but she was wrong. He was moody and lacked the spark in his eyes as if he always had something else or someone else on his mind. She wondered if he was saving all of his prison visits for Beverley Childs because their own were mainly about the money, the house, and the kids. Not that she was particularly bothered: she had Geoff, anyway, to satisfy her needs.

* * *

Geoff arrived within ten minutes, shortly followed by Davey and Kai in Davey's new electric-blue BMW.

Dionne had expected Geoff to fly off the handle and steam into Nicki for taking Hudson out and getting themselves into serious trouble, but she had a shock.

Letting himself in, he stormed into the kitchen. 'Davey's just told me what's happened.'

'Aw, Geoff, don't shout at Nicki. He didn't mean it.'

The evil glare he gave her almost took her breath away.

'*What?* Why the fuck would I blame him, eh? That boy of yours has stabbed a kid in the neck, who, for all we fucking know, could be brown bread. My boys are not gonna take the rap for that. Ten fucking years old or not, that kid is a liability, and we both know why.' His deep, husky voice growled like a bear, much to the horror of Dionne.

'What shall we do?' She tried to remain calm, as her brain rapidly worked out all the options. First up was the money. She didn't want to get on the wrong side of her regular monetary poke. The businesses were not making much, not enough to sustain her lifestyle, and now Geoff had two homes to maintain, Scarlett's and his own. So, the three-way cut was less than any one of them could live off.

Miriam had gone downhill and lost her spark. She used to look after the books; however, since the day Luke was locked up, she'd become quiet, withdrawn, and uninterested in the business.

As for Dionne, it was okay all the while Geoff was feathering her nest, but if he decided to cut it all dead, then not only would she lose a chunk of money and be forced to sell the house, but she would also lose the one man who she felt she couldn't live without.

Geoff sat on a kitchen chair and looked at his two sons and nephew, Kai, who were almost as tall as him. The three of them could all have been brothers, as they were so much alike.

Waiting for some answers, the boys eyed their father, eager to hear a solution.

'Well, right now, there's nothing we can do. If the police turn up, then we'll just have to tell the truth. I mean, Hudson was defending himself, right?'

The boys nodded in unison.

'So, then, let's just leave it at that.'

With a deep frown, Dionne, now confused, said, 'Er, what do you mean?' She'd assumed Geoff would have come up with at least something that looked cunning enough to save her son. *Surely, he had the brains to think of a collaborative story to spin?* she thought.

But Geoff's face said it all. He was done, and there was no way on earth he was going to risk his boys getting mixed up in this mess.

Nodding for the boys to leave, he waited until he heard the front door close behind them before he spoke. 'Dionne, one day, those kids of yours are gonna go too far. I can't be a part of mopping up their mess yet again.' His deadpan face gave away no clues as to his real feelings.

Teary-eyed, she searched his face for some sign of compassion, but there was none. 'Geoff, what are you saying? Are you and me . . . ?'

He nodded. 'Dionne, it's wrong what we've been doing. He's my brother, and, despite everything, I do feel bad. And as for those kids of yours, I can't take any more of them.'

Desperate to keep him there, she almost threw herself on him. 'Please, Geoff, you are all I have. And I thought you loved me.'

In a solid movement, he stood up and moved her aside. 'Leave off, Dionne. We don't love each other. You know it, and so do I.'

'No! No! You have it all wrong. I do love you. I always have. I don't love Luke. It's you I want.'

'Shut it, and pull yaself together. Look at the state of you. We aren't a couple and never have been, for Christ's sake. So don't go all fucking Romeo and Juliet on me.'

The tears tumbled down like a waterfall, and the snot bubbled from her nose. 'Please, Geoff, I can't do this alone. I know the kids are hard work. They fucking drain me. But without you, what do I have?'

'Dionne, I love my kids, and I have to put them first. No, I mean I want to put them first. My sons are my life, and I won't have them put in danger by yours.'

He tried to walk away, but she grabbed his arm, and then he saw the malevolent look in her eye. 'Get off me, Dionne. I'm done. I ain't coming back. You will get ya money, but leave me out of your life. Start making it up with Luke, 'cos you'll need him around when those two kids of yours get older. Trust me, you will. I can't take them on. And the truth be known, I don't even like them. They give me the creeps, and it might be best if the police do cart Hudson away . . . He needs help, for fuck's sake.'

Dionne stood there, staring at him in disbelief. She never imagined she would hear those words come out of Geoff's mouth. Not her Geoff, the man who was always there for her. The man who bought her flowers and ravished her body as if she were the only woman alive. Not her Geoff who buried the body and made sure she was safe. The pulse in her neck was beating so fast she felt she would explode. How could he do this to her now when she really needed him? Five years of reliving their youth, snatching time together to spend hours in bed, had it all come down to this? It was insane; it simply couldn't end this way.

Like two magnets, they gravitated towards each other, both sexually charged, and both wanting the same thing – passion.

Dionne couldn't accept it . . . she wouldn't accept it. No way. He was her only piece of happiness.

Walking out of the kitchen, he took one last look at her and felt his heart sink. She was still beautiful, even approaching thirty-seven; in fact, she could have passed as a twenty something. Her auburn air was still long and shone every colour, and her eyes were smouldering, and even more so, now they were red from crying.

But he was battling with guilt. Not only that, but the passion they'd had for each other for the past five years had made him take his eye off the ball. The Allure needed a new lease of life, and he was in debt. Dean had downsized to free up some money, but he was content enough. Luckily for Dean, Tilly was his right arm. She'd never been one for rinsing the credit cards. As long as her boys had decent clothes, she would wear cheap, off-the-peg clobber.

He knew Dionne, though, was a very different woman. One who liked the finer, beautiful things in life and demanded them. He had spoiled her rotten. He knew that. But it had been worth it just to see that smile on her face.

Nevertheless, he thought, *eventually life brings you back to earth, sometimes with a bump, as it was doing now.* He had known all along that what he'd been doing was wrong. Very wrong. There was no way he could excuse his behaviour. So he had to end it before Luke came home. He had to get himself together – concentrate on the business and spend more time with his own boys.

Her kids' behaviour was the final straw. Hudson was the size of a fourteen-year-old, and Harley was becoming very womanly. They were old for their years, and yet, strangely, they were also immature in that they were socially awkward. No child was ever perfect, but the twins were downright peculiar, and he couldn't bond with them. His mother showered them with affection, saying they were just troubled. Perhaps she was blinded by the truth because they were her grandchildren. Still, he had to walk away – for his own sanity.

Just as he was about to get into his car, he heard Dionne rushing onto the drive. 'Wait for me! Please, Geoff. I have got them help!' The words tumbled from her mouth, and she was surprised herself that she'd let that particular cat out of the bag.

Geoff froze. Very slowly, he turned around and walked back towards her. 'What do you mean you've got them help?'

'You might as well know, Geoff. I've tried to keep it a secret, hoping that my kids wouldn't be labelled insane, but they see a shrink and have done for five years. He helps them.' She'd deliberately left out the fact that they were in a study, and she was earning another grand a month.

Tilting his head to the side, his face clearly expressed surprise. 'A *shrink?* Why didn't you say?'

She sighed and shrugged her shoulders. 'Well, after you know . . .' She flicked her head in the direction of the garage. 'After what happened, I thought perhaps they should see someone, in case they were traumatised. And I thought it would help them to get on with the other kids at school. But I didn't want anyone to know because they would get labelled and it wouldn't be fair. Luke has no idea, because as far as he's concerned, they are perfectly normal. But me and you, well, we know differently, don't we? I didn't tell you, either, because I wanted to deal with the problem without you having to worry.' Seeing his face soften, she spun the last few words, showing her consideration for him and weaving in the idea that they were a team.

'So, what does this shrink think is wrong with them?' he asked, not out of concern for them but out of curiosity.

'He said they're missing their father and they need stability. He also said they are very clever and will do well in life as long as they can have a stable and consistent routine.'

Carefully, she watched Geoff's demeanour. He looked to be falling for it, hook, line, and sinker. She thought that that would be what Geoff needed to hear, when in actual fact, Guy had really told her very little to grab Geoff's attention. So, naturally, she embellished the rest.

'Right, well, I'll not tell anyone. At least, Dionne, you're doing the right thing . . . for your own sake, if not for theirs.'

Watching him walk briskly back to the car with a black shroud around his broad shoulders, she could tell they had come to the end of their relationship. She said no more; turning to go back inside the house, she listened, as he started the engine and tore off down the drive.

As soon as she reached the kitchen and turned the coffee machine on, the side door to the garage opened and Harley appeared. Her earphones were still in her ears, and her hands were covered in clay. Dionne looked her up and down and felt for the first time in her life like a lone acorn in a lonely forest. Harley was growing into a very attractive young lady, with a well-defined figure and long thick black hair. If she'd been more like herself, Dionne would have put her in for modelling and paraded her around.

Harley, however, was not even interested in nail varnish, let alone make-up and hairstyles. She consented to having her mane tied in a ponytail to keep it away from her face, but that was it as far as her hair was concerned. Her clothes consisted of a tracksuit, jeans, and T-shirts. Anything that required a zip up or a button down would be thrown to the side. Any material that felt uncomfortable was thrown in the bin, and as for heels, well, they were never entertained.

Dionne watched as Harley methodically washed her hands three times with soap in the utility room sink before rinsing and drying them, only then to repeat the sequence. Once she had finished, she removed her earphones and looked at Dionne. 'Mum, please do not touch the sculpture. It needs a day to dry. Oh, and can you buy me sanitary towels? I think I have started my period.'

'What? I mean, do you understand what that means?'

Years ago, when Harley was a baby, she'd thought about when this day would come and how she would sit down with her daughter and have a bonding session. It would be an opportunity to talk to her about how she would be a woman and how having periods meant she could have children, which would then lead on to a discussion about the birds and the bees. But it wasn't like that and never would be. Harley wasn't her natural daughter, and she was so far from any normal child who she would want to bond with. But notwithstanding those negatives – as she saw them – she had to admit to herself that there had been moments when she wondered if she had ever wanted a mother-daughter relationship.

Harley leaned her back against the sink. 'Of course I know what it means. My body is now developed enough to *bleed*.' The tone was sarcastic, and the word 'bleed' was exaggerated.

Dionne had learned to rise above her daughter's constant arrogance, even though it really pissed her off. And to top it all, Geoff had left because of her children, and so the blame was now firmly on their shoulders.

'Either speak to me with respect or buy your own damn sanitary towels.'

Dionne noticed the intelligence behind her daughter's eyes; it was as if Harley was playing her – this child of hers with a mind of a grown woman.

'Sorry, *Mother*, but I'm not sure what you expected me to say . . . Has Geoff left now?'

Was this brat playing mind games? thought Dionne. She could never tell with Harley.

'Yes, he has.' *No thanks to you or your brother, though*, she thought. 'Anyway, go to my bathroom. In the cabinet, you'll find towels in there, and I'll buy some more tomorrow and put them in your top drawer, okay?'

Harley smiled, which always made Dionne shudder; it was a smile that made her perfectly proportioned face appear stunning, even though it had the effect of darkening her eyes.

When Harley left the kitchen and called out to her brother, Dionne was left with a lot on her mind. Things were spiralling out of control. She needed to consult *the voice of reason*, but then she wondered how on earth she would be able to put it all into words. He would be disappointed if not cross with how she had managed the situation.

When Dionne poured herself a coffee, she noticed that the door to the garage was slightly ajar. It was uncharacteristic of Harley to leave it like that because that room was her sanctuary; she spent nearly every waking hour in there, unless, of course, she was hanging out with Hudson.

For weeks now, Dionne had never ventured into the garage. It was the last place she would go. Luke's car was there, along with his tools and gadgets. She really had no reason to enter it. However, she was suddenly intrigued as to what Harley had been making. Perhaps it was the distraction she needed from everything that was going on with Hudson.

Stepping inside the garage, she flicked on the light. For a second, she fought to recover her balance. There, at the far end, she could see a stunning masterpiece. But it was a severely shocking sight. So absorbed in the object, she just stood there, holding in her breath. Paralysed with disbelief, her heart almost lurched out of her chest. Absorbing the initial sight, she moved forward slowly, almost expecting the life-size sculpture to come alive. With her hands to her mouth, she edged towards it and inspected the intricate detail. It was the sculptured strands of the hair and the eyes that were so spectacular. The proportions were perfect and the height exact. Slowly, she walked around it, drinking in the beauty and the horror of it. Her heart and mind were playing with her emotions – emotions she'd never felt in her whole life. She studied the expression on the figure's face and wondered if Harley had actually captured something she'd never seen before when she herself looked in the mirror. Maybe she did have that presence: perhaps that's how Harley saw her. Suddenly, a sickening feeling engulfed her. It was the way in which her daughter had brilliantly personified her radiating beauty while emphasising an imperfection – an imperfection that she didn't have. Two tiny indented circles just below the hairline on the forehead, where the skin was subtly puckered around the circles, looked so real, and yet they were so strange. Taking a deep breath, Dionne stood back, tilted her head from side to side, and tried desperately to work out what those two perfectly formed circles meant. It was as if the sculpture had been made with two horns protruding from the forehead and meticulously removed to appear as if they had been cut off. *Christ, did Harley really see her like that?* She had to leave the garage and collect her senses. Again using the side door that led into the kitchen, she slipped inside and poured herself a glass of cold water to cool down the burning sensation that was curling around her body.

Perhaps she should call Guy and have him explain it, but even to describe it would sound ridiculous. She rarely had any meaningful conversations with the doctor. She would drop the children off once a month now on a Sunday and collect them at the end of the day. As long as she got her money, she didn't care. And it was a free day for her, and the kids seemed to come home in a happy mood. Dr Reeves did call once in a while to say the children were making good progress, but what that meant she never knew. Maybe if she had shown more interest, then Dr Reeves would have divulged more.

Deep in thought, Dionne didn't hear the front door open, but the voice was loud and brought her to her senses.

'Dionne, love, where are you?' called Miriam.

'Er, in the kitchen.'

'Oh my God, are you all right, love? Geoff and the boys have just told me what happened. Jesus, that's all we need . . . Hudson inside too. Right, where is he?'

Taken aback by the speed Miriam's mouth was moving, Dionne didn't have a chance to think clearly.

'He's upstairs, I think. I told him to get in the bath about an hour ago.'

'Put the kettle on, Dionne. I'm parched. All this bleedin' drama. Jesus, it's like Luke all over again. He was the fucking same. Honestly, you would have thought that Hudson was his biological son.'

Dionne watched as Miriam eased herself onto a kitchen chair and plonked her bag on the floor. She'd aged dramatically over the last few years, as her appearance exemplified. The woman who dressed in the latest fashion, even though it didn't suit her, was now wearing plain grey slacks and a loose thin jumper. And her eyes always seemed to be pulled down at the sides, emphasising her sad expression. Yet, today, she appeared somewhat different. Maybe it was the make-up or a shot of Botox, but, either way, she wasn't wearing her usual gloomy expression.

'Yeah, my Luke was always coming home having duffed someone or other up. See, that's the problem. The little bastard got a name for himself, and then everyone and his mother wanted to take him on. I'm surprised he never told you . . . Mind you, he was always the quiet one in the home. My Geoff and Dean were full of tales of how they won this fight and that fight, secured this deal and that deal. Of course, Archi loved hearing what they'd been getting up to, as he always said they were a chip off the old block. Christ, when I think back, I was run ragged bailing them out of the police station, and there was my Archi, patting them on the bleedin' back. Anyway, enough about them. How's Hudson? I bet he's shaken up, eh?'

Trying to take it all in as she poured out the tea, Dionne's eyes widened. 'I never knew he was that bad. I knew Luke could handle himself. I heard about the Stracken fiasco, but I never knew he was aggressive. Granted, he larruped me one, but was he really *that* violent?'

'Yeah, but only if someone started on him. Geoff said he was ruthless, and I suppose it did the boys a favour, in some respects. I mean, some of the old boys, Archi's old mates, villains back in the day, they told him that Luke was a force to be reckoned with. With his keen eye, he was good for a moneymaking deal. See, you hooked yaself a bit of a face, if the truth be known. But my Luke liked to keep his home life separate. He always did, even when he was a lad. It was Geoff and Dean who told me the goings-on. My Luke was like a mouse indoors. He hardly said two words – a bit like Hudson and Harley. Perhaps his persona rubbed off on them.'

'Yeah, well, maybe, because Hudson hasn't said a word about the stabbing.'

Dionne then handed Miriam a cup of tea. 'So what do we do? The boy he stabbed may be dead, for all we know.'

Miriam shook her head. 'No chance. If he is, this place would be crawling with police. Anyway, listen, don't you fret. Archi reckons if it was self-defence, then Hudson will be fine. I mean, he wasn't carrying a knife; it was a pen, and, by all accounts, the boy attacked him first.'

'So are the boys gonna say it was Hudson?'

With her eyebrows raised, Miriam's tone was less friendly. 'What else can they say? For all we know, the place probably has CCTV footage. Look, it's better to take him down the nick and for him to make a statement, than to let him hide, which will only make him look guilty.'

'What are you saying, Miriam . . . ? That *I* should take him down the police station?'

Seeing the look of pure horror on Dionne's face, Miriam realised she needed to calm the situation down and put her daughter-in-law's mind at ease.

'No, Dionne, love. I can take him. It would probably be too much for you. Archi says the quicker he hands himself in, the better. He don't wanna look guilty . . . No, I can run him down there myself. Lyle Harris will meet us there, and, trust me, love, they won't wanna charge a ten-year-old with GBH. He was only defending himself. I honestly don't know why Geoff was making so much of it.'

Processing the information, Dionne concluded that if Miriam wanted to take Hudson then she wouldn't have to sit for hours in the police station herself. She smiled. 'It's kind of you, Miriam. What would I do without you, eh? You're like a mother to me.'

Sipping her tea, Miriam glared over the cup. 'Talking of which, ya mother hasn't been around for a long time now. Why don't you invite her over?'

'Miriam, I never wanted to tell you before, but, well, back then, you would never have believed me. After all, I wasn't your favourite daughter-in-law.'

Miriam sighed. 'I know, and I'm sorry, love.'

'Me mother wasn't exactly a role model either. You see, she was a nasty bitch. She should have been done for child abuse for what she did to me.'

Throwing her hands to her mouth, Miriam let out a gasp. 'No!'

Smiling sadly, Dionne, who was inwardly elated by this heaven-sent opportunity, said, 'Yes, I'm afraid that woe is me look – her sad expression of being downtrodden – is an act. She's one conniving bitch, and, to be honest, I don't want her around my kids. I took enough beatings to last me a lifetime. It's probably why I love Luke so much – his calm way and endearing nature. But that cocky front I used to have was just that – a front. You see, I used to put it on to show the world I was tough, but, inside, I was a nervous wreck, always waiting for the next backhander off my mother.'

Staring off into space as if she was reliving the hard times, she carried on. 'See, it's like a vicious circle with me. My kids get away with blue murder because I'll never treat them the way my mother treated me. I can't even shout at them. So, I guess they do play up because I'm a bad mother.' She allowed the tears to flow and accepted the embrace from Miriam.

'Aw, Dionne, I had no idea, love. You could have told me. You should have said something.'

'Oh, Miriam, I couldn't. Who would have believed me? My mother is some actress, and, well, I just learned to deal with it, but I'm not having her around my kids, so there you have it.'

'I'll never mention it again, love. And, my babe, if you want to talk, I'm all ears.'

Dionne noticed again how Miriam seemed a little more upbeat than usual as if she'd suddenly got a spring in her step.

'You are looking well, Miriam.'

'Oh yes, the reason I was on me way over, before the boys told me about Hudson, was because I bumped into Lyle, and he said Luke was going to be out on parole shortly.'

'What!' shrieked Dionne. *Sod Lyle Harris*: he was clearly too good at his job.

'Yeah, apparently, Luke didn't want us to know, just in case he didn't get it, but he did, and he'll be out next month.' The excitement in her voice took her tone up an octave.

Dionne was dumbfounded and stood with her mouth open, her eyes like saucers. She was having difficulty in processing the information. So much was whirling around in her head that she needed time to get herself together.

'That's fantastic. I need to get the house cleaned up, the kids sorted out. I-I need to get this business with Hudson . . .'

'Stop panicking, Dionne. Look, the house is immaculate. You look as gorgeous as ever, and, well, leave Hudson to Geoff and me. You just calm down.'

The thought of Geoff came back to her – her Geoff, the man she wanted, not Luke, the cold, heartless husband, who she detested now. Darkness spread across her face.

It was picked up instantly by Miriam. 'Look, love, I know things have been strained this last couple of years, what with Luke not sending you any more VOs, but once he's back home, you could make a fresh start. What more could he ask for? His Dionne waiting for him, looking after his kids, and keeping a clean home. Most women, well, except for my Tilly, would have done the off and shacked up with another bloke by now, but not you, eh? You did good by him, and he'll know that. I'll be surprised if he doesn't whisk you away for a second honeymoon.' She grinned and raised her eyebrows.

Dionne responded with a nervous giggle.

'Right, call Hudson down. Let's get this over with.'

When Hudson appeared, he was wearing a grey tracksuit, and he'd combed back his hair with his fringe flopping forward.

Miriam noticed how handsome her youngest grandchild was becoming. With his dark features, he looked like her others; in fact, except for his size and that cold, dark expression he wore all the time, the likeness was uncanny.

Harley skipped down the stairs and joined her brother. 'Oh, Nan, I didn't know you were here.' Her face seemed to soften and appear younger.

'I guess Hudson told you what happened today?'

Harley nodded at Miriam. She and her brother always told each other everything. With her eyes beady, she growled, 'Yes, and if I'd been there, he'd be *dead*.'

The coolness in her tone ran through Miriam like shards of ice. 'Harley!'

'Well, Nan, look at Hudson's ear. The boy nearly ripped my brother's ear off.'

Miriam jumped up from her seat to inspect it, while Hudson remained still and allowed her to separate his hair and take a closer look. Sure enough, there was a deep tear that perhaps should have had stitches, but the cut looked clean.

She turned sharply to Dionne. 'Didn't you see this?'

Dionne shook her head. 'No. I took the pen and sent him to the bathroom. I never noticed any blood, though. Perhaps because his hair is so dark and thick.'

'Right, well, that proves he was attacked. And I'm assuming the trip down the station will be a formality. Right, Hudson, are you ready? We need to tell the police what happened before they come knocking.'

'I'm coming too, Nan.'

Miriam stroked Harley's rosy cheek. 'No, my babe, you can't come, but don't worry. I'll look after your brother and bring him straight back home.' Miriam observed the dark cloud that moved across Harley's face. 'Listen, babe, this is no outing. It's really serious, so you just let Nanny take care of it, so we can get back here as soon as possible.'

Unexpectedly Hudson spoke up in French. It was a habit that both children had still not grown out of.

'I will be okay. I will tell the truth. You just wait for me.'

Miriam was in too much of a rush to care about their private conversation; she had a job to do.

* * *

Bromley Police Station was quiet, except for a scruffy-looking family in the corner of the waiting room. The woman, in her late fifties, was chewing her nails that were bitten to the quick, while her husband, dressed in a dirty tracksuit, baggy at the knees and worn at the collar, paced the floor.

Miriam ushered Hudson over to the glass screen and whispered to the officer behind the desk. 'I have brought my grandson in. He was attacked outside The Glades and suffered a terrible gash to his ear.'

The young WPC raised her eyebrow, and in a monotone asked, 'Did he know who did it?' She'd overheard murmurings from colleagues about an incident at the shopping centre, but, from what she'd gleaned, it wasn't worth the paperwork.

'No, he didn't, but the other boy was taken away in an ambulance.' *There, that should prick up her ears*, thought Miriam.

WPC Blane jolted upright. 'Er, when did this happen?'

Miriam shrugged her shoulders. 'Sometime, this morning. My grandson came home and . . .'

Blane tutted. 'Why didn't he wait for the police?'

Her curt question riled Miriam. She hated snotty-nosed people, especially the police. ''Cos he's only bleedin' ten years old, *that's why*.'

Blane looked past Miriam and sized up the boy. At almost five foot and heavily built, he looked a lot older than ten years old. Without thinking, she said, 'Are you sure about that?'

'Of course, I'm fucking sure. He's my grandson. Now, can we make a statement? I need to get back home. Oh, and my solicitor should be here any minute.'

Blane wrinkled her forehead. 'Why would you need a lawyer if you just want to make a statement?'

Miriam gave the officer a fierce scowl. The tone and questioning were really beginning to stick in her craw. 'Because I wanna make sure he's represented before you lot try anything silly.'

Blane rolled her eyes. 'Take a seat. I'll call Sergeant Coots.'

Miriam guided Hudson to a seat, well away from the shoddy family.

Just as she sat down, in walked Lyle Harris. 'All right, have you been seen yet?'

Miriam snorted. 'Only by some snotty knickers WPC who has called for Sergeant Coots.'

Harris took a seat next to her and opened his briefcase. 'So tell me, Hudson. What happened?'

Hudson looked at his grandmother and remained silent.

'Babe, listen to me. You need to tell Lyle, here, what happened. Now all you need to do is just tell the truth. Tell him exactly what happened.'

Hudson gave the solicitor a quick glance but then kept his head down. 'The boy standing next to me, when Davey and Nicki were fighting with some other boys, grabbed my hair and ripped my ear. I tried to push him away and forgot I had my pen in my hand. I hit him in the neck, and then Davey pulled me away. That's when I saw the boy bleeding, and then Nicki took me home.'

Harris was astonished that Hudson was so cold and factual when he spoke; it was as if he was reading from a book. 'Okay, let's get this over with.' He'd seen the sergeant open the side door.

They were escorted upstairs and into one of the interview rooms.

Hudson looked nervous and kept his head down, which gave Sergeant Coots the impression he was just shy. Straightaway, he conjured up a vision that the boy had been bullied.

'Let's start by taking your name and a few details.'

Miriam answered all the formal questions while the sergeant filled out the form.

'So, tell me in your own words what happened.'

Miriam nudged Hudson to answer.

Hudson, though, couldn't respond. The fluorescent light above his head was flickering, and he couldn't concentrate.

'Hudson, answer the policeman, will you?'

Hudson turned to his nan. 'I don't like the light.' His eyes flicked up to the ceiling.

'Never mind the light, son,' said Sergeant Coots. 'Please tell me what happened today. Start from when you left your house.'

Hudson bit his lip and looked up to the ceiling again.

'Hudson! Answer the question, please. What did you do when you left your house this morning?' Coots was getting impatient. He disliked kids at the best of times.

Unexpectedly, Hudson jumped up from his seat and tried to flee from the room.

But Coots managed to stop him.

In a sudden frenzy, Hudson wriggled and struggled his way free and managed to push the sergeant aside.

Miriam was aghast, and her heart rate went through the roof.

'Hudson!' she hollered, but Hudson was still fixated on getting out of the room. Like a caged animal, with Coots as the lion tamer, Hudson lunged forward and tried again to barge past, but, this time, Coots grabbed him by his wrists and physically sat him down.

'Now, you, son, will be charged with assaulting an officer, if you don't calm yourself down this bloody instant.'

Miriam gripped Hudson's knee and said in a low tone, 'Please, Hudson, just stay still. Answer the policeman's questions, and then we can go home, but if you show off like that again, then they may keep you longer.' She glared at the sergeant. 'And you, you had better remember the boy's only ten years old.'

Harris was on his feet and standing in front of Hudson before another attempt to escape could be made. 'Look, sergeant, the light is clearly distracting him. He may have epilepsy, for all we know. Can we use another room?'

Coots rolled his eyes and gathered up the forms. 'Follow me.'

They eventually settled in the next room. It was much bigger, and to one side higher up, there was a window that looked like a large mirror. Harris could see the calm spread across Hudson's face.

Hudson was straightforward with his statement until he was asked how he felt.

'Nothing,' he snapped back.

'I mean, Hudson, do you feel any anger or animosity towards the lad who split your ear?'

'No.'

Harris put his hand up. 'Hold on, Sergeant Coots. Hudson is here of his own free will to give his account of the fight. I can see where you are going with this, but Hudson has no reason to seek revenge. Must you be reminded again that the boy is only ten years old?'

Coots sniffed the air. 'That may be so, but he hardly looks ten, and I have a fourteen-year-old in hospital suffering from an almost fatal attack, so it's my job to ask the questions.'

Harris smirked. 'Yes, and it's my job to ensure this juvenile is properly represented. So now you have your statement, I wish to take my client home.'

Coots stared at Hudson. He didn't like the dark anger emanating from his eyes.

'Wait! You can't go yet. We don't know who started this, and the victim is still in the hospital and not able to provide us with his account of the fight.'

Harris now felt hot under the collar. 'Well, I'm sure you have CCTV footage that will clearly show the incident.'

Coots shook his head. 'No, actually, we don't. That part of The Glades has no cameras.'

'Well, we have three witnesses who saw what happened, and I can call them here right now to give a statement. So, as I said before, Hudson came here of his own free will. He is not under arrest at present, is he? So mark my words Sergeant Coots, with Hudson so very young, arresting a juvenile willy-nilly will not look good for your records, will it?'

Coots chewed the inside of his lip. Harris was right, of course. The boy had come in voluntarily, there was a worrying tear to his ear, and the weapon was a pen, not a knife.

'Okay, you can go, but don't leave the country. I may call you later, once we have a statement from the other lad.' He gave Hudson another look-over and almost shuddered when he met his intimidating eyes.

CHAPTER FOURTEEN

After two weeks, Dionne received a call from Lyle Harris who told her that Hudson was clear of all possible charges; the boy in the hospital, on advice from his mother, who had learned the truth about what had been going on at The Glades from one of the other boy's parents, had given a fair account of the incident, and so the case was closed.

September was nearly approaching and the twins were due to start secondary school.

Dr Reeves had continued with the therapy sessions, and Luke had called to say he would be due home in the first week of September.

It was Sunday afternoon, and Dionne had finished making the beds, when she looked over at the clock. It was late, and she had to pick up Harley and Hudson from the clinic. After slipping her feet into her new high-heeled black shoes, she ran a brush through her hair and smoothed down her dress. She'd planned to go to the supermarket directly afterwards to buy some milk and also a bottle of wine – her regular partner in the lonely evenings.

By the time she reached the clinic, the heavens had opened, and the car had its wipers on full speed. She waited in the car outside. Ten minutes turned to fifteen, and now she was annoyed. She'd never been the most patient person. Huffing aloud, she stepped out of the car and placed her bag above her head. As she hurried in through the double glass doors, she immediately shook her new designer bag and wiped down her figure-hugging green dress.

Samantha was at the desk talking to a middle-aged doctor, who was a heavyset woman with thick-rimmed glasses. As Dionne approached the desk, the doctor looked up and smiled.

Glancing at her Rolex, she realised the twins were very late. Normally, they would be sitting in reception by now. 'Aren't Hudson and Harley ready to go home?' asked Dionne.

The dark-rimmed glasses belonged to Dr Renee, formerly Dr Tavon, before she was married. She was in stark contrast to the young woman she once was. Having suffered from colon cancer, she'd put on four stone. The chemotherapy had made her gorgeous rich brown hair fall out, and now, having grown back, it was completely white. Very few people recognised her former self, but she wasn't bothered – she was just happy to be alive.

'Oh, you must be Mrs Mason. I'm Dr Renee. I am working with Dr Reeves. Yes, Hudson and Harley are just taking an exam. They shouldn't be too long. Oh, er, while you are here, could I take a blood sample from yourself? I've been meaning to call you about that.'

Uneasy, Samantha slowly looked up.

'Er, well, I-I dunno. What's it for?' stammered Dionne.

Renee waved her hands in encouragement. 'Oh, it's nothing to worry about. It's just a section of the study we have to include. You know, a routine tick-box exercise.'

Now appearing visibly nervous, Dionne replied, 'Well, the thing is, I hate needles. I'm also not sure what this has to do with my children. I gave permission for you take *their* blood, so what do I have to do with it? I mean, it's the twins who are in the trial, isn't it?'

Samantha had watched the exchange between the two women and could see that Dr Renee was going to be faced with a problem. Not entirely sure how to handle the situation, Samantha hurried away to speak to Dr Reeves.

Renee put out her hand to touch Dionne's arm to give her reassurance. 'It's nothing, Mrs Mason. All our subjects have a sample taken—'

Dionne pulled away. 'But I'm not *your* subject, am I?'

The harsh response caused Renee to retort back. 'Oh, no! Not at all. And just to assure you, Hudson and Harley are not in a trial. They are simply in a study, but this requires that we have a blood sample from one of their parents, nothing more than that.'

Dionne's shoulders tightened up. *Christ, I don't need all this*, she thought.

'There's no point actually because the twins are adopted, so our blood doesn't match anyway.'

The inquisitive expression on Renee's face deepened. 'Oh, I see. So they obviously don't share your DNA, then?' She took a deep breath. 'Okay, well, actually, there is nothing on the form that requires the subjects to be born from their mother, so, like I said, it's just a tick-box exercise and a formality to process the findings.'

Dionne bit her lip and flared her nostrils.

Renee could sense Mrs Mason was angry and took a step back, studying her expression.

'Well, I can't see, then, why you need a blood sample from me.'

Renee nodded. 'So to sign the study off and for the children to continue for the next five years, we will need a sample. It is as simple as that. Now I can see you are very nervous, but, I can assure you, I am very good, especially with patients who experience needle phobia.'

'Yes, but I'm not a patient here at this clinic, am I, Dr Renee?'

'No, of course you are not. But we do need to get this blood sample taken. As I have tried to point out, I am very good at putting people at ease. Come with me, Mrs Mason. We can get this over with in two minutes, I promise. At least, then, the study can continue, and I am sure the extra money will come in handy.' Ultimately, she knew the financial reward for such a study was always the dangling carrot.

Reluctantly, Dionne decided to agree to do as Dr Renee asked. She followed the doctor into the first room on the right. It was small with just a chair and a rack of blood tubes on a single shelf.

While Dr Renee prepared the label for the collection tube, Dionne looked around. With the thought of a huge needle sliding into her arm, her breathing intensified, and she felt hot and queasy. The idea of jumping up and off the seat and then running for her life circled her mind, but, within a second, the needle was into her vein, and it was all over before she could blink.

'There, see, not so painful, was it?'

Nervously, Dionne laughed. 'No, I suppose not.'

For a moment, Dionne stared at the woman and wondered how she had managed to talk her into something she really didn't want to do. There was only one person in her whole life who she would ever listen to and who could talk her round, and it certainly wasn't this doctor. She sighed and jolted upright when Dr Reeves entered the room.

'Well, hello, Mrs Mason.' His over-the-top voice seemed somewhat contrived, but his smile looked genuine enough.

'I was hoping to catch you. Have you organised a meeting with the new teachers at their secondary school? I feel it would be extremely beneficial if the school was aware of what we are doing here with Hudson and Harley.'

Of course not, Dionne thought. 'Well, what should I tell them?' Her reply was sharp, almost combative. 'Except for the fact that they are unusually quiet. They only bloody mix with each other, and they can probably read, write, and add up better than any teacher in the school.'

Reeves cleared his throat. 'Hmm, yes, Mrs Mason, but, intelligent as they are, they are still children, and, yes, they do like each other's company as they are twins, and some children tend to be happier in smaller groups. I really would suggest the school is informed so that—'

That was it. She was seriously pissed off now on several counts. The kids were late coming out of the clinic, the scheming Renee woman had pressured her for a blood test, there was now all this talk about what the school should know, and, to cap it all, she noticed her new shoes were ruined from the downpour.

Dionne's eyes flashed with rage, as she snapped, 'Yes, Dr Reeves. Why not say it as it is? Come on, then. What you *mean* to say is that my children could potentially be a danger to society – that they're possibly psychopaths. *Right?*'

The room fell silent. Renee's eyes widened, and she shot her colleague a concerning look.

'Mrs Mason, I have never said your children are *psychopaths*. Where on earth did you get that from? I mean, their brain functions slightly differently from the majority of the population, but no one has said anything about psychopaths.'

Taller than the average woman, Dionne used her height to maximum effect as she studied the doctor. 'Dr Reeves, I am not stupid. I know those twins aren't normal, and you know they aren't. You must be looking for something or why have a study, or whatever the hell it is you do here.'

'Yes, we are trying to isolate a gene that can cause the brain to function at a higher level, but that doesn't mean we associate that gene with a psychopath. Without being disrespectful, Mrs Mason, not all abnormal cognitive functioning points to psychopathic behaviour.' He quickly changed the subject. 'Oh, and by the way, Hudson and Harley took an exam today, and their intellect is on a par with someone in their late teens, so they should sail through their studies at school. I am very impressed, and they appear to be taking an interest in separate subjects, which is also good to see. Remember, that when they first arrived here, they were inseparable, but now, they are comfortable spending some time apart. I think, as they mature more, they will eventually lead separate lives, but that very close bond will always be there.'

At last Dionne was able to give him a genuine smile. 'Have you been teaching them to be independent? Is that what you also do?'

Reeves nodded. 'Yes, that is precisely what we do. Whilst we have to spend time with them, of course, for the study, part of my role is to help them to become independent thinkers, to be able to cope with other people outside of their immediate comfort blanket, and, so far, they have made great headway.' He gently tapped her on the arm and left the room.

Dionne turned to Dr Renee. 'So are we done here?'

With a firm nod, Renee indicated she could leave. Renee's eyes followed Dionne Mason along the corridor. She wanted to see how the twins responded with their mother. And what she saw didn't surprise her. Not in the least. She knew why, though. The children acted as if their mother was a stranger to them. There were no smiles or hugs, just a blank expression. And as they walked on ahead, Dionne casually took her time.

* * *

Reeves returned to the reception area and tapped Katherine Renee on the shoulder, making her jump.

'Well?'

Renee gave him a sad smile. 'Let's just hope we are wrong about the psychopathic diagnosis. But you handled the situation very well, Guy, I must say.'

Reeves winked and replied, 'We cannot mess this up, not at this stage.'

Renee was staring into space, deep in thought. 'No, you are so right. I am thrilled about the children's test results. Now we need to do whatever it takes, and I, for one, am eager to see the blood results. I believe we may have just found our Gemini Gene.'

Reeves squeezed her shoulder in excitement. 'And, Katherine, I couldn't wish for a better doctor to share the results with.'

Renee patted his hand. 'You, Guy, were always my top student, and I am honoured to be working with you again. It's been many years, and yet it seems like only yesterday we were on the verge of isolating that gene.'

She stared ahead as Dionne and the twins left the building, her mind preoccupied with so many 'what if' thoughts that they began to scare her.

* * *

As the day of Luke's release from prison rapidly approached, Dionne's mood darkened. She was becoming more short-tempered with the twins, and she'd also declined to go out to lunch with Tilly and Miriam, making an excuse that she felt ill.

The truth was, of course, that she was dreading Luke's return. Her main concern was what he would say about the kids going to see a shrink, and when he eventually found out, would he put his big, heavy foot down and stop it all? Her life would be ruined if he did. Her Sundays, which she cherished for herself, would be over. No doubt, he would want things to go back to how they used to be; yet he had no idea how much had changed. Sunday dinners with the whole family were a thing of the past now. She swallowed hard. Would Luke try to revive the old family way of life or just accept it as it was now?

Perhaps, she mused, it might help if she explained to him that life now had to be a certain way and that she'd gone to extreme measures to ensure it was, just for the sake of the children. She'd kept the house in a neat order, sticking rigidly to times and routine. Although he was an organised man, he wouldn't understand the lengths to which she'd gone to make sure everything ran shipshape just for her own peace of mind. The tins had to have their labels pointing the right way, the plates had to have a paper towel separating each one, the cushions had to be in threes on the sofa and not squashed flat, the soap had always to be wiped dry before placing it in the soap dish, and the children's books had to be displayed in order of size.

But if these conditions were not met by Luke then everything would go to pot. There was no way that life could return to how it was before Luke's arrest. And if he tried to disrupt their current lifestyle, he would cause an explosion, and then, no doubt, he and the kids would blame her.

Harley and Hudson became increasingly anxious. Change made them that way. And Dionne could feel the tension building up. For much of the time, the twins stayed in their bedrooms. They constantly babbled away in French. It irritated her, but at least they were out of her way.

Listening to classical music in the kitchen, to drown out their noise, she placed the last of the vol-au-vents in the oven and then stood back to admire her work. The worktops were laden with food from sausage rolls to overloaded French sticks, freshly baked apple turnovers, and a deep-filled sherry trifle.

Looking at her watch, she realised that the family would be here any minute, in anticipation of Luke's return. She poured a large glass of wine and savoured the cold, crisp sensation on her tongue. She needed to be half-cut to show any emotion towards the man she'd gradually learned to despise.

Today something had changed. For the first time in her life, she questioned *the voice of reason*.

What were the actual words? She couldn't remember. But she did recall the persistent and clear message that Luke was supposed to be the perfect match and that she would have such a good life with all the things she could possibly want.

She gulped another mouthful of wine and tried to think why she'd always listened to that *whisper in her ear* telling her what to do. Granted he had been right in the past, but was he right now? She wasn't so sure. He'd told her that she would grow to respect Luke, that Geoff was just an obsession, that she couldn't possibly love Geoff. But, in her mind, there was no such thing as obsession. Of course she loved Geoff; that wasn't fake. However, what she had with Luke definitely was fake.

The one saving grace was her home – her beautiful home. The money, the car, and the freedom away from her mother's shoddy house had made living with Luke worth it. But things had changed: she wanted Geoff not Luke. Luke was in the way.

* * *

Miriam was the first to arrive, of course, followed by Archi, who kissed Dionne on the cheek and whispered, 'She's brought half the fucking contents of the fridge with her.'

Dionne chuckled and looked down at the spacious holdall filled with plastic cartons.

Miriam was in her element. Her son would be home at long last. Her sleepless nights would end, along with the continuous anxiety. 'Pour us a glass of wine, Archi, while I unload the food,' she called out.

'Fuck's sake, Mir, I've just sat down.'

Dionne smiled, as if to say 'No chance. You'd better do as she says.'

Archi heaved himself from the sofa and waddled into the kitchen. 'Christ, girl, we ain't feeding the British Army.'

'Just you shut it, Archi. I bet you won't moan when you stick ya false gnashers into a sausage roll.'

'I don't like to see food go to waste, Mir.'

'Nah, Archi, and you don't like to see yaself get up off ya fat arse and help either, do ya?'

'Gawd, you can fucking rabbit, woman. 'Ere ya go. Get ya laughing gear around that. And don't call me again. I'm looking at the betting results on the telly, and I don't want to be disturbed.'

He headed back to the sofa and flicked on the TV, leaving Miriam chuckling to herself.

Geoff didn't knock. He spotted his mother's car and let himself in. Under his arm was a crate of beer. As he entered the hallway, he saw Dionne heading towards him. 'Where do you want these, Dionne?' Although he looked her way, his face held no affection.

She lowered her gaze and nodded towards the kitchen. It would be so hard with Luke and Geoff in the same room. Looking at Geoff's handsome face and then reminding herself of the sharp features of her husband, along with his dull, lifeless eyes, it would bring home how much she wanted Geoff for herself.

A commotion outside caused Dionne to retrace her steps to the front door to face Dean, who was carrying cards and presents wrapped in foil. Tilly followed him with a home-made quiche.

'All right, Dionne? Any news what time the jailbird's due home?'

Relieving Dean of some of the gifts, she replied, 'In about an hour or so.'

Tilly excitedly pushed past Dean. 'Oh, Dee, I bet ya can't wait, eh?' She giggled and moved close to Dionne's ear, whispering, 'You got ya sexy lingerie sorted? 'Cos he will be on fire tonight, babe. No sex for five years! Jeez, my Dean can't go fucking five days.'

Dionne wanted to laugh along with her, but the thought made her want to puke. After having Geoff's hands all over her, and loving every second, her husband's cold stares and icy hands would seem like a death sentence.

The boys arrived a few minutes later, and Dionne could hear the popping of the ring pulls. They were obviously getting ready for a big celebration. If only she felt the same, but she didn't.

Nicki and Kai pulled out the centre panel and extended the long dining room table, while Miriam and Tilly began laying out the food. Spirits were high – until Nicki asked about Hudson, which seemed to attract a black cloud into the room.

Dionne wasn't surprised because she felt the same and was relieved that the twins spent most of their time in their bedrooms or in the garage. A cold chill rushed through her body: she hoped no one would venture in there. The sculpture was still in the corner; only, now, it had a glaze over it, and the detail was even more evident.

''Ere, Dee, are you okay, my love?' Miriam asked, as she followed Dionne into the lounge. 'You look peaky.'

Archi laughed. He hadn't moved from the armchair, still watching horse racing. 'She's probably shitting herself. After all, Luke's been away from his woman for six years, so she knows what to expect.'

Miriam slapped his arm. 'Gawd, Archi, you're a fucking dirty old man. A shame you can't get it up.'

Listening to the banter, Tilly laughed and was joined by Dean, who had just entered the lounge.

But Archi was not amused and came back with a stinger. 'I would, my darlin', if ya were twenty years younger, and didn't have such saggy tits.' He chuckled.

Tilly looked at Miriam and gave an exaggerated gasp, knowing they always bantered like that, and, indeed, they loved each other to bits.

'Archi, I can assure you there's nothing saggy about any of my bits. I took your credit card and had them all made like new, and, no, you can't cop a feel.'

Archi laughed and pretended he was choking on his Guinness. 'Yeah, I had to remortgage the flaming house to cover the cost to have you made like new. It would have been cheaper to have traded you in for a younger model.'

Miriam stood with her hands on her hips. 'And what younger model would give you the bleedin' time of day? Look at ya. You're an overweight, balding, lazy bastard.'

'Shut up, Mir. Look, if this horse comes in, you won be slating me then, eh? Not when I collect me winnings.'

Miriam took another gulp of her wine, leaned over the chair, and snatched the betting slip clean out of Archi's hand. 'My winnings now.' She laughed.

Just as the gathering was becoming a laugh a minute, the front door opened and everyone stopped what they were doing.

Dionne's heart was in her mouth as she stared at her husband for the first time in months.

Luke's hair was long and tied back, but he was bigger, broader, and toned. Even his face was fuller, but his eyes still had that shadiness. It was evident that prison hadn't damaged him. It was as if he'd just returned from holiday without the suntan.

Although Dean and Geoff had both offered to pick him up on his release, Luke had told them that he'd things to do. What Luke said went as far as his brothers were concerned.

Miriam was the first to embrace him. 'So glad you're home, Son.' Then she took him to one side. 'Did you,' she whispered, 'tell Beverley it's over now? Because, like I told you, you have a family to think about.'

'Yes, Mum,' he whispered back, 'that's why I was late. It's finished. Are you happy now?'

'Your family need you, especially the kiddies.'

'Okay, okay,' he muttered sharply, before he pulled away.

Miriam knew he'd been getting visits from Beverley Childs simply because he had sent a visiting order in her name to his parents' address by mistake. When she'd taken him to task over it, during one of their regular phone conversations, he'd also admitted that Beverley had received a letter from him that was obviously meant for Harley, which would suggest that the visiting order for Beverley had gone to his home address. As much as Miriam liked Beverley, she had grown fond of Dionne. And while she wanted her son to be happy, he had a responsibility to his family.

*   *   *

So this is it, then, Dionne thought. She knew it would be awkward because everyone would expect her to hug him like Miriam had. But throwing her arms around him and crying with joy was the furthest thought from her mind; instead, she inclined her head as if she was shy.

The family clocked her expression, and it was Archi who said, 'Come on, guys. Let's go outside and let these two lovebirds have a few minutes of privacy.'

Before they left, the men all took it in turns to hug Luke with their own messages of 'welcome home'.

Dionne leaned against the back of the sofa, still looking the shy doting wife.

Miriam ushered everyone outside where she'd set out all the drinks including a Pimm's punch.

For a few seconds, while Nicki grabbed his phone, they waited, until the French doors were closed.

* * *

And then Luke turned to her. Taking a deep breath, she managed to give him a wavering smile that exaggerated her nerves. Slowly, with calculated steps, he went to her, with his eyes still focused on her face.

She searched for a glimmer of happiness, relief, or even love, but his expression said nothing: it was just a blank canvas with two dark piercing eyes.

She froze as he leaned into the side of her head and whispered, 'You, my dear wife, don't fool me, but you *are* my wife, and I expect from now on for you to behave like one.'

He pulled away and smiled, and then he gently put his arms around her and kissed her lips.

She wanted to feel something, but there was nothing; there was no warmth, no tingling feeling, just dread. Did he know what had been going on between Geoff and herself? Surely not, unless he was planning some kind of revenge, once the homecoming was over. For a moment, she studied his face. His intense stare and thick, smoky voice would have perhaps stirred excitement in her ten years ago, but not now. Now that look and voice were like a nightmare of a man who would haunt her. As if an elastic band had just snapped, she shook from the strange trance and giggled, 'Welcome home, Luke. I've missed you. We all have. Let me get you a nice cold beer, and I'll get the kids down. They've been dying to see you.'

The sudden change of tone made Luke step back. 'Didn't you hear what I just said?'

She giggled again and nodded. 'Of course, my darling.' Her voice was upbeat and with a higher tempo now.

*　*　*

With her nose almost pressed up against the window, Miriam watched what was going on in the lounge. She could see Dionne smiling and giggling, and she clapped her hands together. 'Right, come on, then. Let's go back inside and share a dinner together.'

As they piled back in, Luke began to mingle, although he would give Dionne an occasional glance from the corner of his eye. Then he watched her disappear, presumably to go upstairs to call the twins down.

Dionne found them in Hudson's room, both sharing an earpiece and each listening to some music. She pulled out their earpieces and smiled. 'Right, you two. Your father is here, and he'll want to see you, so come on downstairs.'

Hudson curled his lip, and Harley pulled him up. 'Let's go, Hudson,' she said, much to the reluctance of her brother, who was slow in getting to his feet and clearly demonstrating he would rather not go anywhere.

As the twins descended the stairs, they heard the rapturous laughter, and, for a second, they froze.

Dionne urged them on. 'Go on, you two. It's only family, no one else.'

Luke's face lit up when he saw his two children standing there. He hadn't seen them in almost six years, except in photos, and he was astonished at how big they had grown.

Hudson was stocky and tall, with the semblance of a handsome and manly face, and Harley was so attractive, he knew he would worry when she got older. Not put off by their unhappy demeanour, he hurried over with outstretched arms and embraced them, almost crying.

Miriam could see he was emotional, but she could also tell the twins were so cold towards him, it was almost embarrassing. Although they allowed him to hug them, there was no reciprocation. Her heart sank. She'd hoped that at least one of the twins would have shown some emotion. A lump lodged in her throat when she thought back to when they'd been so close to their father. She'd heard from Dionne how Harley had nearly ripped a prison officer's eyes out when he'd dragged Luke away. *Six years was a long time in a child's life*, she thought. Perhaps it had been too long, and her son would have to work hard to gain their trust again.

Feeling the distance between them, Luke glared over at Dionne and frowned. In turn, she gave him a sad smile and a slight shrug, as if to say 'It's not my fault. You left your kids.'

The atmosphere changed when Archi leaped from his seat. 'Yes, get in there!' he shouted. Blue Diamond had crossed the finish line and had just won him five hundred pounds.

Kai was laughing, and Lee gave their grandad a high-five.

Luke turned to laugh at his father and removed himself from the intense hostility of his kids.

The family's comical banter and teasing began again.

Dionne cut the cake and handed Luke two plates. ''Ere, give the twins these. They love cake.' She winked.

Hudson and Harley were sitting in silence on the sofa. To any stranger, they would have looked like two sulky teenagers.

Luke kneeled down and offered them some cake. 'There you go. A piece of homecoming cake.'

Harley pushed herself further back, against the sofa, as if he was offering her a plate of spiders.

Hudson, though, instantly shoved the plates back at his father. 'Take them away,' he screamed.

Luke jumped to his feet, at a loss to understand what had just happened. He looked at Dionne with a deep concern channelled across his brow, but she merely shrugged again and shook her head.

'What's the bloody matter with them, Dionne? I only offered them some cake. It seems as if they fucking hate me for leaving them.'

Inwardly chuffed to bits but outwardly smiling, she nodded. 'Give them time, Luke.'

'Dionne, this cake is beautiful. It's like the song "Tie a Yellow Ribbon Round the Ole Oak Tree." It's been three long years, do you still want me?' sang Archi, as the others joined in.

The cake was covered in bright-yellow fondant icing with a huge bow and it cost a fortune, but Dionne wanted to make an impression.

Archi, over the moon with his winnings, called out, 'Get some of that 1970s music on. We can all have a sing-song, and while you're at it, Mir, get us another Guinness.' Once again, the atmosphere was good.

But an hour or so later, the chit-chatting was interrupted by a fierce banging on the front door.

Tilly stopped the music, and the boys simmered down.

Archi, once again nine sheets to the wind, said, 'That'll be the stripper.'

Dionne looked at Luke. His face was drained of all colour and his eyes were wide. 'Expecting anyone, Luke?'

He shook his head, but, Dionne thought, too profusely, as if he was willing the intrusion was not down to him. She guessed why. He looked so worried, and as she opened the door, expecting to see Beverley, to her horror, it was Scarlett who stood there, almost foaming at the mouth. She didn't wait to be invited in; instead, she pushed past Dionne and stumbled her way into the lounge, to the shock of everyone. Dressed in a skimpy tube dress, which exposed her white mottled legs, she looked a mess. Her hair needed a good wash and colour, and her eyes were black from crying. But it wasn't so much her appearance or even that she was clearly as pissed as a newt that concerned everyone. It was the fierce look on her face that said she was ready to cause trouble.

Geoff, who was at the far end of the room talking to his sons, was horrified to see her there with wrath stamped across her face, but he wasn't quick enough to get to her before she opened her mouth.

'I came to welcome you home, Luke,' she said, as she threw six envelopes on the coffee table. 'I wanted to let you know that I didn't forget you, mate. There's your birthday cards.'

Miriam was the first to grab her arm. 'Get out, Scarlett. You've had far too much to drink.'

But judging by the aggression shown on her face, Scarlett wasn't going anywhere. Shaking herself free, she said, 'Get your fucking hands off me. You sodding well knew what *they* were up to.' She pointed an accusing finger at Dionne and then at Geoff. 'That slut and *my* fucking husband!' she shouted.

'That's enough, Scarlett. Get out.' Geoff's voice bounced off the walls as he marched towards her. 'Shut your vile fucking mouth and get out.'

'Frightened Luke will know the truth, then, are you?'

Suddenly, she took a tumble and landed against the side table, knocking the Tiffany table lamp over.

Miriam again grabbed her arm, but Scarlett pushed her away, and this time she tripped on the edge of the sofa and landed on her arse, by Hudson and Harley, who just stared with astonishment, not knowing what to do.

As Scarlett's eyes met Hudson's stare, she flew into a temper. 'And you, ya little fucking weirdo, getting my boys into trouble, you need locking up.'

Geoff decided to take prompt action and grabbed hold of Scarlett, who was still kicking and screaming.

'Let go of me. This house is the fucking house of horrors. Look at you all. And' – she pointed at Dionne – 'it's her fault, I tell ya. She's making them all evil. I know what you're all about, Dionne, *and* your two psycho brats.'

Geoff still attempted to drag Scarlett to the front door, but, somehow, she managed to break free and decided to launch herself at Dionne, throwing a punch at her.

But Harley was infuriated that she'd dared speak to her brother like that. In a flash, she hurled herself off the sofa and grabbed Scarlett's hair and instantly floored her. Then, when she viciously clawed Scarlett's face and tried to sink her teeth into her neck, Geoff pulled her off, before she did any serious damage.

It was Tilly, though, who leaped off a dining room chair and pushed Geoff aside, lifting Scarlett by her hair, dragging her from the lounge, and shoving her out of the front door. 'Now, do one, Scarlett, you fucking nutjob!'

Just as Scarlett hobbled away, dragging her shoeless foot, she caught sight of Harley in the lounge window. When their eyes met, she saw the girl run a finger along her neck. The action was slow, meaningful, and sobering.

She never thought she would ever fear an eleven-year-old, but, in that moment, she did, despite all the vodka running through her veins.

The house now in chaos, Harley marched to her room, with Hudson on her heels.

Geoff did his best to console his two boys, while Kai fussed over his mother, making sure Scarlett hadn't hurt her.

Luke stared at the family, each in turn. He wondered what the hell had been going on while he'd been inside. The one person who couldn't lie to him was his father. He looked over at the sad expression on his father's face. 'What's been going on, Dad?'

Archi shook his head. 'I dunno, Son. But Scarlett's a penny short of a pound. Okay, so Hudson did *almost* get the boys nicked, but it wasn't his fault . . .'

'No, Dad, I'm talking about Geoff and Dionne!'

'Oh, for Christ's sake, don't listen to *Scarlett*. She's accused everyone of sleeping with Geoff, from your muvver's hairdresser to our Tilly. If you ask me, the bird needs help – psychiatric help.'

Geoff watched from a distance, gauging Luke's reaction. He was unsure whether to broach the subject or just ignore it and pretend to dismiss it as a puerile dig from a jealous wife who wanted to cause a rift in the family.

When the party was over, and they'd all said their goodbyes, Luke was left to settle back into home life. His initial confident manner had dissipated to the point that he seemed almost humiliated by the twins' withering glances of dismissal. He didn't bother questioning Dionne about the accusations from Scarlett. His father's comment had satisfied him, and he would never believe that his brother would do that to him anyway. Then his thoughts turned to what he'd been doing behind *Dionne's* back. Did she know what he'd been up to with Beverley all this time? The chances were she may have if she'd seen the visiting order that had been sent to the house by mistake.

His mind went back to Beverley. He could still see her on the bed with her robe revealing her bare shoulders and the hurt expression on her face when he'd said his goodbyes. She'd tried not to cry because they both knew the affair couldn't go anywhere, but, still, the pain was immense – for both of them.

As the evening drew to a close, Luke switched off the television.

Dionne felt her heart pounding like a jackhammer. Was he going to expect a romp in the sack? Yet, there had been no passes, no sexy smiles, or even innuendos.

Luke yawned and stood up. 'I think it's best that I sleep in the spare room tonight.'

Relaxing her shoulders, she wanted to laugh with relief. 'Yeah, okay, mate. It's an early start tomorrow. The kids start secondary school, and they have . . .' She paused and asked him to sit back down. His former harsh expression had gone, and this was her cue to deliver the news.

He sat on the edge of a chair with his hands clasped in front of him. 'Yes, Dionne, they have what?'

After a big intake of air, she gave him a soft smile. 'While you were away, I struggled, babe. I struggled a lot with the kids. At one stage, they nearly got expelled from school. Now, before you bash me one again, I need to tell you something. I love the kids, I really do, and as their mother, I know there is something . . .' She didn't want to use the words 'not right' or 'abnormal'. 'They're troubled, and as their mum, I wanted to get them help, before the school kicked them out for good. So . . .' Dionne took a deep breath and looked him straight in the eyes. 'So . . . anyway, they go every month on a Sunday to see a Dr Reeves.'

She waited for a reaction, but Luke just sat there stone-faced. 'He has helped them an awful lot. They interact better now and have learned to be independent of each other. Not completely, but he's working on it.' She kept her voice soft and caring, and she decided to keep the fact that they were in a study out of the equation.

'D'ya know what, Dionne? I had a lot to think about in the nick, and you were always at the forefront of my mind. I never really knew you, did I? I thought I did, but when the babies arrived you seemed to be moody, and I had this feeling you would hurt them. I dunno why I thought that. Maybe it was 'cos I loved them so much, I just couldn't imagine anyone else loving them the same way I did. But you did ya best, and I was wrong about you.'

Sipping the last of her wine, she turned to him. 'Luke, what did you mean when you said to me earlier "You don't fool me"? I laughed it off, hoping it was a joke, but . . .'

He held his hand up. 'I got it wrong. I thought you were gonna act all fake and pretend you had missed me and start showing some affection of your undying love and make a real show of it, like ya used to. But you didn't. You were serene and sweet, not full of shit.'

He said his goodnights and got up to leave.

Dionne watched him. His shoulders were slumped, and it was then that she saw the broken man he was. But, strangely, she found his dispirited demeanour all the more attractive. Not that she would fancy any man who wasn't tough and virile, but perhaps his personality change had sparked something inside her. She looked at her empty glass and smiled. It was probably just the alcohol.

* * *

By the time the alarm went off, Dionne was all ready and had breakfast on the table.

Luke had enjoyed a peaceful night's sleep in a luxury bed, and he was refreshed and eager to begin his new life, starting with taking the children to school. He slid out of the soft sheets and made his way to the bathroom. The hot power shower was such a stark reminder that he was now in his own home. Prison life had been tough, for no other reason than he couldn't stand to be told what to do. As the piercing sprays massaged his back, he sighed. It was good to be home, even if Dionne wasn't his first choice of a wife. But holding inside regrets would do him no good. He would work with what he'd been given. Climbing into his jeans, he puffed out his chest, pulled his shoulders back, and joined his wife in the kitchen. 'Smells good.'

Dionne handed him a full English breakfast and placed a coffee on the kitchen table under his nose. She stared at her husband's appearance. The wisps of grey in his hair and his fuller face, along with those mysterious shifty eyes, which for some reason women found attractive, suddenly became even more alluring to her.

'It's gonna seem strange driving again. Is my car still in the garage? Has it been properly serviced?'

Suddenly, horror gripped her. The garage floor! He would see it screeded and the pit filled. And then there would be questions . . . loads of them. And the sculpture, of course. What would he make of that? She had to divert his attention before he went into the tomb of secrets.

'Take my car, babe. It's running like a dream, and the petrol tank is full. We don't want the kids to be late on their first day, eh?'

Luke nodded. 'Okay.'

Dionne was still staring at her husband. She liked the way his hair hung loose and long and how it tumbled about his shoulders all thick and wavy. She had to admit he did look more handsome with it styled that way.

Blinking, she snapped out of her trance and instantly thought about Geoff. No matter how handsome and sexy her husband was looking, she wanted Geoff – no one else.

Harley was the first to appear, dressed in her school uniform, blue blazer, and A-line skirt. Her tanned skin and deep blue eyes stood out against the pale blue shirt. Her hair was tied away from her face, and she looked perfect.

Luke's eyes lit up. 'Wow, you look lovely. Look at you, all grown up.'

Dionne saw a small glimpse of a smile as Harley sat at the table. It irritated her because she assumed that Harley would forever hold a grudge towards her father. How could she forgive him so easily? It wasn't fair. Harley certainly never smiled at her, even though she had been the one holding the family together.

As Dionne handed Harley her breakfast, Luke glanced over. 'What, no eggs?'

Dionne, with her back to Luke, answered. 'She doesn't eat eggs.'

His face soured. It was like being a visitor in his own home. He knew he had a lot to learn about his children, and he would have to be patient.

When Hudson appeared, he looked sullen.

'What's up, Son?' asked Luke.

Buttering her toast, Harley said, 'He doesn't want to go to school.'

Luke placed his coffee down beside his plate and pulled Hudson towards him. 'Now, Son, we've all been through this. Starting a new school *is* nerve-racking, but once you meet new friends, you'll have the time of your life.'

In between mouthfuls of her toast, Harley remarked, 'He doesn't like meeting new people.'

Luke looked back at Hudson. 'You can join the football team or rugby and—'

'He doesn't like sports.'

With a vast sigh, Luke turned to Harley. 'And it sounds to me that he doesn't like to answer for his bloody self either.' He let go of Hudson and tutted.

'No, you are right. He doesn't like to talk much either, not when he is being treated like a five-year-old.'

Now gobsmacked, Luke looked at his daughter. 'Okay, Hudson. I will talk to you like an adult. Now then, Son, whether you like people or sports or not, you have to go to school and mix with the other kids and do PE. We all have stuff in our lives that we have to deal with, so man up.'

He turned to Dionne. 'Christ, is this shrink any good or what?'

Out of the blue, Hudson leaned forward to within an inch of Luke's face. 'Don't you *dare* say anything about Dr Reeves. He's been there for us when *you* haven't. You left us alone, and now you come back and expect us to be someone we are not. So, *Father*, watch what you say in future.'

Astonished, Luke sat back. He'd never expected his son to sound like an adult. His son's whole disposition, with his shoulders slouched and with his chin on the floor, was like that of a moody kid, but it was his words – they were so undeniably cutting.

'Watch ya mouth, boy. There's no need to be rude. Now, if we're done, you need to get ready for school. I'm taking you today.'

* * *

No sooner were her family out of the door than Dionne decided to call Geoff. She had the phone in her hand as she watched Luke drive away.

'Geoff, listen, Luke will go into the garage sooner or later, so what should I tell him about the pit?'

'Dionne, don't panic. Just tell him I carried out a few jobs while he was away. He wanted that pit filled in anyway because his last car had damaged the axle when he came home pissed. Er, listen, Dionne. I don't want you to call anymore.' His voice was soft, and all she wanted was to hang on to his every last word. That sexy, husky voice had her weak at the knees.

'Why, Geoff?'

He heard her voice crack. 'Dionne, I told you before, I can't do this anymore, for many reasons, but after last night, and Scarlett showing up like that, I feel bad.'

'Oh, Geoff, it's all right. Don't feel bad. Luke didn't jump on it. He assumed she was just a bit of a fruit loop.'

'No, Dionne. I mean, I feel bad seeing Scarlett like that. She was so upset, and, well, you're with Luke, so I feel I should make another go of it with Scarlett, for the kids' sakes.'

There was a long pause before Dionne replied, 'It doesn't have to be that way, Geoff. We both know that . . .'

'No, Dionne, it does have to be that way.' His tone was sharp.

She wasn't going to plead, not over the phone. She would talk another time – face to face.

'Of course, Geoff, you're right. I mean, it was good while it lasted, but I have Luke, and you have Scarlett. Is she okay now? It *was* horrible to see her like that.'

'I don't know. The boys are away in Spain, and in a few days, I'll be picking them up from the airport and taking them home. I'll talk to her then.'

Dionne let the tears fall down her cheeks, but she kept up the brave voice. 'So are the boys okay seeing their mum like that?'

'Well, they flew out early this morning, so I haven't had a chance to talk. Anyway, listen, Dionne, I had better go, love. Luke's meeting me at the club. We have a lot to talk over. Er . . . let's just pretend me and you never happened, for all our sakes, yeah?'

A tear dripped from the end of her nose, but she managed to hold herself together until the connection was cut. Then she broke down, sliding into the comfort of an armchair and sobbing until she could cry no more. It was really over. The man she'd always wanted was now history.

CHAPTER FIFTEEN

The older students started an hour before the new ones, so that they were not overwhelmed by the amount of pupils descending on the school all at once.

Hudson curled his pen in between his thumb and index finger, which had always been a nervous habit of his.

Harley watched as the children began piling in through the main gates. It was so much bigger than her junior school, and the children were much older, of course. Opening her passenger door, she nudged Hudson. 'Come on, then. We'd better not be late.'

Luke watched from his rear-view mirror. His heart went out to them. It wasn't comfortable starting big school. He'd been lucky having his elder brother Geoff already at his senior school, and so he sailed through, but Hudson and Harley were alone in this. He knew, from his regular phone conversations with Dionne, that his children had issues when mixing with the other pupils. He just hoped they would get over their awkwardness and not find what should be a fun time a hideous five years of suffering.

Hudson clambered across the rear seats and then stepped out of the car onto the pavement. He ignored his father, but she gave him a respectful wave and then dragged her reluctant brother by his rucksack, whispering words of encouragement in his ear.

The twins had already met some of the teachers at the open day. Mrs Finch was Harley's form tutor, and Mr Magpie was Hudson's. Harley still thought the tutors' names were amusing. *You couldn't make it up*, she thought.

The first part of the school day was morning assembly in the main hall. Hudson sat on the floor in his form row and held his rucksack in front of him. His breathing was shallow, but his heart raced. The hall was filling up, and the air seemed to be stifling. The smell of wood polish from the parquet flooring gave him a sickly feeling in his stomach, and he had an urge to run from this monster of a room. He took a few deep breaths and fiddled with his pen to calm his fears. As he glanced across the aisle, he saw Harley, also cross-legged, who was looking decidedly more confident than he was. *But then*, he thought, *she was the more assertive of the two of them.* He was grateful for her smile of encouragement.

The head teacher gave a lecture and then the pupils were led to their classes. Some looked excited, some daunted; for the nervous ones, the jump from their primary school to this one seemed to be massive.

Although, academically speaking, Hudson suspected he was leaps ahead of most pupils in the school, he definitely knew his social skills were below par. And he realised he stood out like a sore thumb – something his classmates had instantly picked up on because he could see them nudging each other. Aware he was by far the biggest in the class but also a target for bullies, he couldn't help but shrink in his chair and look at the floor.

Mr Magpie was also alert to the fact that Hudson was very different in so many ways from his peers, but, nevertheless, he had assured the boy's mother that he would do his utmost to integrate him and bring him out of his shyness. However, as he watched Hudson clutching his rucksack and spinning his pen, he knew he had a big job on his hands.

The first lesson was English and the set text for the year, *The Crucible*, by Arthur Miller, was handed out. The children sighed and moaned; it wasn't their sort of thing. Hudson had already read the play, though; he had a fascination with all things that defied logic.

'Right, please start reading act one, and I will be back.'

Once he left the room, the class began nattering. Hudson spun his pen and stared out of the window and across the field. By the time the teacher returned, armed with two packs of exercise books, the children had already formed relationships, all except for Hudson, of course, who was still in his own little dreamworld.

'Right, I am going to ask you what your thoughts are of act one.' His eyes roved around the classroom until they focused on Hudson Mason, who was clearly not paying attention.

'I will start with you, Hudson. Please tell the class your first thoughts.'

The words were ringing in his head, and he felt the heat rising up his spine into his neck. He couldn't speak in public.

Mr Magpie was old school. A man in his mid-fifties, desperate to retire from his job, he had a reputation for being inflexible and strict.

'Hudson, pay attention. Tell us what you think of act one.'

What Andrew Magpie really wanted to do was to go in at the deep end with the boy. No one had ever got the better of him, and his reputation for running a tight ship with above average results was not going to be undermined by this socially awkward pupil.

'Hudson! Will you pay attention and do as you are asked!'

The class were almost shell-shocked by the teacher's firmness. Twenty-six pairs of eyes were focused on Hudson.

Tutting with displeasure, Mr Magpie walked from around his desk and stood in front of Hudson. Snatching the pupil's copy from his hands, Mr Magpie looked through the pages for any obvious signs that this brand-new edition had been opened. It hadn't. Slamming it down and making all the pupils jump, except for Hudson, who didn't even flinch, he said, 'You haven't even opened this. Why is that, Hudson?'

With a gradual movement of his head, Hudson looked his teacher in the eye.

'I don't need to read it.' His voice was deep and cold.

'Oh, yes, you do. It is part of the curriculum, so I suggest you open it now and read it, or you will fail before you have even started.'

Hudson shook his head defiantly. 'No, I won't fail.'

Such directness was perceived by Mr Magpie as impertinence, and it got his back up.

'Hudson Mason, I won't tolerate misbehaviour in this class. Do I make myself clear?'

'Yes, but, Mr Magpie, I wasn't misbehaving. I just said I won't fail because I've already read the play.'

Mr Magpie was both embarrassed and annoyed. He was not going to be shown up by a pupil; however, it was the first day, and he had plenty of time to pull the lad into line.

More worrying for Hudson, though, was how he would be perceived by his classmates.

They had summed him up good and proper. He was clearly a loner and an ideal candidate for the butt of their jokes that in turn would make them look good.

Taylor Croft wanted to make a name for himself. Living on the Mottingham Estate with his mother and four brothers, he was used to a hard life. He got hand-me-downs, and if there was any knocked-off gear going, then his mother was first in line. And he could fight; he was respected for that at least. At four feet five, he looked fairly stocky, but, in comparison to Hudson, he was a waif. That wouldn't stop him, though. Like his mother had said, 'Take no shit, Son. Make sure those kids know who you are. I ain't bringing up no fucking fairy.' Those exact words were said before she handed him a fiver and sent him packing off to school. Taylor had already made friends on his estate who were going to his school, and so, luckily for him, he already had a gang.

When the bell for break sounded, the dragging of chairs rang like needles through Hudson's head. He didn't dash out like the other children; he took his time, allowing the rush to die down.

Just as Hudson reached the door, Mr Magpie threw him a question. 'So what was the main effect in the play, Hudson?'

Mr Magpie expected him to say witchcraft or something along those lines.

'Mass hysteria, Sir.'

Mr Magpie grinned. He knew then that the kid was smart, and he would treat him carefully from now on.

Harley's first lesson was art, which she enjoyed. The new art room was like a candy store to her, until, that was, Alice Montgomery-Blythe walked in. At the junior school, Alice was moved to another classroom away from Harley, for both their sakes. Now at nearly twelve, Alice still had a really spiteful tongue and walked around with an overconfident attitude. Harley smirked when she spotted her, and as their eyes met, Harley ran a finger across her throat that made Alice feel sick.

Alice looked away in fear and shuddered. As soon as the bell sounded for morning break, she was the first out of the door to get as far away from Harley as possible. She'd watched enough horror films to laugh most scary things off, but not Harley Mason. The intense look in those dark eyes was a horror story all of its own making.

The playground was buzzing with pupils either huddling together and chatting away or searching for their siblings. Harley spotted Hudson alone, leaning against a wall and spinning his pen. As she edged her way through the crowd, eager to see if he was okay, she spotted a crew of lads surrounding him. The ringleader was saying something to her brother, but Hudson had his head down, and all she could make out was that he was lightly rocking on his feet. Knowing the telltale signs of stress building up inside him, she sprinted over the playground, pushing students out of her way, until she reached him. That was when she could hear a lot of name-calling and chanting aimed at her brother. With her heart racing nineteen to the dozen, her anger was reaching an uncontrollable pitch.

Taylor Croft had already planned his target and was now ready to start a fight and show the other kids he was no pushover. He would make his mark by kicking the hell out of the weird kid, and everyone would then know never to mess with Taylor Croft. It would be the best way to start his school career.

'*Hudson Mason!* What sort of a fucking name is that?'

Hudson didn't respond; he kept his head down and carried on spinning his pen.

'Fucking weirdo, ya shouldn't be in my class. The dummies classes are up the road in the window lickers' school.'

The word 'weirdo' hit a nerve, and Harley felt it as much as she knew her brother had. She should have controlled herself, but something inside snapped. Pulling her rucksack off her back, she launched it at Taylor and followed up with a punch aimed at the side of his head.

Taylor didn't see either blow coming. While they hurt, they weren't sufficient to knock him over. With a nasty sneer, Taylor spun around to find he was nose to nose with a girl. His mother had always said if a bird can dish it, she can take it. Taylor wasn't going to be shown up by anyone, not least a girl. Guessing who she was, he spat in her face and yelled, 'Fuck off, ya freak. You're both fucking weirdos.'

Harley clenched her fist, bit her lip, and flared her nostrils. 'No one calls us weirdos,' and with that, she threw a punch that landed on Taylor's jaw and nearly knocked him out.

Hudson tried to pull Harley away, but Taylor was no pushover. Leaping to his feet, he cracked Harley's cheek, knocking her off balance, and then swung another punch, which, this time, hit Hudson in the stomach.

Hudson initially doubled over in pain. But then he suddenly straightened up, and with a look of anger in his eyes, his face tightened. He pulled his fist back and smashed Taylor so hard in the face that the lad fell onto the ground. Immediately, Hudson was on top of Taylor, now mental with anger.

Glen, one of Taylor's friends, tried to pull Hudson off by pulling his hair, but it had no effect. Even when he punched Hudson in the back of the head, it did nothing except hurt his own hand. No one, it seemed, could stop Hudson.

And now, Harley was out of control. She jumped onto Glen's back and bit hard into his neck.

Hearing the sound of a whistle in the distance, it acted as a switch in Hudson's brain. He stopped and jumped up, his body shaking all over.

A teacher pushed his way through the crowd only to find a bloody mess.

Harley looked down at Taylor's face, which was ripped to ribbons, and realised that Hudson had gone too far. She grabbed his hand. 'Run, Hudson, run!' she cried.

Hudson let go of her hand. It was as if he'd woken up from a bad dream. He headed for the school entrance and then disappeared into the surrounding woodland.

Harley scooped up her rucksack and tore after him, the trees and branches whipping at her face. Within minutes, they managed to outrun the overweight member of staff, who had tried but failed to keep them within eyesight.

Now, in the middle of woodland, Harley finally caught up with her brother, and they both slumped onto a pile of dry leaves.

Harley looked over at Hudson. His breathing was heavy, and there was sweat dripping down his neck.

'Oh, Hudson, are you all right?' cried Harley, as she saw his face crippled in terror. 'Are you hurt?'

He shook his head. 'Harley, I have done it this time.'

Harley sat next to him, leaning against a tree. 'Why didn't you count to ten like Guy told us to?'

A tear trickled down his face. 'I did! I counted to a *hundred*, but those kids back there, they wouldn't stop. They called me a weirdo, but I'm not, Harley. I'm not weird.'

Stroking the hair away from his face, she huddled close to him. 'No, Hudson. You're right. You're not a weirdo or a freak. We are different, but they just don't understand us.'

'What shall we do, Harley?'

'I'm hungry. Let's eat first and then make a plan.' She opened her rucksack and cursed. 'My sandwich is squashed. I hate that boy. I'm gonna make sure no one ever calls us weird again.'

Hudson pulled a sandwich from his bag. 'Eat this one. Mine is still square and straight.'

Harley checked it was perfect before she took a bite.

'What do you think I did to him?'

She looked up from her sandwich and smiled. 'You have probably scarred him for life.'

They waited in the woods, for hours, listening to the sounds of suburban life, and then, when the sky began to darken, Harley pulled Hudson from the ground. 'Come with me. We can go to the clinic.'

'But Guy will call Mum and Dad, and we will be in trouble.'

Harley looked at her watch. 'No, he won't. Look, it's now approaching seven o'clock. He and his staff would have left by now. Listen, Hudson. We can get into the storeroom at the back of the building. We'll be safe there. I won't let anyone hurt you, I promise.'

They walked with their heads down for about three miles through the woods and away from the road.

As they approached the clinic, Harley was pleased to see that she had been proved right: there were no signs of cars in the car park and all the lights in the building were off. She was the first to climb over the wire fence, followed by Hudson. She held his hand and hurried to the back of the building and stood in front of the storeroom. 'Hudson, do you still remember the code? You are well good with numbers.'

Hudson tapped in ten digits, and the door clicked open.

They hurried inside, shut the door, pulled the blinds down, and flicked the light on. The room was the size of their bedrooms. On one wall there were cleaning supplies, and on the other there were racks of games and stationery. But it was at the back of the room that interested the children. Here, there were two old-style ward beds, ready to be disposed of.

Harley pointed to the beds and said, 'We can sleep here tonight until I decide on a plan. But I will need to go out first.'

Hudson looked at her, visibly shaken.

'Don't worry, Hudson. I'll be back. Besides, we have no food or drink. I need to fetch some.' She looked at his hands trembling and pulled open one of the stationery boxes. Inside, she found pens, rulers, rubbers, and piles of notepads. She grabbed a pen and placed it in his hand. A sudden calmness came over him as he spun the pen. But then he shivered.

'See those white lab coats, Hudson? Pull them over yourself. You look cold.'

He was silent but did as she said.

'Aren't you afraid, Harley?'

She frowned. 'No, not at all. Why would I be scared?'

'Because we're in trouble, Harley. Serious trouble.'

She pulled another lab coat off the hanger and placed it on top of the two he had covered himself with. 'He deserved it, Hudson. No one calls us names like that. And it won't stop either, unless we do something about it.'

Hudson lay down on the bed and curled into a ball. 'You'll come back, though, Harley, won't you? Promise me you will.'

She nodded and replied. 'Always for you, Hudson, always.' With those words, she popped outside into the fresh air and took a deep breath.

* * *

It was 6 p.m., and Detective Inspector Jacob Forbes, a fresh-faced man in his early forties, with a slim frame and thick chestnut hair, sat in an armchair opposite Luke and Dionne Mason. Brett Nelson, the younger officer, remained standing and took notes.

* * *

Geoff was in the dining room of his brother Luke's house, pacing the floor. The news was certainly disturbing. The police had informed them that they were treating this incident extremely seriously. Hudson was being accused of a grievous assault on a boy in his class. The lad was now hospitalised due to severe puncture wounds caused by a pen. It gave him an awful feeling of déjà vu. Yet he had to be there for Luke. So many times, he'd wanted to confess to his brother that he'd been sleeping with Dionne, but he couldn't. He would destroy the family, and the closeness between them all would be gone. Not only would Luke probably try to kill him, but his mother and father would never forgive him and neither would his sons. Luke needed him now, and so he decided to find other ways to make it up to him. As much as he disliked the twins, his brother loved them. He thanked God, however, that his and Dean's boys were well out of the picture.

* * *

'So, Mr Mason, you dropped them off, as usual. Were they in fine fettle this morning, or, like many youngsters on their first day, were they worried about starting school?'

Luke's dislike for the police was legendary. He was annoyed that the filth were wasting valuable time asking him daft questions, when, if they only used their heads for once, they could be out there looking for his kids.

'Look, I've already told you. I dropped them off, and then my wife called to tell me to come home 'cos the school had called to say our kids had run away after some fight in the playground.'

Forbes nodded. 'Mr Mason, it was hardly a playground fight. This was a grave assault, and with a weapon. A weapon that your son used not so long ago that resulted in a previous serious injury.'

Luke jumped up. 'Well, unless we find the twins, I don't know what else you want me to say.'

Forbes had to agree and so stood up to leave. 'I'll get the station to file a missing persons report. But I've no doubt once it gets cold and your children get hungry, they'll be home, and I want you to call me the minute they do. Are we clear about that, Mr Mason?'

Dionne saw the officers to the door and hurried back to the lounge where Luke looked frantic with worry.

'What the fuck. Those idiots are complete arseholes. They should be concerned for our twins' welfare. Christ, they are only eleven, not seventeen. They could have been snatched or they're hiding, terrified somewhere.' He looked up at Dionne. 'Can you think of anywhere they might go? Friends? Anyone at all?'

Dionne tried to think but shook her head. 'Luke, they don't *have* any friends. I'm gonna drive around to see if I can find them.'

Geoff came in from the dining room to hear the tail end of the conversation. 'They'll be back. It's not late yet. They've probably gone somewhere to cool off and think over what they've done. They're bright kids, and I bet they'll come home before bedtime.' He tried to sound reassuring, but, in the back of his mind, those last two incidents – Curtis Stracken found in the kitchen and the boy stabbed in the neck in the local shopping centre – were giving him even more cause for concern about what the twins were actually capable of doing.

'I know, Geoff, but I feel responsible. I mean, I did give Hudson a hard time this morning, and, really, I should have been more caring. They hate me, Geoff. I mean, you should have seen the way Hudson and Harley looked at me. The boy was nose to nose with me, gritting his teeth. I swear, I saw pure hate in his eyes. But I can't blame them. They don't fucking know me, do they? They were five when I got put away. Out in six years on good behaviour.' He snorted. 'I tell ya, Geoff, there were many times when I nearly lost it in there, an' all. But I bit my lip and counted to ten, thinking of the twins.'

Geoff patted his back.

* * *

Scarlett was nursing a hangover, but she decided to ease the pain with a large shot of vodka; it was her favourite livener. She flicked the channel over to some love story; it was an old classic film. *Don't torture yourself*, she said to herself. A sudden cold breeze blew in through the lounge, and she pulled her tatty dressing gown around her bare legs and gulped back the drink, gritting her back teeth. She should have added a drop of Coke, but the bottle was in the kitchen, and she had neither the strength nor the energy to get up and fetch it. Instead, she poured herself another glass of the liquor – this time a bigger shot and gulped it back. The second breeze gave her a chill, and she shuddered. She couldn't be bothered to get up and close the window either.

Another lonely night was on the cards, she reckoned. Not even her boys were here to make any noise and make her feel human again. The only light cast in the room was from her table lamp. The curtains were still closed from yesterday. It was as if time was standing still, and apart from getting up to use the toilet, she hadn't ventured from the armchair. Last night was a drunken mistake, and she felt a sick sensation when she went over it in her head. Geoff would never want her now; it was clear the family despised her, and as for calling the twins 'weirdos', well, that was very cruel and so out of character.

As she wiped her eyes with the back of her sleeve, she winced; they were so sore from the endless crying that the skin was swollen and thin. Looking down at her wedding ring, she cringed at the sight of her puffy, fat fingers and chipped nails; she really had let herself go. No wonder her husband looked at her with utter contempt. She was a wreck compared to a few years ago when she was the heart and soul of the party. Her Geoff would follow her around the room with his eyes, and she knew he'd loved her then. But, somewhere along the way, he'd changed overnight. She swallowed another large glass of vodka, hoping to clear away the memories that were dragging her down into that deep black hole where a box of pills and a bottle of spirits would be her way out. She looked at the litre bottle, and through blurry eyes, she tried to work out how much she'd drunk, but the room was spinning a little. Was this her chance to fall into a stupor and black out the pain for a few hours?

Unexpectedly, the table lamp went out and she found herself in total darkness. For a second, she thought she could hear breathing, but then she decided it must be coming from her. A chill hit her again, and there in the shadows, she thought she saw someone, but she couldn't work out if it was the alcohol that was playing tricks with her mind.

Then she saw something. A figure moved, and the sudden fear almost sobered her up. In the darkness, the face of the intruder appeared, looking menacing. Throwing her hands to her face, Scarlett screamed, 'Oh my God. What are *you* doing here?' She tried to get to her feet, but she was struck in the chest and pushed back down. The thump hurt but it was more than a thump; it was a strange sensation that caused her to lose her breath. Then came another thump. Scarlett tried to cry out, but her throat was tight, and she felt as if she was choking to death. 'Please, no,' she gurgled, but it was too late. She knew the injuries she was suffering from would kill her. As she tilted her head to the side, all she could manage to say was 'Why?'

The reply was brutal. The last words she heard were, 'Because you are cruel with your words.'

*   *   *

At 11 p.m., Hudson heard a rustling sound outside. He sat upright, straining to hear. Then, as he crept towards the door, it suddenly opened, and in rushed Harley, out of breath and shivering. Proudly, she held up two bags. As she closed the door behind her, she noticed the worried expression on her brother's pale, sickly face and instantly tried to soothe him by rubbing his arms.

'Hudson, everything will be okay. I've food and drinks here, and I think I know where we can go.'

Hudson pinned all his hopes on the confident look in his sister's eyes.

'First thing in the morning, we'll leave here and jump on a bus. No one will take any notice of us. We'll just be like two kids going to school. I have some money in my rucksack, so we can get over to London. I think it's three bus rides.'

'Where are we going?' he asked, in between shudders.

'Nanny Lilly's. She won't turn us in. I just know she won't. Look at you, Hudson. Why are you so cold? You're shaking.'

'I feel sick. I don't like this feeling. Can't we just stay here and wait for Guy and Dr Renee? I feel much safer here. I'm sure they'll protect us.'

Harley threw him an impatient glance. 'Hudson, for God's sake, you're supposed to be the intelligent one. Figure it out yourself. Anyway, we have to get away.'

She watched as his eyes moistened and his head drooped. She knew then that he was having a meltdown, and she would have to take control. It had always been the same from as far back as she could remember. They looked after each other.

While Hudson was the really clever one, he'd also always looked out for her. His strong, protective arms would shield her from harm's way.

But now, it was her turn to look after him. While he was weak, she was strong.

He lay down on the bed and covered himself with the lab coats, and she lay beside him, staring at his floppy fringe and swollen eyes.

A sudden rush of adrenaline surged through her body, and for the first time, she felt annoyed. She needed him to be strong, like her. Still, he was all she had; no one else understood her like he did.

* * *

As soon as Dionne came through the front door, Luke recognised the despair across her face.

'Where have you been?'

The tear-stained face and grey complexion played with his emotions; he was gripped by an incredible urge to hold her tight and kiss away the pain on her face.

With shrunken shoulders, she replied, 'Everywhere. Every street around the school, every open café, in case they were cold . . . They must be terrified. They don't even go to the shops alone, and it's so dark, so frightening for them.'

Despite what he'd said to Dionne that the affair was over, and ignoring for the moment his feelings of guilt for betraying Luke, Geoff wanted to go to her. And if his brother wasn't there now, he would have. Her sweet face and freckled skin were so childlike.

But Luke embraced her, allowing her to cry in his arms.

Geoff looked away in shame because *he* wanted to be the one holding her. His thoughts turned to Scarlett and the state she was in yesterday. Overwhelmed by his iniquity, he'd taken the decision to go back and rekindle their marriage. The more he'd thought about Scarlett, the more he realised that the reason he was drawn to Dionne was because he couldn't handle Scarlett being so needy and tearful, along with the constant spying and accusations. However, Scarlett had every right to spy and to accuse him of being unfaithful because he'd been cheating. And his constant denial of another woman had sent his once attractive and confident wife around the flipping bend. Dionne stirred his sexual cravings but that was where his desire for her ended.

He saw Dionne peer over Luke's shoulder. Her brow was furrowed in sorrow. Was it for him that she looked so sad, or was it for the twins? He really didn't want to know now. His mind was clear at last. As he walked past, he squeezed Luke's shoulder. 'I'll go to Mum's and let them know.'

Releasing Dionne, Luke, with hope in his voice, said, 'Maybe they have gone there.'

'No, they won't have. They know our mother would call us right away. What about your mum, Dionne?'

'No, definitely not. They wouldn't know her if they saw her, and they certainly don't know where she lives.'

Geoff gave Dionne a compassionate smile and left.

* * *

Dionne left Luke in the lounge. 'I'm going to get changed.'

He watched her, still dressed in her coat and shoes, begrudgingly head upstairs. She was a good mum, and the way he'd treated her before he went to prison and even on the few visits while inside had been wrong. She'd held the fort, and now she looked like she had the world on her shoulders.

Approaching midnight, Dionne and Luke sipped the last of their brandy and left the glasses in the lounge. The two of them were both spent. They'd exhausted all options of where the twins were, and Dionne had concluded that they'd found some refuge somewhere and would probably come home the next day.

Luke walked her up the stairs.

As they lay together on the bed, he held her loosely, not wanting to make her feel uncomfortable.

His body so close to hers stirred something in her; was it a sexual urge or disgust? It didn't matter. She wanted to sleep and blot everything out of her mind, just for a moment, at least.

* * *

By the morning, Harley and Hudson were aching from a cold and disturbed night's sleep. The beds were hard and Harley liked her own home comforts. She looked at her watch. It was 6 a.m., and the dusky dawn held a chill that made her shiver.

'Right, straighten your hair, Hudson. We need to get out of here and get on a bus. It's early, so we won't be noticed by any other schoolkids.'

Hudson slid off what felt like a solid blue mattress and tried to smooth down his unruly fringe.

Harley passed him a drink. 'Drink this. We need to go now.'

He took the Fruit Shoot and gulped it back. The drink was welcome, and as he shot a look at his sister, he couldn't be more proud of her. She was proving to be mentally the stronger of the two of them at a time of crisis.

As Harley predicted, the bus stop was deserted, and when the bus arrived, she relaxed her shoulders. They were heading in the opposite direction from the school, so, she reasoned, they were hardly likely to see another pupil.

'Harley, do you know where Nanny Lillian lives?'

'Yes, Nanny Miriam took us there a few years ago, remember?'

Hudson stared out of the window. 'Yes, but how do you know how to get there?'

'Oh, Hudson, you need to learn to be a jump ahead. I study maps, you study puzzles. I study bus journeys too, ready for when I leave home and become totally independent, away from Mum and Dad.'

She noticed he was twiddling his pen again and it irritated her. 'What's bothering you, Hudson?' she said, as she grabbed his hand to try to stop him.

'Mum will never let us go, Harley. Never.'

She squeezed his hand. 'One day, Hudson, I will make sure we are free. *No one* will stop us. We have a plan, remember? You and me, our very own flat, with a huge art studio, and you working from home making money from the stock market. Remember what Guy said. You will be a millionaire with your brain for numbers. We can have a dog, but I guess I will have to walk it, and we'll have fish tanks from wall to wall. The rooms will be green and blue, or even red, and the music will play soft classical or heavy metal, and you, Hudson, will never have to do anything you don't want to, and I can make an entire army of sculptures.'

Her words seemed to soothe Hudson, and the nervous pen twirling finally stopped.

The journey from Chislehurst to Greenwich was a trek, with bustling commuters entering the bus at nearly every stop. Hudson curled in a tight ball as he watched people pushing and shoving to find a space. He went back to staring out of the window until Harley nudged him. It was time to get off. She waited for him to follow, glaring at a man who was so fat he was taking up most of the aisle to allow them room to pass. Once he caught Harley's glower, he soon moved aside.

The houses in the streets were so different from their own, where each dwelling was detached and surrounded by thick foliage and high hedges, and where many of the properties had gates and intercoms to deter unwanted visitors. Here, though, the streets consisted of row upon row of old small Victorian houses, with sash windows and concrete windowsills.

As Harley and Hudson walked along a street that was littered with rubbish, they were met with the sound of two dogs barking and graffiti on the rendered garden walls. The old paint and grey net curtains were the norm on the estate because most of the homes were rented out from the housing association, and the houses, even as small as they were, had been divided into flats for temporary accommodation.

Harley drank in the gloom of it and mentally noted that this part of Greenwich wasn't the place for her. Although some parts were highly affluent, this street was not.

Now, standing outside, eyeing up their nan's house, which was clearly in need of some TLC, Harley said to her brother, 'That's where our Nanny Lillian lives.'

Hudson noticed the dandelions growing through the cracked concrete, and the square lawn with grass as high as his waist. The paint was peeling off the front door, but the net curtains were clean; although they were old-fashioned, they at least dressed the window nicely. But what wasn't so pleasant was the sight of bluebottles buzzing above the overflowing bins. They made him screw his face up.

'Go on then, Hudson. We'd better knock at the door.'

They waited until the door finally opened, and there in a pinny and holey slippers stood their grandmother. She'd certainly aged from the last time they'd seen her. Her hair, which was always untidy, was longer, and her facial wrinkles had deepened.

Tilting her head to the side, she smiled. 'Can I help you?' Then it dawned on her who the two children were. Feeling her whole body tremble, she couldn't hold back the tears, and, instinctively, she held out her arms. Pulling both grandchildren to her, she hugged them, stroking the back of their hair, while allowing the tears to tumble down her face.

'Don't cry, Nanny. It's okay,' said Hudson, in his deep voice.

After taking a deep breath to get her emotions in check, she stepped back. Her face shone from tears and that rosy countenance beamed as she smiled.

'I can't help meself. It's been so long, and, well, I just hoped for the day, before I push up daisies, when I would be able to have one more cuddle.'

Harley and Hudson, both sensing the sorrow in her voice, flung their arms around her again. And it seemed to be the most natural thing to do.

Lillian felt more tears cascade down her cheeks before she released the twins again.

'Well, I'll be buggered. Look at you two. Ya must have grown four inches.' She looked over their shoulders expecting to see Miriam, but the street was empty. 'Er, come in. Where's ya nan?'

With no response, she stepped aside as they shyly entered.

'Go on, loveys. Go through to the living room.'

There were only two doors: there was the one on the left leading into the small living room and the one opposite that opened into the kitchen.

Hudson could smell a lavender air freshener, a cheap one from the Poundshop. With his head down, he looked at the swirls of gold and yellow in the hall carpet. He'd never seen patterned carpet before. His home was fitted with beige carpet in the bedrooms and solid wood flooring with large cream rugs downstairs. The wallpaper here was woodchip that looked to have been painted thirty times. But, somehow, the 1970s decor had a homely feel.

Harley pushed her brother into the living room.

He stood trying to recall the place from a few years ago. He was good at remembering detail, but, for some reason, he was struggling this time. But when he spotted the swing in the garden, his memory came back to him. He recalled it had been hot the last time they were there, and so they'd played in the garden, sipping Cherry Coke and enjoying the swing.

'Sit, sit, let me get you a drink.' Lillian clapped her hands in excitement. She'd dreamed, prayed, and imagined for this day. She'd been desperate to see her grandchildren, even for a minute or two. It had been so long, and yet not a day had gone by when she hadn't thought of them.

Miriam had visited a couple of times, and Lillian had been told that Dionne didn't want the twins coming over.

As Lillian hurriedly left for the kitchen, Harley eased herself onto the sofa and nodded for Hudson to do the same. The swirly patterned carpet theme continued into the living room. The sofa was covered in a mustard coloured throw to hide the worn-out seats. A fluffy bright-red rug lay in front of the coal fire that over time had blackened the fire surround. This was so far removed from their own home; yet, oddly, each of them felt comfortable. Perhaps it was the smell of furniture polish, mixed with remnants of the previous evening's fire, and the soothing tones of hearing some chat show host on the radio mumbling away in the background.

Harley watched as Hudson stood up again, removed his blazer and rucksack, and then, surprisingly, removed his shoes.

As soon as Lillian returned, she clocked his shoes placed neatly by the side of the chair and his jacket folded methodically, where it rested on the arm of the sofa.

'Here you go,' she said, as she shuffled over to the coffee table, which had a ring mark that no amount of polishing would remove.

'I've biscuits and chocolate bars. Go on, help yaself. Now, what do I owe this pleasure?' She sat on a chair close to the window.

Harley tried to crane her neck to see into the kitchen. 'Where's grandad?'

Suddenly, Lillian looked uncomfortable. She fidgeted in her seat, and a sad expression crossed her face. 'Oh my, didn't your mother tell you? I mean, I did call and write to her to come to the funeral.'

Hudson gasped. '*What? Did he die?*'

'Oh, yes, my angel. He died a few years ago of cancer, the poor old bugger. I thought ya mum would have told you. I'm sorry it's such a shock.'

She moved closer to the coffee table and picked up the plate of biscuits. 'Would you like one, Harley? And before you check,' she giggled, pausing for a moment, 'they are all chocolate digestives or pink wafers.'

Harley shook her head. 'I'm fine, Nan . . . Nan, you don't talk to Mum anymore, do you?'

Lillian raised a concerned eyebrow. 'Well, no, I think I've upset her somewhere along the line. Why do you ask?'

Harley looked at Hudson who was nibbling on a biscuit. 'We have run away, Nan, and we don't want her or anyone to know we are here. Can you promise not to tell?'

Lillian bit her lip and sighed. 'I should really let someone know, or they'll be frantic with worry . . . Did your mother do anything to upset you, then?'

Harley shrugged her shoulders. 'No, not exactly, but we will be in so much trouble if we go back.'

Lillian studied their faces and concluded that whatever trouble they were in it was serious because Hudson looked sick with the stress of it all.

'Okay, but you need to tell your mother you're fine. We don't want her pulling her bleedin' hair out. If she knows you're here, she'll be knocking at the door, quick sharp.'

Harley smiled. 'Nan, do you have a phone?'

Lillian nodded and pointed to the phone on the side table. The phone was probably worth money as an antique.

'Babe, dial 141, before the number, and then it will show up as being withheld.'

Harley pulled the phone onto her lap. 'Hudson, what's our phone number?'

Like a robot, he reeled off the digits.

* * *

Dionne must have been sitting on the phone because she answered right away. 'Hello?' She was hoping it was Geoff.

'Mum, it's Harley. Hudson and I are safe, so don't worry. There's no need to find us.'

* * *

She hung up and smiled. 'Thanks, Nan.'

Lillian wondered if she was doing the right thing, but her grandchildren needed her help, and it had been a long time since anyone had called or even shown an interest in her.

* * *

When Luke stepped out of the bathroom, he called down the stairs. 'Who was that?'

Dionne was in a dilemma. She wondered whether the children were better off where they were rather than face the consequences on their return. Because if the kids were picked up, then they may be interrogated about more than just the playground fight, and she didn't want that to happen. Who knew how the children would react once they were inside a police station? And would the police start checking their property and discover Curtis Stracken's body underneath the garage floor? She shuddered. It wasn't worth the risk to get the police involved just yet.

Dionne called upstairs to Luke. 'It was Harley. She sounded fine. At least they're safe. She didn't say where they were, but she said she and Hudson are okay.'

Luke ran down the stairs with a towel around his waist, still dripping wet. She eyed him over and noticed that he wasn't the skinny man who went to prison; he was chunkier, toned, and now with his long hair, he looked entirely different. For a moment, she wondered if she could fancy him, but when her mind returned to Geoff, there really was no comparison.

'Check the number!'

She shook her head. 'I did, but the number was withheld. As I said, at least they're safe. Harley sounded fine.'

Luke curled his lip. 'That's what worries me. They shouldn't be fine, should they? Most kids their age would be desperate to get home to their parents. I dunno, Dionne, I think you were right when you said they were different. They are, ain't they? Shrinks see all sorts, and when you first mentioned it, I thought perhaps they were just shy and needed to come out of themselves, but it's more than that. I guess their psychiatrist knows what he's doing.' He turned away to head back to the bathroom. 'Leave it for a day or so. They are bound to come home.'

* * *

The afternoon was spent doing puzzles; it put Hudson's overactive mind at rest. 'These are old ones, Nan. Did you love doing puzzles?'

Lillian peered up through her bushy brows and tilted her head to the side. 'No, my darlin'. But your mum did. She was good too. I never had much money for fancy toys. See, when she was a nipper, she loved to get her head stuck into a puzzle. I used to buy them in charity shops or the fêtes. My Kenny used to wind her up something rotten, ya know. He always said she was a weirdo.'

Suddenly, the children stopped what they were doing. They looked up and then at each other in disbelief.

But Lillian was in a world of her own, down memory lane. 'All because he was the outgoing type. He loved to dance, that boy did. He always had a new bird on his arm, a tenner in his pocket, and a cheeky glint in his eye. Mind you, he took after his father. He was the same. I think the old git still had it in him the day he died, having those Macmillan nurses wrapped around his finger . . . Oh, 'ark at me going on. I tell ya what, why don't I go down the shop and fetch us a nice bit of liver for tea, eh? Ooh, liver, onions, and bacon. It'll be a real treat. What d'ya say?'

'I've never had liver before. What's it like? Where does it come from?' asked Harley.

Lillian laughed. 'The butcher down the road, babe.'

Hudson, for the first time in a long while, chuckled. 'No, Nan, she means which animal?'

Lillian was surprised to hear Hudson speak. For most of the time, he'd hardly said a word.

'Well, pigs or lamb, but the best is lamb. I tell ya what. I'll get sausages as well, just in case, 'cos it ain't to everyone's taste. And we'll 'ave ice cream for afters.'

Slowly easing herself off the chair, Lillian straightened her back. Her arthritis had worsened and was crippling her at times, but she wanted to make sure her grandchildren were fed and happy.

'While I'm gone, you two can go upstairs and get yaselves settled in for tonight. Kenny's room is as it was, but I still dust it and keep it fresh, Gawd rest his soul. And ya mother's is as it was, so I'll leave ya to get on with it. I'll only be half an hour.'

Much to the pleasure of Lillian and to the surprise of Harley, Hudson jumped to his feet and helped her with her coat. Rarely did Hudson like contact. He was fussy who he allowed to touch him.

The children watched her waddle down the garden path and then they went to look at the bedrooms. The upstairs landing had four doors leading to three bedrooms and a bathroom.

Hudson looked at the black toilet seat and the high-level cistern with the long chain. A dolly in a knitted dress to hide the toilet roll was perched on a small cabinet between the bath and the toilet and on the floor was black and white chequered lino.

Harley stuck her head in the smallest room. It was a girl's room, so she assumed it was her mother's at one time. The single bed, which was pushed up against the wall, was draped in a candlewick bedspread, which was slightly faded from the sun. An old melamine wardrobe with plastic handles stood against the opposite wall, and on the dressing table, there were bags of make-up and perfume. On one wall were posters of aliens. She chuckled at those. 'Hey, Hudson, look at these! Mum must have liked star stuff.'

He joined her in the room and gazed around. 'She didn't have much. They must have been poor. Look at the worn-out books in the corner.'

Both children looked at the girls' annuals and more puzzles, all neatly piled.

Harley brazenly opened the wardrobe to find dresses and blouses. She stepped back in surprise. The clothes were evenly lined up in order of colour, from black to green and then to red. There were no other colours. Harley grinned. 'Well, I think maybe I do take after Mum with my favourite colours. Only, I don't like red much.'

'Nine,' said Hudson.

Harley frowned. 'Nine?'

He pointed to the books. 'Look. Nine books, nine puzzles, and nine dresses.' He pointed to the nail varnish. 'And look at those. There are nine of those too.'

Giggling now, she tapped him on the arm. 'You and numbers. You see a pattern in anything. It's just coincidence, surely? I guess you are looking for things in common. I wonder if we take after Dad too?'

Hudson shook his head. 'No, I think we're more like Mum.'

Plonking herself on the bed, Harley suddenly shuddered. 'No, Hudson, we aren't. We are not like anyone.' She noticed a deep sadness creep over his face, and she held his hand. 'We are like each other, though. Let's check out the other bedroom. I guess that will be yours tonight. I hope it's a lot nicer than this one.'

'What's that on the bedposts?' asked Hudson, looking at the bolts.

Harley screwed up her nose. 'I don't know, but it may have been a bunk bed at one time.'

They left the bedroom, none the wiser, to investigate the next one.

That door was shut, and as Hudson turned the handle, he paused. 'What did Nan mean when she said "God rest his soul"? Is Kenny dead?'

Harley shrugged her shoulders. 'Mum's never spoken about any of her family.'

He pushed the door open and crept inside as if he was doing something wrong. His eyes widened. 'Wow, this is different. It's more modern, at least,' said, Hudson, as he looked at the blue quilt cover and grey curtains. The wardrobe was made of wood and seemed relatively new. The carpet was immaculate. It was a soft grey colour, and there on the wall was a montage of photos. One showed a teenage boy holding a fish. Others showed the boy with friends at scouts, clubs, and on holiday.

Harley tilted her head to look at each picture. It was definitely the same boy in each one, and in some, he was hugging their grandmother. And she looked younger but so much happier.

Harley laughed. 'Well, you got the long straw.'

Hudson bounced on the bed and nodded. 'Yes, I will like this room.'

As Harley opened the wardrobe, she stepped back. It was packed with clothes, jackets, and shoes. Instantly, she had a sense that this older boy would walk into the room at any moment. She felt uncomfortable and suggested they returned to the living room to wait for Nanny Lillian.

It wasn't too long before Lillian put her key in the lock. Quickly, Hudson hurried to help her with the shopping. 'Oh, good lad. I ended up buying half the shop. Now then, you carry them through and put them on the counter while I stick the kettle on. I got some iced buns. Go on, lovey, help yaself. Christ, it's getting nippy outside. I'd best get that fire going before night falls. This house gets a tad chilly, but I have hot water bottles and electric blankets, if you feel cold.'

Hudson was bemused by her prattling away and in some ways comforted by it. To him, she was an honest woman, and he knew where he stood.

He knew his honesty, however, always got him into trouble, but like Guy had said 'It's not a bad thing, Hudson. You just have to think if it is appropriate before you begin to speak.' Having worked on his thought processes for months, he was beginning to find it easier not to speak unless he had to. But Nanny Lillian was different: he felt he could say what he wanted to her, and she wouldn't be angry.

'Nan, is that room with the blue quilt on the bed and all the clothes in the wardrobe Kenny's room?'

Pulling out the food from the plastic bags, Lillian laughed. 'So you've had a good nose through, then?'

'Yes, Nan, we did. Did he die?'

She placed the kettle on the stove and turned to face him. 'Yes, my lovely. He died when he was sixteen, an accident.' She didn't like to talk about how he died; it was too disturbing, so she spoke about the wonderful memories she had of him instead.

'How old was Mum then?'

Lillian looked to the ceiling. 'Um, twelve. Now then, Hudson, take these buns to your sister. See if she would like one.'

Lighting the fire and sitting by the soft golden glow of the lamp was a new experience for the twins, and one they enjoyed, to the point that Hudson left his pen in his rucksack and dozed like an angel on the sofa. Harley listened to her grandmother waffling on about how she met their grandfather and the little dog they had. She watched the flames flickering, dressed in her mother's old nightdress, until, she too, became heavy-eyed and ready for bed.

CHAPTER SIXTEEN

Three days had passed, and although Harley made a daily call to say they were okay, the police were now concerned.

Taylor Croft's mother was in uproar that Hudson had, as she put it, 'mutilated her son's face', and she wanted someone to be held accountable.

Detective Inspector Jacob Forbes had been remiss regarding finding the missing children. He'd assumed they would turn up eventually, probably hiding out at a friend's house; however, a subsequent visit to the Mason family's home had pricked his attention. They were not as bothered as they had been when their children were first reported as missing. He concluded that the parents had a pretty good idea where their kids were. If that was the case, then they were harbouring a criminal, even though Hudson was eleven years old.

Forbes had to be seen to be making headway since Taylor's mother, Kitty, was not one for taking this lying down. She was going mental in the station and making all kind of threats including going to the media. With a mouth like hers and her distinct lack of decorum, she would be the type to do it and make a mockery of the whole police station.

And the photos of Taylor's face would be a shocker if printed in the local rag. His blue bloated cheeks, which had severe puncture wounds, looked horrific. What was more troubling, though, was when he showed the photo to the Masons. Luke Mason, a well-known criminal, and not long out of prison, actually looked physically sick and threw his hands to his mouth; but Mrs Mason, in contrast, appeared totally emotionless and distant. Either she wasn't surprised, which would suggest she'd seen her son do something like this before, or she found it inconceivable that her child would commit such an atrocity.

With so much going on at the station – a sudden rise in knifings and other violent assaults had become a top priority to deal with – he had to be seen to be making headway.

Detective Chief Inspector Lewis Sanders, a middle-aged man of shoddy appearance but with a keen eye for detail and an impeccable record, strolled into the custody suite, just as Forbes was rubbing his temples and staring out of the window. 'Hello, Jacob. You look stressed, mate. Wanna go for a beer later? I'm scratching my nuts trying to find any cold case to satisfy my interests.'

Forbes, recently promoted to the post of detective inspector, was a well-educated man and found Sanders amusing with his choice of words. 'Actually, Lewis, I would love to . . . And I could do with your advice.'

Sanders winked. 'Holding out in the bedroom department, is she?'

'That would be nothing new.' He looked at his watch and could see it was approaching 6 p.m., well after his shift finished. 'Come on, then. Let's go to the pub. I could do with a cold beer or three.'

At fifty-two years old, with no children himself and no woman who would put up with him, Lewis Sanders was married to his job. He didn't want to climb any more ladders, and so just being a detective chief inspector suited his needs. He loved the work – even the stress that went with it. What he couldn't stand, though, was being bored, and, right now, there were no murder cases he could get his teeth into. His record for solving particularly difficult murder cases was exemplary. Not the type of man to follow the rules, he went by his gut instinct. He didn't care for modern police methods, and so, although he'd been offered a place on numerous training programmes such as profiling, and even the opportunity to go on advanced IT workshops, he'd never been interested.

His idea of being a good copper was that policing was either in your blood or not. Thirty years ago, his brother had been murdered. The case had never been solved. That determination had led him to become a detective, and once he had reached the position, he began opening cold cases, and, naturally, his brother's was the first. Within a month, to the astonishment of his colleagues, he had the murderer in custody. The need to solve serious crimes became an addiction. He could handle himself and never worried about getting his hands dirty. He knew he was fearless and reckless at times, but the superintendent always found a way to cover up his little cock-ups because he knew that he was the best they had.

* * *

The Sydney Arms in Chislehurst was ideal for the two men to have a conversation without being overheard. They decided to sit in the garden out the back, which was small but empty.

Forbes had changed into his jeans and check shirt. With his slim frame and dewy complexion, he looked like a regular punter and not a washed-out, overworked detective.

Sanders, however, with his five o'clock shadow, messy hair, and broad shoulders, wore the aura of a copper, although he didn't care what he looked like. He knew he looked scruffy in his tatty mac, yet he wasn't in the least bit slovenly and wasn't one to be taken for a fool.

'So, what's on ya mind, mate?'

Forbes nervously giggled, a bad habit of his. 'So, there are these twins, eleven years old. The boy, Hudson, has attacked a kid at school with a pen.'

Sanders laughed, thinking it was some kind of joke. 'Playground bullying, right?' But then he saw the serious expression on Forbes' face.

'Okay, so what's the big deal? A kids' fight, was it?'

'Do you remember a few weeks ago when a kid was rushed to hospital with a stab wound to the neck, and, by all accounts, it was done with a pen? Well, the case wasn't taken any further because the kid who stabbed him did it in self-defence.'

Sanders looked to the sky in recollection. 'Oh, yeah, I think so.'

Leaning forward, Forbes said, 'Well, it's the same kid, only, this time, it *wasn't* self-defence. The lad, Hudson, has made a real mess of Taylor Croft's face, to the extent that we nearly had a murder on our hands.'

Looking perplexed, Sanders replied, 'I don't get it. I mean, I have loads of little shits out there who have committed two, three, sometimes four stabbings. They're teenagers who don't give a flying shit. It's all about gang culture, and it's getting worse. So why is this kid so different?'

Taking a large gulp of his beer, Forbes shook his head. 'Going back to the incident at The Glades, I just happened to be upstairs when Bill Coots took the boy, who was accompanied by his grandmother and the family's solicitor, into the main interview room. Out of curiosity, really, I watched the interview take place. And I was pleased I did. I saw something in the boy's eyes that made me go cold. He was strange, and you know when we say that someone isn't "the full ticket"? Well, I can honestly say that about this kid. He's a size as well. He doesn't look eleven. More like fourteen. And, Lewis, I think there's more to him – a dangerous side – and he is out there somewhere. And another thing: the parents are acting odd. They were frantic when Hudson and his sister first went missing, but, now, they don't seem bothered.'

Sanders shrugged his shoulders. 'They must know where he is, then. So, if I were you, I'd have them followed . . . What's their surname?'

'Mason, as in Luke Mason.'

'Well, that explains the boy's temper. Fuck me, Luke Mason is one violent fucker. I was warned by my mates in Greenwich that he'd moved here and to watch out for him. Geoff and Dean Mason are his brothers. They own a club called The Allure, but they are into other rackets. Luke was nabbed with two guns and a hundred grand in cash. He got a twelve-stretch. He's a very violent man. I've seen first-hand what that bastard is capable of, but no one will grass him up. They're all too shit-scared of the repercussions. You won't have heard of the Strackens, boys out of Bermondsey, will you?'

Forbes shook his head.

'They never pressed charges and refused to say what happened, but the three of them are not pushovers either. They took a beating from Luke, and when I say a beating, he nearly killed them. The eldest boy, Ryan, had brain injuries and later died. The middle lad, Callum, will never walk properly again. As for the youngest, Curtis, he also sustained terrible injuries, to his right shoulder and shins. He still won't leave his house, as far as I'm aware.'

Forbes finished his pint and rose from his seat to get them both another one; he wanted to process the information.

As soon as he returned, Sanders looked as though he had something on his mind.

'Penny for them?'

'Jacob, a while back now, I got a call from DI Shaver, an old pal of mine at the Met. He was the one who was always pulling the Mason files. He didn't like to see them doing so well outta dirty money. He was always itching to bring them in, but they were particularly smart, especially Luke Mason, the middle lad. Anyway, he asked me if I could keep my ear to the ground. Curtis Stracken, after years of being a recluse, suddenly snapped when Ryan died. He was mouthing off that he would find Luke and kill him. He blames Luke for his brother never being the same, and the damage to his brain was the likely cause of his death in the end.' Narrowing his eyes, he stopped and took a swig of his beer and then leaned back on the garden chair.

Seeing his friend perturbed, Forbes, now intrigued but confused, asked, 'Yeah, so what are you saying, Lewis?'

'It's odd because Callum Stracken filed a missing person report. Curtis Stracken is on the missing list.'

'Hmm, that's not so strange, is it? The man may have just upped sticks.'

Sanders shook his head. 'No. Callum reported that although Curtis had been a recluse for many years after his brother died, he did venture out to the local pubs but never further than that and never for more than two hours. Apparently, after Callum called the office for an update on his missing brother, he also added the fact that Curtis had gone after Luke Mason to seek retribution.'

'So, do you think Luke had anything to do with Curtis' disappearance, then?'

'Nah, I don't think so. Luke was inside at the time, but who's to say the other brothers didn't have. We can't go in and make accusations, but with this young lad on the run, you could do a bit of fishing.'

'Like father, like son, possibly.'

'I would agree with you, if they were still living over in Greenwich and running amok, but living in a mansion in Chislehurst, you would think they would want their kids to be a pillar of society and get a good education, which, if they wanted to, could buy them a crime-free life,' replied Sanders.

'The problem is, Lewis, I need someone like you on this case. I know it's not murder but. . .'

'Oh, I see, you want me to stick my nose in?'

Forbes beamed and his cheeks reddened.

'Hmm, so the pints were just to soften me up, then?'

Forbes nodded and laughed.

'Okay, okay, I'll get the boss to sign it off, and I'll do some digging.'

* * *

It was 6.30 a.m. on the fourth day, and Luke was annoyed. He looked at the phone and then at Dionne. 'If that phone rings, don't you answer it. I will. I'm not having my kids dictate to me. I wanna fucking know where they are and what the fuck they're up to.'

Dionne nodded. 'Be careful, Luke, or they'll just cut you off.'

'When I get my hands on them, I swear to God, I'll give them such a hiding! I have been home less than a week, and I had far less grief inside. What the fuck is the matter with them?'

Thirty minutes later, the phone rang, and Luke snatched it before Dionne had a chance to blink. 'Right, no more nonsense. Where the hell are you?' he scolded.

'Mr Mason, it's DCI Sanders here. I take it the children still haven't arrived home. I'm on my way, so please don't go anywhere.'

Luke's eyes were wide and his breathing was fast. He looked at Dionne in shock. *'What?'* he snapped.

'Mr Mason, I will be with you in ten minutes. I suggest you don't make plans to go out.'

Luke sighed. 'Fine, whatever,' he replied, before he replaced the receiver.

'That's just fucking great. We've got a detective on his way now.'

Dionne felt her throat dry up and her hands shake. She wanted to be out of the picture, so she excused herself to take a bath.

'Dee, don't you think it'll look odd, you casually soaking in the bath when he arrives?'

'What the hell have *I* got to hide? Me kids are missing, and the filth ain't done fuck all to find them. We should be pointing the fingers at *them*, for not getting off their arses and going out there to look for them.'

Luke rolled his eyes. 'Ha! That finger-pointing won't work now, will it? The copper heard me shouting down the phone.'

She tutted and headed upstairs. 'Well, I'm gonna get dressed!'

'I wouldn't bother now. This copper will be here any minute.' Luke was sharp. He hated the Old Bill, and having some detective on the case had now put the hairs on the back of his neck on end.

Dionne ignored him and hurried up the stairs.

Less than ten minutes later, DCI Sanders was at the front door. Like the detective he was, his inquisitive eyes surveyed the outside of the house. He noticed that the bushes needed a trim and the doorstep needed a repaint, but what took his breath away was the sheer size of the house. The wide block paved drive swept up to the front door and was big enough to house ten cars. He could guess it was a six-bedroom property, just by the windows at the front alone. The double garage had cobwebs on the frames and leaves had gathered in the corners, so he surmised the building wasn't in constant use.

When the front door was opened in one fluid movement, he assumed the gentleman was Luke Mason. He could tell the man was tall just by comparing him to the height of the door. With broad shoulders and with his hair neatly tied back, Sanders noticed his expression was tight and his eyes moody. Yet after hearing about the description of the Strackens' beating, he would have expected a chunk of a man with a bald head, tattoos, and hands like shovels.

'You'd better come in,' stated Luke, standing to the side to allow the detective entry.

'Go in the lounge. Wanna drink?'

Sanders shook his head. 'No, thank you, but thanks for offering.'

Taking a moment to size up Luke Mason, he concluded that the man was certainly no pushover. Confident and yet harshly serious, yes. There was no doubt in his mind that Mason was a man who he could be quite direct with.

'Now then, Mr Mason, I'll get to the point—'

'Take a seat,' interrupted Luke.

Sanders nodded and got a sense of the real measure of the man; Mason was clearly used to being in charge. So he did as he was asked.

'I can assume from the way you answered the phone that you were obviously expecting a call from your children.' He stared at Mason's expression. But there was nothing, just a deadpan face.

Mason's slow nod had Sanders wondering if he was saying 'Carry on' or 'Yes, I've received a call.'

'Oh, sorry. I'm Detective Chief Inspector Sanders. Call me Lewis. I hate formalities.'

Luke sat down, opposite, still stone-faced. 'They only called to say they were fine and not to worry.'

'You were expecting that call, though, weren't you, Mr Mason?'

Luke nodded. 'They've called every day but they've said the same thing.'

'No idea where they are, then?'

With a questioning look, Luke glared. 'If I knew where my kids were then I would have them back home. They wouldn't be bloody missing, would they?'

Sanders smiled sarcastically. 'Would you, though, Mr Mason? Because you're no stranger to the law and neither are your brothers, and, funnily enough, your ol' man. So, I'm guessing, you like to sort things out your own way.'

Leaning back and grinning, Luke gave a false laugh. 'You're right, Lewis. It's no secret me ol' man was a bit of a lad and got himself into trouble. And, yeah, me and me brothers were no angels, and, as well ya know, I've just served six years for a couple of guns, but, come on, mate, these are kids we're talking about. They ain't running around causing fucking mayhem with a shooter. Me lad's just had a fight. Maybe he did do some damage, but he's still only a nipper.'

Sanders sniffed the air and looked around. The room was spotless and not what he expected with young children living here. No PlayStation, no Nintendo, no kids' trainers in the hallway, and no family photos.

'He didn't just have a regular fight, though, Mr Mason. I was shown the photos, and I have to say it doesn't look good for him, not with the previous assault as well.'

'What's this really all about? I mean, they are only fucking *eleven*. I had worse rucks when I was seven.'

'Whether they are eleven or not, they need to be brought in, so let's start by trying to track them down. Now, where's your wife? I need her here too.'

Dionne was listening at the top of the stairs and decided to join them. After all, she would have to meet this detective sooner or later.

'So, give me the names of their friends, family, addresses, phone numbers, everything you have.'

Upon hearing that the twins had no friends, Sanders was now intrigued. Usually, any kid, no matter how bad they were, had friends. 'And their cousins?' asked Sanders, glancing at Dionne Mason, as she entered the room.

'The boys are all in Ibiza. They flew out on Monday. They should be back later today, so they're not with them, unless they grew fucking wings.'

Sanders watched Dionne. She remained expressionless, giving nothing away, until he asked after her family.

Her eyes widened. 'I don't have any.'

Luke was taken aback and turned to face her. 'You have your *mother*.'

'Yeah, but we don't talk, and the twins wouldn't know her if they bumped into her in the street. And besides that, my mother would call me right away if the twins were with her. Plus they don't know where she lives. The last time they set foot in her house was years ago.'

Sanders stood up. 'What's her address because I can guarantee that's where they will be, if they don't want you to know where they are, and since you're estranged from her, what better place to run to?'

Luke snatched his coat from the back of the chair. 'Right, I'll fetch them, if you're sure that's where they'd go.'

Sanders waved his hand. 'No, Mr Mason. I will go. Once I have them, I will call you, and you can meet me at the station.'

Luke was too tired to argue; he'd wound himself up over the last few days. He decided perhaps a stint in the station might buck up their ideas. As the detective left the house, Luke shot his wife a glare. 'Why didn't you think of her? Didn't you even call her?'

Dionne shook her head. 'Of course, I bloody called her. She said that they weren't there. And there's a lot you don't know, Luke. While you were away, I broke all ties with the woman. She was horrible to me growing up, and I didn't want our children to be subjected to her spiteful ways, like I was.'

'Really? She's always come across as such a sweet person.'

'Huh, yes, that was her facade. She had everyone fooled except me because I was the one she abused.'

Under normal circumstances, Luke would have grilled her over a statement like that and even accused her of bullshitting; right now, however, he was anxious about his kids. So much had happened in a short space of time, he was beginning to wonder what planet he was living on.

* * *

Geoff picked up the boys from Gatwick. He waited at the arrivals point and beamed when he saw the four strapping lads tanned and full of excitement. He also noticed how a group of young women were eyeing them over, and he was proud. Not an ugly one among them, and confident too, even little Kai was now a hulk of a lad and walking with a swagger, not tied to his mother's apron strings as he was as a kiddie.

His thoughts turned to Hudson, and a sudden sadness drained his happiness. Poor Luke was plagued with a lad who was so far removed from his four nephews. How could he enjoy being with his son now or in the future – going to the footie, having a beer, teaching him to drive, and helping him to fix his own cars? He hadn't called the boys while they were on holiday to tell them the goings-on because he hadn't wanted to let the issue regarding Hudson ruin their trip.

The drive back was filled with non-stop chatter about the girls they had pulled and the antics they had got up to. Geoff laughed along, with his spirits high. They reminded him of Dean and himself at that age. Luke was the more serious one, but even he engaged in a good night out at times.

After dropping Lee and Kai off at their home, he headed for Scarlett's house. The boys were living with her for half the week and with him for the other half. However, Davey had his eye on a flat above the shop in the high street and Nicki was after renting the second bedroom. Unbeknown to them, Geoff had saved the deposit to help them on their way to becoming independent. And next month, he would surprise them both with the keys.

He pulled into the drive of his wife's modest house and lifted the boot. 'Oi, boys, I ain't your footman. Get the bags yaselves.'

Nicki came back to the car and grabbed both the cases while Davey marched on ahead.

But as soon as Davey put the key in the door, he staggered back. 'Jesus, what the hell is that smell!'

As the door widened, the stench reached Geoff, and he hurried over, moving the boys away. 'Go back to the car!'

Davey and Nicki looked at each other and stepped back, while their father covered his nose with his T-shirt and entered.

He knew he would expect to find someone dead because the smell was the worst thing in the world. It was so bad, it made his eyes water. He had to look, though; he had to be sure.

The doorway to the lounge was the first on the left. It was open, but the room was dark, very warm, and the curtains were still drawn. His heart pounded wildly, believing he would find his wife had taken her own life. Extreme thoughts hurtled through his mind. He tried to flick on the light. Realising that it wasn't working, he opened the curtains. The shock caused him to jump back and cover his mouth before the scream escaped. He'd never seen a decomposing body, and he would never wish to again. He'd seen a dead body, even buried one, but this was on a different level. And nothing would ever shock him more – not the grotesque expression on his wife's half-eaten face, the bloodstained dressing gown, and her empty eye sockets crawling with maggots. Stunned, he couldn't move but only stare in horror. This wasn't his wife with the pretty face. This was a monster – an incongruous, indescribable, hideous thing. And the buzzing of the thousands of flies mixed with an unholy sensation made him want to leave his own senses. Then he felt the vomit violently make its way to the back of his throat and project through his mouth and nose. He gagged and gasped for air as he staggered to get away from the vision that would run like ice through his veins.

Hearing their father scream, both boys ran back up the drive and entered the house.

'Dad?' called out Davey.

Geoff spun around and held his hands up for the boys to stay back.

Seeing the look of sheer terror on their father's face, they grabbed him to hold him steady. 'Dad?'

'Don't go in there. Please don't go in there.' He was still trying to catch his breath, but the vomit rose up again and instantly covered the floor.

Nicki jumped back. 'Dad, what is it?' His voice was now frantic.

Geoff was shaking his head and coughing, pushing the boys ahead of him out on to the drive.

'Get in the car.'

Looking at the state of their father, they did as they were told.

Geoff, now weak at the knees and visibly shaking, looked back at the house and then patted his jeans for his phone. He dialled 999. 'Hello, er, er . . . My wife, she's dead, she's in the house . . .'

'Sir, please calm down. Are you sure she's dead? Can you see if she's breathing?'

'Christ, no, she's dead . . .'

'Please, sir. Take your time. How do you know she's dead?'

'I, er . . . I found her just now, in her house. The place stinks. Oh my God . . .' He felt vomit rising again and had to take a few deep breaths.

'Okay, sir. What's your name?'

'Geoff Mason. My wife, er, is Scarlett Mason. I have to go. My sons can't see this. I have to take them away.'

'Mr Mason, please tell me the address. We'll have someone over right away.'

After Geoff gave the details, he ended the call.

He had to get away, get his boys away. They could never see that; it would haunt them forever and remove their spirits, along with their dreams for the future.

Davey didn't hear the call to the police. He and his brother were already in the car, but as soon as their father hopped into the driver's seat and began to tear away, driving like a lunatic, he knew his father had witnessed something that would put the wind up any grown man.

'Dad, what's going on?' cried Nicki.

Geoff pulled the car over to the side of the road and turned to face the two innocent faces of his children. 'I'm so sorry, so sorry, but your mother is dead. I didn't want you to see her like that . . . Oh, Jesus.' He banged the steering wheel and collapsed in a heap, crying like a baby.

Davey jumped out of the car, opened the driver's door, and held his dad. He'd now become a man, helping his distraught father into the back seat and taking over at the wheel. Nicki was in shock and stared ahead in silence. This would shake them to the core, and it would be hours before any of them could comprehend it.

CHAPTER SEVENTEEN

Sanders had left his phone in the car. As good as he was at his job, he was slovenly at times around formalities.

However, for once he wasn't alone. Normally, he preferred it this way. It suited him. He could think more clearly, and, importantly, his instinct – and no else's – was what set him apart from his colleagues. Having someone else accompanying him hampered his style because as far as he was concerned policing was about risk-taking, and if he had someone with him, they would, in all likelihood, want to do everything by the book. But, very reluctantly, he'd decided today to bring with him a female PC. It was for the best, he'd decided, since there were two children involved.

As per usual, he surveyed the outside of the house and summed up the occupant. She was apparently unable to mow the lawn, probably suffering from some ailment, yet he suspected she was probably house-proud from the perfectly hung net curtains. It also appeared that she liked animals because beside the bin there was a small bowl of cat food, which he presumed was for the strays. An empty carton of raspberry ripple ice cream was just visible from the refuse bin, along with a party size crisps pack. A woman on her own would hardly buy a twenty-four-pack of crisps.

He knocked before he stepped away from the small glass pane, but he was still close enough to the door so that the occupants couldn't see him from the living room window.

* * *

Lillian got up from her seat as her grandchildren looked nervously at each other.

'Aw, don't you go worrying. It's probably Hettie from next door wanting to borrow sugar or something. The woman's lost her marbles and is always on the scrounge.'

As she opened the door, Sanders stepped in, not even waiting for an invite. WPC Tara Willis followed nervously. She'd only been in the job for three weeks and was wary of Sanders. He had a reputation for speaking his mind whether the person liked it or not, and she was a very timid soul.

'Lillian Stuart, I'm Detective Chief Inspector Sanders. I've come to talk with Hudson and Harley.' He didn't wait for an answer; instead, he walked directly into the living room and smiled at the two children who were sitting at the coffee table drawing pictures.

'Well, this is cosy.'

Lillian hurried past him. 'Look, Mr Sanders, they just wanted to stay for a while . . .'

He held up his hand. 'It's all right, Mrs Stuart. No one is in any trouble. You did what all grandmothers would have done in the circumstances – protect your own.'

Lillian cocked her head to the side. 'What do you mean?' she said, as she gave Hudson and Harley a deep creased frown.

Ignoring her, he stared at the twins. *Jacob was right*, he thought. Hudson was certainly a big lad, and he had an arrogant sneer across his face, yet Harley was the one with pure hatred behind her big round eyes.

'Right, you two. Your parents have been worried sick, and I need you to come with me now.' His gravel voice, from too many cigarettes, commanded attention.

Before Lillian could even ask for proof of ID, he'd pulled out his warrant card from his mac and shoved it under her nose.

'I'll come with them. They are only young. They need me with them and—'

Sanders stopped her. 'They will have adults with them, I can assure you of that. There's me and WPC Willis here. Anyway, their parents will be at the station soon.'

Too nervous to say any more, she hugged her grandchildren and watched them as they held hands, in defeat, and followed the officer and the detective to his car. She could see Hudson spinning his pen in his other hand.

Sanders expected the kids to ask questions or argue, or at least to do something. However, when he looked in the rear-view mirror, all he saw were two pairs of dark foreboding eyes. He shivered and drove faster. His phone was face down in the front console, and so he didn't see it flashing with all the missed calls. He ignored WPC Willis as she sat in the front seat. As far as he was concerned he only had her along because of the children.

After driving down the ramp leading to the police station, he parked up and held open the door for the kids to follow him.

Harley spoke to Hudson in French. *'Everything will be okay. Don't worry. You were just defending yourself against the bully at school.'*

With a look of indignation, Sanders rolled his eyes. 'I *can* speak French. Just so you know.'

Harley clammed up and squeezed Hudson's hand.

The corridor was lit by fluorescent lights, which upset Hudson, especially since the last incident where they had flickered, causing him to go into panic mode. Now his throat was dry, and his heart raced.

As Sanders led them into an interview room, he spotted Brett Nelson, who, at only twenty-eight, was itching to become a detective and so was always eager to please. 'Brett, do us a favour. Can you watch these two? I need to contact their parents.'

Brett Nelson stepped inside the interview room. 'Gov, are they the Mason twins?'

Sanders nodded. 'Yeah. Just keep an eye on them for a mo, will you?'

'Oh, did the sergeant get hold of you, Gov?' asked Nelson.

Sanders shook his head. 'No, why?'

'Well, Gov, I think you'd best be advised to go to the custody suite. The Super has been trying to contact you. There's been a serious incident, and I do believe it's in connection with the Mason twins – well, at least a family member.'

Sanders hurried along and skidded into the room where another DI and the chief superintendent were gathered.

'I know you're involved now in the Mason children's disappearance, Sanders, but we now have a murder on our hands. A young woman's been found dead in her home. She's been identified as a Mrs Scarlett Mason,' stated Chief Superintendent Tristan Clark. In his late fifties, he had a shrill voice that would leave you with a ringing sound in your eyes, if he was in one of his moods.

'So, what's happened?' asked Sanders.

Clark looked up from a folder on the table. 'A Scarlett Mason was found dead a few hours ago. Forensics are at the scene. The coroner reckons she was murdered because of the fatal stab wounds, and . . . interestingly enough, the puncture wounds were caused by a small pointed object. Hudson Mason, Scarlett's nephew, is on the missing list for another assault using a pen.'

Sanders' mouth dropped open. 'Gov, I have Hudson and his sister in an interview room.'

The chief superintendent threw Sanders a look of shock. '*What?* Have you made an arrest?'

'No, Gov. I was going to call in their parents. I haven't had a chance yet to interview them over a playground fight.'

As Clark looked up from the folder, Sanders could see that the man's cheeks were rosier than usual. And he realised he'd just put his foot in it with his choice of words.

'A *playground* fight?' said Clark. 'I would hardly call it just a playground fight. The victim was brutally attacked. I presume you've seen the photos? That boy will be lucky if he manages to live his life normally ever again, without people gawping at him like a circus act.'

Sanders held his tongue before he had a go back. Clark could be a tyrant, when he wanted, and their polar opposite personalities clashed more often than not.

The silent pause gave both men time to reflect that now was not the best time to have another argument with each other.

'Okay, Sanders, keep them there. They are not to leave, not until we have this issue settled. I have Geoff Mason, the husband, in Room Two. He's really shaken up. I'm no psychologist, but my gut tells me he didn't kill his wife. Give him a going over, Sanders, and, yes, get the kids' parents here asap. This is such a fucking mess. Christ, if that boy is now a suspect in his aunt's murder, and we're found to be slow off the mark in not doing enough to track him down, we're going to look like imbeciles.'

'Righto, Gov.'

Clark handed Sanders a folder. 'Here's the file. Take a quick look before you question Mr Mason. The photo will give you an idea of what the man faced when he entered his wife's house.'

Sanders looked at the gruesome picture and swallowed hard.

* * *

Sanders expected Geoff Mason to have his lawyer there. So when he walked into Room Two, and he saw the man alone with his shoulders slumped and his face red and swollen from crying, he was very surprised. 'Where's your lawyer, Mr Mason?'

Geoff shook his head. 'Don't worry about a lawyer. I never killed my wife, but I'll tell you everything I can. I want to help in any way possible because I just want the fucking killer caught.'

'Let me get you a drink. It must have been a shock, finding your wife like that.'

Geoff's eyes were wild as he looked up. 'A shock, a *shock*? I'm glad it was me and not my boys that found her. Those maggots and her face, her dear, sweet face . . . I want who did this found, and I wanna kill the evil son of a bitch with my bare fucking hands!'

'All right, Mr Mason, calm down, please. Right, I'll fetch some tea.'

Geoff was holding his head as if he was in pain. 'I don't want any tea. I want to know what happened to her, and who fucking murdered her!'

Nelson popped his head around the door. He was waving a folder. 'Er, this is the forensics report, Gov.'

Sanders got up from the table while keeping an eye on Mr Mason. He took the folder and sat back down, opening it on the first page.

Geoff tried to read the information upside down. 'Well?'

'Your wife died on Monday at eight forty-three p.m.'

Geoff tried to absorb the information. 'How do you know it was eight forty-three?'

'The electricity was cut to your house at that time. We can only assume the crime took place then, and, in any case, other evidence also points that way. So, you know my next question, Mr Mason.'

Geoff knew he would be a suspect: the spouses always were. 'That was the night my niece and nephew went on a disappearing escapade after the incident at the school. I was at my brother's house. He was worried, you see, and I stayed with him while his wife, Dionne, went out searching the streets.'

'And he will confirm that, will he?'

Geoff nodded. 'Yes, of course, he will.'

'Good, because he's on his way to the station. I have his children in an interview room.'

Geoff suddenly took a deep breath and relaxed his shoulders. 'Oh my God. Do you think they did this?'

With a look of surprise, Sanders leaned forward. 'Why do you ask that . . . ? Mr Mason, do you think they had anything to do with it?'

Running his hands through his hair and flicking his eyes from left to right, Geoff recalled the night Scarlett turned up at Luke's homecoming. She'd called the twins vile names and Harley had gone for her. Niece and nephew or not, he wouldn't protect them again. He'd done it once over the murder of Curtis Stracken. But not this time – not over his wife.

'Maybe.'

'You must have a strong suspicion to say that, Mr Mason. I mean, being that they are *family*. I know you and your brothers are close. I know how you guys operate as well. Grassing goes against the grain.'

As Sanders studied the man opposite him, silent in thought, he could almost see the wheel of thoughts working overtime behind Mason's eyes. And he wondered if the man would suddenly clam up.

Sanders urged him to talk. 'Mr Mason, you want your wife's killer caught. Now come on, mate. Why do you think it was Hudson or Harley? They're eleven. Are they *capable*?'

Observing Mason's reaction, Sanders witnessed a resigned expression of sadness. 'Come on, Mr Mason, you need to talk to me, for your own sons' sakes. This is their mother we're talking about. They'll want answers too.'

Geoff found Sanders' words and tone calming, as if he was confiding in a friend. There was also something else about him that made him warm to the man. A natural empathy perhaps. When Sanders spoke, he gave the impression he was one of the good guys who genuinely wanted justice. He wasn't a jobsworth, ticking boxes to work his way up the ladder. Then his thoughts turned to his sons; their hearts would be breaking right now.

Nephew or not, if Hudson had killed his wife, then he deserved all he got. Besides, who was to say his boys wouldn't be next.

'I broke up with Scarlett a few years ago. We sold the house and bought two separate homes. She had my boys half the time, and the other half they were with me. She was convinced I was having an affair, you see. I couldn't take it anymore – all the accusations. I still popped in and helped her out, you know, for the boys' sakes. But she began drinking heavily, and so I stayed away more and more. I couldn't stand to see her drunk like that. Sunday night, we were celebrating Luke's prison release, and she turned up pissed and started shouting her mouth off, and then, as she toppled over, she looked at the twins. She called Hudson a "weirdo" and then both of them "psycho brats". That was when Harley went for her, you know, aggressively. It was like she wanted to kill her. But it wasn't how fiery the kid acted that bothered me – it was the look of evil in her eyes that disturbed me the most and stuck in my head.'

'But kids always give dirty looks. That doesn't mean they're capable of murder.'

Geoff knew it sounded stupid, but he couldn't tell the DCI about the murder of Curtis Stracken.

'Look, Hudson stabbed a boy in the neck. My son Nicki was there, and although it was self-defence, my Nicki said Hudson looked deranged.'

Sanders eyed Mr Mason with an expression that suggested there was more to it than this. 'Come on, I need more than that.'

Watching the man biting his thumbnail, Sanders knew there was something he wasn't being told. 'I need more, mate, 'cos just an angry boy fighting won't cut it.'

'But he *is* strange. I can't explain it. The boy's super intelligent but he's also odd. I mean *creepy* odd.'

'Okay, I'll take a statement from you. Are you sure you don't want a drink because you could be here for a long time?'

'No, I'm fine. Just find the killer, will you?'

Sanders left the room feeling uneasy. In all his years, he'd never known an eleven-year-old to kill anyone, especially under these premeditated circumstances. But, as he passed the other interview room, he glanced in, and his eyes met Hudson's. A cold shiver suddenly ran through him. The boy didn't have a cocky attitude, but he did have something else – a dark cunning about him.

By midnight, he had the parents in one interview room and the twins in another.

In the serious incident room, forensic evidence was being pinned on the board. Sanders read and reread the details. The woman died of stab wounds to the neck and chest. The puncture wounds were from an instrument, possibly a pen. Whoever had entered the house knew exactly where the fuse box was, so he or she was no stranger to the place, and there was enough booze inside Scarlett Mason to make it difficult for her to have the foresight and strength to fight off her attacker. So that meant a kid could have been the perpetrator – and Hudson was a likely suspect.

As Sanders entered the interview room, where the twins' parents were waiting, he was confronted by Luke Mason, who looked absolutely livid.

Luke jumped up from his seat and demanded to know exactly what the hell was going on. 'I've been waiting here for fucking hours. Where are my kids?'

Sanders waved his hands for Luke to calm down. 'Mr Mason, it's more complicated than that. Your brother Geoff is here. I take it, you've no idea what has happened to his wife?'

Luke looked at Sanders in disbelief. *'What?'* Sitting down quickly, he inclined his head, now totally confused. 'No. What do you mean? What's happened?'

Sanders looked at Mrs Mason and then back at her husband. 'Geoff found her murdered a few hours ago, when he took his sons home from the airport.' He paused, gauging their reaction.

With his mouth gaping, it was obvious that Luke was in shock. *'What?'* he yelled. 'Scarlett's *dead*?'

As Luke tried to take it all in, his brain struggled to absorb the news. 'Is my brother okay? Jesus, what happened? Why didn't he call me?'

Coldly, Sanders replied, 'He called *us*, and we brought him straight in. I guess he didn't have time to call you.'

Luke stared with a deep frown, waiting for Sanders to carry on.

'She was murdered by a sharp instrument in the chest, and her other injuries showed puncture wounds, possibly from a pen.' He said no more and waited for Mr Mason's reaction. Then his eyes shifted to Mrs Mason.

'Who would do that? Was it a break-in? . . . Was it rape or what?' The words tumbled from Luke's mouth.

'No, not rape, not burglary, just cold-blooded murder, possibly from using a knife, or, more likely . . .' He paused. 'A pen.' *Surely, the words would resonate?* thought Sanders.

As if Luke had been hit with a brick, he jolted upright. 'What do you mean by "a pen"?' Slowly, his head twisted in disbelief and then the penny dropped. He had been told about the incident at The Glades, and, of course, he knew about the fight at the school – both involving a pen. 'You're not suggesting my . . . Fucking hell, please don't tell me you think Hudson had anything to do with it, surely to God?'

'Did Scarlett turn up at your house on Sunday evening hurling abuse at your children?'

Luke jumped up from his seat. 'Get my kids. This is fucking mental. I ain't having this bollocks. You wanna pin a fucking murder on my son? Jesus. You really *are* scraping the fucking barrel.'

He pushed past the detective and almost ripped the door off its hinges. 'Where are my kids? I'm going home. I ain't listening to another word of your crap.'

Sanders followed him out of the room and called after him. 'You do that, Mr Mason, and you'll be arrested for perverting the course of justice, and you can add to that accessory to murder, if you like!'

Luke turned and punched the wall in frustration. He knew he wasn't going anywhere. Sanders was deadly serious; his son was going to be arrested and possibly charged with murder.

'Mr Mason, please come back into the room. We need to talk.'

Feeling as though he had the weight of the world on his shoulders, Luke reluctantly went back into the interview room and sat heavily on a chair.

Dionne leaned across and held his hand, letting him know she was on his side.

'Right, Mrs Mason, if you want to take Harley home you may do so. She isn't involved in this matter. It's late, and she looks tired. Also, I don't want to waste any more of your time. Mr Mason, I believe your lawyer is on his way, and I have called in social services. We have a member of the team who will also be present because firstly we have to assess if Hudson is mentally stable. If we feel he isn't, then he will be sent to a hospital where he can be assessed to find out if he is able to stand trial, if, of course, we do charge him.'

Sanders held up his hands. 'But those are all formalities. I'm not saying for one moment that Hudson *is* under arrest for murder, not at all. But, he certainly needs to answer questions about the attack on the boy at school. The offence is serious. I need to tell you that much, and so a consenting adult will be present during his questioning. I suggest we use social services rather than either of yourselves. I also want his mental health assessed before he's questioned.'

'What? Why his mental health? There's nothing wrong with my son.'

Sanders raised a questioning brow. 'Really, Mr Mason?'

Luke glared in defiance. 'And no, you fucking ain't questioning my boy without me there. He's a minor, and I'm his father, end of, mate!'

'I want to see my son first,' spat Dionne, expecting to be denied.

Sanders looked from one parent to the other and nodded. 'Okay, for a few minutes. But, and I mean but, do not mention Scarlett Mason's murder. I would like to think you would not pervert the course of justice.'

'Aw, fuck off, Detective. I take it, you don't have kids? I want to see my son's okay.'

Sanders shrank into himself. 'Sorry, yes. Look, of course you can, Mrs Mason. And you can also take Harley home. She is in the room with him now.'

As Dionne was being escorted from the room by WPC Willis, Luke stared into space. Words were twirling around in his head: freaks, weirdos, shrinks, mental health assessed . . . Was he really the last person ever to imagine his child was not normal? He now questioned himself as to whether he'd ever really wanted to admit to his son's peculiar traits and unusual personality. He should have tried to understand both of the twins for who they were. An unexpected tear ran down the side of his nose. The guilt for being out of their lives was hard, but denying there was a problem other than just shyness was unforgivable. He'd let them down – badly.

* * *

Two police officers had to prise Harley away from Hudson.

As Dionne stood in the doorway, she could see the absolute fear in Hudson's eyes and the anger in Harley's.

Harley whispered something in his ear, and instantly he turned to his mother, and his bottom lip quivered.

Dionne had never seen him cry, not with real tears. She did, however, clock Harley look back one more time and mouth the words 'I'm sorry, Hudson.'

Dionne couldn't wait to get out of the police station and to her home, away from this awful place. She was tired and hated the surroundings; she just wanted to curl up on the sofa and down a bottle of wine.

Harley was quiet all the way home, worried sick about her brother.

Dionne had no intention of interrogating her, except to ask why she'd gone to Lillian's.

Harley's answer was short. 'Because, Mother, she's a real person.'

'Huh, a real person? As in someone that crawled from under a rock and who likes to live in squalor. If that's what you call real, then I guess she is. And tell me, Harley, what did my mother have to say about me?'

Harley sat like a sulky child with her arms crossed and her eyes beady. 'Nothing. She was more interested in us, *her grandchildren*.'

Ignoring her daughter's dig, she drove them home and prepared herself for the phone calls, no doubt, from Miriam and Tilly, and whoever else wanted to stick their oar in. Deciding to unplug the phone and switch her mobile off before the calls came, she poured herself a large glass of chardonnay and made herself comfortable on the sofa.

Harley stormed off upstairs. She tried to phone Nanny Lillian but the phone line was dead. She lay on Hudson's bed, fretting. He couldn't handle all of this, although she could because she was the stronger one, and she knew it. He may be more intelligent than her, but she understood how people worked, and she could play their game, but not Hudson. His terrified face would prey on her mind and make her angry, and she didn't like to get angry.

* * *

Luke was anxious to see his son. A social worker and a mental health worker were standing outside the room waiting to be called in.

Lyle Harris came hurrying along the corridor, still trying to straighten his tie. Out of breath, he stopped dead in front of Luke. 'I'm sorry I'm late. Listen, Luke, what they have is only circumstantial evidence, and if Hudson just answers the questions, we can get him out of here. But the minute they think he's not up to it or not fit for any trial, they'll put him in a secure unit, like a hospital. We don't want *that*.'

Luke was even more afraid for his son. 'I'll talk to him first, *alone*.'

Harris insisted he came in too.

Being a fair man, Sanders accepted that it would probably be for the best to let Hudson have some private time with his father and the family's solicitor, but only for a few minutes.

As soon as Luke entered the room, his heart sank. Hudson was curled in a ball on a chair. His face was white, and his eyes were wide. 'It's okay, Son. I'm here now, but you have to listen to me. They are going to ask you questions, and you'll have to answer them clearly and truthfully. Let these people know you understand what they're saying. It's the only way they'll let you out of here. Do you understand, Hudson?' He was dying to put his arms around his son, but the distant look in Hudson's eyes, and the way he turned away from him, led him to believe he didn't even trust his own father.

'Hudson, do you understand what I'm saying?'

Very slowly, Hudson nodded.

'Good. Now straighten yourself up and don't look at the floor.'

Watching the interaction between Hudson and his father, Harris felt distinctly uneasy. The lad was away with the fairies. *No,* he thought, *worse, he actually did look mentally unstable.*

The door opened and in walked Sanders, who was followed by Edward Smithson, the mental health worker, a man in his thirties, who had a balding head and an eager grin, and Pat Sykes, the social worker, who looked to be in her fifties. Both sat down opposite the family and introduced themselves.

Luke felt his anger rising, just watching all the eyes fixed on his son as if he were an animal at the zoo.

'Right, just so we're clear, I'm Detective Chief Inspector Sanders, the detective who brought you in. But we already know each other, don't we, Hudson?'

Hudson nodded but chewed the inside of his lip.

'Now, Hudson, we need to know where you went after you left the school on Monday.'

Hudson's eyes glanced across to the adults. 'We went into the woods.'

Harris was on the edge of his seat, hoping against hope that Luke's lad wouldn't put his foot in it; they both needed Hudson to remain calm and answer the questions as any child would.

'Where did you go after you left the woods?'

'To the storeroom behind the clinic.'

Luke's heart was in his mouth. He never expected his son would be stupid enough to mention the fucking clinic. His own son had completely blown it.

'What clinic?' The questions were short and sweet.

'Dr Reeves' clinic.'

'Who is Dr Reeves, Hudson?'

Luke rolled his eyes, wiped the perspiration from his brow, looked at Lyle Harris, and shook his head.

'A psychiatrist.' Hudson felt proud of himself. He just assumed he was doing as he was told; after all, his father had said if he told the truth and spoke up, he could go home.

'Is Dr Reeves your own psychiatrist?'

Hudson nodded.

Sanders gave Hudson an approving smile. 'Thank you, Hudson.'

Turning to Mr Mason he said, 'A word in private, please.'

Luke felt as if he wanted to die. The lad may be intelligent, but he didn't have an ounce of common sense. He gave his son a rueful smile and followed the detective outside.

'So, Mr Mason, your son is under a psychiatrist. You didn't tell me that. We'll have to keep him here for the time being. Then, he'll go to a secure holding for juveniles until we get his report. I want a full assessment carried out, and we'll go from there. He can't go home.'

Luke felt a lump in his throat; he knew that if he tried to speak, he would choke.

'Do you want to tell me his condition?'

Luke shrugged. 'He's a little socially awkward and shy.'

Sanders laughed through his nose. 'Is that what they call it?'

Luke knew that it was game over: all he could do now was say goodbye to his son and hope they could get Dr Reeves to turn things around for him.

* * *

Totally drained, mentally and physically, Luke climbed out of the cab and took weary steps towards the front door. The outside sensor lights didn't come on, not that he'd noticed until then, but parked by the bushes was Geoff's car.

As Luke put the key in the door, Geoff jumped out from his vehicle and confronted him.

* * *

Hearing loud voices outside because the front door was open, Dionne dragged herself away from her comfortable sofa position to see what was going on. Expecting to find Luke and Hudson, instead, she saw the raging, angry face of Geoff. But he wasn't shouting or screaming, he was growling in a deep voice, demanding to know what Hudson had done.

'Please, Geoff, come in. This isn't a conversation for the street.'

Looking over at Dionne, he spat, 'Who gives a shit? My fucking wife is dead, and it's your son's fault.'

Grabbing Geoff's arm, Luke said, 'Go indoors, Geoff, for fuck's sake.' He pulled him inside and kicked the door shut behind him.

The sound of the door being slammed brought Harley tearing down the stairs hoping to see her brother. She stopped halfway and desperately looked around; her heart sank, and her fury rose.

'Where's *Hudson?*' she bellowed.

The sight of her almost feral-looking face made Geoff feel nauseous; he had vile visions of the twins killing his wife, in some sick, twisted fashion.

'Locked away for a fucking long time, I hope,' he screamed back at her.

Ignoring him, she turned to her father. 'Where is he?' she yelled again.

Luke shook his head. 'They're keeping him in, until——'

Harley's face was contorted with rage. 'Until when? For *ever*? Will I ever see my brother again? I hate you, I bloody hate you! You should've brought him home!'

Geoff was shocked that such a young child could have so much venom in her voice and violence in her eyes. The sight was disquieting, to say the least, and left him speechless. He turned to Luke, waiting for him to take her to task.

Instead, Luke lowered his head and walked into the kitchen, away from the wrath of Harley.

'You evil child!' spat Geoff, glaring back at her, but then he saw her eyes soften.

'*Why*, Uncle Geoff? Why are they doing this to us?'

So taken aback by the instant change in her tone and appearance, he thought for a second *he* was going mad.

'Because your brother murdered my wife. He stabbed her and left her there to die. She bled to fucking death.'

Harley's eyes widened, and she paused, looking at her mum, before she focused on her uncle. 'No! He *didn't!*' she said, quietly, before turning away and heading forlornly back to her bedroom.

Dionne put her arm around Geoff, who now looked ready to collapse. 'Come into the lounge. Let me get you a drink.'

Her soft words should have been a comfort, but it was all too strange. In fact, finding his wife dead and the killer his nephew – and possibly his niece too – it was totally bizarre. Shrugging her off, he made his way into the kitchen. 'You know, don't ya, Luke? Ya fucking know your kids are killers, don't ya?'

Sensing that Geoff was about to blow the lid off about the body in the pit, Dionne rushed into the kitchen and pulled him away. 'Come on, Geoff. This will do you no good. The police have Hudson in custody now. Go home, for your boys' sakes. They'll need you, right now.'

Geoff took one last look at Luke, shook his head, and left.

Dionne felt her whole body ease with relief; yet she wanted Luke to be the one who stormed out, not Geoff.

* * *

That night Luke tossed and turned; he was racked with so many mixed emotions, but it was guilt that was making him feel sick. Had he raised a killer or was his dear little boy just caught up in a murder that had nothing to do with him? And as for Harley, the little girl who he adored and who he thought at one time adored him, she'd just looked at him with so much hate.

By the morning, his body ached with stress; every fibre in him felt as though it was on fire.

* * *

Harley heard her father get up, but she lay there going over in her mind the last few days' events. They'd had to run away because Hudson had been picked on, yet no one would believe them except Nanny Lillian. She'd listened to her and grasped that her grandmother was so different from her mother. Now, she longed to run back there and live with her because out of all the members of her family, it was only her Nanny Lillian who truly understood her and Hudson.

Lying on her bed and staring up at the ceiling, she heard the sound of the garage door being opened. It creaked every time. *What was her father doing in there?* she wondered. Perhaps he was meddling with her sculpture or her tools. He shouldn't do that. That was her space, her work, *her* project. She concluded that he didn't care, and so she assumed he wouldn't give any thought to hurting things that belonged to her; after all, he'd hurt Hudson, by leaving him at that awful police station, knowing full well he was scared.

* * *

After the disturbed night's sleep from all the shit that had been going on yesterday, Luke decided it was high time he got his car out of the garage. He'd thought about it while he had been waiting for a cab at the police station to go home. As the car had been sitting in his garage for many years and Dionne had assured him she would keep it in good nick, he hoped she'd made good on her promise.

As he flicked on the light, he was surprised to see it so tidy. The house was always spotless, but the garage was his domain, his man cave, so neither Dionne nor the kids, he assumed, had a good reason to go in there.

The tools were all arranged neatly on the racks, the fishing rods and canoe were held secure by the ties in the wall, and the floor was spotless. When he looked more closely, he realised that the floor wasn't just immaculate, it was new. Someone had screeded it. The surface was so smooth and polished. Then he looked under the car and saw that the pit had been filled in. Standing back, he scratched his chin. He had every intention of filling it in one day because it was a pain in the arse having to manoeuvre his car above the pit, and, in any case, if he wanted work done on the vehicle, he would take it to the local dealer's. In the early days, before his time in prison, he'd hoped that Hudson would show an interest in cars, which was why he'd delayed filling in the pit. But it seemed that Hudson never liked anything else that other boys enjoyed. It had crossed his mind that the boy may be gay – not that he minded, if this was the case.

He would ask Dionne about the pit. Maybe she had plans for the garage herself. He tried to start the car, but the clicking sound confirmed the battery was as dead as a dodo. Lifting the bonnet, he looked down at the battery and wondered for a moment which spanners he would need to remove it and put it on charge, but the newer engines were complex. He saw a small nut that held down the battery cover and then searched the racks on the far wall for a tool of that particular size. But his eyes were drawn to a tall object in the corner of the garage that was behind neatly stacked boxes. He was intrigued because not only did he not remember it being there before, but it was covered in a sheet.

Carefully, he removed the boxes one by one, not knowing what was inside them, and as he lifted the last one, he saw a small stand with tools he'd never seen before. The tools were all odd shapes and sizes, along with files, a small hammer, and chisels.

Curiously, as he slowly lifted the bedsheet the sight before him left him almost paralysed in shock. There, one foot away, stood a sculpture in its finished state of perfection. For a second, he had to hold his breath. He'd never seen anything like it, and it took him a few seconds to process what he was seeing.

The detail was spectacular and yet hideous. He was looking at his wife but with an expression he couldn't comprehend. It was dark . . . it was repugnant . . . and yet it was stunningly beautiful. He peered at the indented circles – at what looked like puckered skin surrounding them – and marvelled. The imperfection of the two oddities made the piece even more interesting. So drawn in by the sculpture, Luke didn't hear the footsteps behind him. But he sensed breathing. For a moment, he thought it was the sculpture itself. As absurd as it was, the lifelike detail played tricks on his mind.

'Perfect, isn't it.' The voice behind him was emphatic, surreal, and yet evil.

Gripped by the sight of the piece of art and overwhelmed by its creepiness, Luke's mind was in a state of shock. So many thoughts were being propelled through his brain at meteoric speed. Previous conversations retold, personal grievances remembered, odd expressions recalled, he found himself now in another place – a dark place – where dreams ended and nightmares began. But the dark place was just the beginning. The vision before him was demonic, cold, and devoid of life. Behind those eyes was a soul that could conjure up demons.

Luke's jaw dropped, still trying to comprehend what was happening. But the person holding the long thin metal rod and the expression that told him 'I'm going to kill you' left him in no doubt that his time on this earth was about to end – and end painfully.

As he staggered back, the attacker, in one fluid movement, savagely thrust the metal object in through his stomach and up into his heart, as though they were spearing a fish.

Total shock and disbelief rendered Luke incapable of fighting back. The tool was ripped out and shoved into his chest again and again. He stumbled back and landed beside the sculpture. The accurate and precise stabs had hit all the relevant organs sufficient to kill him.

CHAPTER EIGHTEEN

Beside herself with grief, Tilly sobbed into Dean's shoulder. 'I hit the woman. It was the last time she saw me. I fucking smacked her one and threw her out of Luke's house. How will I ever live with meself?' she cried.

Teary-eyed, Dean tried to calm her sobs. 'Babe, you weren't to know, eh?'

Miriam sat with Geoff in her kitchen, dumbfounded. *How could this have happened?* she thought. Was it their love for the twins that had made them all blind to what had been going on?

'Aw, Son, I just can't get my head around it. That poor woman. Whatever possesses a kid to do that?' She blew her nose and wiped her eyes. 'I just don't know what to say, babe. I'm so sorry.' Her red eyes met Geoff's.

'Son, you need to have a lie-down. You look exhausted. Take a couple of me sleeping pills and lie on me bed. You'll feel better, I promise.' She knew he wouldn't, but she'd reached the point where she had nothing left in her to console her grieving son.

'I won't, Mum. How the fuck can I? Her face! It haunts me. It fucking haunts me.'

Archi looked at his grandsons all huddled together around the dining room table, tears endlessly flowing. He got up and left the room; he needed to have a sniffle himself. In the corner of the lounge stood a cabinet. He pulled open the top drawer and removed a photo album, which contained Geoff's wedding photos. Slowly, he headed back to the kitchen, placed the album on the table, and opened it to the page he wanted of his daughter-in-law's wedding day. There, radiating so much beauty, with that familiar bright, beaming smile, Scarlett stood proudly.

'Here, boy, keep looking at that, eh? Remember how she was before . . .' He stopped. In that second, he pulled his son close and hugged him. He wasn't one for a public show of emotion, but nothing had ever hurt him more. As tough as he was, and as hard on all his sons as he saw fit, inside, he was soft and loved them more than life itself. He couldn't stand to see his eldest sick with grief. If he could swap places with him, he would.

'Dad, please do as Nan says. Take the tablets. You look tired,' said Davey, standing in the doorway.

Miriam gave him a soft smile and nodded. He was growing into a man and taking control. Her younger grandsons looked up to him as a good role model – someone who worked hard and was going places. *Why couldn't Hudson be the same?* thought Miriam. She rose from her seat, opened the kitchen drawer, and handed Geoff two tablets. 'Take these, my babe, and get off to bed.'

Staring at the two pills in his hands, Geoff realised that his wife's death had shown him that he'd made a colossal mistake. Why had he allowed himself to be drawn to Dionne? He would never really know, but there was one thing he was sure of: the affair had been the biggest mistake of his life. Swallowing the sleeping pills, he picked up the album and left the room. Walking up the stairs was like carrying two lead weights, but he knew he must rest and pull himself together for his sons' sakes, if not for his own. His parents' bedroom was calming with muted colours and inviting pillows. The tablets were quickly taking effect because his stomach was empty. As he lay there staring at the photo and drifting off, he could hear a buzzing sound and a light flashing. He tried to focus on the number on his phone. It was Dionne. Not wanting to talk to her, he put the phone on the bedside table, let his head fall back against the soft pillows, and focused instead on the pretty face of his wife.

* * *

Dionne tried again to phone Geoff but to no avail. With her husband lying dead in the garage and Harley nowhere to be found, she decided to call the police. Reluctantly, she dialled 999.

'Please hurry! My husband's dead!' she cried, frantically, almost out of breath.

'Okay, please calm down. Are you sure he's dead, madam? Can you feel for a pulse?' urged the operator.

'He's been murdered! Come quickly. Please!'

'What's your name?'

Briefly, Dionne spat out her name and address.

'Okay, madam, the police and ambulance are on their way.'

'Please come quickly!'

'Madam, is there anyone else in the house?'

'No!' she yelled, before slamming the phone down.

* * *

The information from the call was passed to Bromley Police Station, and it was instantly picked up by the serious incident room.

Sanders was sipping a cold coffee and wolfing down a cheese and pickle sandwich while he waited for the arrival of Dr Reeves. He needed answers to so many questions.

Nelson appeared in the doorway, out of breath. 'Gov, a call's just come through from Dionne Mason. Apparently, she's found her husband dead.'

Sanders jumped up from the table and reached for his mac. 'Jacob, you're coming with me. And, Nelson, when Dr Reeves arrives, he's to stay and wait for me. I need to talk to him. Where is Mrs Mason now?'

'At her house. A squad car's on its way,' replied Nelson, excitedly.

Sanders wasted no time and almost pulled away without Forbes completely in the car. 'Hurry up, son. I want to get there before the fuckwits do anything stupid, like tamper with the evidence. Fancy sending a squad car. They're all like a bunch of farts. Jacob, call through. Tell them not to go anywhere near the body. Tell them not to even go in the fucking house.'

Forbes radioed through to the squad car. 'DCI Sanders says don't go in the house.'

The muffled spitting sounds of radio static suddenly cleared. 'Tell the DCI we have to. The killer may still be in the house, and our main concern is the wife. She could be the next victim.'

Sanders heard what was said loud and clear. 'Tell them to use their loaf. If she answers the fucking door, just pull her out. I don't want those plonkers traipsing through with their fucking great size ten boots cocking up any chance we have of catching a potential killer.'

'I heard that, Jacob. Tell the DCI we understand.'

Sanders was not the best of drivers, but he managed to swerve in and out, jumping two red lights in the process, before arriving in record time. He spotted Mrs Mason sitting in the back seat of the squad car, with a blanket around her shoulders and being comforted by a female officer.

Sanders stepped out of the car and surveyed the surroundings. Then it hit him: where was Harley? He hurried over to Mrs Mason, almost pushing the officer out of the way. 'Where's your daughter?'

Dionne looked up, wiping her nose with the back of her hand. With tears streaming down her face, she shook her head. 'I don't know. I woke up late. Harley wasn't in her room, and I called out, but there was no answer. So I went through the whole house, but there was still no sign of her. Then, I thought Luke had taken her somewhere in my car, the shops maybe, but my car was still out at the front. And there was no sign of Luke either. So I went into the garage to see if he'd taken his car, and that's where I found him.'

Sanders stared for a few seconds. He hadn't requested an account of the situation; he'd only asked where Harley was. But then, he realised from the state of Mrs Mason that she was still trying to process what she'd done and what she'd seen. He couldn't be too hard on her.

Nodding to Forbes to stay with Mrs Mason, he tutted loudly when he saw more blue lights appear. 'That's all we need – hundreds of bloody footprints and finger marks.' Hurriedly, he put on his rubber gloves and made his way to the house. Treading carefully, he walked along the hallway and into the kitchen and stared at the door leading out to the garage. He looked around the kitchen. It was spotless. There was not a dirty cup or saucer, not a crumb anywhere. As his eyes swept the floor, he noticed that in between the tiles the grouting was damp. He knelt down, running his fingers along the grooves. He then grabbed a piece of kitchen towel and wiped his hands to see if there was any moisture. There was. The floor had been washed, and, clearly, very recently. He peered into the sink and could smell the bleach. That was when he heard running water.

The door that linked the kitchen to the garage was only ajar, and so with a pen in his hand, he opened the door fully and stared in disbelief at the body on the floor, which was almost floating in a three-inch pool of water. He traced the hosepipe to the wall and hurried over to turn off the tap before the water destroyed any more evidence. A long sharp tool lay by the side of the body, and he could see the blood was being washed away by the water. Carefully, he retrieved it, with his thumb and forefinger, making a mental note as to its original place on the floor. He pulled a large plastic bag from his pocket, placed the instrument inside, and carried it back into the kitchen. He was almost certain now that the wet kitchen floor was due to water seeping from the garage and not because it had recently been washed, as he'd first thought. Looking down at his wet shoes, he cursed, took them off, and headed back to the front door in just his socks, only to be met by Josh Stark, the coroner.

'Ah, Lewis. So what do we have?' asked Stark. He liked Lewis Sanders and saw a lot of himself in the DCI. They were both open, frank, and honest men who had worked well together for many years. He looked down at Sanders' feet. 'There must be some claret, yeah?'

Sanders shook his head. 'No, we have a wet floor in the garage. My guess is the culprit tried to wash away any evidence by leaving a tap on.'

Stark peered inside. 'There's money here, and then some, I take it?'

'Yep. Luke Mason was a bit of a crook. He'd just served six years and had only been out a week.'

'What are your thoughts, Lewis? Do you think it's a revenge killing, a gang war, perhaps?'

Sanders bit his lip. 'No, Josh, I think we have something more disturbing going on, but let me know what you find, mate.'

In his mid-forties, Stark wasn't your typical coroner; he was a leading professor too, but he spoke like an East Ender and stood no nonsense, much like Sanders. So they often drank together.

Two identification officers directly behind Stark were already gowned up in their white SOCO suits, gloves, and shoe covers.

'All yours,' gestured Sanders, before he made his way to the car where Dionne Mason was being comforted by the female officer. Carefully, Sanders eased himself inside the car and nodded for the WPC to leave. 'So what time did you find your husband lying dead in the garage?' he enquired, not wasting time to beat about the bush.

Snivelling, she said, 'Er, what? I don't know. It was just before I called the police.'

'Okay, Mrs Mason. I'd like you to come down to the station. Let's get a statement.' He knew he was pushing his luck; usually, he would wait a few days while forensics gathered the evidence, but he wasn't comfortable leaving her in the house.

Looking visibly shaken, Dionne nodded.

Sanders helped Mrs Mason into his car, with the WPC accompanying her, and arranged for Forbes to stay behind to make sure no one except the team entered the property. A serious concern was weighing on his mind as they drove to the station – Mrs Mason didn't seem preoccupied that her daughter was missing. He would wait until he could question her, so he could analyse her expression. Another one of his attributes was body language interpretation.

The serious crime investigation room was a hive of activity. The inquiry was given its operation name – Operation Wasp – and pictures, photos, and a map were arranged on a large board. The particularly gruesome photo of

Scarlett was placed in the middle, and those of both Harley and Hudson were pinned at the top.

Sanders called for a PC to fetch some tea for himself and Mrs Mason. Holding her arm, he guided her into the interview room. He watched her take a seat.

'Right, do you want to call your solicitor?'

With eyes like saucers, she suddenly sat upright. 'Why? Do I need one?'

'Well, you probably should, Mrs Mason, for many reasons. Your husband is dead, and it doesn't look like natural causes. You were in the house at the time. You found the body and called the police, so, yes, I suggest you do.'

'But I didn't kill him! It wasn't me. I just woke up and found him like that.' Her words flew out in a panic.

Holding his palms up, he replied, 'No one is saying you did. However, under the circumstances, you should have your brief here with you. It's just a formality, you understand.' He didn't have time for all the niceties. He had a job to do. The younger PCs could babysit Mrs Mason if she needed it, but, right now, he wanted answers.

She looked into his eyes and wondered if he knew something she didn't, but all she could see was a bottomless pit.

'No, it's fine. I really don't think I need one. I'm happy to tell you all I know.'

'Okay, then. Do you mind if I record this as your statement? It's just routine, really. And while it's all fresh in your mind.'

'Yes, that's fine.' Her face was now dry of tears, and the pink glow had returned to her cheeks.

'Okay, then. So from the beginning, when you left here last night having taken Harley home, talk me through the events as they happened to you.'

Dionne took a deep breath. 'I drove home, I got changed into my nightclothes, and Harley went to her room. Shortly after, Luke came home. Geoff, his brother, met him at the doorstep, and they started to argue. I asked them to come inside, and that's when Harley came down the stairs screaming at Luke because he'd returned home without Hudson—'

She was stopped in her tracks.

'Hmm. Okay. Let's deal with what you've just said point by point. Can you tell me why Geoff was at the house and what the argument was about?'

Ashen-faced, Dionne gave herself time to think. 'Geoff had arrived earlier in his car, waiting outside on the drive for Luke to return because he was angry and believed that Hudson had killed his wife.'

'That was the sole reason for Geoff coming to the house, then?'

'Yes.'

'You also mentioned that Harley screamed at her father when he arrived in the house, right? Was there something else I should take from what you said?'

Her eyes flicked from left to right. 'Er, no, not really. I, er, it was just an outburst, that's all. Harley screamed at him. It was something like "I hate you." And then she returned to her bedroom.'

'Did she shout at you or Geoff?' Sanders asked, in a low tone.

'No. It was just Luke. I guess she was angry because she assumed he would be bringing Hudson home.'

'What gave her that impression? Did you tell her he would?'

Her eyes narrowed, and her lip curled up. 'No!'

'Okay, then. Please, carry on.'

She paused, searching his face, before she said, 'Geoff left, and Luke and I went to bed. I woke up mid-morning, I guess, and then, as I've already told you, I went to find Harley, to see if she was okay after her temper tantrum.'

Sanders noticed her deadpan face. She seemed to be focusing a great deal on Harley's state of mind. This was the second reference to Harley, and he wondered if she was deliberately trying to plant what amounted to another seed. He couldn't tell whether this was the case. He indicated she should continue.

'I assumed she was downstairs with Luke or had gone out. I saw my car was out at the front, so I guessed they were both somewhere in the house. But when I called, there was no answer. I searched upstairs and downstairs but she wasn't there. I even went down to the end of the garden. So then I went from the kitchen into the garage to see if Luke had driven his own car out and that's when I found him and called 999.'

'Where do you think Harley is now?'

'I have no idea,' she replied, nonchalantly.

Sanders studied her face, deep in thought. 'You don't seem too worried either, do you?'

Those words caused a look of spite on Dionne's face, and she quickly redeemed her expression.

'Right now, Detective, I'm too upset that my husband has just been bloody murdered.'

He nodded and gave her a cold look. 'Has the thought not occurred to you that whoever murdered your husband may have kidnapped your daughter?'

'What? Oh my God! No!'

'Who would have wanted to hurt your husband, Mrs Mason?'

She stared blankly. 'I don't know. But he had plenty of enemies. He worked in a club and apparently he had a few fights when he was younger.'

'What about Geoff? Would he have wanted to hurt your husband?'

She shot him a harsh glare. 'No way, not Geoff . . . I, er, I mean, he was his brother. They were close.'

'And you, Mrs Mason? Were you close to Geoff?'

She didn't like his insinuation and leaned back on her chair. 'As a brother-in-law, yes, of course,' she spat.

As the time went on, he concluded he'd nothing to hold her for. He informed her that she could leave but to remain in the locality, as the murder was still under investigation. Also, she was to contact him immediately when Harley returned home. His offer of a lift back to her house was declined, and she shortly left the station. He would have liked to have kept her longer because there were still so many unanswered questions. First and foremost was the whereabouts of Harley Mason. He couldn't ignore the fact that Mrs Mason seemed more interested in telling him about her daughter's state of mind from the previous night. She certainly didn't seem concerned about Harley's present whereabouts. It seemed very odd. Did Mrs Mason think her daughter had murdered her own father because he'd had the temerity to return home without her brother? And if that was the case was Mrs Mason possibly hiding the child or was there something more sinister afoot? He would get Jacob on the case to have Mrs Mason followed and to organise a small team to search for Harley.

Just as Sanders left the room and was making his way to the incident room, Nelson called him. 'Gov, we still have Dr Reeves here, but he said he really must get back to work. Shall I ask him to come back later?'

Sanders sighed. 'Oh, bollocks. I had completely forgotten about him. No, I'll be along. Just give me two minutes.'

'Gov . . . I may have spoken out of turn.'

Sanders turned to face Nelson. 'What do ya mean?'

Nelson looked for any signs that Sanders would shout him down. 'Well, Dr Reeves arrived a while ago, and he asked me lots of questions. I told him that Mr Mason was dead, that it was possibly a murder case, and, well . . . he said he needed to get something. He went back to his clinic, but he's now in the interview room and looking very anxious.' He waited for Sanders to snap at him, but, instead, the detective merely nodded and smiled.

'I think we need all the help we can get on this case. Good lad.'

CHAPTER NINETEEN

Guy Reeves was concerned. He'd waited at Bromley Police Station for three hours, anxious to get Hudson out of the secure unit. He knew the boy would be suffering, and that being the case, it could send all his hard work out of the window.

Sanders was tired. He thought he should apologise to Dr Reeves and arrange to meet later, perhaps next time at the clinic. Nevertheless, he was still keen to hear what the man had to say.

Walking into one of the interview rooms, Sanders quickly appraised Reeves.

'Hi, I'm Detective Chief Inspector Sanders. Call me Lewis. I'm very sorry, Dr Reeves, for delaying you. We've had another incident. I'm afraid Hudson's father has been murdered. It happened this morning. I believe Nelson kept you updated. Anyway, as you can imagine, it's been bedlam here. Oops, sorry. That was the wrong choice of words. Oh, and please keep all of this to yourself.'

Reeves still looked shocked and bewildered. 'My God! Do you know who was responsible?'

Sanders was unexpectedly comfortable in the doctor's presence. It wasn't often he instantly liked a person, but there was something sincere and kind about this man. He could tell Dr Reeves was younger than he looked, and his sharp eyes told him that he was very bright.

'No, not yet. Anyway, I understand you have a clinic, so I guess Hudson's files can wait for the moment.'

He looked at the bulky brown manila folder with CONFIDENTIAL stamped across the front.

'Lewis, under the new circumstances, my clinic can wait. In fact, I have asked my secretary to cancel all my appointments.'

The tone in Dr Reeves' voice made Sanders raise his brow. Promptly, he gestured that they should take a seat.

Reeves spun the folder to face Sanders. 'I think you really need to read this. Hudson is no murderer, but *she* may well be.'

Sanders got up from his seat and closed the door. The soft yet firm voice of Dr Reeves commanded attention. Sanders felt like he was back at school when his eyes landed on the folder again. It smelled old.

The number stamped across the first page was in bold. At first, the words looked very scientific, and then, as Sanders reread them, they all began to make sense.

Patient 2316

Female – Age: 6 years 6 months

Blood test shows - Gene (101) positive – *twin sibling (patient 2317) gene (101) negative.*

Patient demonstrated a clear lack of understanding between wrong and right (too young to conclude findings).

Showing abnormal regulation of morally appropriate behaviour (too young to conclude findings).

Her emotions have little role in guiding judgement for dilemmas that pit highly diverse action against utilitarian gains, suggesting she will favour the outcome.

Her emotional processing plays no role in her moral understanding (emotionally immature to conclude findings).

Has no fear of consequences with an embryonic view yet to mature.

Age: 8 years 6 months

High-functioning – intelligence at an optimum level.

Obsessive thoughts observed through drawings.

Showing signs of personality disorder manifesting in compulsive disorders.

Demonstrates fixations on people who appear to be a threat.

Will react negatively to particular colours.

Beginning to detach from people yet will fixate on a single individual.

Developing host-like tendencies.

Age: 10 years 6 months

Has mastered the art of manipulation.

Is aware of herself and how others perceive her.

Presents with fake emotions.

She now knows what she is and has become a master of disguise.

Demonstrates exceptionally high levels of planning skills.

Remarkable eye for detail.

Age: 11 years 6 months

Shows complete lack of fear.

Can morph into her surroundings.

Has evident psychopathic traits on a level higher than has been seen before in the study.

Findings – a danger to society.

Sanders' heart was racing noticeably as he studied the notes. When he read and then reread the last line, he thought he could even hear his heart pounding.

Never, in all his years in the force, had he ever come across something like this. And he had been played – completely. He had been sure that he'd got the right twin. Convinced he had. One hundred per cent. He had never been wrong. But he had been this time. So Harley was out there, in the public domain.

Two murders in two days, she would be onto her next victim. His eyes slowly roamed over some of the words and phrases: 'mastered the art of manipulation', 'intelligence at an optimum level', 'developing host-like tendencies'. Was he really reading information on a human patient? He'd never read a clinical study paper before. So, to him, it was so cold and almost alien. The patients were treated as objects and labelled as numbers. Just those few words had his brain firing in all directions. He should have known Harley was too calm. Hudson was her host. She was fixated on him.

'Christ, Dr Reeves. She is out there, and probably onto her next victim. Tell me, who would she target next . . . ?' He paused and caught his breath. 'Sorry, Dr Reeves. We obviously need your help. You know her better than anyone. Where would she go?'

Reeves sat back. 'Well, firstly, she is not reckless. Anything she does will be done with precision. Her brain can work out puzzles quicker than most, and she will not run around harming unimportant individuals. She will have a very targeted approach and may even be acting very innocently and unsuspectingly.' He paused for the detective to grasp the information before he carried on. 'She is a genius at manipulation and can turn on an emotional act at the drop of a hat, but she has no soul, no fear, but, obviously, she has a fixation on someone, and until we know who that is, we will not be able to understand why she has killed, if, of course, it *is* her.'

Sanders swallowed hard. He had a flashback to *The Silence of the Lambs*, and although he'd seen many nutcases in his time, this was on a different level. Maybe reading the top page of the monstrously thick file had left his brain to wander down a horror story of a road.

'Your report mentions "psychopathic traits". Are we talking about a psychopath as in *serial killer*?'

Reeves nodded slowly. 'And not just a serial killer but a highly intellectual one. This type of disorder is more complex and dangerous than you could ever imagine.'

Sanders put his hands to his mouth; it was beyond comprehension. 'I just cannot believe it – an eleven-year-old——' He stopped when he noticed the frown on Dr Reeves' face.

'No, Lewis, not an eleven-year-old. Look at the date,' he replied, as he tapped his finger on the date of the file – it showed 1986.

With his mouth open, as if he was catching flies, Sanders stared in total confusion. All of this made no sense: the twins weren't even born then. His eyes flicked up to Dr Reeves for clarification.

'Who did you think I meant?' Reeves' voice was slow and precise.

'Harley Mason, obviously. I mean, the report refers to twins . . . I assumed, because, well, aren't you the Mason twins' psychiatrist?'

Reeves almost laughed out loud at the confusion on Sanders' face. Of course, they were talking at cross purposes. It was his fault, though; he should have explained first before presenting the file. 'Well, yes, the twins are in a study. The original study began back in the early eighties, under the initiation of Dr Katherine Renee, or, more accurately, Dr Tavon, as she was then. I was a mere junior then. But this patient' – he pointed to the file – 'was a subject in the original study. It was only when Dr Renee came by my office to go through the recent findings that she happened to recognise her. It was quite concerning at the time because I had no idea that Harley and Hudson's mother was patient number 2316; namely, one Dionne Stuart, now Dionne Mason.'

Sanders' shoulders slumped, and he ran his hands through his receding hairline, his face staring at disbelief at the patient's name: Dionne Stuart. For the first time in his life, his body became covered in goosebumps, and he visibly shuddered.

'Oh no! I have just let her go. Are you certain? I mean a hundred per cent?'

'I can never be a hundred per cent, but with someone like her, I would never second-guess.'

Sanders jumped up from his chair and asked Dr Reeves to wait. Then he ran along to the incident room. 'Everyone! Get all available officers on high alert. Dionne Mason has just left the station, and she may well be our killer. Tread very carefully. She is dangerous. Jacob, you go to Archi and Miriam

Mason's home. Inform them that Luke has been murdered, and if Harley shows up, they are to call us immediately.'

Forbes gave a confident nod, but, inside, he was dreading the visit. He hated giving the solemn news to anyone that a loved one was dead. However, he wasn't going to argue. Sanders was on his way to cracking the case, and if he had a suspect, he was usually right on the mark.

* * *

Forbes had decided to ask if he could have Tara Willis to accompany him, obviously for some support, and Sanders had sanctioned it. Neither of them said a word as Forbes drove over to the Mason family's place.

By the time he'd pulled into the Masons' driveway, he'd rehearsed the words over and over. As they approached the front door, it opened, and there stood Geoff Mason with anxiety written all over his face. 'Any news?'

For a second, Forbes had forgotten about Scarlett. Then his heart sank; his rehearsed words went out of the window. This family were facing a second sucker punch. Slowly, he shook his head.

Geoff looked ragged; his face was almost white, and his lips were tightly pursed in anger.

'I am sorry, Mr Mason. Geoff, is it?'

Geoff nodded and held the door open for Forbes and Willis to enter. Just as they stepped into the hallway, Geoff spotted a squad car pull up behind Forbes' vehicle.

'What's going on?'

'Please, can we talk inside?'

'Yeah, go on in through to the lounge.'

Forbes entered the large room on the left and was suddenly faced with four pairs of eager eyes. As he scanned the room, his sharp brain began to match the family members here with their names on a list in the incident room at the police station, so he guessed right away who everyone was. The older woman sitting on the sofa was obviously the mother. Next to her, a younger woman with thick dark hair was almost certainly Dean's wife, Tilly. By the fireplace stood a younger version of Geoff, who Forbes assumed was Dean, so the older person sitting in the armchair was the father, Archi.

'So what's going on?' urged Geoff.

Before he could say anything, Miriam politely offered him a seat.

Forbes didn't sit down. He had to tell the family their son was dead. 'I'm so very sorry, but your son Luke has been murdered.'

No one said a word. Archi looked over at Miriam. Geoff and Dean just stood there like statues. The silence seemed to last for an eternity. Then all hell broke loose.

'Noooo!' cried Miriam, her face drooping in pain. 'Noooo! He can't have. I don't believe it.'

Instantly, Archi jumped up from his armchair and made a beeline for his wife. Gripping her hands, he knew the news would have her hysterical, but he couldn't process it himself.

'What did you say?' asked Dean, who was in a trance-like state.

'Luke was found dead a few hours ago, at his home.' Forbes was aware that he should not pussyfoot around with the facts. He could tell the family were shocked to the core and the information wasn't quite resonating.

Tilly ran to her husband's side and clutched his arm, while Geoff stood in the middle of the room, his arms hanging loose by his side, as if his body had gone limp. 'No, this can't be right. There's gotta be some mistake.'

Like Dean, Miriam was now staring into space, almost in a trance, her brain unable to accept the news.

'Who's done this to our Luke, Detective?' snapped Geoff.

Forbes wondered if he should divulge what he knew, but it wasn't his call to make.

'Sorry, Mr Mason. We don't know at this time, but I have two officers on your drive as a precaution because your wife's murder and Luke's may well be connected. So for now, please be cautious. I would suggest none of you leave this house until we know more.'

Miriam, who had been staring into nothing, suddenly snapped out of it. Speaking in a calm, almost monotone voice, she asked, 'How did he die?'

'I'm sorry, Mrs Mason. The investigation is at a very early stage, but please be assured, you will be informed once the formalities have been concluded.'

Dean was at boiling point. 'Oh, come *on*! Was he stabbed? Was he shot? How the fuck did he die? And I wanna know this. Who the fuck killed him?'

'Yes, er, sorry, Mr Mason. Look, he was killed with a sharp instrument, that's all I know. And we do not know as yet who's responsible.'

'And what about Dionne and Harley? Are they okay?' asked Geoff.

Forbes took a deep breath. This meeting with the Masons was proving to be a lot harder than he'd anticipated. He was beginning to think he was out of his depth.

'I can only inform you that Dionne Mason has given a statement, but Harley is missing. If she turns up here, we need you to call us right away. I have to go back to the station now. Again, I am very sorry.'

Miriam was now wide-eyed. She leaped up from her seat. 'Oh my God, please, don't tell me that Harley may have been killed. She's only a kid. No, please . . .'

Seeing the extreme anguish on the woman's face, Forbes' reaction was to jump in quickly and calm the situation. 'No, we don't think that, but she is missing, so if she comes here, please call us. We need to speak to her as a matter of urgency.'

Miriam lost her balance but was instantly steadied by Geoff. 'Mum, sit down.' He helped her back to the sofa where his father pulled her close.

'Why don't you think,' asked Geoff, 'whoever killed my brother didn't kill Harley? Unless you have an idea who killed him!'

'I'm sorry, that's all I've been told. I'll keep you updated, but, please, if you can, stay together for now.'

Geoff grabbed the detective's arm before he could leave. 'Now, hang on a fucking minute, mate. You can't just leave us like this. We're going through enough heartache as it is. I wanna know everything you know. Starting with who the fuck do you think killed my brother?'

Forbes looked at Geoff's hand gripping his arm, and, instantly, Geoff let go. 'Well?'

Sighing, Forbes looked at all the questioning faces around the room. It was clear that he wouldn't be able to leave the house without divulging what he knew. 'Okay, we aren't a hundred per cent sure, and this is still an inquiry, but we cannot rule out Mrs Mason . . . er, I mean Dionne. She left the station a while ago, but—'

'*Dionne?*' questioned Geoff.

'All I can say is that since leaving the station, she has become a person of interest. If she arrives here, you need to call us right away.' He looked out of the large bay window overlooking the garden. 'You'll have an officer inside the house and one outside at all times until we find the killer. Look, at the moment, that's all we have. Just stay together.'

No sooner had he and WPC Willis reached the front door than he heard a high-pitched scream of pain. It was a scream that would only come from a mother who had lost her child.

CHAPTER TWENTY

Sanders stared at the investigation board, biting his lip. He'd decided to ask Dr Reeves to join him. Perhaps he was the best hope of catching Dionne Mason. Guy Reeves was sad yet excited that he was being asked to help on the case. It was a new experience for him, working as a profiler, instead of testifying in the courtroom as an expert witness. He stood back and stared at the photos pinned to the board. He scrutinised each one but one in particular drew his attention: the tall, handsome man with alluring eyes. Then he read the name below: Geoff Mason.

Sanders watched a genius at work.

'Initially,' said Reeves, 'I think she became fixated on Geoff. If I am right, then I believe she would have killed his wife and then her husband, if she wanted him that badly.'

Sanders scratched his chin, a habit of his. 'Well, when I questioned her and asked if Geoff would have hurt her husband, she instantly snapped at me, saying "No, he wouldn't."'

'It's him. She wants him, and if his wife and her husband were the reason she couldn't have him, then she would do something about it. She'll target anyone who stands in her way. Even her own kids.'

'Harley is out there somewhere. She wouldn't have hurt her already, would she? Only Mrs Mason called us when she found her husband dead. She wasn't too concerned about her daughter's whereabouts, which seemed odd. She mentioned that last night Harley was annoyed because Hudson was still at the station.'

Reeves nodded. 'Yes, because I suspect she might have been feeding you, making you subconsciously believe it was her daughter. Think back, Lewis. Did she put that thought in your head?'

'Yeah, I did feel at the time she was keen for me to know her daughter's state of mind rather than worry that she was missing. Christ, most mothers would be hysterical, worrying that whoever killed their husband would have hurt the child.'

'Yes, Dionne was definitely feeding you. She is clever, but I feel troubled because from Dr Renee's notes, Dionne is extremely clever and manipulative. Hmm . . . I wonder if she's distracted? I'm surprised she made it so obvious.' His eyes focused on the board and the two weapons – a knife and a pen. 'And Scarlett Mason was killed by those two weapons, was she?'

Sanders nodded and sighed. 'Not those two actual items, but the coroner suggested a knife and possibly a pen.' He inhaled deeply. 'Christ, I should retire. Why didn't I see that? I automatically thought of Hudson—'

'Because of the pen,' interrupted Reeves.

'Yeah, how stupid of me. A knife alone would have killed her, so why add a pen?'

'Hudson always carries a pen. He constantly fiddles with it and of course anyone who knows him would know that.'

'I should have sussed that. It was too obvious,' replied Sanders, totally deflated.

'Lewis, she timed it to perfection. She didn't kill Scarlett opportunistically: she waited. And her ideal time was the night the children fled after a fight involving a pen. You already had the thought in your head. It was all too carefully planned. I told you she's an expert in the art of manipulation. Tell me, was there an altercation between Harley and her father, prior to Dionne finding her husband dead, and was there a witness present to the altercation?'

For a second, Sanders frowned, deep in thought. 'Er, yes, there was. She said Geoff was there when Harley screamed at her father . . . Again, why didn't I see it? I thought it was odd, but I just didn't quite get it at the time.'

Looking at the bulky file that was now tucked up under Dr Reeves' arm, Sanders asked, 'What else is in there that I need to know?'

'If you don't find her or Harley then perhaps you need to read this. But, for now, I think our key objective is to track down Dionne before she gets to Harley. My guess is, if she is becoming out of control, which is all in the folder, she'll go for Harley. For now, though, she seems to be calculated. Let's hope it stays that way because Dionne Stuart is probably the most dangerous woman in this country – at the moment, that is.'

A clammy sweat covered Sanders' body, and the hairs on the back of his neck stood on end.

'Right, I have an idea where Harley is. I need to reach her before Dionne does. Please give me your mobile number. You never know, I might need some expert advice.'

* * *

The small radio on the 1970s sideboard was playing 'Just the Way You Are' by Bruno Mars as Lillian polished the lounge for the umpteenth time. She was worried sick and knew damn well her daughter wouldn't call her to update her. She stopped and sighed. Dear little Hudson. He was such a shy and sweet child, yet he had an awkwardness about him. Of course, he was odd, but sometimes something extraordinary can be found in something imperfect. That was her Hudson to a T. And then there was Harley, with her dark eyes that held so much love behind them just waiting to come out, and it would, one day, when she was ready.

The banging on the door startled her, and she peered out of the window. To her amazement, Harley was standing there.

She smiled; perhaps if she thought about a pile of money, then that would appear too. She hurried to welcome her granddaughter.

Harley nearly flew through the door, anxiously peering over her shoulder. 'Nan, please help me!'

Lillian grabbed her shoulders. 'Of course, babe. What's going on?'

Harley skipped over to the window and looked up and down the road. 'Nan, they've got Hudson in prison, or somewhere, but he didn't murder Auntie Scarlett. I *know* he didn't. He *couldn't* have.'

'What?' shrieked Lillian, throwing her hands to her face.

'Someone killed her, Nan. Someone killed Auntie Scarlett, and they think it was Hudson. But it *wasn't*. He wouldn't kill a fly.'

'Where's ya mum and dad, sweetheart?'

'I don't know. As soon as I got up, I packed a bag and headed here. The bloody bus broke down, and it's taken me ages. I don't know what to do. Mum doesn't seem to care, and Dad . . . Well, I'm so angry with *him*. He didn't bring Hudson home last night. I can't go back, Nan, I just *can't*. I hate it there, I hate it. Mum is so well . . . I dunno. She's just so *cold*. She acts like I don't *exist*.'

Trying to take it all in, Lillian knew she had to have her wits about her, if she was to inspire any confidence in her clever granddaughter. 'Darling, listen, we need to get away from here.'

Screwing her nose in confusion, Harley tilted her head to the side. 'But why?'

Lillian was looking very flustered, her mind in turmoil. 'Look, let me get me shoes. I'll tell ya later, but you have to trust me. We need to get away. *Now!*' She grappled with her old boots and reached up for her overcoat.

Just as Harley headed for the front door, Lillian hurried back into the kitchen.

'I left me bag. Hold on, Sweetie.'

Suddenly, Lillian heard a skidding of car tyres and a door slamming. In a panic, she nearly tripped over some loose carpet in her rush to prevent Harley from opening the front door. But it was too late; there on the doorstep stood the same detective who'd been to the house earlier, with another officer.

Harley was glued to the spot.

Sanders gave her a reassuring smile.

'It's all right, Harley. You are not in any trouble, none whatsoever, so don't look like that.'

He then looked beyond Harley to Lillian. 'I need to take Harley to a safe place, but I want you to come too.'

Lillian didn't question him; she followed the detective and a WPC and climbed into the back seat with Harley.

'What's going on, Detective?' asked Lillian, as she fastened her seat belt.

'I have some awful news, and I'm just so glad you are with your granddaughter right now.'

'Please, can you tell me what's happened?'

Sanders didn't have the time to consider the feelings of the child. He needed to inform them of their possible danger, and so the words just blurted out. 'I'm afraid, Harley, your father was found dead—'

He almost jumped out of his seat when he heard the scream. There was a guttural, deep heartfelt cry of pain.

'No! No!' She shook with anger, throwing herself around, as if she was in agony.

Lillian allowed her to punch and kick the front passenger seat until her screams and thrashing around slowly receded to a pitiful sob. Then she put her arms around her granddaughter and rocked her as if she were a baby, stroking her hair and kissing her forehead. 'It's okay, my darling. You let it out, there's my girl.'

Sanders felt a lump in his throat. He'd never heard such grief in a child. He'd somehow expected her to take a while to absorb the information silently before shedding a few shy tears and a gentle sob. As he looked in his rear-view mirror, the dark, threatening eyes of Harley's were round and extremely sad. In her present state, she was like a toddler who seemed so vulnerable. He knew at that precise moment she hadn't killed her father.

'Please, Detective, take us somewhere really safe. And Hudson, where is he?'

With Sanders' mind so distracted, what Lillian had just said seemed almost irrelevant. Then everything clicked: Lillian was worried about her daughter.

'Don't you worry about Hudson. He's fine, and I'll have him with you as soon as we can get this mess over with. I think we should go to the station first. Perhaps, Mrs Stuart, you can help us.'

Lillian didn't need it spelling out to her; she knew exactly what he was getting at, and, this time, she would get everything off her chest. She had two grandchildren to think about now. There would be no more making excuses and no more hiding the truth.

The evening was drawing in, and the sky was black, heralding rain. It lashed down onto the windscreen, and the wipers thrashed furiously, as Sanders weaved in and out of the traffic. When they came to a set of traffic lights, he checked his phone, but no one had called. So Dionne Mason was still on the loose. His thoughts returned to the conversation with Dr Reeves. Was the psychiatrist's assumption right? Could or even would Mrs Mason really have killed her husband? After all, she had appeared to be so concerned over his death, more so than with the disappearance of her own daughter. However, there was one phrase that rang in his ear – 'mastered the art of manipulation'.

The past two days had been long and tiring, and he tried to remember if he'd actually had any sleep. Two, maybe three hours, perhaps, but the days were rolling into one. This case was sending him down a road he didn't want to go. Psychopaths and sociopaths were not his thing – well, not serial killers, anyway.

CHAPTER TWENTY-ONE

Once they reached Bromley Police Station, Sanders offered Harley a bed in one of the cells, just to rest.

She accepted; she knew she would be safe there.

Lillian was more than happy to join Sanders in an interview room. He looked at the hard plastic chairs there and decided to take her to the incident room where the chairs were softer. There was also a couch for those who worked late. Forbes was on the computer, and other officers assigned to the case were reading through notes. They stopped what they were doing and waited for him to explain why he'd allowed an elderly lady into the incident room.

'This is Lillian Stuart, Dionne Mason's mother. She's here to help.' He gestured for her to take a seat, but her eyes were drawn to the grotesque photo of Scarlett and now the new one of Luke.

She ignored the others in the room and walked towards the investigation board, still clutching her tatty old bag in front of her. They watched in silence as she stared at the photos. Then she turned to face them. 'My Dionne did that!'

Forbes' jaw hit the floor.

Sanders went over to her and carefully held her arm, leading her away from the board and to the couch. 'May I get you a tea, Mrs Stuart?' he asked, politely.

'Oh, er, yes, please.'

He nodded to Nelson to fetch Mrs Stuart a cup of tea. 'Why are you so sure?' he asked, in his gentlest tone.

'Where do I start, Detective Chief Inspector? It's a long story and one that I should have told many years ago, but I was afraid, you see. I was so sure that my little girls would be like me. They were so beautiful when they were born, with fair hair and the biggest blue eyes . . .' Her voice trailed off as if reliving a memory, but then her face tightened when reality came back. She looked at Sanders and smiled.

'Sorry, Detective Chief Insp . . . er, Mr Sanders. Where should I begin?'

Seeing all the signs of exhaustion on the kind woman's face, he placed a hand on her arm and smiled. 'Begin by calling me Lewis and just start from as far back as you can remember.'

Lillian shuddered with the memory of that time. She'd always hoped never to relive it to a living soul, but now she thought it might help her family.

'I was twenty-five years old, and Thomas and I had been married for four years. He was a looker back then, you know, all trendy and stylish. Kenny was almost four years old, a real cutie, with big brown eyes and fair wavy locks. He looked a bit like a girl, I suppose. Anyway, we went to a party, not far from where we lived. It was someone's birthday, but I can't really remember whose. Thomas left early. He said he felt unwell. I think he had a bit of a chest infection. Anyway, I loved to dance, ya see, and so I stayed on. But then, when it got late, I decided to head off home. I was a little tipsy, or maybe quite a bit tipsy, and I chose to take a shortcut through the churchyard. I had done it many times before but not in the dark. I remember hearing heavy footsteps behind me and then this person's hand was shoved across me mouth. So hard it was, it nearly knocked me teeth out. Then I was lifted up in the air. I was petrified and thought I was gonna die. This man, he had a knife, you see. It was a large blade that shone in the moonlight. I couldn't take my eyes off it. The man knew I was scared. I never did see his face, but he was a big man, though, a huge man . . .' She stopped and took a deep breath.

As Nelson approached her with a mug of tea, Sanders took it from him and held it until Mrs Stuart was able to stop shaking. Nelson then left the room to see how Harley was faring.

'It's all right, Mrs Stuart. Give yourself a moment before you continue with your story.'

Sipping the hot tea, she then took another deep breath and composed herself, sitting upright. 'I can't get the smell out of my head, ya know. Mad as it seems, he smelled like death. Anyway, he did what he needed to do, and then he raised that knife and plunged it into my leg. Why he stabbed me in the leg, I haven't a clue. He could just as easily have stabbed me in the chest, so I guess he didn't want to kill me. The wound was bad, though. A while later, as I dragged myself across the path, a passer-by found me, and I was rushed to hospital, where I had to stay for a few weeks. It was all the shock of what he'd done to me, ya see.'

Two officers, seated at their desks, began scribbling notes, while Forbes and Sanders remained totally attentive.

'The months rolled by, and then I discovered I was pregnant. Of course, my Thomas knew what had happened and begged me to have an . . . well, you know, not to continue with the pregnancy, but I just couldn't do that, you see. I was too far gone, in any case. I mean, those babies were a part of me too, and God must have had his plan. Well, at least, that's what I stupidly thought at the time . . . I don't know if I believe in God now, though. The Devil, I do, but God? No.'

On the edge of his seat, in fascination at this woman's harrowing story, Forbes said, 'So what you're saying is that Dionne was actually a *twin?*'

Annoyed, Sanders held up his hand in Forbes' face to shut him up. He wanted Mrs Stuart to ramble on in her own words – at her own pace – because this was her story and not an interrogation.

'Yes, two little girls. I called them Dionne and Jenny. My Thomas didn't want anyone gossiping about us, and so the twins took his last name, and, in their first few years, he treated them much like Kenny, as if they were his own.' She stopped and had another sip of her tea.

The men were all enthralled by this story. It was something so incredibly moving, and one they felt privileged to listen to. They watched Mrs Stuart take a moment. Her eyes were watering, and they guessed she was coming to the most painful part.

'Jenny was the smaller child. She was the quiet one. Dionne bullied her. She would rip a toy from her hand, and if Thomas told her off and demanded she handed it back, she'd fly into a temper. And not as you imagine a two-year-old would, mind. She was fierce and violent. She would backhand all the cups, ashtrays, and anything else from the coffee table. God help anyone who tried to restrain her. She'd leave a nasty mark, she would. She'd kick and scratch like a wild animal. By the time they started school, my Jenny, bless her heart, could already read, write, and add up better than my Kenny. And according to the teachers, Dionne was also a model student, bordering on being a gifted child, she was so bright. I said I wanted them separated because they didn't get on. That's when my little Jenny was at her happiest – when she was away from Dionne. Kenny didn't like Dionne and spent all his time with Jenny; they were that close. It was hard to really bond with Dionne, ya see, and my Thomas, in the end, well, he just gave up. He was strict and kind, like, as any parent would be, but he never bothered with the hugs – he only had them for Kenny and Jenny . . . Don't get me wrong. It wasn't his fault. Dionne hated being touched. Then, one day, she got in a fight with Jenny and broke her arm. That was it, then. I took Dionne to the doctors and told 'em she needed some kind of medication to calm her down.'

Lillian finished off her tea, found a tissue in her bag, and wiped her mouth.

The men in the room anticipated that this might be the precursor for something startling to come.

'That was when a doctor sent her to a shrink, ya see.'

Nelson tapped on the door, interrupting the moment, and Sanders shot him an annoying glance. 'Gov, the forensics report has just come in, and there's a doctor here to see you. Shall I send her home, or . . . ?'

'Her?'

'Yes, Gov, a Dr Renee. She says she may be able to help with the Mason case.'

Sanders got up from his chair. 'I am so sorry, Mrs Stuart. Please would you just give me a moment. I am very interested in hearing the rest of your story.'

'How is Harley doing?' asked Lillian, as she looked over at the young officer.

Nelson smiled. 'She is weepy, but we've been playing chess. She beats me every time.'

Sanders stood up. 'Nelson, I suggest you get some burgers or whatever Harley wants to eat. Then, find out if we have any leads on Dionne Mason, would you. Also, when you bring Dr Renee in, please fetch another tea for Mrs Stuart.'

Lillian smiled. She liked the DCI. He was a kind and caring man, ensuring her granddaughter was being properly looked after. It took the worry from her, but, right now, she was more worried than she'd ever been. She'd brought a monster into the world, and she knew she had to do whatever it took to protect the innocent.

Nelson wanted to work his way up the ladder to become a DCI himself and was eager to please Sanders, so he hurried off and brought Dr Renee to the incident room along with a fresh round of tea.

Then, as Renee entered, she looked straight at Lillian. 'Lillian, hello, do you remember me?'

Everyone looked at her in astonishment.

Lillian's face was a picture of surprise as she gasped. She hadn't recognised the lady at first. The woman was older, larger, and her hair was white.

'*Katherine?* You were my daughter's psychiatrist, weren't you? So you've changed your surname, then?'

Renee nodded. 'Divorced.'

'Well, hello, Kate,' greeted Lillian, nervously. They'd been on first-name terms ever since Kate's involvement with Dionne.

'Oh my gosh. How are you?' asked Renee.

'Very worried, I guess.'

'Hmm, yes, me too. That's what brought me here.' Turning to the others, she said, 'I know Dr Reeves came earlier to present information regarding Hudson to help secure his release, but when he came back to the clinic, he told me what had happened. I appreciate that it's all confidential at this stage, but I won't be able to sleep tonight unless I give you the background on Dionne. Whether it helps or not, I don't know, but, well, I am here if you need me.'

At that point and with a confident aura about her, she introduced herself fully, giving a brief résumé of her qualifications and experience, after which she placed a large manila folder on the desk, opposite the investigation board. After scrutinising the photos, she said, 'I was Dionne Stuart's psychiatrist for a few years, until she went off the radar.'

She pointed to the folder. 'That contains the data from the original study.'

Sanders offered her a seat. 'Yes, I don't really know too much about clinical studies.'

'I don't want to jump to conclusions, but Dionne fitted a particular profile of a study we were conducting.'

'What study, exactly?'

'Right, this is confidential, Detective Chief Inspector Sanders.'

'Please call me Lewis.'

'Yes, Lewis. Well, over many years ago, when we became more advanced in understanding and identifying genes, we began to look at the myth, or not, of the Gemini Gene. It was supposed to be a gene found in the strongest of men and one that led onto one being found in psychopaths, and so it was said the serial killers had this Gemini Gene. However, there is more to it. We have found similar traits in people who are ruthless, who may be moneylenders, bank managers, and certain businessmen, and who are not dangerous as such but show less regard for people's feelings and lack a common level of empathy. The study looked at a higher level of intelligence of the Gemini Gene trait. We recruited mainly children who demonstrated intelligence and unusual levels of violence. You see, children who have psychosis will not present as an adult would, and so we could follow them over the years and watch how the traits develop.' She paused, hoping the DCI was keeping up.

'So, you wanted to see if these kids would turn into serial killers?'

She smirked. 'Not exactly, Lewis. The Gemini Gene is found in high-functioning children who will fight for what they want. Now, that doesn't mean they would kill for what they want, but they have the ability to never give up. Nothing will stop them. For instance, if they want to achieve an honours degree they will work all day and night to achieve it. If they want to swim the channel, they will die before they fail. Nothing will distract them. We see it at a young age when they attempt a puzzle. They will complete it, even if they have to stay up all night. But there is also the darker side of the Gemini Gene profile, which exists for those who have the same determination but who have a total disregard for others, as if they don't exist. They are the dangerous ones, the potential killers.'

Sanders and Forbes were hanging on to her every word, now completely intrigued.

'Dionne and Jenny were both enrolled in the programme, and you don't mind me being frank do you, Lillian?'

She smiled. 'I think we need to be honest, Kate. Earlier, I was telling them about Dionne, but, I think, maybe, you could fill in the gaps.'

Renee nodded.

'Mr and Mrs Stuart fell on hard times, shall we say, and the study paid them well, so the Stuart twins were enrolled. Dionne was so typical of all the traits at a young age, but, obviously, we couldn't confirm this was the case because of her immaturity, so we just monitored them. Jenny functioned at a higher level but showed obvious regard for others, so we knew she didn't have the psychopathic element. What did concern us, though, was the fixation Dionne had with her sister, and as the months rolled on, this fixation increased, and it reached a peak when, suddenly, her intelligence went out of the window, so to speak. She was planning – no, actually, she was scheming – and she would find ways to have Jenny take the blame for her wrongdoing, but as soon as that wasn't working, she would fly into an uncontrollable rage, causing more damage than any normal six-year-old would. She also possessed unbelievable strength, and my assistant, Clive Black, would have to restrain her. She was too much for me. And then came the terrible news.'

She looked at Lillian, who was reliving the story, her tears falling down her cheeks and her lips quivering, but the truth had to be told.

Renee smiled and nodded encouragingly for Lillian to take over the story.

'I thought the girls were getting along. Dionne was being really nice. My Thomas said she must have grown out of her tantrums because she was sharing nicely, not screaming and fighting . . .' She took a deep breath to steady her voice. 'And then, one Saturday afternoon in August, I needed to get some shopping, so I left Thomas to look after the kids. It was easier than taking them with me. I remember returning and struggling with the shopping bags as I walked up the garden path, but, more than that, I remember the smell.'

Forbes, forgetting himself, said, 'Smell?'

Sanders raised his hand again. 'Sorry, carry on, Lillian.'

She coughed and held back the sob lodged in her throat.

'Yes, this odd deathlike smell that I had often encountered. Anyway, no sooner had I put the key in the door than I knew. Don't ask me how. I just knew something was wrong. Thomas was asleep in the armchair, Dionne was at the coffee table doing a puzzle, and my little Jenny was nowhere to be seen. I don't know why, but I flew up the stairs and that's when I heard the water dripping. And there in the bath, along with a bloody hairdryer, was my little angel – dead.' She stopped and wiped her eyes.

'So, you reckon Dionne was responsible for Jenny's death?' asked Sanders, gently.

Lillian's sad face said it all. 'It couldn't be proved, and the coroner said it was just a misfortunate accident. But my Thomas was never the same with Dionne after that. He wasn't abusive or anything like that – he just paid her no attention. He even said once that Dionne was her father's daughter. Ya know, meaning she took after the monster who raped me. You see, just before the girls went upstairs to play, Dionne made Thomas a cup of tea. I believe she laced it with my sleeping tablets because there were a few missing, and I was always careful with any medicine, you know. And my Jenny wasn't stupid. She would never have put the hairdryer in the bath. She could even have survived that, but the coroner's report showed a weakness in her heart, Gawd love her.'

Renee sensed that Lillian needed a break, just by the way her face sagged and her brows had become hooded over her eyes. She took over from Lillian.

'So, we continued seeing Dionne on a weekly basis until we felt she was showing signs of being more in tune with a normal six-year-old, but by the time she reached eight years old, we had guessed that she was managing to manipulate people. She'd cleverly learned to mimic normal behaviour. So she taught herself by copying others. Her reactions to bad news were fake; they were not real at all. Her tears were forced, and even her friendly disposition was just a front. She simply mastered every normal reaction to every scenario. It was pure genius.'

Sanders was enthralled, and totally in awe of the story, but he was puzzled, and, like a student, he had to ask her something. 'How do you know she was faking it?'

'Good question,' replied Renee. 'It was only because we had a mirror room installed and we monitored her. The obvious sign was when we placed a gerbil in there.'

Sanders frowned. 'A gerbil?'

'Yes, it was part of the programme. Anyway, we told the children that it was a pet. We showed them how to handle the gerbil. Having an assessment window, we were able to watch. We wanted the kids to nurture the animal. We needed to record how the subjects reacted. All the children in the study either had no interest in the gerbil or showed normal signs of interest. Some wanted to hold it, stroke it, and feed it. However . . .' She paused and sighed. 'When it was Dionne's turn, she snatched it from the cage, and, of course, naturally, it bit her. We expected her to throw it to the ground or scream like any other child would; instead, she placed it back in its cage and sucked the blood from her finger. I decided to leave her alone, and I left the room to study her behaviour from behind the mirrored window.' She paused again and shook her head.

'She looked around the room, and then she snatched the gerbil, holding it by its tail. Then, with one solid movement, she bashed it against the table, killing it instantly. That done, she smiled and placed it back in the cage and covered it with sawdust. I immediately entered the room and went over to see if it was, in fact, dead, and then I turned to her and asked if she knew how it died. Pretending she was distraught, she covered her face and began crying. When I asked her if she had anything to do with it, her face fell, and her eyes looked genuinely sullen. She replied, "No! No! I loved that gerbil." But then she turned her back on me and waved at the mirror. You see, she knew then we had been watching her.'

Renee looked across at the manila folder. 'There is a stack of files inside there that would make your toes curl, but I think it's better that we concentrate on sourcing where she might be.'

Sanders agreed and returned to the board. 'Any clues?'

Renee collected her thoughts. 'When you interviewed Dionne, did she seem to be calculated in her responses to you, or did she make any slip-ups?'

Sanders had a thought in the forefront of his mind. 'Yes. She completely disregarded the fact that her daughter may have been kidnapped by the person who killed Luke. I was surprised myself because any parent would have panicked, but she dismissed the idea and left the police station.'

'That's the worrying thing. You see, when she's fixated, she'll be scheming and planning. Once she goes beyond that point, she'll develop a rage, and that's when I believe she'll slip up. Her anger will supersede her intelligence, and that, my friend, is the point at which she'll become reckless. She'll go after Geoff. Dr Reeves is convinced that Dionne is fixated on him. If she wants him, she'll have him, and she'll destroy anything and anyone in her path. As a matter of interest, does he have children?'

Sanders pointed to Forbes. 'Jacob, get a squad car over to Geoff Mason's now. I want Davey and Nicki found and removed to safety.' He turned to Renee. 'Will she hurt Geoff?'

Renee shrugged. 'That I don't know, but if she can't have him, she may destroy him.'

Lillian unexpectedly spoke up. 'She'll kill him. She did my Kenny. I'm sure of it.'

'How old was she when Kenny died?' asked Renee.

'She was twelve.'

Sanders remembered the last entry in the file when she was eleven and a half years old. It said 'Findings – a danger to society.'

'Why didn't you have her committed?' asked Sanders, as he glanced at Renee.

'Because she was in a study, and the downside of that is our findings are confidential, and so they cannot be used to make an official diagnosis. Ipso facto, she couldn't be certified as a psychopath. Even if she wasn't in the study, we couldn't label juveniles as psychos – only as having social or behavioural problems.' Renee sighed.

'Oh, I see. Well, that's a bloody shame.'

Lillian was fidgeting. She asked if she could be excused to use the bathroom. Sanders nodded to Nelson. 'Please escort Mrs Stuart to the restroom . . . *our* restroom.'

Nelson smiled. He knew that the officers' toilets were far better than the ones used by the public.

Once inside, Lillian closed the door and looked in the mirror. She stared at her aged face and recognised her submissive appearance. As a large tear fell down her puffy red cheeks, her eyes welled up again, and then another tear tumbled. Opposite the toilets were shower cubicles and slatted benches where the officers dried themselves.

She slumped down on one of the benches and stared at the white tiled wall. A sick feeling – one of guilt mixed with anger – consumed her body. Why had she protected Dionne so much? Why hadn't she left her in the study or pressed for her to be locked away in a secure unit? Her little Jenny, Scarlett, and Luke would still be alive. Her Kenny, who'd been the apple of her eye, had been so full of life. A generous boy, with many friends and so much to give and to live for, it had all been taken away in the blink of an eye. She allowed the tears to continue falling as she recalled that day. Not that she'd ever pushed it to the back of her mind, but with the past coming back to slap her in the face, the vision of him lying there, dead, was still there – and it was so crystal clear. His dear, sweet face in death was frozen in fear as if he'd been terrified in the last few seconds of his life. Lying at a peculiar angle, his head was so far back it was almost upside down. She remembered hearing a high-pitched scream that echoed inside her head until she realised that blood-curdling cry of total despair had come from her own voice box. But there was something else she remembered: it was that sickly, sweet smell, that reminder of death, the same odour that had burned her nose on the day she was raped – and the distinct stench that clouded the day Jenny died.

Oh Kenny! He lay there at the bottom of the stairs staring up at the ceiling. Then she saw Dionne standing almost in shock herself at the top of the stairs, by the pile of dirty washing. But it was the quilt cover partly draped down the stairs and wrapped around her son's foot that stood out now in her mind. Kenny had bought it specially for Dionne. It had beautiful yellow flowers, and he'd been so excited to give her the gift. He'd bought it for next to nothing from his friend who was selling them as knock-offs from Arding & Hobbs. Unable to get rid of the flowered ones, Kenny's friend had been almost giving them away. But Kenny thought of his sister as he'd always done. He wasn't close to her, not like he had been with Jenny, but he still treated her with respect in the hope that one day she would change her moody, nasty ways and be nice to him. But as her son lay there, her daughter's cold, expressionless eyes just stared at him. There were no tears – no emotion.

Perhaps she had been paranoid back then. Nevertheless, she'd always had that feeling that her own daughter was responsible.

The coroner had said he'd fallen, and although his neck had snapped, and it was unusual to see such a clean fracture, no one could find any reason to think that a twelve-year-old girl could be capable of using enough force to snap a neck. Apart from Kenny, she was the only one at home, and therefore the only witness, so they had to dismiss foul play and conclude that he'd died by tripping over the pile of dirty washing and then falling heavily at an awkward angle. Perhaps the force and weight of his own body had caused the break.

Lillian couldn't cope at the time, conjuring up evil thoughts about her daughter, and so she headed for the church to absolve her sins. But as she reached the building, she was met by a crowd of people all in black. They were carrying in a coffin, and as the pall-bearers marched by, the smell of death laced the delicate skin just inside her nose. That distinctive smell again. She looked up at the cross, and the sun began to shine. Deep in grief, she made a life-changing decision not to lose another child. So, she forced the evil thoughts from her head and decided to love the child as much as she could. But, of course, it had been a monumental mistake. Why hadn't she gone with her instincts? Why had she let her own daughter manipulate her?

Putting it down to the loss of two siblings, she tried to ignore Dionne's strange behaviour: all those times when she would wander off in the dead of night, the weird fascination with anatomy, and her imaginary friend.

But this cruel, violent kid never stopped being anything other than evil, despite all the love she'd given to her. She had prayed to God on the day of her daughter's wedding that she would change and become as beautiful on the inside as she so obviously was on the outside. But God, apparently, hadn't listened. So how could she believe in God now? Why would she even want to? And even more recently, with a loving husband, a beautiful home, and two gorgeous children, Dionne had still not been satisfied.

* * *

Sanders was looking at the investigation board. He then asked Renee if she would add her bullet-pointed notes from her study of Dionne. He thought it might help if he could see them in black and white.

She scribbled down, on the left-hand side, Dionne's state of mind at each age and added a few notes.

Sanders felt uneasy with what he read of Dionne at the age of six. *Christ, it was as if he was seeing a psychopath unfold*, he thought. Then he frowned. At the age of seven, she had an imaginary friend. *What?* He was intrigued, if nothing else.

'I have a niece,' said Sanders, conversationally. 'She is seven, and, funnily enough, she has an imaginary friend. I guess that's pretty normal, isn't it?'

Renee stopped writing and stood back. 'Yes, it can be perfectly normal, and, at the time, we assumed in Dionne's case that she'd developed this friend as a substitute for her sister. Which would be understandable, except her imaginary friend wasn't set a place to join a tea party with her teddy bears. Because in her head, this friend of hers was a real person. Her friend told her to do things. He or she apparently whispered in her ear, but you see, by the age of eleven, she was functioning at a higher level of intelligence, so her friend was never mentioned again.'

'So is she schizophrenic or does she have multiple personalities, then?'

'Funny you should ask that, Lewis . . . We did test for that, but, no, she has one personality, but she can master her character to give off a pretence of being someone she certainly is not. I wanted to explore that possibility because there was a lot that simply didn't add up. I have to say, she was our most fascinating subject by far, but she was also the most complicated . . . *and* alarming.'

As Renee continued with her note writing, and as Sanders watched and read each bullet point, he gained a sense of this child, and he imagined a different world – a sick, dark place in Hell. He was especially disturbed when he read of 'an unhealthy fascination with anatomy, advanced level'.

'What does that mean?' he said, as he pointed to the words.

Renee turned to face him. 'Yes, well, most children are usually grossed out, as they put it, by internal body parts. Our old research unit was based at King's College Hospital. That's where we started the study. There was a room with pickle jars containing all sorts. It was shut off to the public. Anyway, one day, while we were in session, the fire alarms went off, and we were told to gather outside the front of the building. But Dionne was missing. When we found her, she was in that very room, and a porter couldn't get her to leave, so they called me. She was drawn to the jars, and I assumed it was just curiosity, but then she gave me a tour, talking me through each specimen, and in great detail too. At first, I assumed she was reading about the body or she'd done some project at school. However, that wasn't the case. It puzzled me because her knowledge was indeed exceptional. So, I then brought into the session an anatomy book, and she was totally focused on it, absorbing the knowledge like a sponge, but she already knew how to pronounce the words. It was as if she had some prior knowledge. I thought at the time she could become a doctor, but she had a detachment, as though the specimens were objects and not part of a person. You see, psychopaths see people as inanimate objects. I guess, it was at that pivotal moment, I suspected she had psychopathic traits.'

'Nelson, could you fetch more tea, please? And check on . . . Oh, Mrs Stuart. I didn't see you standing there. Please come in and take a seat. Are you feeling okay?' asked Sanders, feeling his mouth drying up.

Lillian nodded. She shut the door quietly, walked across the room, and sat back on the couch. She'd heard the tail end of the conversation between the two professionals. 'I asked her once where she'd learned so much about the body, and she told me that her friend had taught her. Anything that was unexplainable, she would say it was this friend of hers.'

Renee nodded. 'Yes, I never diagnosed her with multiple personalities, and yet I did believe that perhaps her imaginary friend was potentially one of them. It was a worry. However, until she showed a definite sign, something that we could establish, we couldn't add that to the traits we already knew about.' She sighed and looked at Lillian. 'You see, she suddenly stopped coming to the clinic just before she reached twelve. So that's why there is no entry for the next year.' Renee held her hands up, indicating that Lillian could continue because only she could give the reason for the discontinuation of the study.

Fiddling with her bag, Lillian was unsettled, but her daughter was out there somewhere, and she couldn't live with herself, if she didn't tell the truth, whether it helped or not.

'After my Kenny died, she ran away. I was beside myself because the coroner said my son's death was an accident. I blamed her, but not blatantly, like . . . But I just couldn't bring myself to talk to her. And then, one morning, I got up to find her gone. That's when I went to the church to pray for forgiveness and wash myself of all the bad feelings I had for her. She was only a child, and with that smell of death, as the pall-bearers held that coffin as they went past me, I knew that I couldn't lose another one. So we called the police, and for a week, I was frantic with worry. We thought she was dead, and then she came home as if she'd just been out for a stroll, and yet she was so different. I asked her where she'd been, and she said in her words "Just with a friend." I didn't want to push her, she appeared unharmed, and so we left it at that. But her sour expression vanished. She seemed cheery, somehow uplifted, so when I said it was time to go back to see the doctors, that was when her face changed, and she turned back to being cold and harsh. So . . .' She stopped and gave Renee an embarrassed look. 'We decided to take her out of the study. And for a year or so, she just got on with life, and there was no trouble, no hiccups at school, and yet she would often disappear, not for days, this time, but a few hours, here and there, and she would say she was with her friend.'

'Did you ever meet her friend?' asked Sanders.

Lillian shook her head. 'No. I did suggest her friend came for tea, but Dionne could be cruel. She told me that her friend wouldn't want to come to our house because it was . . .' She paused and choked back a tear. 'Because, in her words, "It was disgusting."'

The phone rang, and one of the officers took the call. As far as those in the room were concerned, the distraction was a welcome one from hearing such a morbidly fascinating account from a member of the public.

'Gov, they've found all the family safe at Miriam Mason's house. I've requested two officers to stay with them.'

Renee raised her eyebrow. 'Let's just hope it's enough.'

CHAPTER TWENTY-TWO

Switching the last of the lights off, Guy Reeves punched in the code for the alarm. He was eager to get home and join his wife for a glass of wine perhaps, if she wasn't already in bed.

It was 1 a.m., and he should probably have taken the notes from his most recent study of the twins home with him, instead of staying at the clinic to read them. However, he felt part of the investigation, and he'd bonded with the children and wanted to help them as much as he could.

Just as he was about to punch in the last digit of the alarm, he could hear breathing. A cold feeling swept through him, as if someone was behind him. With his senses already on high alert, he detected an unusual odour. Wondering who that heavy breathing belonged to, he turned slowly, his heart now pounding, hoping that the cleaner had turned up extra early.

But as he locked eyes with his soon-to-be killer, he froze in shock. The evil in those eyes was almost inhuman. Holding his breath, he experienced an overwhelming feeling that this dark and foreboding silhouette would be responsible for his demise. Suddenly, he dropped the file, trying to ward off the attacker. Desperately, he struggled to protect himself from the long metal object that was thrust so fast into his stomach, then into his chest, and finally though his pounding heart. He was dead before he slumped to the floor.

* * *

As the hours ticked by, Sanders could see that Lillian Stuart was looking tired and particularly sickly, and Kate Renee was drinking more and more coffee to stay awake. 'Let's call it a night, shall we? The Mason family are safe. Hudson and Harley are under our watch, so we'll just keep searching, and hopefully, Mrs Mason will turn up.'

'She knows you are searching for her,' uttered Renee.

Sanders inclined his head. 'Well, her disappearance says as much, but why didn't she just keep up the pretence of an innocent woman? She insisted she wanted to be alone and declined my offer of a lift back to the house or anywhere else, for that matter.'

Renee gave him a sad grin. 'Because, like I said, she's not stupid, and she would have cottoned on that she'd slipped up, by her disregard for her daughter's welfare. You see, she has no feelings for anyone, and if she showed she had, then it would be an act, and that's where the slip-up occurred. She'd dropped her guard, causing her to flee as soon as possible. Dionne would have sussed you out, Lewis, in a heartbeat. She would have known that you would have picked up on it. I would suggest that she's watching what is going on from a safe distance, and she's either planning her next move, or, as I said, she's ready to wage war on anyone who gets in her way. Either way, she's very gravely dangerous.'

'I'm glad we have you to help us, Kate. You don't think she would hurt you, then?'

'Yes, she will, if she's seen me coming here to the police station. She didn't appear to recognise me at our last encounter, though. Sadly, I have changed a lot from my younger days. But she will suss me out soon enough, no doubt.'

Sanders frowned. 'What do you mean?'

'As I'm sure Guy Reeves explained, the Gemini Gene Study, or, as we now call it "The Higher Functioning Level Gene Study", was set up a long time ago. After I left the job, Hudson and Harley were enrolled, merely because of their unusual behaviour. I was the lead in the first study many years ago, but I was married then, using my husband's name Tavon, and then, when Dr Reeves secured funding for the second study, he called me in to look over the findings. When Dionne showed up to collect the children, we made eye contact. I knew it was her. It was those eyes . . . Well, it was more the expression. It was unmistakable. I had to be sure, so I asked for a blood sample. I claimed it was necessary for the study.'

'And you say she *still* didn't recognise you?' asked Sanders, intrigued.

'When I took a blood sample, I pretended I didn't know who she was. The sample was just to confirm it, you see. I knew she'd go ahead with it because she's also driven by money, and money can mean power. When she thought we could stop her payment, she allowed me to take her blood. Her excuse for having needle phobia was just an act. She's not afraid of needles at all. But, to answer your question, it's very hard to tell if Dionne recognised me or not. She gives nothing away.'

'So, is that why Dr Reeves let you in on what's going on?'

She smiled. 'Yes, that's why I rushed over here because I know Dionne more than anyone. After all, I studied her closely for years.'

Concerned that she was also at risk, he assigned another two officers to protect her. She offered to take Lillian and Harley to her home. Living in a large five-bedroom house alone, Renee was more than happy to provide a place for them to stay, much to the relief of Sanders, who was running out of officers to use as a safeguard.

*　*　*

Sanders didn't leave the station. He slept on the couch in the incident room. If there was any news, he would be there ready. He lived alone, and with no pets, he was free to do as he pleased.

At 6 a.m., Sanders was awoken by the incident room becoming active again. He'd managed to sleep for three hours and was rudely poked by Chief Superintendent Clark.

'Sanders, in my office.'

Wondering what he'd buggered up this time, he eased his aching body from the couch and followed his boss.

As they stepped inside the office, the bright light from the window made Sanders squint, and after blinking furiously and attempting to straighten himself, he sat down.

'What the hell is going on? I have turned up this morning to find out that you've had a grandmother and a doctor in the incident room drinking a hundred cups of tea and coffee and filling the investigation board with notes.'

He was well aware that Sanders never did anything by the book. However, the man still had to be brought into line at times, and the incident room was entirely off limits to the public, as, of course, Sanders knew very well.

Sanders ran his tongue around his teeth and smiled. It must have been a hundred cups as well because all he could taste was stale tea and coffee. 'Um, yes, Gov. We have a dangerous psychopath on the run, two dead bodies – as well you know – and a whole fucking family on the hit list.'

Clark looked particularly well; his break had left him sun-kissed and rosy-cheeked. 'Hit list?'

'Look, Gov, I need a shower, and, yes, another cup of tea, but listen. Dionne Mason is somewhere out there and more bleeding dangerous than the fucking Hiroshima bomb at the moment. Dr Renee and Dionne's mother, Mrs Stuart, are helping us to put the pieces together, to be one step ahead. This ain't no fantasy idea of scheming to find a serial killer, like hunting down Hannibal Lecter. This is real.'

Clark sat back and pressed his fingers together in contemplation. 'Sanders, I hope you know what you're doing. I have four officers standing around scratching their nuts and countless others all assigned to track her down, and they're all signed off by you. I just hope you weren't taking advantage, or on the piss, while I was on my break.'

With a heavy sigh, Sanders replied, 'Gov, you may think that—'

He didn't finish. Forbes ran into the office, out of breath. 'Gov, she has struck again. Dr Reeves was murdered, found by the cleaner this morning.'

Both Clark and Sanders almost bounced off their seats and hurried back to the incident room.

Forbes was already putting his arms into his jacket, ready to escort Sanders to the scene.

'No, Forbes, you wait here. I want Dr Renee brought back in. I want every available officer from the force assigned to track Mrs Mason down. I want her credit cards, bank cards, even her fucking gym membership checked. I want her found and now,' Clark ordered.

He nodded to Sanders.

There was a measure of respect there that Sanders hadn't seen from his boss until this moment.

'Sorry, you carry on. See what forensics have over at the clinic and then get back here.'

Clark flicked the tail of his jacket aside, placed a hand on his hip, and paced the floor.

'And, Sanders, get them to hurry up. I want everything, every shred of a clue in this room up on that board. I want the officers looking after the entire Mason family upgraded to three. And make sure the boys don't go out. You know what teenagers are like. They think they're invincible.'

Sanders nodded, pleased that his boss was upping the game.

Officer Briggs, a man in his late forties, with a cocky attitude and a smug face, had recently transferred from Croydon. He stood in the incident room with his shoulders back and a self-satisfied smirk plastered across his face. 'And knowing the Masons, they'll think they can take her on. They are no small fry. With their club and illegal activities constantly shoved under our noses – and nothing we can do about it – well, this may be our chance, since their eyes will be well and truly off the ball. We can uncover what they're really up to inside The Allure. Money laundering, I reckon.'

'What did you say?' spat Sanders, with a look of complete contempt.

Briggs looked distinctly uncomfortable in his own skin. 'I was just thinking two birds, Gov, one stone.'

'Well, do yaself a fucking favour and *don't* think. Let me do the thinking, and you do what you're told!'

Sanders turned his collar up and mumbled under his breath. 'Fucking Croydon twat.'

Embarrassed, Briggs lowered his gaze. He assumed the Bromley police were idiots. He hadn't considered that Sanders was no fool and his methods may not be by the book. But he, himself, was like a bloodhound. To redeem himself, he offered to take over from one of the duty police at the Masons' place.

On his way out, Sanders stopped in his tracks, turned on his heel, and strode towards Briggs. 'No, actually, I want you to study the board and make a list of anyone who Dionne Mason could have a grudge with. And I mean anyone – school friends, former work colleagues. Also, check if any of them are missing. For all we know, these murders may be the first of a whole series.'

Briggs hated computer work; he would much rather be on the road or interrogating suspects.

* * *

The clinic had been closed for the day. Samantha Kidman was inconsolable. Her eyes were red from crying, and she had been taken to the police van outside the premises. The police wanted to keep the entrance clear for the forensics team to seal off the entire clinic.

The cleaner, Lita, a small Filipino, was being questioned.

Pulling up in the driveway, he could see the lady was shaken. He hurried over and asked her one question. 'Did you touch anything?'

She looked terrified. 'N-No, I opened the door, and found him there, with blood all around him. I was too frightened to go in. I hurried back to the road in case whoever killed him was still in there, and then I called the police.'

Sanders looked at the officer who had been questioning her. 'Okay, please take her home.' He placed a hand on her arm. 'Thank you. You've been very helpful. You don't need to stay.'

His attention turned to the tall young blonde woman who was sitting in the police car. As he opened the door, he could see then how distraught she was. 'Have the officers taken your details?'

She nodded, and her whole body shook as she sobbed. 'Who would do this? Guy was such a good man, you know, a real gentleman. He would never hurt anyone.'

Sanders nodded. 'I know. I met him. He *was* very much a gentleman. Look, I don't think there's any need for you to be here. Please, let one of the officers take you home. If you think of anyone who may have been hanging around, any unusual visitors, call me. Here's my card.'

She nodded furiously. 'I will. I just can't think straight, right now. I said goodbye to him yesterday. He was coming to see you, and that was the last I saw of him. Oh my God, it's so awful.'

He nodded to another officer to take her home.

* * *

Never before had Sanders really felt much when he'd seen a corpse, unless, of course, it was a youngster, but this time it was different. He'd liked Guy, so he hadn't tried to be polite when he said he was a gentleman. A strange feeling gripped him; this situation was darker than any other he'd been involved in, and the thought that a seemingly innocent young woman could carry out such atrocities deeply disturbed him. He took one last look at the claret covering the body of Guy Reeves. *What a waste and what a shame*, he thought.

His attention was distracted by the sound of car wheels on the gravel drive. He turned and smiled. It was Josh Stark and the SOCO team ready to get to work. Josh got out of his car and headed straight towards Sanders and nodded in acknowledgement. 'The same killer, then?'

With a heavy sigh, Sanders replied, 'Unbelievable, eh? A woman, capable of this. Jesus, it makes no sense.'

Josh frowned. 'Are you sure, Lewis?'

'I detect an air of doubt, Josh.'

'Hmm, yes. Only, whoever killed Luke Mason needed to have some force behind them. The weapon used was blunt. It *looked* sharp, though, but, inside, his injuries were not as clean as one would first imagine. The stomach, liver, and lungs were puckered before they were torn. There was no clean slice, and it would have taken a great deal of force. We are not that easy to penetrate. Muscles get in the way.'

'I have known many a woman to stab their ol' man.'

Josh raised his eyebrows. 'But how hard is it to skewer meat with a blunt skewer? Think about that next time you invite me over for a barbecue.'

An officer opened the door to the clinic, and Stark stepped inside, followed by Sanders.

'Early to tell, I know, but do you think this was done by the hands of the same killer?'

Kneeling carefully, so as not to disturb the black pool of blood, Stark moved the man's bloody shirt up to his neck. Using his long plastic tool, he exposed the entry wound. Standing up, he pulled a small camera from his pocket and took a picture. Then he scrolled back to the photo he'd taken of Luke Mason and compared the entry wounds. They were identical. He leaned towards Sanders. 'What do you think?' asked Stark, showing him the screen on his digital camera.

'That looks like it was almost measured out. Surely, if you were going to use an implement to kill someone, you would never be that precise?'

'And you wouldn't be so lucky as to strike in exactly the same place either, Lewis.'

'Josh, I need help with this one. The killer, if, of course, we have the right woman, is high-functioning and super intelligent, and so she'll not leave any obvious clues. Therefore, anything you find questionable, no matter how small, please let me know.'

'Are you talking about the woman in the car outside Mr and Mrs Mason's house yesterday? I'm assuming that was Luke Mason's wife.'

'Yeah, why?' questioned Sanders.

'I don't know, but did you see the sculpture of her in the garage? A real piece of work, that is.'

Sanders glared. 'No, I didn't see it. I just wanted to turn the bloody hose off before it destroyed any evidence, and I guess my eyes were drawn to the body on the floor. So what's this sculpture thing about, then?'

'Well, you know me. I love a good piece of art. The statue or sculpture jumped out at me right away, because, for a second, it was as if there was another woman in the room. It was so lifelike and brilliant, and I *mean* brilliant. The detail was so intricate that it drew me in. But I'm guessing you didn't turn the centre light on in the garage because it bloody lit the statue up and illuminated it. Between you and me, Lewis, I was spooked at first. It's eerie, I tell you. Oh, hang on. I took a picture. Look at this.' Stark scrolled back to the photos on his digital camera and stopped at the one of the sculpture.

'There, what do you think?'

He was right; it was in fact quite odd and morbidly beautiful. 'That's Dionne Mason. Well, at least it looks like her.'

'Yes, that's what I thought. An absolute brilliant piece of work.' He sighed. 'Anyway, about this mess. I'll make sure the team are meticulous, and I will get back to you with any results as soon as possible.'

Sanders gave Stark a salute and left.

The drive back to the station was gloomy, the skies dark and depressing, much like his mood. This case was becoming more confusing as the day went on. In particular, that sculpture was almost unholy. Perhaps he'd drunk too much tea, and the stimulants fighting with his tiredness had left his brain in an addled state. Suddenly, a cat shot out in front of him, and he had to brake. The adrenaline felt like needles pricking his skin, and, in that second, he snapped out of his haze and took a new perspective on the situation. *Perhaps Dionne Mason wasn't the chief suspect in these murders. So if not, who could it be?* he wondered. After all, she was still missing, or possibly dead.

Kate Renee was already at the station when Sanders arrived. She looked much like himself – washed out.

He greeted her warmly. 'I am so sorry about Dr Reeves. It must have been a shock.' He could see the pain behind her eyes and knew she was trying to hold it together. 'How did Harley take it? He was a big part of her life as well.'

'She's quiet. A lot has happened. I think she needs Hudson, but one consolation is having her grandmother with her. Oh! Thank you for the extra protection.' She smiled. 'Harley has already beaten one of the officers at chess three times.'

Sanders nodded. 'But what about you? Do you still feel able to help us?'

'As you may know, I worked with Guy for years, on and off. He did so much for the future of mental health. He was a very well-respected man and a dear friend. So, of course, I will, for the sake of another life, do everything I can to help.'

With a sympathetic smile, Sanders escorted her to the incident room, where she was met with fresh faces. He politely introduced everyone and then made it very clear that they were listening to her, and they should take what she said exceptionally seriously, as this wasn't the USA, where a criminal profiler was attached to every serial killer investigation. So, Dr Renee, he told them, was a key player in this case.

All eyes were on him as he wrote notes on the board for everyone to see. They included the vital point that the killer was exceptionally strong and had not only made almost a carbon copy of the second murder but they must have got their hands on another long tool and inflicted the same fatal wound. He then added question marks and turned to Renee. 'Are you so sure that this is Dionne Mason's work?'

Twisting her head to see the scribbled notes, she slowly pushed herself up from her seat and walked towards the board. No one said a word. They all just stared, including Sanders. He watched her demeanour change. It was as if she'd suddenly seen a ghost. As her eyes shifted from one piece of information to the other, Sanders could see she was gluing the pieces together.

She turned to face the team, with her hand over her mouth, her eyes wide in shock.

'What?' urged Sanders.

'Oh my God. We have it all wrong.' She picked up the marker pen and circled the words 'imaginary friend' and 'host'. Then she underlined the words – 'precision wound identical in both victims'.

'What is it, Doctor?'

'I have a strong feeling that this friend is *not* imaginary. Dionne Mason is symbiotic, so she needed a host when Jenny died or was killed. She needed another host – an accomplice – or as kids would say a sidekick, but she needed one like her, with the same mentality. I should have guessed, when her mother mentioned that she would often go out alone and come back in good spirits. Why? Because she didn't need her *own* family: she had someone she could relate to – someone like her.'

'Any idea who that could be?'

Renee looked at the board again and focused on the words 'fascination with anatomy'.

'It's someone older, much older. It's someone who could have been teaching her. I never could get to the bottom of her depth and breadth of knowledge around the human body. I probably should have explored it more. But this host could be a teacher of sorts.'

The quiet, shocking atmosphere was cut with a knife when Briggs jumped up. 'Gov, she's used her credit card.'

'When and where?'

'At 2 a.m. at a fuel station in bloody Hastings.'

'Right, Briggs. Organise for the footage from the CCTV camera to be emailed over and check the picture to see if it is her,' ordered Sanders.

Pulling his mobile from his back pocket, Sanders called Josh Stark. 'Do you know the time of death for Dr Reeves?'

'Yep. It was between 2 a.m. and 2.30 a.m.'

'Thanks, buddy. Speak soon.' With that, he placed his phone in his back pocket, ran his hands through his hair, and looked at Renee, who was eager to know what was going on.

'You were right. She's either innocent, or she has a friend as dark as her, because *if* it's her on the CCTV footage at 2 a.m., then we have another killer on our hands.'

'She has planned this deliberately, you know. She wanted to be seen at that time, to put her out of the picture. She knows who the killer is. Why 2 a.m.? Why not 1 a.m., or even 4 a.m., for example? No, she's playing a game now.'

'Kate, would you be so kind as to work with the team? I'm going to pay the Masons a visit. They've been part of her life for many years, so they may have some idea if she has a so-called friend.'

* * *

Sanders parked up on the roadside opposite what appeared to be a sizeable property belonging to the Mason family. On either side of the long drive stood tall trees and thick bushes. The front lawn appeared pristine as if it had been cut with a pair of scissors, with each blade of grass no more than a centimetre high. Sanders sat back, impressed, and admired the various coloured bricks and wide wooden exposed timbers on the facade. The chunky oak door, with a small pillared veranda, had two long windows on either side, and in front of the door there was a red flagstone doorstep. To the right, there was a double garage separate from the house; it was built like a log cabin. The garage was larger than his own dwelling.

Clearly, crime does pay, he thought. The Masons had money and plenty of it. They were not to be underestimated. Sanders knew they were involved in serious organised crime. Without the tip-off, they'd never have caught Luke Mason and have had him bang to rights.

As he walked towards the property, a police car was parked in the drive for all to see, as a warning. WPO Mary Cruickshank answered the door. 'Morning, Gov.'

She took him into a large and airy lounge.

Dean Mason looked up and frowned. 'Please don't give us any more bad news.'

'Gov, this is Dean Mason,' stated Cruickshank.

Shaking Mr Mason's hand, he said, 'I'm DCI Sanders. I'm very sorry for your loss, and, no, I haven't come with bad news, but it's not good either, I'm afraid. Mr Mason, do you think your family are up to talking with me?'

Chewing his lip, Dean got up from his seat. 'If we can help, we will. I'll call them in.'

Sanders flicked his head for Cruickshank to leave. He wanted to be alone to get a sense of the sentiments of the family – to gauge the dynamics.

As Sanders waited for Dean Mason to return, he heard mumblings, possibly from the kitchen. Surveying the room, he looked at the photos everywhere, each one in an expensive frame. He focused on just one on a side table: it showed Dionne Mason in her wedding dress standing next to Luke. Carefully holding the photo in his hands, he stared at her face, hoping to find something about the real Dionne Mason, formerly Stuart. She looked like any woman would on her wedding day, but was that a happy smile or a conceited grin?

'I should throw that bloody thing in the bin!' came the husky voice of a middle-aged woman.

Sanders returned the photo to the cabinet and pivoted to face Miriam Mason. Behind her, he assumed, was Archi, and then Geoff appeared. Their eyes were filled with pain and anger. Sanders knew the stages of grief and how it affected people differently. Some cried, some remained quiet, and others, like the Masons, were angry.

They all took their seats and Miriam gestured for Sanders to join them. 'So Mr . . . ?'

'Detective Chief Inspector Sanders, but call me Lewis. I'm not here to interrogate you guys, so, please, don't feel you're on trial.'

'Have ya found that bitch yet? 'Cos, Lewis, if ya don't, and I do, I'll kill her meself. As God is my fucking witness, I'll rip her head clean off her shoulders,' replied Miriam, in a caustic tone.

Archi patted her shoulder. 'Leave it, Mir. You can see the man's got a job to do, and you can't make threats, my gal.'

'It's no fucking threat, Archi. It's a bleedin' promise.'

Archi searched Sanders' face to see if he was a jobsworth and would read the riot act to her for making threats to kill his daughter-in-law.

'Well, let's hope *we* track her down. I have all available officers on it. I would love to say she won't get far, but she's reached as far as Hastings, we believe. Right, here's the thing. We believe from the evidence that she had something to do with it, but we also suspect someone else is involved.'

Sanders clocked the look of shock on their faces and held his hand up before they all began to bombard him with questions.

'The twins, your grandchildren's psychiatrist, Dr Reeves, was murdered at around 2 a.m. this morning at the same time as Dionne Mason was on CCTV footage in Hastings. We're just awaiting the pictures to confirm it's definitely her. You'll know very well that we don't give out our information, we collect it, but, in this case, I want you to know everything, in the hope that you may be able to shed light on anything that may help us, and I mean anything. Dionne is a psychopath. She was under a psychiatrist herself as a child. She stopped seeing the shrinks and went off the radar, so to speak, but this is where you may be able to come in. Lillian Stuart has had minimal contact with Dionne over the last ten years, and so she hasn't been able to tell us much. However, you were obviously a big part of her life, so we now need your help.'

Sanders waited for them to absorb the information; he knew it would take some time before these latest developments sank in.

'Do you have any idea who else is involved?' asked Geoff.

'We think it's a man, because of the strength needed to murder the victims . . . Oh Christ, I'm sorry. I mean your son Luke and Dr Reeves. I can sound cold at times. Please, forgive me.'

Miriam's eyes filled up again, thinking of her Luke. The news had hit them all hard, and they were finding it so difficult to comprehend everything. No one knew what to believe. Having to come to terms with the possibility that Hudson had killed Scarlett was one thing, but now finding Dionne was also in the frame – and for two further killings – it was all too much.

'Not Harley or Hudson then?'

Sanders nodded at Geoff. 'No, Mr Mason, and why would you still think that now?'

He shrugged his shoulders and looked at his parents. 'Well, like I said to you before. They're strange, they aren't normal. It's hard to describe, but, trust me, I wouldn't be surprised if they are behind all of this.'

Miriam cried openly, and Archi shoved a tissue under her nose. 'They are different, but I never believed for one minute that our Hudson would do such a thing.'

'For fuck's sake, Muvver,' said Geoff, with a raised voice. 'Why can't you open your eyes and see them for what they are? They ain't right in the head.'

Sanders felt the tension rising. This family was not just suffering a loss, they were being ripped apart.

Dean got up and leaned against the back of his chair. 'Muvver, he's right. The twins *are* mental.'

'Don't be so bloody cruel. They're your niece and nephew. Imagine what they are going through right now. Some evil bastard, possibly to do with their own bleedin' mother, has killed their father.'

Sanders could see Dean Mason's face had noticeably tightened. It was clear that he wanted to argue the point and was biting his tongue to keep his mouth shut.

Geoff just shook his head. 'Muvver, they are under a psychiatrist themselves, not a bloody psychologist. They have *mental* issues, and I wouldn't put it past one of them or both to have killed the shrink. Jesus, Muvver, open your eyes, will ya?'

Sanders coughed delicately. 'Harley and Hudson could not have murdered Dr Reeves because they were in a safe place under police watch.'

Sanders assessed right away that Geoff and Dean had it in their heads that the twins were in some way involved. However, while the twins seemed to have a dark side to them, their whereabouts were accounted for at the time of Dr Reeves' murder.

Turning to Geoff Mason, Sanders said, 'Dionne has deliberately put it in your mind, Mr Mason, that the twins were responsible, because, as her psychiatrist pointed out, she will give you the impression she's an innocent victim, and yet she's very manipulative and cunning. So she cannot be underestimated, and also, to add fuel to the fire, she's a class act at disguising her emotions. Her emotions are fake; she can turn them on and off at the flick of a switch.'

Geoff shifted his eyes towards the floor.

Sanders guessed then that he had some guilt somewhere in the back of his mind.

'So what I need you to do is to try and remember if you've seen Dionne with a friend, a confidante, someone she would meet. We think it could be a man.'

'I knew it! I bet she was seeing someone. I begged my Luke to kick her to the fucking kerb, the no-good slut.'

Sanders nodded. 'Why, Mrs Mason, did you think she was seeing someone? Did you ever see him?'

'No, I never saw him, but she was so secretive, it's hard to explain. But I never saw her with friends as such, apart from a handful of snooty bitches, but, even then, I don't think they were friends. Yet she was always out and about and telling my Luke she was this someone's friend or that someone's friend, but, of course, Luke had never met them. At our summer barbecues, she never invited her so-called friends, even though Luke encouraged her to, all except her mate, Josey, the bridesmaid at the wedding. The poor cow, she was being bossed about by Dionne. She married my Luke for . . .' Swallowing back the tears, Miriam took a deep breath. 'She married him for his money. She never loved him. I know for a fact she never. Dionne turned my stomach when she first met him. She was all over him, and I know he wasn't interested at first, but, then, her persistence paid off, as if she'd cast a fucking spell. He was like a lapdog, trying to please her at every turn. Then, she moved into his house and started spending his money by turning his home into *her* home. She changed the decor, the furniture, and was racking up heavy bills. My Luke was working day and fucking night to please that . .

.' Miriam stopped and sighed. She looked over at her two sons. 'My Luke was the tough one out of them. They'll tell ya. He was the hardest of the three.'

Sanders turned his attention to Dean Mason. 'I've heard the rumours he had a temper.'

'That's an understatement. My brother could take out any man, if he was in a rage. As much as I loved Luke, he wasn't like Geoff and me. He was the serious one. He always wore a blank look and very rarely laughed unless he was with his kids. That was when he seemed more relaxed. But Mum's right: he didn't take any shit from anyone,' said Dean.

'So,' Miriam continued, 'as you can imagine, Lewis, when my Luke was acting like a fucking lovesick teenager pandering to her every fucking whim, it pissed me off because I knew, I fucking knew, she didn't love him. When she wasn't looking, I watched her face change. She looked almost repulsed by him, if he hugged her or showed her any affection. Not like Scarlett, God rest her soul, or our Tilly. Nope, she was cold, and, as you say, Lewis, she could be very cunning.'

Wanting some facts, he pushed Miriam again. 'Did you ever see her with anyone, anyone at all?'

She clicked her finger. 'Well, yes, I did. Well, no, not a person, but, years ago, before my Luke got arrested, I saw her just up the road from her house. She got out of a car. Now, I thought back then it was strange. I mean, if someone dropped you off near your home, why wouldn't you ask them to pull into the drive? So, anyway, I mentioned it to my Luke, who was probably getting fed up with me always moaning about her spending money and disappearing on her mysterious shopping sprees or her cocktail evenings with her snotty friends. He shrugged me off. I think he was working too hard by then. It was the time when he was waiting to adopt, and so his mind was on other things. Of course, I pulled her up about it. She laughed in my face, would you believe. And she had the fucking *audacity* to say she was saving on the cab fare! I said to her, "Often get the *same* cab, do you?" 'Cos, although she never knew it, I'd seen her jump in that black car before and never thought much of it. Nevertheless, Luke wasn't bothered, so I shut up about it in the end.'

'Would you by any chance remember the car at all?'

She didn't have to think. 'Yes, I do. It was a black Audi.'

'What?' snapped Geoff and Dean, in unison.

Removing his jacket, Sanders made himself comfortable. 'What was so special about a black Audi?'

Dean explained that before Luke was arrested, they'd clocked an Audi parked up that had been following one of their employees. He couldn't say to the detective that they were really gunrunners. At the time, they'd assumed it was the police and the reason for Luke's arrest.

Sanders could tell that Dean Mason was looking somewhat shifty at that point. Straightaway, he made it clear that he'd no interest in any of their business interests. He was at their home purely to solve three murders, and nothing more.

'Could you think of anywhere she would go in Hastings?'

Geoff remembered Scarlett's parents' cottage in Winchelsea that wasn't far from Hastings. He shook his head, as did the rest of the family. Of course they would never have thought of that place. Geoff felt his heart beating so fast, his cheeks were flushing, but he had to keep calm and wait for the detective to leave, and then he would do some searching himself.

Sanders got up from his chair to leave. 'I need to head back to the station, but if you can think of anything else, no matter how small, please don't hesitate to call me. And, trust me, we are doing all we can to find her.'

* * *

Assured that Sanders had left, Geoff asked for another sleeping tablet, making the excuse he needed to sleep again. No one noticed him sneak out of the back door. The officers on watch were at the front of the house. So after climbing over the neighbour's side fence, he hurried through to their front garden and onto the road where he had parked his car. He could see Sanders hadn't pulled away just yet, so he waited.

* * *

Sanders tapped his back pocket and found his phone was missing; he'd left it in the car again. By the time he had started his engine, the phone was bleeping with messages. He stared down at the number. Not recognising it, he listened to his voicemail. 'Detective, it's Samantha Kidman from Dr Reeves' clinic. You said to call you if I remember anything. Well, it may be nothing, but yesterday morning when I arrived for work, there was a man . . . Oh, um, it sounds stupid, now I think about it. He was standing across the road from the clinic. When I stared back at him, he hurried away, well, limped away. Sorry. It's probably nothing.' The call ended.

Wasting no time, Sanders called her back.

She answered right away, obviously recognising the number. 'Hello, Detective. I'm sorry. I hope I'm not wasting your time, am I?'

'No, not at all, Miss Kidman. Can you describe this man for me?'

'Yes, I can because he looked so strange. He was roughly sixty years old. He was a big man, probably six foot plus and wide. I wouldn't like to guess his weight, but, without being rude, he was a lot bigger than you.'

Sanders was a size himself, a good forty-six-inch chest, and, sadly, a belly to go with it. 'Any other distinguishing marks?'

'He had dark hair brushed behind his ears, but it was his eyes. They were dark and . . . well, it's hard to explain. He looked angry, his forehead was thick, almost as thick as a Neanderthal, and yet he was wearing a very smart black suit. I don't know, it's as if his face didn't fit the suit. I only noticed him because it was early and there was no one around. The gates were locked, so I had to open them. I was conscious he was across the road, and I felt uneasy, you know, being alone, so rather than keep my back to him, I turned to face him, and that's when he hurried away, but, as I said, he hobbled away. He seemed to be dragging one of his feet.'

'Did you see him get into a car, or . . . ?'

'No, once he was out of sight, I hurried into the clinic. To be honest, I wouldn't have mentioned it because I'm a worrywart, anyway, and, stupidly, I'm addicted to horror films, so, anyone who appears like Freddy Krueger or Michael Myers always gives me the creeps.'

'Did he look like Freddy Krueger, then?'

'No, he just seemed dark and intimidating. Perhaps because of his size and his cold expression.'

'Thank you, Miss Kidman. You have been a real help. I promise you, you haven't wasted my time. The opposite, in fact.'

* * *

As soon as he saw Sanders drive away, Geoff sighed with relief. He had to head home to collect a tool, a grey sweatshirt identical to the one he was wearing, another pair of Levi's, and white trainers.

CHAPTER TWENTY-THREE

Visibly seething, Dionne drove back towards the cottage. She was angry that he'd spoken to her that way, as if she was a naughty schoolgirl. He'd demanded that she went to a cash machine bang on 2 a.m., no earlier, and no later, and not to go back to the cottage. She was sick of it, doing as she was told, month in, month out. She wasn't a child; she was her own person. And she sure as hell didn't need him anymore.

Scarlett was dead, and so was Luke. Geoff could have been hers; he should have been hers. There was no one to stand in her way, except her children, but with them locked away, her life would be perfect: her house, the money, and her Geoff. With every breath, her jaw clenched tighter; her patience was wearing thin, and the anger was rising to a pitch. She had to stay in control and not slip up again.

The dark sky and the howling wind would normally calm her temper. She loved the wind – the way it took no prisoners – ripping the leaves from the trees, the tiles from the rooftops, and how as an invisible force it could cause so much devastation. Pulling up outside the quaint cottage, she stared at the front door and thought back to her time with Geoff – the power of the man as he took her like the wind itself and ravished her body.

Her lips tightened and her eyes twitched. 'Fuck you! All of you!' she bellowed, as rage coiled around her stomach. Visions of Miriam, Archi, and the boys – all the boys – lying dead in pools of blood, or their headstones all in a row, would be her only comfort. There had to be no one left to come between her and Geoff. She watched the leaves fiercely whirling around as if a mini tornado had just whizzed by. She smiled to herself. One by one, she could easily pick the Masons off. Jenny, Kenny, and the others had been a walk in the park, and she'd been so young then.

But she was a grown woman now. She would do things *her* way, not *his* way. He'd put the thoughts in her head. He'd been the one who told her to marry Luke. But she'd wanted Geoff. She could have killed Scarlett years ago, and there would have been no one to stop her, but, oh no, she went along with his wishes and married Luke instead.

'Damn you. Why did I tell you about the police interview? I should have kept my mouth shut. Now you, *the voice of reason*, are making me even doubt myself,' she said out loud. But she had told him, and he'd made her feel like she had failed, and it had then forced her to go over the conversation she'd had with DCI Sanders a hundred times in her head, questioning herself.

Would DCI Saunders have recognised that she had deliberately implicated her daughter? Had she overdone the seed planting. Even if he had realised that was the case, what was her excuse for not returning to her home? She could cross that bridge, if questioned. She would say she went for a drive because she was so consumed in grief. Besides, people do all sorts, once they are bereft. Her own parents changed when they were grieving. She wondered just for a moment what it was like to grieve. She could only liken it to having something taken away that she wanted. Yet it had never happened to her. Except for not having Geoff. She wanted Geoff. But she knew she wasn't allowed to have him. Maybe it was Geoff who had actually brought her in touch with an emotion that she'd never experienced before. It was addictive, a calling, a longing.

She stared at the front door of the cottage and removed the key from the ignition. Perhaps she could phone him. In her dark moment of grief for her husband, Geoff would console her. She would have him to herself in the cottage away from everyone. As she slipped out of the car and breathed in the cold air, she cleared her mind and began to form a plan.

Once inside, she drew the curtains, flicked on the side lamp, put the heating on, and sat in the armchair that was placed close to the fireplace. She needed to get all the doubting thoughts out of her head and think of what she would say if she dialled Geoff's number.

That was it, she would tell him that she had to get away, away from the house and the vision of Luke lying dead in the garage. And she would feed him the idea that her own daughter was responsible. How could she cope with so much heartache in such a small space of time? It was a reasonable notion. He would understand. They could pick up where they'd left off, in each other's arms and with wild, passionate nights in bed. He wouldn't have to think about his dead wife, as he would have her. A noise disturbed her from her thoughts and sent a rush of anger through her veins.

She listened, but there was only silence. Perhaps it was the old floorboards settling after the long hot, dry summer. Closing her eyes, she went over the planned conversation in her head. She could cry, even sob. She knew how he felt losing Scarlett, so they would grieve together, alone. He would understand, surely? The second creak made her open her eyes, annoyed that she was being pulled away from her thoughts just as she was making headway with her plan. She strained her ears once more and looked around the room, but there was nothing to suggest another presence there. Annoyed that she'd been disturbed from her place of comfort, she pushed herself out of the chair and switched on the main light. 'If you are here, then show yourself, damn it!' She spun around, but all that was behind her were the drawn curtains. She stepped into the hallway and looked up at the top of the stairs. 'Show yourself!' she bellowed. The quietness made her mad. 'Fucking show yourself. I ain't afraid of you, whoever you are.'

The hallway mirror caught her eye, and she stared at her own reflection, instantly admiring her soft, smooth skin and her long hair that fell in waves shaping her face. She closed her eyes as she visualised Geoff kissing her. He would stand behind her with his arms around her and gently kiss her cheek while undoing the buttons of her blouse. She looked at her face and smiled, but then her lips fell into a grimace. There at the corners of her eyes were lines. She peered closer and could see from the light in the hallway the thin wrinkles. She couldn't see them in her own bathroom mirror, but the light in here showed them so clearly. Her breathing intensified as she spun around to find something – anything, in fact, to smash the light. Geoff could never see her wrinkles. But there was nothing in sight for her to use. She had to look one more time. Perhaps she was wrong. Again, she stared in the mirror and moved closer, scrutinising those crow's feet. She had to blink twice. Had she just seen a figure lurking in the background? The floorboards began to creak again. He was here; now she could smell him.

Slowly, she turned to face him. Somehow, he seemed bigger than ever, and darker; perhaps it was due to the light, which was diffused through the hallway window.

'I'm surprised, Dionne that you haven't demolished this house.'

She didn't move. His voice seemed different, somehow.

'You're angry, Dionne, aren't you?'

She raised her eyebrows.

'Yes, you are. You're raging, in fact.'

She shook her head. 'No.'

He nodded slowly, deliberately. 'Yes, you are. I can feel the heat coming off you. I can see rage weaving its way through every nerve and muscle fibre. You have lost control.'

His deep voice and firm words pricked an unusual feeling – fear. She was never afraid. She didn't know how to be, but he was the one person who could evoke unease. She tried to shrug off his serious tone. 'No, I'm not angry. Anyway, we don't have time for therapy. What should we do?'

'We?'

'Well, yes, we.'

'There is no "we", Dionne. I was wrong about you . . .' He stared, his eyes cold.

She knew he hadn't finished talking and she dare not interrupt him.

'Being wrong about who you are is the only mistake I've ever made. You do not have the Gemini Gene. You are merely a psychopath. A clever one, but not a genius, not high-functioning, like me.'

'If you don't believe that I possess the Gemini Gene, then why kill Guy Reeves and ensure I was here when you murdered him? Why still bother with me?'

'Because, Dionne, I was protecting myself. He had information that must never be shared with anyone, and the first person they would go to is you. And we both know that you cracked in the interrogation room. You were distracted, Dionne. You told me the conversation you had with the detective, and we both know you messed up. You may be clever, Dionne, but you've let your emotions and impatience get in the way. Emotions, Dionne!'

'No, no, you have it all wrong. That detective is stupid. He'll arrest Harley. The finger is pointed at her. I made sure of that.'

His face took on an expression she'd never seen before. He seemed angry, or perhaps disappointed.

'You were not supposed to implicate Harley – ever!' He stepped forward.

Looking up into his eyes, she spotted the evil Fiend – the Devil – that lurked behind them. 'I had to. I had no choice. Harley and Hudson are surplus to requirements. They're just getting in the way.'

Shaking his head, he coldly replied, 'You should never have implicated Harley as the murderer.'

'Well, it doesn't matter. She is a killer anyway. She killed a guy in my kitchen with my gun.'

'No, she didn't, Dionne. That was me. I came to protect you because, once again, you were distracted. You never noticed a man hanging around or that you had not locked the back door or French doors. And, more seriously, *you* had left a loaded gun for anyone to use. Luckily, it was me who was there to protect you all, or that man could have shot you as you slept. So, frankly, Dionne, your stupid obsession with Geoff is leaving you open to mistakes.'

'No, I wasn't distracted by a bloody obsession!' she bellowed in frustration.

'Look at you, Dionne. Look in the mirror. You are raging. Your nostrils are flared. Your breathing is faster. Your face is red and your jaw is tight.'

In a flash, she spun around and stared at herself. He was right. She could see it, but she had to prove to him that she could control it. Yet that ugly expression on her face and those wrinkles pushed her to a place she had never been before. Like a volcano erupting, she couldn't pull back the reins. Gripping the sides of the huge mirror, she ripped it from the wall and threw it onto the stairs. The ornate wooden banister broke away, and she lunged forward, grabbing a protruding pole and tearing it from the floor. Raising it above her head, she smashed the mirror again and again, until it shattered into a thousand pieces. Then she turned to him, her eyes red, her face taut. 'And you, too, are surplus to requirements.'

Still gripping the pole, she daringly faced him. But he didn't move. He seemed unafraid.

'No, Dionne, *you* are surplus to my requirements.' His eyes narrowed, and his pupils widened, giving his eyes the appearance of black pools of emptiness.

'No! You're wrong . . .'

'I am never wrong.'

'Without me, your work, everything, it will amount to nothing!' she screamed.

'You, Dionne, are narcissistic.' Shaking his head, he huffed, 'Why would you think that *you* are the only one out there who has all the attributes to confirm that the gene, *my* gene' – he poked himself in the chest – 'really does exist?'

She narrowed her eyes in puzzlement. 'What do you mean?'

'You were merely one subject of many. And you have shown me that although I am never wrong, I was wrong about you. You could have been someone, Dionne, a doctor, a scientist, but, no, you just wanted money. Now you just want Geoff, and you were not supposed to be distracted merely by a man. Tell me, did you recognise the psychiatrist at the clinic who, I am guessing, was assisting Dr Reeves? Did she take a blood sample, Dionne?'

Dionne's pulse quickened and a sick feeling came over her. The doctor had been adamant that she should take a blood sample, and, for a moment back then, she'd thought she seemed familiar. *Dr Tavon!* She gasped.

'So, no and yes in that order. Is that right? She was your *psychiatrist*, Dionne, and if you gave her your DNA, then she will also know who you are!'

Unexpectedly, Dionne's stance changed when she heard a car pull up directly outside the cottage. She glanced through the hallway window and her heart skipped a beat: it was Geoff. She watched him get out of the car and look around. Excitedly, she glanced back, but all she saw was the mess she'd made. She was now alone, and the back door was wide open, swinging in the wind.

She didn't have time to do anything except to rely on her instincts. As soon as Geoff opened the front door, she threw herself at him. 'Oh my God, Geoff, I'm so glad you're here. It was awful, so awful. I thought he was going to kill me.'

Geoff grabbed her arms and pushed her away from him. His face was white and his lips were tight as he glared at Dionne and then at the state of the banister and the smashed mirror. His brain couldn't instantly comprehend it all. He'd driven all the way to the cottage, to face the murderous bitch, but he never expected to find her like this, or the cottage wrecked to pieces.

'Geoff, please don't push me away. I was attacked. I was so terrified. Oh my God, who is this man that is after our family, my Luke, your Scarlett, and now me? I'm just relieved that you turned up when you did.'

She looked around her at the shattered glass on the floor. 'God knows what he would have done to me.' She spoke so fast that the words tumbled over one another.

'Who, Dionne, who?' questioned Geoff, with a face like thunder.

'I don't know, Geoff.' She stepped towards him. 'I have no idea, but I do know he wanted to kill me.' Fearing he wasn't believing her, she made puppy-dog eyes at him and put on the waterworks.

Geoff stared unblinkingly as the detective's words 'her emotions are fake' circled his brain. He watched her angelic expression change as if she was pulling faces to get a reaction. She was raising her brow and smiling, giving him her best come-to-bed eyes. He couldn't believe what she was doing. Her husband and his own wife had been murdered, and here she was acting as if they meant nothing. And how could she suddenly look so calm if, as she'd said, she'd just been attacked? A dark, eerie feeling crept over him, and it was at that moment he knew the truth.

'What is it, Geoff? Come on. Please, you know it's always been me and you.'

'What!' he yelled. As if she had a disease, he stepped back. 'Get the fuck away from me.'

She stepped closer. 'No, Geoff, you don't mean that. Come on, you know you love me. You never loved Scarlett, and you know I never loved Luke. It was always meant to be me and you.'

Just the mere mention of Scarlett's name sent Geoff into a rage. 'You disgusting fucking bitch. You evil whore.' As he cursed and called her every name under the sun, she tilted her head to the side, but Geoff was fuming, and, effortlessly, he pulled his fist back and punched her clean in the face. She fell to the ground. But to his horror, she jumped back onto her feet. A fully grown man would be wobbling. He watched her wipe her mouth and smile.

'You didn't mean that, Geoff.'

He was angry and a little uneasy. Instinctively, he threw another punch that should have sent her senseless.

But to his amazement, she got up again, like a jack-in-a-box, and this time she laughed. She should never have done that because the one thing that he found antagonising was being laughed at.

'I'm sorry, Geoff. Look, I mean it. I am so sorry, but it wasn't me. Someone is trying to kill me.' She wiped the blood away from her mouth again as she took a step forward.

When Geoff didn't move, she stepped forward again, but he remained still.

He sighed and held out one arm for her to fall into.

Gladly, she embraced him. 'Oh, Geoff, I missed you so much.' Suddenly, she felt a solid object being thrust into her ribs and her eyes widened. 'No, please, Geoff, please.'

Geoff held her close so that she could not move.

'It's over, Dionne. You should never have killed my wife, and I won't let you loose to kill my sons.'

She didn't even have a chance to answer.

Geoff fired his gun, but before she collapsed, he kissed her on the lips. 'Now die! Bitch!'

CHAPTER TWENTY-FOUR

The serious incident room was hot, and the smell of eagerness was in the air. Sanders had his back to the door and was facing the investigation board. Standing beside him was Dr Renee. They were both staring at the map of South-East London and Kent, while Nelson stuck a pin in Sundridge Park.

Sanders had a file in his hand. 'Nelson, is this the only victim connected to the Stuarts and the Masons who has been found dead in the last fifteen years?'

Nelson nodded. 'Yes, Gov. Briggs and I searched the database. Beverley Childs is the only one.'

Sanders opened the folder and peered at the photo of the stunning woman with long blonde hair. 'Shame, she was a good-looking woman . . . Not that it means anything. And are you sure that there is a connection here with Dionne Mason?'

Sanders was taking a liking to Nelson. He'd noticed that the lad was putting his heart and soul into the case.

'I took the liberty of calling Mrs Miriam Mason, and she confirmed that Luke had once been a close friend of Beverley's, and, apparently, she was visiting him during his time in prison. And, Gov, Dionne Mason may have known about her husband's affair with Beverley Childs. Mrs Mason said it was something to do with visiting order mix-ups.'

Renee nodded. 'If Dionne felt her idea of a life plan was in any way threatened, she would focus on the threat and find a way to remove it. So she could have killed Beverley.'

Sanders looked at the notes. 'It said Beverley fell down a flight of stairs. An accident?'

Renee gave a confirmatory nod. 'Of course, like I said, Dionne is very clever. If she murdered her, she would have ensured it looked like an accident.'

'Gov, can I just add something? I spoke with Beverley's mother on the phone, and she said that it was a terrific shock because Beverley was pregnant at the time – the father of the child was unknown. She wouldn't tell anyone.'

'Thank you, Nelson. Good job, mate,' said Sanders.

Renee walked over to Sanders. 'If Dionne thought for a moment that the child was Luke's, she would have killed her. I'm sure of it. Can I see the photo?'

Sanders flicked through the file and came to the photo taken at the scene. His eyes widened as he stared at the grotesque angle of the woman's head. It was as if her neck was completely snapped and bent so far back it was almost upside down. 'Jesus, this looks horrific!'

Renee leaned into Sanders to see for herself, but Lillian intervened.

'Please, may I look?'

Sanders glanced at Renee, who nodded.

'Lillian, this is particularly gruesome. Are you sure you want to?'

Gripping the sides of the chair and slowly getting to her feet, Lillian took a deep breath. 'My Kenny died from falling down the stairs, as you're aware, but I know there was more to it. Please, let me see.'

Hesitantly, Sanders turned the photo around to show it to Lillian.

Everyone in the room watched her reaction. But there wasn't one. She just stood there silently, her eyes moist with tears. 'That's just how my Kenny looked. His head was twisted back, just like that poor woman's head is.'

Sanders, out of character, put his arm around Lillian's shoulders. 'You've been more help to us than you could possibly imagine. Thank you, sweetheart.'

Lillian sat back down. This time, a tear did begin to trickle down her cheek. 'I have to help. I raised a monster, and so it's my responsibility to help cage her . . . for all our sakes.'

Renee took a seat opposite Lillian, and with her hands clenched together, as if she were praying, she leaned forward. 'I promise you, Lillian, this is not your fault. I'm afraid this isn't about nurture: it's about nature.'

* * *

Forbes was in his office when he took a call from a DCI in Hastings.

'Hi there, it's DCI Rampart. We have been informed that Mrs Dionne Mason, a person of interest, under Operation Wasp, was last in the Hastings area using her credit card.'

'That's correct. What have you found?' said Forbes, jumping up from his seat.

'We received a call from a concerned pensioner who lives in Winchelsea. She informed us that the cottage next door to hers had been empty for over a year, and that she heard an awful lot of banging, smashing, and screaming. I sent two officers over to check it out and we found a woman dead – a gunshot wound. The team are there now, and forensics are on their way. It may be Mrs Mason.'

Forbes held his breath. 'Jesus, are you sure?'

'Well, no, not one hundred per cent, but the car parked outside is registered to a Mrs Dionne Mason. I can have a photo of the dead woman sent over to you.'

'Yes, please, right away, if you can. Was anyone else there at the scene? Is there any CCTV in that area?'

'No, no one was there, and it's a quiet area, so we have no cameras. It's strange because there is evidence of criminal damage inside the house, but the victim had no injuries except from a single gunshot wound.'

'Okay. Thank you.'

Sitting back down, Forbes tapped his fingers on the table while he waited for the email to come through. He was exhausted. This was the first real case of this nature that he'd been involved in, and he was determined to put the hours in, even though his missus had been on the phone moaning that there were chores at home that he still hadn't finished. Working with Sanders was a breath of fresh air because although Lewis didn't follow the rules, he still got things done. It made him wonder if the reason for his own previous failings was due to so much red tape.

With the evidence in his hand, Forbes made his way back to the incident room. Not realising that Lillian was sitting in the corner on their lounge suite, he blurted out, 'Gov, you may as well add another photo. Dionne Mason is dead. They found her at an address in Winchelsea. She's been shot through the chest.'

The room fell silent as they absorbed the information. Their prime suspect was now a victim.

As soon as Forbes realised Lillian was there, he gasped, 'Oh, Christ! Forgive me. I'm so sorry.'

Sanders instantly took a seat next to Lillian. 'I'm so sorry, love. When all's said and done, I know she was still your daughter.'

Lillian tapped Sanders' knee. 'She wasn't my daughter. She was evil, and so please don't get all soppy about me. I'm all right, love.' She paused and took a deep breath. 'I want to 'elp, if I can, or, as Gawd is my witness, I'll never sleep again.'

'Let's get you back to Dr Renee's house. Harley needs you.'

Lillian was about to protest, but Sanders gave her a sad smile.

'Lillian, you've been brilliant, but you're tired and you need a break. I'll get one of the officers to take you there. As I've just said, Harley will need you all the more now. I should imagine she's feeling just as anxious and confused.'

Lillian nodded. 'Yes, you're probably right, but I'll be back tomorrow, just in case you need me.'

* * *

As the day turned into evening, the team worked tirelessly trying to put the pieces together, but nothing made any sense. The murders were all focused on Dionne Mason, and now she was dead.

* * *

It was 7 a.m. Renee had slept on the couch in the incident room, and Sanders had caught forty winks on the sofa in the Chief Superintendent's room. The bright morning light shone on his face and woke him up. He stretched and rubbed his eyes, but when Nelson appeared with what looked like a wash bag and a cup of coffee, he was pleasantly surprised.

'I hope you don't mind, Gov, but I thought you might like to freshen up.' He handed Sanders a drawstring bag.

Sitting upright, Sanders gave the young man a generous smile.

'Thank you, mate. I think I could do with a brush-up. I reek.'

Nelson nodded and laughed. 'There's shower gel, a razor, a toothbrush, oh, and deodorant.'

Sanders chuckled. 'I must be stinking the incident room right out.'

'Yep.' Nelson laughed, with the confidence that, so far, he'd gained Sanders' trust enough to banter.

'How's everything?'

Nelson wondered what Sanders was actually asking him. 'Er . . . Well, we're still going over the details of Dionne's murder. We've got the local bobbies in Winchelsea scouring the area, calling on neighbours. You know, the usual.'

Sanders sipped his coffee. 'I meant with you, Brett. I've noticed how hard you've been working, and once this is over, I'll be reporting your good efforts back to the Superintendent.'

Nelson's cheeks flushed bright red. 'Thank you, Gov.'

* * *

Half an hour later, Sanders was back in the incident room refreshed and ready to get cracking. He sat opposite Renee, who was not so tidy in her appearance. Her hair obviously hadn't seen a brush, yet, still, Sanders was grateful that she was giving the team so much of her valuable time. He watched as she appeared to be deep in thought.

'Lewis, you're probably going to tell me my job here is done since Dionne is now dead, but I really would like to stay and help, if I can.' She smiled. 'Sad as it all is, I know that if I go home and try to put this behind me, I will grieve . . .' She paused and swallowed hard, trying to stop the tears from welling up. 'I will have to enter a world of reality, grieving for

Guy, and comforting his lovely wife, but I'm just not ready for that. I feel too attached to this case. I'm not ready to let go.'

For the first time, Sanders noticed that underneath Kate's strict professional demeanour there was a softer woman, with eyes that held a sweetness. He stared probably longer than he should have and then blinked. 'Er . . . Yes, of course, Kate. I've a feeling that we'll need your help, and as the detective leading this case, I feel like you're my crutch at the moment.'

He winked and watched her face light up. Her smile was endearing and made her look very attractive in an unassuming way.

Knowing this wasn't the time or place to get drawn into any awkward tension between them, Kate looked away. In her eyes, Lewis was a handsome manly man. But she was tired. Perhaps she'd just read too much into that wink. She hoped it meant more, but she couldn't go down that road again of thinking that anyone would be attracted to her.

* * *

An hour later, with the incident room quieter than usual, Sanders felt it was time to refocus.

'Okay, I'm going to call in Samantha Kidman, to see if she can help us with a photofit of the man she saw. And I want Lillian back in here. We need to find this nutcase before he harms anyone else.'

Suddenly, Renee put her hands to her mouth. 'My God, that's him, the imaginary friend. So he *is* real. Very real, in fact!'

Sanders frowned. 'Yes, but you've already told us that.'

'No, I mean, he isn't just a friend like a Fred and Rosemary West duo. He needs a host. He's the parasite. This was no symbiotic relationship. He's following the same pattern as I naturally assumed Dionne did. This imaginary friend is the psychopath. He's been in her life since the age of seven – he's been grooming her!' Her voice became excitable. 'Somehow, I don't know how, he knew she had social disorders. He needed someone clever, with no empathy, no natural emotion. But he had to have some kind of gain.'

For the first time in the investigation, Sanders felt as though he wasn't in control of events. That baton of responsibility seemed to have been passed on to Kate Renee. He needed to keep pace with her before he lost where she was going altogether.

'What would be his gain?'

'Perhaps it isn't a gain at all. It could be a need,' she replied, tapping her lip. 'You said that this man Samantha had seen had a limp. That could be a reason. He might be losing his strength. He's getting old. Perhaps he's injured or . . .' She paused. 'Or he just wanted to leave a legacy, like when we want to leave this world knowing our children will pass on what we've taught them.'

As Forbes entered the room, he caught the tail end of the conversation.

'But what did he want to pass on? Because it looks to me as though it's possible Dionne Mason didn't kill anyone. It was probably this nutter, and, maybe, his fixation was on her,' stated Forbes, feeling he'd learned so much from Kate that he could confidently participate in the discussion.

Renee was about to reply when a voice from behind Forbes spoke.

'No, she *was* a killer. She killed my Jenny. I know she did. And she also killed my Kenny.'

It was Lillian. She'd arrived only moments before, eager to help.

'I know you should be resting, love. But thank goodness you are here.' Sanders' tone was sympathetic as he clocked the weary expression on her face.

Forbes stepped aside, allowing Lillian to enter the room. 'Lewis, Lillian wants to help.'

Renee smiled. 'Are you up to this, Lillian?'

She nodded. 'I'm more ready than I ever was. Harley has been telling me how heartless Dionne was. She was cruel in such a devious way. I mean, the poor kid can't stand the colour yellow. It makes her feel ill. Dionne knew that, so she would punish Harley by making her wear yellow or buy her a toy that was yellow, just to get a reaction when they had visitors. I tell ya, my girl messed those two kiddies' heads up. So, for their sakes, I'll do whatever it takes.'

Renee glanced at the board and then back at Lillian. 'May I ask, it's probably nothing, but you mentioned earlier this death smell, as you put it. Can you explain it to me again?'

Lillian shuffled in her seat. She appeared uncomfortable. 'It's hard to describe, but it's a sweet, sickening smell. I have smelled it a few times, and, sadly, when Jenny and Kenny died, and as I said, when I passed that coffin, I've always assumed it's a psychological thing.'

Renee pulled up a chair and sat opposite Lillian. 'Think carefully. Where did Dionne learn about anatomy?'

Staring into space, Lillian tried to recall, but, instead, she just shook her head. 'I've no idea.'

'And this sweet, sickening smell. Did you ever smell it at any other time?'

Lillian nodded. 'Yes, sometimes if Dionne came home late, I would get a waft, but she wore perfume, and so I pushed it to the back of my mind. I mean, these modern perfumes ain't nothing like the white linen and musk.'

'One last question, Lillian. Have you ever been to a funeral parlour, a chapel of rest, by any chance?'

As if a light bulb went off in her head, Lillian's eyes widened, and she threw her hands to her mouth. 'My mother! I went to see her body at the funeral home. I . . . I was so upset, you see. My little Kenny was a nipper, and she had been such a great help to me. She died unexpectedly. I still miss her now. Yes, that's it. That's the smell. I knew I associated it with death, but I never knew why until now. Oh my Lord.'

Renee's mind was suddenly trying to piece the puzzle together. 'Sorry, Lillian, just one more question, if I may. Were you attacked after your mother died?'

With her bottom lip quivering, Lillian nodded. 'Yes, I was, two weeks after the funeral.'

One of the younger members of the team returned with teas and coffees.

Lillian felt tired again, due to the stress, fear, and guilt. All she could do was answer the questions put to her. Never clever at school, she found it all too much to follow, but the expression on Kate Renee's face gave her a clue that they were definitely onto something.

A buzzing sound could be heard coming from Sanders' phone, which was resting on the table in front of him. Glancing down at the number, one which he didn't recognise, he, nevertheless, decided to press the accept key.

'Mr Sanders, it's Dean Mason here. That black Audi that was mentioned on your visit. I have the registration number. I remembered after you left that I wrote it down on a car park ticket in my car. I've just found the ticket in my glovebox.'

Sanders punched the air. 'Thank you so much, Mr Mason.' He wrote down the details. 'I'll be in touch soon.' With that, he hung up. 'Right, we have a registration number of the Audi. Nelson, run a plate check for me. This could be a red herring, but run it anyway.'

* * *

The artist arrived and took Samantha off to an interview room, and the two of them began to rifle through pictures to try to put a photofit together.

Samantha's memory was remarkable, and between them, they managed to have the work completed in record time.

* * *

Once the drawing was placed on the board, the team felt uneasy. The man wasn't just an ordinary-looking person. Far from it. His features were very distinctive, with his sheer size and darkness across the eyes. The forehead was big and bulbous, and the dark hair parted in the centre was dead straight and combed behind his ears.

Sanders stared for a while, and then he slowly turned his head to see if Lillian recognised the man in the photofit picture.

She had her hands to her mouth, and tears began to flow down her face. She knew him all right.

'Gov! We have an address for the car. It's registered to a Mr Nyall Grant Seymour, 16 Vanbrugh Hill, Greenwich. It's the flat above the funeral directors' place.'

Sanders was still waiting for Lillian to speak. Smiling at her in encouragement, he asked, 'Lillian, who is he?'

Snapping out of her vacancy, she looked up. 'He was the undertaker at my mother's funeral. He was younger back then, but it's definitely him.'

Renee scrutinised the picture as the name Nyall Grant Seymour whirled around her brain. Where did she know that name? She pushed the thought from her mind. Besides, the name 'Seymour' wasn't exactly uncommon.

CHAPTER TWENTY-FIVE

An armed response unit headed to the Greenwich address; it was followed by Sanders and Forbes.

'I swear, Lewis, you need to retake your bleedin' test or get some glasses.'

'If I buy glasses, I'm admitting I'm old, so buckle up and let's make sure we get there in one piece. I want this monster captured. I tell ya, Jacob, this has been one hell of a fucking journey. I think I'm ready to retire.'

Forbes chuckled. 'I tell ya what you're ready for, mate, is a steaming hot bath. Have you even been home yet?'

'Nope, and I probably won't until we catch this bastard. I did have a wash though, you cheeky sod.'

Squad cars sealed the street from traffic. Armed police jumped out of their vehicle, and like soldiers, they went about their business without breaking a sweat. Ready to seize the building in question, they hurried along in two columns: one went around the back, and the other went up a staircase at the side of the building.

The front of the funeral parlour, like all such premises, conveyed a sombre tone. The black shopfront, with gold writing and a horse-drawn hearse as the company logo, and the window display, which showed a headstone and a large bunch of faded silk flowers, said as much to the passer-by.

Sanders slowly got out of the car and stretched. 'Come on then, Jacob. Let's do this. I want Seymour captured, placed in police custody, and me back home, in, as you put it, "a steaming hot bath".'

Forbes pulled the collar up on his tweed coat. A cool, damp gust of wind blew through the open part of the shirt, and the inclement weather matched his mood. He felt a chill of foreboding run down his spine.

A loud bang confirmed that the armed police had bashed in the door.

'Our cue, I think,' said Sanders, marching ahead.

Forbes was not far behind. He watched his governor climb the stairs two at a time, noting just how athletic he was, despite his weight.

The armed police had done a sweep of the flat; they came out shaking their heads.

Vernon Walsh, the lead officer, looked hesitant. 'There's no one in there, Gov. But that flat is . . .' He sucked his teeth and swallowed a gulp of air. 'Well, all I can say is, you'd better see for yourself.' Walsh shuddered and stepped aside for Sanders to go in.

A slate tiled floor and white plastered walls gave the hallway a clinical feel. To the left was a small kitchen. It comprised a row of white cabinets, a cooker that had never been used, a glass fronted wall unit that contained white cups, an even assortment of glasses all neatly placed, a white microwave, and, pushed against the wall, a table with two chairs.

Sanders checked the cupboards and the fridge, but there was no food of any description, implying that no one lived here. Sanders shrugged his shoulders. 'Is the man a fucking alien? It doesn't make sense.' But the officer's uneasiness bothered him.

In contrast, the next room was a whole other story. It was large, dominated by a wall covered in bookshelves with hundreds of books – scholarly, heavy tomes – bound in leather. Standing on the wooden floor, which was probably from the Victorian era, was a chunky oak table, with four chairs around it. A rug on the floor had two oversized tapestry cushions and a chessboard was already set up for a game. The walls themselves were papered in a deep burgundy, and the only window was the skylight. The bed was a single four-poster, also dressed in deep red, with green bed covers; it looked plump and inviting.

It took a while for both Sanders and Forbes to absorb the shocking contrast from the previous room. It was as if they had entered a Victorian playroom. The ambience felt distinctly creepy as if time had stood still.

The more Sanders tried to take it all in, the more he felt he was being sent into another era. The wooden rocking horse in the corner of the room, the mahogany writing desk, the gilt-edged pictures on the wall of troublesome portraits – all reinforced this impression.

But it was the set of early Victorian pictures showing the internal organs of the body that left Sanders dumbstruck. His eyes opening ever wider, he turned to Forbes, who was wearing the same shocked expression.

'What the fuck!' he said, slowly.

'Lewis, this is a museum, surely to God.' He tried to swallow but his throat was dry. 'This is freakish. And it makes no sense.'

'Yeah, you're right. It doesn't. You know, I feel like I am in a dream. This fella is someone very fucking strange. Let's see what's through there.' He pointed to the door in the far corner of the room.

Forbes took a deep breath, unsure if his brain could handle this much peculiarity. But as soon as they pushed the door open, their sense of strangeness increased tenfold.

On the floor were green and yellow tiles from around 1920. To Sanders, it looked like an old tube station. Then he realised that what he was seeing in the middle of the room was a stone autopsy table and above it a body lift. The metal T-frame had four adjustable leather belts that hung from it, to accommodate a heavy body, equally balanced to move the weight up and down. Above that, there was a long lamp, similar to the ones found above a snooker table. There was no mistaking what it was; yet, strangely, it was not in keeping with the modern facilities located in a coroner's lab or an embalming room. *This was the stuff of nightmares.* He shuddered and felt a sick feeling in the pit of his stomach.

Behind the table against the wall there were shelves with row upon row of pickle jars. Slowly, as Sanders' eyes wandered from jar to jar, he wondered if his freaked-out mind was deceiving him. As he looked down, he noticed haberdashery cabinets with thin drawers – not stainless steel ones but wooden – much like one would find in a men's department store back in the forties. Sanders pulled out a pair of gloves from his pocket and put them on. He was careful where he walked, but he was itching to see what the cabinets held.

As he slid open the top drawer, he glanced at Forbes. 'Jacob, this will turn your stomach. Look at these. They're embalming tools, probably late 1920s, I should imagine.' He huffed. 'Looking at them, you'd think they were torture weapons.' He stared at the long thin trocar, an instrument used much like an internal cannula, but it was so worn that the three sharp edges were blunt. He pulled open the next drawer and gazed at the Spencer Wells artery forceps, used for clamping during an operation.

Forbes shuddered. 'Fuck me, is this what happens when you die? They hoist you onto a slab like that and cut you about with those tools?'

Sanders frowned. 'No, Jacob. You've been to the fucking mortuary hundreds of times. What's the matter with you?'

'I mean, once you get released to the undertaker, is this where they prepare you for the coffin?'

'No, Jacob, this here is the monster's fucking experimental room. The proper embalming rooms must be downstairs, in the actual funeral parlour. I've been to a couple, and I can promise you this: they don't look anything like this den of horrors.'

Forbes steered his eyes away from the cabinet and focused on a blackboard on the opposite wall. He twisted his head from left to right, trying to determine the drawings and scribblings.

'Lewis, can you make out what this is?'

Closing the drawer, Sanders spun around to see what Forbes was looking at. He smiled, hiding his unsettled feelings. 'That is a cross-section of the brain, and those' – he pointed to the notes – 'are labels of the various parts, you see. Look, there is the frontal lobe . . . He has written what its functions are. Look. It says "emotion", "decision-making", "expression", "problem-solving" . . .' With confusion spread across his face, he stopped and tried to spell out the last sentence. It was written with hard, aggressive strokes, as if the writer was angry. 'Look what has been written here. "Shows signs of risk-taking behaviour, becoming environmentally dependent – remove and qualify new subject."'

Sanders pondered for a moment before he said, 'I don't know what that means, but, Jacob, I don't have a good feeling about it.'

'A good feeling? Christ, Lewis, this is like nothing I've ever seen before or even read about. I don't reckon I'll get much sleep tonight.'

Sanders looked at the desk below and pulled open the drawers. Inside there were pens, pencils, a calculator, and general stationery, all neatly arranged. But below the drawers, he noticed a filing cabinet. It was locked.

'I need that lock busted because the answers may lie in there.' Sanders pointed to the cabinet.

Forbes obliged by pulling his key ring from inside his jacket pocket. On it was a gadget he used to open locks; it had been confiscated from a well-known safe-breaker. He inserted the tool and fiddled for a while until the lock suddenly opened.

Sanders crouched down and removed some files and placed them on the desk. When he inspected the cabinet further, he found an album. *This is more like it*, he thought. Grabbing the leather-bound heavy book, he opened it.

The first picture was of an elderly man. He was tall with a broad forehead. The photo was in sepia, probably around 1920. Sanders squinted to get a better look, and he had to admit to himself the man in the picture was very similar to the photofit back at the station, but this one was obviously taken almost a hundred years ago. The next page showed a man and a woman, and, again, the male was tall, and he had a very large forehead. Sanders could only guess the year to be around 1940, just by the clothes they were wearing. Curious, he flipped to the next page showing black-and-white photos of mental asylums. Some of the photos even depicted surgeons carrying out lobotomies. They were gruesome and typical of Victorian times – an era when the middle class knew how to frighten people, with their tales of Jack the Ripper, and Edgar Allan Poe's classic horror stories. The photos typically lent themselves to a dark, monstrous time of poverty and gruesome murders.

Sanders then looked at what he assumed was the next family portrait. This one was of a boy dressed in grey shorts, and beside him, on a velvet couch, were, he assumed, his parents. As Sanders stared for a while, he realised the image of the two parents was slightly blurred, yet the one of the child was so clear. He concluded that it was a photo of the child who was dead and propped up. Not knowing an awful lot about photography, he did, however, learn years ago that photography was expensive and sometimes families would have a photo taken if their child passed away. It was to provide a memory of the way they looked. The boy was perfectly in focus because he couldn't move: after all, he was dead.

While Sanders turned each page, he was building a picture in his mind of the family history. Then he was faced with an up-to-date picture, a close-up of the face of their killer. It wasn't a pouting selfie but an angled photo that somehow defined the size of his forehead. He looked fearless and behind those dark eyes there appeared to be a soulless being.

Two pages were blank and then a small picture, obviously taken from an Instamatic camera, showed a woman who was approximately thirty years old. She was not particularly tall, slim, or beautiful – just rather plain in appearance and going about her business. It looked as if it had been taken in the seventies. She was wearing a frilly blouse and bell-bottomed jeans. Turning to the next page, she was there again, this time in a white mini dress. She seemed prettier, with her hair long and shiny, and her dress outlined her curvier figure. The third picture showed her close up, and he thought he recognised her. 'Jacob, pass me your glasses.'

Forbes was now staring at the pickle jars, trying to work out their importance. He wandered back and slapped his glasses in Sanders' open hand. 'Found anything, Lewis?'

Sanders had an idea, but he couldn't be a hundred per cent sure. He turned to the next page and sighed. Then he flinched in surprise. Pushing a pram with two little girls upright was the same woman. She was holding the pram with one hand and a little boy, who looked about four years old, with the other. Eager to see the next page, his heart began to race as he flipped over the stiff cellophane sheet. Standing in a school playground were the same girls – twin girls. He could only guess the ages of them in the following photos as they became older. They were possibly four or five, and then maybe seven years old. Then he noticed a young teenager, with long auburn hair, her head innocently turned to the side but with a malicious grin spread across her face. The stark difference in this picture was the way in which she was clearly posing for the person taking the shot.

'Jacob, look! That's, er . . . that's Dionne Stuart as she was then.'

Both men struggled to contain their excitement in case what they thought they were seeing was an utter fabrication.

With his shoulders slumped, Sanders slapped the album on the desk. 'My God, Jacob, the monster could be Dionne's father, the man who raped Lillian. His eyes flicked towards the blackboard. Look, Jacob, that drawing is of Dionne's brain. He was describing her. The writing says "remove and qualify new subject". What the hell was he doing in here?'

Tapping the top of one of the files, Forbes said, 'I reckon, Lewis, it's all in there.'

Walking around in circles, with a bemused frown, Sanders threw his arms up in the air in frustration. 'There must be another room, unless, of course, he slept next door in The *Princess and the Pea* bed.'

Forbes shrugged his shoulders. 'It doesn't look like there *is* another room.'

'Jacob, I *know* these buildings. There has to be another room at the back. Push those cabinets to see if they move.'

Forbes looked at the floor-to-ceiling cabinets and noticed that one in particular had two very large doors. On opening them, he found another door concealed inside. 'Here, Lewis, it's like opening the fucking door to Narnia.'

Much like the Victorian room with the single four-poster bed, this was decorated in the same red and green colours. The queen-sized bed was nothing like as impressive, though. A small fireplace, a patterned rug in front of it, two armchairs upholstered in deep red velour – everything was in keeping with the charm of a grand house. The oak carved wardrobes were unusual, and Sanders assumed they were probably from India or the Far East. In one corner, there was a small kitchenette, with a sink, a microwave, and a kettle. The kitchenette was tidy and clean, just like the whole room.

Curious, Sanders opened the wardrobe to find black suits hanging neatly. He noticed the size of them: they were huge. He then looked down at the shoes polished to a high shine, and he conjured up a picture of a giant.

The recess on the left wall from the doorway was dark, and Forbes flicked the other light switch on to look more closely at the pictures.

As the room was now wholly illuminated, they could see everything, but their eyes were drawn to a set of framed pictures in the recess. Like the album in the lab room, some of the portraits were old and some were new, but there was something familiar about them. All the children in the framed photographs seemed to have larger foreheads, although these were not as obvious as those contained in the album. The photographs had been organised like a family tree, with the older Victorian pictures at the top. Six rows down, the officers were drawn to a photograph of Dionne and Jenny.

A separate photo showed a little boy. Below were more photos of twins, some with bulbous heads and some normal in appearance.

The cogs were turning in Sanders' head now. He was putting the pieces together and was overcome by a very cold, unholy feeling. It was time to go. He'd seen enough. If he was ever to sleep tonight, he needed to erase the images from his mind. But as he turned away from the recess in the wall, he noticed a large framed photo. It was grainy, but from a distance, the image was obvious, although why anyone would want such a photograph adorning their wall was a surprise to him. Four men, with wide eyes and self-satisfied smiles, posed over a gruesome mess of a cadaver. The top of the head was removed and the brain exposed. The limp waxy body was lying on a dark wooden table, with its head turned to face the camera. Sanders was glued and didn't blink. The four men were obviously wealthy, if their attire was anything to go by, and yet there was something odd about them. As Sanders scrutinised the picture, his eyes focused on the cadaver's face. He unexpectedly winced. The subject was alive – it was no cadaver. Inhaling deep gulps of air, he left the room, feeling entrenched in Victorian gore and mentality.

It was late enough. The suspect was still at large, and there was nothing they could do except wait until the morning to talk with the funeral directors and put out an APB.

The police had raided the funeral parlour for any signs that their suspect was perhaps hiding inside one of the coffins, but the place was clean.

CHAPTER TWENTY-SIX

By the next morning, Harley had been reunited with her brother, who had been quiet and saddened by the whole situation. She'd been allowed to explain what had been going on, despite, she understood, this not being standard protocol. But, then, their situation wasn't normal by any stretch of the imagination.

Harley knew her mother had led a very secretive life. She had watched her sneak out of the house at different times and return hours later, perhaps with a jar of coffee or a loaf of bread. As she became older, she suspected her mother had some secret liaison with someone – perhaps a friend or a secret boyfriend – but because this occurred on a regular basis for years, it wasn't something she found odd. However, the fact that she had never had a one-to-one conversation with her mother certainly was.

And as far as Harley and Hudson were concerned, their mother had never shown any interest in them, had kept physical contact to a minimum, and, they knew only too well, she had been cruel at the drop of a hat. She would promise to take them to the zoo or the park, and then, as they sat on the bottom step dressed and ready for their outing, she'd laugh in their faces, telling them the trip was cancelled, for no reason at all.

Harley couldn't understand why her mother used her own peculiarities to hurt her. Why, for instance, had she shoved the colour yellow under her nose to get a reaction from her? And as her attention turned to her brother, why had she strapped Hudson's hand in a boxing glove so that he couldn't twirl his pen?

As she was growing up, she would look wistfully at the other children's mums when they came out of school, who were waiting excitedly to hug their loved ones. She would hear the other kids talking about what their mums did for them. Her mother was so very different.

When she cast her mind back, two particular episodes in her life stood out – two that she really was not proud of. Her mother had promised them treats if they did awful things. For example, when she gave Davey a peanut butter sandwich, and when her brother shot at Kai with his BB gun.

Conversely, her mother never rewarded them when they were good. She would tell them they were not good enough, that they were evil and wicked, and that one day they would end up being locked away in a mental asylum for the insane and strange. To drive the point home, she showed them pictures of what it looked like in those places back in the 1900s and told them they would go there one day.

When all the horror stories of the sick and mental abuse that the twins endured were relayed to Sanders, it made him want to leave the room.

He had been one of many who had found Harley's dark, lifeless eyes sinister, and yet now he knew why. He suspected that behind those dark pools of sadness, lost hope, and faded dreams, the never-ending fear of being locked away in an old Victorian asylum would always be on her mind.

Her words resonated with Sanders, and he thought he would never forget them. 'I wanted to love Mummy, I really did, but she wouldn't let me.'

It was then that the tears pricked Sanders' eyes, and, unexpectedly, he broke all the rules by holding out his arms for her to be hugged.

Slowly, she stepped into the comfort of the big man with the deep voice and floppy hair, now, perhaps, her saviour.

He stroked the back of her head and whispered, 'I'm so sorry, Harley. I wish I'd been in a position to help you sooner.' Guilt glared at him like an invisible demon.

Renee had advised that the children be informed of everything. Notwithstanding their young ages, they were intelligent and mature enough to understand the danger they were currently in.

* * *

Lillian had agreed to move to a safe house with the children and was accompanied by a female officer to a country cottage in Devon, far enough away to provide the safety and anonymity they all needed. And the property also benefited from having cameras and alarms installed.

* * *

It was Sanders who informed the Mason family that Dionne had been murdered and the suspect was a man called Nyall Seymour. Although under any circumstances the death of a young woman would be terrible news, it came as a relief to the Masons, none more so than Geoff. He was shocked.

And before Sanders had taken a seat, Geoff assumed the detective was there to arrest him for Dionne's murder. Even after carefully concealing his tracks, by changing his clothes and throwing both the bloodstained garments and the gun into the River Rother near the cottage, he still believed he would get caught. But at the time, he couldn't care less: he just wanted the bitch dead. And as it turned out, no one in the family had even realised he'd been missing. They'd all assumed he'd taken a long much-needed nap.

Even though Miriam was upset that she couldn't visit her grandchildren, as there was a risk that the suspect may follow her, she understood why this was the case and nodded quietly in Sanders' direction.

'Before I leave you,' said Sanders, 'I need to show you all something. We have a photofit of the man we think is responsible. I would like you all to have a good look at this person. Be vigilant if you see him, and don't approach him.' He raised his eyebrows, glaring at Dean and Geoff. 'We don't want another murder on our hands, so call us right away. However, I suspect he won't come for you.'

He slid his hand in his inside pocket and removed a folded piece of A4 paper.

He passed it first to Geoff, who scrutinised the photofit. *Was he the man who had watched us from afar and who had appeared in my nightmares? Surely not.* He shook his head. 'Nope, I've never seen him before.'

'No, I ain't ever seen him either,' said Dean, as he looked over Geoff's shoulder.

'I'll get some more copies for you, so you can have one each.'

He passed the picture to Miriam and was about to hand it to Archi, expecting the same response from her as her sons.

Surprisingly, her hands trembled, and her eyes widened.

Sanders knew then she'd seen him before. Her frightened expression spoke volumes.

'Mrs Mason, have you ever seen this man?'

She looked like a rabbit caught in the headlights, but, suddenly, she blinked and shook her head. 'No, no, never.'

Sanders knew Miriam was lying. Sensing she was holding something back because her family were there, he handed her his card. 'If you ever see him, or remember seeing him, please call me.'

* * *

He returned to the station to find the incident room was quieter today. The team were out tracking down the Audi, collecting information and sharing the photofit with those who they felt may have come into contact with the suspect.

Renee was still there at one of the desks and reading through the files that Sanders had collected from the strange lab in the suspect's flat. So deep in thought, she almost jumped when he said, 'Fancy a coffee?'

Her eyes looked tired; she'd been reading so much. 'Yes, that would be lovely, Lewis.'

He looked at her, and for the first time, he noticed how, under those thick rimmed glasses, her eyes were very pretty and young. She was wearing a light-blue fitted dress.

He smiled. They had worked hard together, often until the early hours, missing a decent meal and a bath, for that matter, and yet, today, they were fresher, having both spent what was left of the evening at their homes.

She noticed his smile and took off her glasses. 'Shall we go out for coffee, Lewis?'

He chuckled. 'Amazing how a smile can change things. Yeah, Doctor, a breath of fresh air will do us good . . .'

'Lewis, call me Kate will you. I always feel like a character when people call me "doctor", when, really, sometimes I want to feel like a woman.'

She got up from her chair and giggled. 'Why not? I'm drained, and I think I need a tipple to unwind from that horror story I've just read. I'll tell you about it, but I'm not at the end just yet. I have to warn you though, Lewis, you'll be shocked. I don't want to give too much away, unless, of course, I'm wrong, because as far as disturbing facts go, these are on a completely new spectrum.'

He opened the door and gestured for her to walk ahead. 'Kate, nothing after what I saw yesterday in that flat will shock me. Christ! The photos were obviously taken by Nyall. He followed a young Lillian. He then raped her. But more than that, he somehow brainwashed Dionne, who I can only assume is his child. And those pictures, it was like an old Victorian museum.

I half-expected Anthony Hopkins, who played Hannibal Lecter in *The Silence of the Lambs*, to suddenly appear.'

She giggled. 'I'm afraid to tell you this, but our suspect would give Hannibal Lecter nightmares.'

The lunchtime rush at the Bricklayers Arms was over, and Sanders pointed to a table in the corner by the window. He ordered a large whisky for himself and a double G & T for Kate.

With two bags of crisps under his arm and his wallet in his mouth, he held the two glasses and carefully returned to their table.

Renee released him of the drinks and chuckled. 'Gosh, you know, I haven't been to a pub in years. Well, this *is* nice.'

Sanders was intrigued by her. She was confident and in control in the incident room, but here in the pub, she seemed self-conscious, to the point where she looked completely out of her comfort zone. But then, he hadn't really had the chance to get to know her as a person.

'Like me, I guess you're married to your work.'

She sipped her drink and shuddered. 'You can tell I'm not used to drinking. Still, I think I need this, and, yes, I'm afraid I am. I was married many moons ago, but work took over, and that was that. And what about yourself? I assume you're also single?'

'Oh, well, I'm hard to live with. I smoke too much, I drink too much, and I work too much, so who would have me?'

A little fidget and a slight blush made it apparent she was feeling an attraction. He changed the subject, to save her from any embarrassment. 'I think Miriam Mason knows the suspect.'

Renee bit her lip. 'Well, if she does, then it will solve the missing piece in the puzzle. You see, this suspect, "the monster", as I call him, had big plans. He wasn't just leaving a legacy or a protégée, he was carrying out his own experiment. A very sick and dangerous one too. Oh, listen. I said we should have a nice drink, and later on this afternoon, when I've finished reading all of the monster's files, I'll tell you the full story.'

Sanders leaned across and patted her hand. 'We both know that until this case is closed we won't really have a sociable drink. I have to say, this case has consumed me, even to the point where it is disturbing my dreams.'

Renee nodded. 'Yes, I am breathing this case, and it's so odd because I'm not really even part of it, well, not officially. I just seem to have got caught up in it, somewhere along the way. But I have no regrets. Guy was a good friend of mine, and I want to make a difference, if I can.'

'Kate, you *have* been a real help. We would never have got this far without your input . . . It's funny how life throws people together.'

Noticing her cheeks flush in response, he knew he'd nearly crossed that line again.

Deciding on a leap of faith, he said, 'But, Kate, I think it's a good thing. Maybe, once this is over, we could perhaps make the G & T a regular get-together.'

'Well, Lewis, I think I would like that very much.'

Just as Sanders was about to order another round of drinks, his phone rang. He looked at the number and saw it was the station.

Clark sounded harsh, but he always did on the phone. 'Sanders, I have a Miriam Mason here. She says she can't wait around and wants to speak with you.'

'I'm on my way. Give me five minutes.' He looked at Renee. 'Bingo! You might just have your missing piece in that puzzle. Miriam Mason's at the station.'

In short order, Renee shuffled across her bench seat and threw her jacket over her arm. 'We'd better not waste time, then.'

*   *   *

Clark had taken Miriam to one of the interview rooms and he'd offered her a drink. Nodding to a WPC to fetch the teas, he sensed she would be here for some time.

While Sanders hurried along the corridor, Renee made her way back to the incident room to continue reading what she assumed to be the monster's research notes. Although the records found in the flat were pointing towards the culprit, Renee was totally fascinated by his research. The project was apparently handed down by the man's forefathers, but there were many crossovers between her study and his conclusions. She hoped she'd be able to fill in the missing part of the puzzle, providing, of course, Miriam Mason's information gave them what she was looking for.

As Sanders entered the room, he gave Mrs Mason a generous smile. 'I see they got you a drink. Are you okay, Mrs Mason?'

Her smile hid a deep sadness. 'Look, I'm sorry, Chief Inspector. What I mean is, I should have said right away, but . . .' Pausing, she took a deep breath. 'This chat . . . it's just between you and me, right?'

'Of course it is. I guessed you knew him, and I'm also guessing it was under circumstances that you would prefer your family to know nothing about. Am I right?'

Coyly, she nodded. 'Yes, you are. They must never know. I mean, never *ever* know.'

'I understand, Mrs Mason. You have my word.'

She sighed and looked uncomfortable. 'It's hard, ya know. I thought I could've put it behind me. I really believed I could put what happened out of my head, and I did, after a time. I just pretended it never happened, but seeing that picture was like seeing the fucking Devil himself.' She coughed, realising she'd sworn.

'It's okay, Mrs Mason. You just tell me in your own words. It's just you and me.'

'It was shortly after me dad passed away. My little Geoff was a babe in arms, and I was out one night. I used to go out every Thursday, with girls from the bus garage. We all worked there, ya see. We went to The Cat's Whiskers. My Archi was at home with Geoff. His night out was Friday, with his mates. Anyway, we all shared a cab back, but I was feeling a bit sick. I'd drunk far too much. Well, I did, back then. Me mate Yvonne lived only a few streets from my house, so when the cab dropped her off, I got out as well. I said I wanted to walk. It wasn't that Archi would mind me being pissed as a parrot, but, then, I was young at the time and wanted to, ya know, look ladylike, and I was still after his affections. So, I took me shoes off. It wasn't cold, late September, and I dawdled along. Just before my road was a small park. I never thought much of it. I was never one to be nervous of me own shadow, like. So, I didn't see – until it was too late – this man lurking in the dark by the entrance. Well, not until I felt this hand over my mouth. And it was a big hand, an' all. He dragged me into the park. I was so frightened, and then as if I was a puppet without strings, he threw me to the ground. Christ, he was huge, and I *mean* huge. He would make two of my Archi. I was too petrified to scream. That's unlike me, I know, because I've always been a mouthy cow, but I never felt fear like it. He had this hooded jacket, so I couldn't see his face. At first, I didn't want to see who was going to kill me, 'cos I felt like he was definitely going to do away with me. For some reason, raping me never entered my head, and then, as I lay on the ground, he dropped to his knees and pulled out a knife, or something shiny. I can't remember every detail. Then I shook all over, and all I could think of was my Geoff would not have a mother. I then tried to scream, but he put his hand over my mouth and waved this metal object under my nose. As he let go of my mouth, I bit my bruised lip to hold back even a gasp. Because he would have killed me. Suddenly, he ripped me knickers off. It all happened so fast and so violently that I couldn't fight back. I couldn't even scream, I felt so helpless. Then, when it was over, he stood up. At that moment, the wind blew and pushed his hood away from his face. That's when I saw him . . . properly, like. He was a monster,

Detective, an ugly monster. I closed my eyes thinking he was going to stab me, but when I opened them again, he'd gone.'

She took a deep breath and sniffed back the tears, determined not to cry. 'I straightened myself up and went home. It's funny, because I remember looking at my Archi and little Geoff, asleep on his chest. They looked so peaceful, they were my family, and I wouldn't hurt them. If I'd told Archi, I don't know what would have happened, so I never said a word. I crept upstairs, had a bath, and curled up in bed. In the morning, Archi laughed at me. "Good night, was it?" he said, pointing to my bruised lips. He'd assumed I'd fallen over in a drunken stupor or got rucking. Then he handed me tickets to Spain. We were off on a surprise holiday. The trip was so relaxing that I managed to put the incident behind me. That was, of course, until I found I was expecting. I kept looking at my little Geoff. He was such a beautiful baby that I couldn't consider having an abortion. Well, me and Archi were in love, and, ya know, I guess we went at it a bit like rabbits. So, I hoped that this baby was his, and if it was born like a monster, then I would know it wasn't Archi's, and so I decided to cross that bridge, as they say. Then Luke was born. He didn't look exactly like Geoff, more like me, and he was far from any monster. From the day he was born until now, he was my Luke, and I never thought any different.'

Seeing Mrs Mason covering her face, Sanders could feel the sorrow. Her middle son was dead, and whether he was the rapist's son or not, he could tell she'd always loved him. Paramount in his mind, then, was that he needed to tread very carefully because he didn't want to hurt her any more than she was already suffering.

'I think you were and are very brave, Mrs Mason, and, again, you have my word: no one will know.'

She stopped the tears and took a deep breath. 'It never stopped me loving him, ya know.'

Sanders' ears pricked up at what she'd just said. Was she saying she knew Luke wasn't Archi's?

'Of course not. He was still your son, though, wasn't he?'

'I knew he wasn't Archi's when Dean was born because Dean was Geoff's double. But my Luke, was different. At least he *behaved* differently, what with his moody expression. He was always so serious, a real mystery kid. He never had decent friends, but he didn't need them, because he loved his brothers, and God help anyone that got in his way or theirs, for that matter. He could fly off the handle and create mayhem, but he never did at home. The boys said he had a rage that when unleashed was like ten men going into battle. I used to say the quiet ones are always the worst.'

He could tell she was reminiscing. 'Do you remember anything about how he met Dionne?'

Miriam stared over Sanders' shoulder. 'Actually, I do. I'm sorry, but I don't feel bad that she is dead. I never really liked her. Oh, I tried to when Luke went away, but she was too premeditated for my liking. She arrived at The Allure when it had been open for about a year. I called into the club one evening to collect the receipts. There she was, all done up to the nines, ya know, like a bleedin' dog's dinner, with this low-cut top and a skirt up her arse. I warned him. I told him she was a gold-digger, but every night, there she was, in there, flirting over the bar, until she ended up on a date, and I can only imagine what was on offer, because after a few weeks, he was hooked, and before I knew it, she'd moved into his place. I remember asking the boys if she was genuine. Do you know what my Dean said? Well, he just laughed, and his exacts words were: "Yeah, Mum. She's a genuine parasite."'

Sanders couldn't keep a straight face. He loved her terminology. 'Thank you, Mrs Mason. You've been more helpful than you could possibly imagine.'

She looked into his eyes and asked, 'What exactly is going on? I mean, first our Scarlett is murdered, and we were led to believe it was Dionne. Then my Luke. And then Harley and Hudson's shrink has been killed. But *now* someone's murdered Dionne. Do you think it's this . . . this rapist? It's all so mixed up.'

Nodding with empathy, he replied, 'I know, and trust me when I tell you, it's been a shock to us here too. We do think that Dionne murdered Scarlett, but as for Luke, Dr Reeves, and Dionne, we think it's this alleged rapist. But in order to find him, we need everything we have, including everything you know. In that respect, you've been a great help.'

As she looked down at her hand and twirled her wedding ring around her finger, she asked, 'Is any of this my fault? I mean, that guy was definitely the man who attacked me.' She couldn't bring herself to use the word 'rape'.

He took her hand, gently cupping it in his. 'I promise you, Mrs Mason, this definitely isn't your fault. There's a much bigger picture. I'm afraid, you were a very innocent party in the grand scheme of things, but once we have the bastard, you have my word, I'll tell you all the facts.'

With round, vulnerable eyes, she smiled. 'I know you will. Let's hope it's very soon, eh?'

As soon as Mrs Mason left, Sanders hurried to the incident room to let Kate Renee know the truth, but on his arrival, he was met with pure horror on her face. He inclined his head. 'What is it, Kate?'

She shook her head. 'I think we need to call the team in because this is a long story, and one I only ever want to tell once. I'm guessing that Luke Mason was the result of Miriam Mason being raped by the monster, then?'

He nodded. 'Yes, he was. But how did you know? I mean . . . ?'

Seeing the grave look on Kate's face, he knew she needed a break. But he was just getting to know her now, and so he surmised that she would want to get this story off her chest in her own way. He gathered the team, including Chief Superintendent Clark, as Kate prepared the board with notes and pictures from the file.

CHAPTER TWENTY-SEVEN

The man behind the monster

For someone like Kate Renee, mentally disturbed patients were nothing out of the ordinary. She'd worked for many years in research, identifying factors that would make the sane insane and classifying psychopaths into categories. With her advanced knowledge of the history of psychiatry, she was struck dumb when she carefully studied Seymour's notes. His ancestry had been meticulously documented, going back over a hundred years, and when she realised who his ancestors were, she literally gasped. The diaries and photos were so precise that she felt she was taking a step back in time to a place where the most obscene practices were being carried out in the name of medicine. The 'monster', as she called him in her mind, was a killer, and yet, she had total admiration for him. His actions and the project he was working on were, she was in no doubt, totally alarming, and, even worse, unholy, but his research, methodology, and findings went far beyond anything she'd ever seen. The fact was her research practice was under a strict protocol, and so her hands were tied, and that was why finding the Gemini Gene, if it even existed, was so problematic. Seymour, however, was under no such constraints. He had put his theory into practice, and the results, along with his own methods, were equally utterly compelling and shocking.

For her own interest, she photographed the pictures and relevant documents and uploaded them onto her computer to give the team a slide show.

She looked up from her notes, breathed in the stale air, and blanked out those images, if only for a moment.

The incident room was filled with everyone who had been working on the case, and she was about to deliver a story that would make their toes curl. Battling with the idea of either keeping it simple or going into gory detail, she decided to treat the situation as a lecture, something that she was well used to doing.

Sanders watched her falter for a moment as she gazed at all the eager eyes. 'Kate, your stand,' he urged, gesturing with his hand that she should stand by the table with the projector.

'Popcorn, anyone?' joked Forbes, trying to break the tension in the room.

Declaring his authority, Clark decided to give a speech and forthwith stood up and faced everyone. 'I just want to say that Dr Renee's assistance has been invaluable, and we've been very fortunate to have her with us on this case.' He turned to face her. 'You'll have our undivided attention. Thank you.'

Sanders rolled his eyes, as Renee blushed. He'd got to know her well and was aware that she wasn't the type of woman who would be looking for a pat on the back; not from what he'd seen of her. She was too independent and fully aware of her own self-worth.

Using her remote, she turned on the projector. On the screen appeared the side profile of a man. His forehead was large and bulbous, and his eyes almost narrowed to an ugly squint. With dark hair pulled behind his ears, he was no potential magazine model.

The silence in the room told Renee she really did have their undivided attention. 'This is Nyall Seymour, yes, an ugly brute. This is who I have referred to as the "monster" and for a good reason.'

The beam from her laser pen pointed to the large forehead. 'This area here would give the impression that this man was perhaps mentally challenged.'

'Retarded,' shouted a DI.

'Yes, and that word was used many years ago to describe a person mentally challenged. In fact, Nyall Seymour himself used the same word in his notes. However, Seymour is far from retarded. He is highly intelligent, extremely focused. The way his brain functions is far superior to the average person.'

The room remained silent; she became the teacher. Some were enthralled by the science lesson, others out of morbid curiosity.

The next slide showed another man, who was very similar in appearance to Nyall Seymour. As the image of the front part of the head was enlarged, the officers saw an older photograph from what he was wearing; the photograph was probably taken around the 1950s. 'This is Michael Seymour, Nyall's father, and I must add, this man comes from the aristocratic family of Lord Seymour. And again, this man was not retarded, but a brilliant professor of psychiatry. I can only guess there were two reasons he chose that particular career. Firstly . . .' She clicked onto the next slide of another person. 'This man Edward Seymour, Nyall's grandfather, was also in the same profession, and secondly, Michael would have been subjected to serious harassment in that era, and would have best served working away from the public, either with the dead or the demented. So, I looked deeper into the family tree and did research of my own. Sadly, he was also born somewhat deformed, as you can see from his oversized forehead and heavy brows. Also note his extreme height, giving further support to him being associated with mental retardation. But Michael, as I have just said, was not retarded, and although very shy, his knowledge of the human body, particularly the brain, was vastly advanced. What held him back from working at any research establishment was his appearance, and so he spent his time working in the basements of the asylums, experimenting on those who showed signs of hysteria, schizophrenia, or mania.'

She heard a couple of gasps from the officers.

'So, all three men inherited that large ugly forehead? It's not a condition, then?' asked Sanders.

'Well, in answer to your first question, the answer is yes. With regard to your second question, we think of conditions as a disease or an illness, yet, suffice to say, their disfigurement is not a disease. It is an extension of their brain.'

To add more effect, Renee's next slide demonstrated the experimentation of a conscious patient with the brain exposed.

The sight had one officer up off his seat and hurrying away to spill his guts.

A few choice words were said before Renee smiled and returned to the history lesson.

'Now, this slide shows a very famous man called Walter Jackson Freeman II, from whom we've gained the term "ice pick lobotomy". He has, as you can imagine, received mixed reviews. But what we didn't know was he had a partner in crime, excuse the pun. His partner, or, more accurately, his mentor, was Nyall's grandfather, Edward. Now, as I mentioned, the Seymours were wealthy and respected, so it was very difficult to slur the man's name. It just wasn't the done thing back in that time. So, when Edward pursued his own work, away from Freeman, no one questioned it. In fact, he kept his work so secretive that he built a laboratory inside his huge Victorian mansion.'

She clicked to the next slide showing the inside of Nyall's flat.

The officers who hadn't seen it were totally moved. It really was like stepping back in time.

'These were some of the original pieces from the Seymour family home,' she continued.

'Dr Renee, I'm confused. So, tell me, what has all this got to do with this monster, Nyall Seymour?' asked Clark, who very rarely admitted he was baffled.

'Yes, well, I'm getting to that part. I just wanted to give you some idea of the type of family Nyall came from. His forefathers were professors, men who were determined to make a discovery, which, as a scientist, I can readily identify with. However, unlike myself, they were so driven that they would go to any lengths to achieve their hypotheses. You see, science is the pursuit and application of knowledge and understanding, which, in my case, is mental health, following a systematic methodology based on evidence.'

Clark tilted his head to the side, still confused, only this time, he decided to keep his mouth shut.

Renee, however, clocked his puzzled expression. 'Okay, what I mean is this. As a scientist, we have theories, but without experimentation and evidence, they will remain as just theories. In my work, I have to follow strict protocol, which . . .' she sighed, 'can hold me back at times, but it's to protect the patients and the outcomes.'

The next slide showed four boys, two with the large foreheads, and two without who looked normal. 'This slide' – she pointed, using the laser beam – 'shows Michael Seymour and his brothers.'

Sanders was on the edge of his seat. 'So, Nyall's father had two normal siblings? I mean, they weren't all monstrous looking, then?'

Renee held up her hand and flicked to the next slide, a later photo showing this time a girl and a boy who both looked normal, and, beside them, two young lads with the pronounced foreheads, one being Nyall himself. 'Not only did Nyall have two normal-looking uncles, he had one brother like himself but another brother and a sister who also appeared, as we would say, in proportion.'

'And the lad next to Nyall with the big forehead, who is that?' asked Forbes.

'He is Nyall's twin, Simon.'

Sanders and the team were intrigued as they watched Renee zoom in to show a close-up of the four children's foreheads, and just below the hairline, they all saw the scars. 'Christ, did they have a lobotomy? Was this Michael Seymour operating on his own children?'

Renee turned to face Sanders. 'Yes. When I said the Seymours would do anything to find the answers, they did. Even Nyall, as you can see, was subjected to such tests.'

The following slides showed details of the operations, which would make the most hardened of coppers want to puke.

'Was Michael researching to find answers as to why he, one of his brothers, and only two of his children were born with a huge forehead?' asked Forbes, who was so engrossed that he was oblivious to those around him.

'No. He wanted to carry on his father's work to study his own bloodline. His own had come from a long line of aristocrats. All of the family were either businessmen or in the medical profession, all intelligent and successful. He noted that some were far superior intellectually, and yet they did lack something that their friends had, and that was empathy. So much so, that he observed their lack of emotion and disregard for people outside their own interests. It was at that point, he began to study what we would call today *psychopaths*. He was fascinated and intrigued by the level of skills in planning, problem-solving, and untapped intelligence.'

'Is there anyone else in the Seymour family still living?'

Renee shook her head. 'The notes and the albums continue without their mention. I couldn't find any more information in his files. They probably died from being experimented on.'

'Who the hell would use their own kids for experimentation like that?' pointed out Clark, shaking his head in disgust.

'A high-functioning psychopath.'

'Bloody hell, I've never heard of such a thing,' replied Clark.

Nelson was scribbling notes, when, suddenly, he looked up and without thinking blurted out, 'Hitler.'

Renee gave him a generous grin and nodded. 'Exactly. He would have been classed as one, and, in fact, in some of Michael's notes, there are references to the man. Which brings me on to the next part, and like Hitler, who was obsessed with the superior race, the Seymours were equally fixated with their own bloodline.'

The words 'superior race' and 'bloodline' had Sanders feeling uneasy. 'Sorry, Kate, we keep butting in, but how obsessed? Can you elaborate?'

Renee nodded. 'I don't mind questions. Please feel free to ask whatever you want. I shall explain about the obsession. When I mentioned high-functioning psychopaths, there is another type. We in the profession have been working on isolating a particular gene called the Gemini Gene. We have thought for many years that there are a few individuals who possess this gene and although they are high-functioning and intelligent, with no empathy, they also have an uncontrollable rage. Left to their own devices, without the ability to focus intensely, their anger reaches a frightening level. They're stronger than most and extremely aggressive. I believe that the Seymour family were tapping into that specific trait, but, of course, back then, they didn't have the technology we have today – like DNA profiling.'

All eyes were glued to the screen and all ears were hanging on to her every word.

'So, what are we dealing with? Well, let me take you back. Nyall was obviously very close to his father. The photos show them working together. But when his father was taken ill, the large mansion fell into disrepair and the money dwindled away. Nyall took a job at a funeral directors', where he secretly continued his father's research. His monstrous looks made him unsuitable for a job with the public, and so he worked with the dead. Nyall was so good at his job that when the flat above the funeral parlour became empty, the company gave it to him. So attached was he to his family history, he moved in his father's belongings, his original old tools, and all the research files, in order to carry on from where his father had reached.'

The room was silent until Nelson asked the obvious question. 'And what exactly is the work?'

Renee switched the slide projector off and sat on the corner of the table. 'He wants to prove that there is another race of people living amongst us, a forgotten species of human being, who have evolved thousands of years ago with abilities that the general public do not possess. He wants to secure the future for what he believes to be his own kind. This monster wants to leave a legacy.'

'But how? I mean, in this day and age?' questioned Clark.

'By breeding in any way possible and raping vulnerable women who wouldn't abort their baby. In his younger years, he would have tracked his offspring, using his intelligence and his skills in manipulation to study them and even train them, as he did with Dionne.'

The words 'forgotten species' made Sanders' blood run cold. Everyone in the room sat silently in contemplation. This was a story that would go around in their heads like a carousel, keeping them up at night and haunting their dreams.

Suddenly everyone in the room began to clap, and the officers rose to their feet.

Clark smiled and mouthed a 'thank you' to Kate and left the room.

Sanders then waved his hands for the team to sit back down. 'Thank you, Kate. It's been so informative, it gives us an insight into the man we need to track down, and fast. Right, everyone, I want Nyall Seymour's picture put out and every bloody camera this side of the water checked. We have to find this monster and bring him in!'

There were no huffs and puffs or dragging of heels; the information regarding Seymour's story had disturbed the team enough to have them jumping like Mexican beans.

As Renee packed her computer away and Sanders pushed his arms into his jacket, Nelson came bounding into the room waving a fax. 'Gov, Gov, we've got him!'

'What, how, where?' demanded Sanders, breathless with excitement. After all he'd just heard, he was eager to meet the infamous monster in person.

'We got a call from the police station in Folkestone. They've found Seymour's car, with him dead inside. They reckon exhaust fumes caused it. A pipe was still attached through the window.'

Sanders punched the air. 'Thank you, God, for that. I thought this Seymour geezer was gonna give us a right runaround.'

Renee stared at Sanders with a blank expression.

Forbes skipped out of the room to let the Chief Superintendent know the good news, leaving Sanders beaming.

But Renee was in a world of her own. 'I don't believe it's him!' she said, with a cold warning in her voice.

Sanders instantly stopped smiling. 'What? Why?'

'Because, Lewis, I know this man better than anyone.' She pointed to the files. 'I've studied every diary that tells every dark thought he ever had, and there were many, and all recorded. So there is no way he would have taken his own life. He wouldn't have the emotion to feel suicidal.'

Annoyed that she'd suddenly thrown a bloody great spanner in the works, he said coldly, 'Well, when they send over the photo, we'll know for sure.'

'Okay, I want to believe it myself, Lewis, but . . . Look, let me tell you what else I know about this man. And it's not just my opinion; he logged it all down. He's too calculated, too focused, suddenly to top himself.'

'But, if he reached the end of the road, and he is insane, then perhaps . . . ?'

Renee shook her head. 'Please, Lewis, take a seat. Let me explain more about him.'

Sanders drew in a deep breath and sat patiently opposite. 'Go on, then, Kate.'

'Right, Nyall was a very determined man, in a field of scientific interest that we would never comprehend. During his free time, he spent it watching people, studying and following them to the point where he was stalking them. Successful, men, with money and confidence, he admired from a distance by making detailed notes, but he would always be lurking in the shadows. By 1961, he was ready to take control and define what made these people intelligent and rich. The only way to know for sure was to look inside their brains and then dissect and record his findings. But he could also hide his work from the authorities. He had the perfect job. Who would suspect that inside the coffin of a Mrs Smith was also a Clifford Slithers or a Peter Danson? He recorded everything in meticulous detail, and his records went on for years. By the late seventies, he wanted to procreate and test his own offspring, but he had to ensure that his unsuspecting victims would not abort his children.'

Sanders frowned. He still wasn't convinced by what Kate had just told him. 'He was a serial killer, and I've known serial killers to take their own lives in jail, never mind committing suicide in a car.'

'No, Lewis, he was clever. Look at what he did. He prayed on the emotionally vulnerable – the mothers who already knew what it was like to love a child. A woman like Lillian, whom he met on her saddest day when her mother was in the chapel of rest – a young virile woman who was already nurturing a son. And then there was Miriam Mason when she mourned over her father's grave, clutching her little boy. And a third woman, Jackie Rice, who buried her three-year-old daughter and was desperate to push around a newborn. There were probably many others too. He could make an educated guess that these young mothers would first not go to the police, and second, they would still bring up his children, probably because they were already married and dependent on their husbands, and so would not want to rock the boat.'

Sanders scratched his head. 'Well, yes, but, Kate, he may have realised he was too old to be a father and would rather end it all. I mean, he was hardly a slippers-and-bedtime-story man.'

Frustrated, Renee continued. 'No, *listen*. He'd carefully selected his women and stalked them tirelessly until he could impregnate them. As all these children were born, some adopted out, others raised by the mothers, he watched them from the dark hidden trees, the lamp posts, the recesses in the shop doorways, or through the windows. He kept a diary of each child, scoring them.'

Wondering if he could handle any more of this man's antics, Sanders sighed. 'Please, Kate, let me just see if it's him. I'm not sure I need to know all of this right now.'

Renee cast Sanders a look of annoyance. 'I have worked bloody hard on all of this, Lewis. I'm not giving up now. You need to know *everything*.'

Offering her a sympathetic smile, it was her cue to continue.

'Then there was Dionne, the child who was his protégée but also his host. The girl who had taken on his genes. The one who would understand him to learn and grow from his wealth of knowledge and experience. She was wild and would go off on her own. He saw the way she dismissed her mother, and then he saw her being taken to the psychiatric clinic.' She stopped and looked at Sanders to establish if she was wasting her time by continuing, but he nodded for her to carry on.

'This was Nyall's chance to gain her trust. He would be her saviour, be the man who understood her when everyone else wouldn't. He would be her mentor and would take away any discomfort caused in her life, any burden and anger, and help her remove anyone who got in her way. Knowing her as he did, his relationship started when she was seven. It was a whisper in her ear, a chance meeting, and then he saw an opportunity for him to satisfy her needs. She was hungry to learn, and anatomy was her interest. He taught her many things and how to kill was one of them. He showed her how to use a victim's own weight to tumble dangerously down the stairs or how to electrocute her twin sister, the twin who was no use to him. She listened and did everything he said without question. You see, Nyall was taking his study to a whole different realm, to see if his subject would kill. But then Dionne became too emotional, fixated on Geoff Mason rather than her own work. She spent more time planning how she would finally have him for herself rather than increase her knowledge.'

'So, do you believe she killed Scarlett and Luke . . . and also Beverley Childs?'

'Scarlett, possibly, based simply on circumstantial evidence, because the method used was totally different. I guess she planned it that way. Beverley she murdered for sure, but as to Luke, I think the monster may have killed him because in his earlier notes he states that Luke was surplus to requirements. But Dionne was strong, and so I wouldn't rule her out. Beverley was killed in the same way that Kenny was. Guy and Luke were killed by a similar implement. Whether the monster killed them both or he taught Dionne how to murder a victim by the method he would have used, God only knows because she's not here to tell us.'

'Maybe he gave up on Dionne? I mean, with us lot getting involved, maybe he saw her as stupid or reckless.'

She shook her head. 'No, that was not the sole reason. He would never have given up unless he had no need for her. If, for example, he found another host.'

Sanders shuddered. He hated that word. 'Well, perhaps he never did, and that's why he killed himself.'

She sighed heavily. 'He was going to kill me too. It's in that diary, the last page.'

With his eyes on stalks, Sanders grabbed her hand. 'Oh my God! How must you feel? Christ, I now know why you are so concerned. But, if it's not him, who . . . ? Hang on. Why would he want to kill *you*?'

Her expression looked uncomfortable, as if what she was about to tell him wouldn't be easy to talk about.

'He killed Guy because he was after some files, and he knows I have them.'

Sanders was confused. 'What files? What is he after, Kate?'

She paused, unsure if she'd said too much already.

'Go on,' urged Sanders.

'He wants to track down the DNA for the twins Harley and Hudson. He needs to make sure they are his offspring from a woman who committed suicide. It was an open adoption. The mother had no family, but the father stepped forward and chose Luke and Dionne as the parents to adopt the twins. I believe the father is Nyall,' she replied.

Running his hands across his bristly cheeks, Sanders sighed. 'So I guess the question is, are they?'

'Sadly, yes, they are. I matched their DNA with Dionne's, and they are siblings. Dionne was their sister, which means that the monster Nyall Grant Seymour must be their father.'

A cold shiver ran through Sanders' body as he stared at the troubled look on Kate's face. 'We need to see if that dead man is Nyall. Like right now.'

As Sanders jumped up from his seat, Renee grabbed his arm. 'His four children were all under one roof. That evil man was so desperate to have his pure bloodline, he bloody brainwashed Dionne into marrying Luke. I'm just so pleased they didn't conceive their own children. Yet, even so, Dionne and Luke were raising their own siblings, the twins, as their own, and neither of them had a clue.'

With his mouth open, Sanders shook his head. 'My God, this is so shocking. Look, I think it's for the best that we don't ever tell the twins. I mean, it's so sordid and . . . Well, I don't think there *is* a word to describe it.'

'Twisted, perhaps?'

He gave her a sad, resigned smile. 'Yes, I guess, you're probably right about that.'

CHAPTER TWENTY-EIGHT

Kate Renee sat staring at the large folder as Sanders hurried to Clark's office. The road had been a long one, and now she wondered if she'd got it all wrong. What if she'd become so obsessed with the identification of the Gemini Gene that she had overlooked vital information? She was so sure that Nyall wouldn't take his own life; indeed, she would have bet her life savings on it.

Her stomach turned over, and she felt the contents rising. Gulping back the excess saliva in her mouth, she jumped up to go to the toilet. Luckily, she made it in time and expelled the contents. Gripping the bowl and gasping for breath, her mind went into overdrive. It was plagued by a myriad of flashing images and test results, which had overloaded her brain like a landslide. She took a few deep breaths, pushed herself away from the toilet bowl, and, shakily, she rose to her feet, wiping her mouth with the back of her hand.

A sudden deep sense of dread caused a wave of adrenaline to sweep around her body, making her palms wet with sweat. 'Christ, what if I am wrong?' she said, aloud. It didn't bear thinking about. Determined to shake the apprehension, she returned to the incident room. As she snatched the files, the weight of the folder bent her fingers back and the loose papers and photographs fell to the floor. Quickly, she got to her knees and began gathering them up. But one photo of a little girl caught her off guard. Peering closer, a cold shiver ran up her spine and her hands shook. 'No, surely not,' she said out loud, as she slid it into her pocket. Feeling another wave of sickness, she took a few deep breaths, forcing the disturbing notion out of her head. She had to get away from the police station and gather her thoughts. Perhaps the last few hours had sent her mind to a place that was filled with the strange, the shocking, and the unthinkable. Once she picked up her bag from the chair and slid the file inside, she grabbed her keys and left.

'Hey, Kate!' called Sanders, whose tone seemed upbeat.

Renee stood dead in her tracks, and the large bag slid off her shoulder. She heard Sanders' footsteps behind her and waited for the words – 'He's dead.'

'Kate, I thought you'd want to . . .' Sanders' voice trailed off, conscious of Kate's ashen-faced expression. 'Kate, what's the matter? You look unwell,' he said, as he made his way over to face her.

Sluggishly, Renee looked into his eyes. 'Don't worry about me. I am just tired, that's all. I want to go home. I think my work is done. You have your man, judging by the joyous tone in your voice.'

Sanders frowned. 'Well, yes, it's him, but I thought you'd be pleased. I, um . . . don't understand.'

Renee pulled the strap of her bag up and over her shoulder. 'I *am* pleased, of course, I am. I'm just exhausted, that's all.' She tried to lift a smile.

'Shall I drive you home?'

She waved him away. 'No, I have my car. I'll be fine. Nothing a few hours of sleep won't cure.'

Awkwardly, Sanders stepped aside. 'Well, look, thank you, Kate. You've been an enormous support . . . Can we kinda, like, stay friends? Perhaps we could have a drink later this week?'

She smiled again and blushed slightly. 'Let's see, shall we? I have an awful amount of work to catch up on, but, perhaps, in a few weeks, we can maybe meet for a drink, if you'd like to?'

'Oh, yeah, sure, well, it's been . . . I was gonna say it's been wonderful that we've met, but, probably, that's not the right choice of words.' He shuffled from foot to foot. 'It's been great working with you.'

She nodded and walked on, not wanting to look back. In deep thought, Renee got into her car and threw her bag onto the back seat. Pulling the vanity mirror down, she looked at her red-rimmed eyes and sighed. It was the first time in her entire career that she was now beginning to question her own ability.

The various studies to discover the Gemini Gene had taken over her life. Now she was devasted because everything she'd studied regarding the high-functioning psychopath was a lie. Nyall had clearly committed suicide because if he *had* possessed the gene then there was no way he would have killed himself – ever.

Had she wanted to believe in the myth around the gene so much that she'd looked at the evidence with tunnel vision? Conceivably, there were psychopaths, and there were *psychopaths*. In that moment of deep reflection, she wished she'd been born later, so as science moved on at the rate the internet allowed, she would have had the chance to isolate the gene. But a darker thought clouded her mind right now and this would no doubt remain until she knew the truth.

A tapping sound on the car window made her jump and instantly pulled her away from her thoughts. It was Nelson the young officer. His boyish shiny cheeks and a twinkle in his blue eyes gave her the impression that he was an eager beaver. She lowered the window. 'Hi, er . . .'

'Brett,' he replied.

'Yes, sorry, Brett. Is everything all right?'

'Oh, yes, I just wanted to say I was blown away with your talk. In fact, it was fascinating. It was such a pleasure, Dr Renee, to be part of it all.'

Renee smiled. 'You are very welcome,' she replied, wondering why Brett looked a little apprehensive.

'Is there anything else?'

'Oh, yes, sorry, I think you may have accidentally taken all the files with you.' His eyes glanced at the large open bag that had partially released its contents across the back seat.

Renee followed his eyeline. 'Uh, sorry. I'm so tired. I must have scooped them up along with my own notes.'

'Easily done, Dr Renee. Er, if you want, I could get authorisation to have them photocopied. I just need Detective Chief Inspector Sanders to sign them off. I'm sure it'll be okay. The case will be closed in a few weeks. I mean, we have our man, after all.'

The words 'we have our man' rang in Renee's ears, bringing home to her the fact that she'd got the profile on Nyall so horribly wrong. 'Er . . . yes, that will be lovely. Thank you.' She struggled to twist around in the car to reach for the bag.

'It's okay. I'll get it for you,' said Nelson, as he opened the back door and helped himself.

Renee stared at the fat manila folder enclosing all the files she had been working on. For a second, she wanted to snatch it back, but, instead, she smiled and nodded. 'Yes, if you could get a copy done for me, it would be such a help for my own records.'

Nelson nodded, smiled, and left.

* * *

The hearse stopped outside Miriam's home. The coffin was completely covered in flowers and was dominated by a huge wreath that spelled out DAD on one side and SON on the other.

Miriam was inconsolable and continually cried into her handkerchief.

Lillian stood by Harley and Hudson, unsure how they would react. They had been solemn that morning as they'd got dressed, barely touching their Rice Krispies.

Days before, she'd decided she would have to go to Luke's funeral, even though she might receive a frosty reception. The Mason family wouldn't be human, she reasoned, if they didn't treat her as the culprit.

So, sick with anticipation and almost shaking to pieces, it had been a huge surprise when Miriam and Archi hugged her, followed by Luke's two brothers.

The whole congregation were beside themselves with grief. The last few months had been nothing but a complete shock coupled with utter disbelief. First Scarlett's funeral, and now, only a week later, Luke's.

Geoff and Dean were so quiet, both distant and almost unrecognisable in their sorrow that even a comforting arm around their shoulders wouldn't bring about a smile.

A complete array of emotions descended on the Mason family. Each member was too ashamed to admit how they felt, except to express an obvious sadness for the loss of Scarlett and Luke. Yet guilt and shame pervaded and would do so for a long time.

Overwhelmed by his conscience, Geoff found it so hard to look the twins in the eyes. Dionne had led them all to believe that the youngsters were a little screwy, but what she'd failed to tell them was they had autism, high-functioning autism, in fact, which accounted for their behaviour.

With his head hung in shame, Geoff watched as the coffin was lowered into the ground. In his mind, he was begging Luke to forgive him for sleeping with his wife, for the lies, and, most of all, for treating his children as if they were dangerous psychotic freaks of nature.

But Luke couldn't answer back: he was lying in that cold wooden box six feet down in the ground.

Under normal circumstances, Luke would have been buried with his wife.

But in a final attempt to get her own back, Lillian had decided Dionne should be cremated. Her ashes had been left with the funeral director, ready for collection. Lillian, however, had no intention of scattering them somewhere holy or beautiful. As far as she was concerned, they could stay there in the mortuary – quite fitting, considering her daughter had spent many hours with the monster. Her aim now was to make sure the twins had a healthy and happy home. Geoff and Dean, who part-owned Luke's house, had given Lillian the keys, since she was now their legal guardian. Miriam was on hand to help if needed.

The funeral was a personal affair, with no reporters or cameramen; it was just a quiet gathering in a local church. The grave lay next to Miriam's father's.

The wake was held in a hall at the back of a pub in Chislehurst. It was a classy room, with a few waitresses handing out drinks and nibbles.

Miriam thanked the priest and stepped forward to join Harley and Lillian. 'So, my darling, when do you go back to school?'

Harley rolled her eyes, like a typical teenager would do. 'Next week. Boring.'

Miriam chuckled. 'Boring, eh? Well, you, my girl, get stuck into your studies and make ya dad proud.'

'Yes, I definitely will,' she replied, with a fully-fledged smile.

'So, what do you want to study eventually, Harley? Your dad always said you liked puzzles and art.'

'Yes, I do love art, and I also love anatomy.'

Miriam slowly inclined her head. '*Anatomy?*' she said, dragging out the word. Her eyes clouded over. 'Er, whatever for . . . ?'

'Because, Nan, I want to be a coroner when I'm old enough.'

Relieved at hearing a sensible response, Miriam was able to relax her shoulders. 'Oh, Christ, I thought you were gonna say an undertaker, for a moment.'

Harley laughed. 'Undertaker? No, Nan, I'm far too intelligent to do that job.'

Miriam raised her eyebrows and laughed. 'Yes, I guess you are. You're a confident little madam.'

Lillian chuckled. 'Oh yeah, a right one, she is. Always putting me to rights.'

'You'd better not be taking bleedin' liberties with Nanny Lil's good nature, my girl.'

Harley rolled her eyes. 'No, Nan, I just help her to get organised, that's all. I do the shopping online for her, so she doesn't have to carry any heavy bags.'

Miriam laughed. 'And I bet you add a few goodies for yourself.'

'Well, only organic food. I'm trying to get Nanny Lil to stop eating processed stuff.'

With a mocking look, Miriam said, 'I think she did fine before all this gluten-free and dairy-free bollocks came out. Jesus, I remember when we just had meat and two veg. Life was simple back then. We didn't have any do-gooders telling us what we should eat.'

Harley once more rolled her eyes. 'Nan, we have come a long way since the war.'

'Ya cheeky mare,' said Miriam, pinching Harley's cheeks. 'So, where's Hudson?'

Miriam turned around to look for her grandson and was pleased to see him talking with Davey and Nicki. It had been a long time coming, but at least her other grandsons now knew the facts about Hudson, and as a family, they'd made an effort to bring him into their fold. It was such a relief because the most important thing was family as far as she was concerned.

She turned back to face Harley. 'Babe, do us a favour, will ya? Go and get me another glass of brandy. I seem to have spilt mine.'

Harley looked at her grandmother's empty glass and smiled conspiratorially. 'Yeah, right, Nan. Okay, I'll go and get one.'

As soon as she was out of earshot, Miriam leaned into Lillian. 'How are they, really?'

Lillian sighed heavily. 'They're comfortable being back in their own home. I'm still getting used to it meself. You know me, Mir. I ain't never lived in such a posh place. It's taken a while to work out how to use the washing machine, and, bloody 'ell, the dishwasher. Cor, what a treat that is. But I think they'll be okay.'

'It'll take time, no doubt.'

'The only time they kicked off was when I said they didn't need to go to the clinic. Well . . . 'cos of that poor man, Dr Reeves . . . Anyway, I let them decide, and they wanted to go back. Somehow, they get a lot of comfort from the place. Familiarity, I suppose. That Dr Reeves taught them a lot. I mean, he was a big part of their life. They still have Dr Renee. She seems to be doing a lot of good, ya know, helping them with grief and stuff.'

Miriam patted Lillian's arm. 'And you, gal, you're working wonders with them. I mean, I never saw Harley smile, not ever, but she does now.'

Lillian looked down, embarrassed. 'I'll always do me best for 'em.'

'And you are, love. Thank Gawd for you, eh?'

*　　*　　*

One year on

Katherine Renee smiled as she watched Harley and Hudson walk along the corridor to the main door. Harley was growing into a beautiful young lady and Hudson now walked with his head up, instead of always staring at the floor. She smiled because Harley still mothered her brother. It was only on the twins' last visit she had seen Harley straightening her brother's scarf before they ventured out into the cold evening air.

As soon as they were out of sight, she returned to her office and began working on her new report. The Gemini Gene study had been stopped because it hadn't reached its primary end point so the funding was denied. Her new venture was under the guise of understanding high-functioning autistic subjects. Hudson and Harley were perfect, and she had helped them advance in only twelve months. They were learning to integrate so much more, and each child had made individual progress in different ways.

Hudson had stopped spinning his pen. But he was still reticent and remained reserved and studious, taking a particular interest in computer programming.

Harley had excelled so much with her art that the sculpture of her mother was presented to the Royal College of Art. It was simply called *Rage* and stood in their foyer to be admired by the students. Yet she was creating a series of incredibly beautiful anatomical drawings, the likes of which had never been seen before. UCL Medical School were already interested in her, if and when she secured the right grades – which looked to be just a formality – and, of course, art college was another option, should she choose to go down a different career path. She had managed to portray a gift of using both sides of her brain in very reasonable equal measure: the creative and the logical.

Just as she wrote the words 'Subject 134 aged thirteen', she stopped. An uneasy feeling crept through her. Then her eyes widened and the hairs on the back of her neck spiked. A strong smell of embalming fluid seemed to pervade the air. Trembling, she got to her feet and stared at the door. With her heart beating furiously, she prayed she was just being paranoid, but the doorknob was being twisted slowly. She held her breath – he was here.

As the door opened, her mind went blank. There was nowhere to run. Petrified, she stood glued to the spot until he was finally in the room. He was bigger than his photo, darker than she'd imagined, and even more terrifying in the flesh.

'Cordelia!'

Renee frowned, but that name – it meant something.

'So you're Katherine Renee now, are you?'

So transfixed by his emotionless grotesque face and his deep hypnotic voice, she didn't answer.

'You know who I am, Cordelia, don't you? You have the photo album and my life's work.'

After swallowing hard, she found her voice. 'Yes, you are Nyall Seymour.'

He stepped closer and unexpectedly grinned. 'Cordelia, Cordelia, Cordelia, how does your garden grow? With silver bells and cockle shells and pretty maids all in a row.'

Like a sharp prod with a hot needle, she almost jumped out of her skin. But it wasn't a needle: it was the missing part of her life that suddenly came to the fore. She ran her finger along the deep scar just inside her hairline. It was shocking to imagine, so hard to believe. The photographs of the children being operated on while they were awake. One of them had been her. No wonder she couldn't recall any of it. A child of that young age would want to bury those memories forever.

'Yes, yes, Cordelia, my dear, sweet little sister. Oh, you look so shocked.'

His voice was so calm and slow. It was then that the past came flooding back, like switching on the TV to find an old movie that she'd long forgotten about. The old house, their father, the cruel operations, and then nothing. She realised at that moment that she had been suffering from psychogenic amnesia. From the age of eight, she had clear memories of the convent, the nuns, and the children's home, but anything before that was blank. Yet as an adult, when she'd tried to find information about her past, there were no records – nothing to explain where she had come from. She twisted her head to the side, trying to piece it all together. Her father, the scientist. No wonder she was so obsessed with the subject herself and the Gemini Gene – the name that *she* thought she had given to the idea of such a gene. It all made sense now because she'd been confused. The name had obviously originated from her father's research. Yet he hadn't called it a gene, he'd called it a species – The Gemini Species Study.

Initially, when she'd seen the name in Nyall's notes, she naturally assumed he'd taken them from her previously published papers. She now realised that he hadn't. He, like her, had found the name from their father's work. It must have been embedded in their brains.

Another rush of memories made her gasp. There were *three* brothers. One of them, William, died. What happened to Simon? She remembered him. Of course, Nyall hadn't committed suicide. She had been right about that all along; he would never do that. So the body the police found must have been Simon. He looked so much like Nyall, with his bulbous head.

'What do you want from me?'

He stared with dead eyes. 'My life's work, which the detective took from my home and which ended up in your hands, and the files that Reeves must have passed on to you with the blood results of my offspring in them.'

'There is no Gemini Gene, Nyall. It doesn't exist!'

'Dear Cordelia, that's why you were sent to a convent, because you were stupid, not one of us, and you were surplus to requirements. Our father was right when he saw that you were not of sufficiently high intelligence. So you cannot tell me that there is no such thing, don't you see, because your knowledge is inferior to mine.'

'No, Nyall. You've worked with the dead, not the living. You may be a psychopath, and, yes, you are very smart. But your brain is flawed.'

Stepping closer, Nyall glared with a look that could kill. *'Flawed?'*

'Yes, Nyall, flawed. But you can have your files back. I have no need for them. My Gemini Gene study is over. Harley and Hudson are in a new study for the autistic geniuses.'

She shuddered when he raised his brow and smirked.

'I'll get your files,' she said, as she stepped away from the desk and walked across to the filing cabinet. She listened to hear if he was behind her. Unlocking the second drawer, she slid her hand down into the suspended file and felt the cold and heavy object. Gripping the weapon in her hands, she looked back at her brother. 'I said you were flawed because, Nyall, not only are you a psychopath, but you are a narcissist. And narcissists can easily be blindsided because they really believe, like you do, that they are superior in every way to everyone else.'

'You are wrong. My children have my genes. They have the Gemini Gene and the traits. I know, Cordelia, because I have been studying Dionne, Luke, and the twins for years. But the twins are something special. They have what our father would have been so proud of. They are proof of his and my life's work. You never had it, and you will never stand in my way.'

Still holding the gun, she watched him take slow and deliberate strides towards her and then pull a long thin metal object from his black overcoat. In that moment, any hesitation she had of killing the monster disappeared. He didn't even see it coming. She ripped her hand from the cabinet, aimed the gun, and fired.

He fell back against the wall, but, unexpectedly, he pushed himself forward, gripping the thin rod.

Renee darted out of his way, and fired the gun again, shooting him in the chest.

He collapsed with a heavy thud as his head hit the desk on his way down.

Holding her breath, she checked for any signs of life. He was dead. She stared for a while. Everything seemed like a dream, or was it a nightmare? She knew in her heart of hearts that he'd faked his death to fool the police, and she'd also guessed that one day he would come for his papers – his life's work. The gun was just a precaution, and, right now, she was glad she'd had the forethought to obtain one.

She had no idea how long she'd been standing with the weapon in her hand. Time had just stood still, as memories of Nyall, her family, and her earlier life came flooding back to her.

Eventually, she picked up the phone and dialled Sanders' mobile. It rang twice before he answered it. She could hear voices, police sirens, and then his voice.

'Hello, is that you, Kate?'

'Yes, Lewis. I need you to come over to my office.'

'Sorry? Say that again.'

Renee could hear the sounds in the background of what could be a helicopter. 'I said, can you come to my office at the clinic?'

'Can it wait until tomorrow? Only, we've just found a young girl, Alice Montgomery-Blythe, in the woods with her throat cut. We're still searching for the killer now. Poor kid, she was still in her school uniform. Sorry, Kate, but I can't hear you very well over the sound of the drones.'

Renee ended the call and looked once more at Nyall's dead body and recalled that smirk on his face. A clammy feeling swept over her. Her eyes shot back to the filing cabinet, and she hurried to dig out some old drawings that Guy had kept. She removed Harley's file and the photo of the statue fell out, which momentarily distracted her. As she bent down to pick it up, she felt cold as if a dark thought had wormed its way through her brain. The sculpture depicted Dionne as being dehorned. It was Harley's way of making a statement that she was the powerful Devil Woman, and not her mother.

But that wasn't what she was looking for. She remembered being disturbed by one very detailed drawing in particular. It was one created by Harley, aged five, which had ended up in Guy's hands. Hurriedly, she delved through all the paperwork until she came to what she needed. She found it. The colourful sketch of Alice – with her throat cut.

How dangerously intelligent was this child? Renee gasped as more pieces fell into place. Scarlett's murder was never really looked at beyond the assumption that Dionne had been the killer. But it looked like they'd all been wrong. Scarlett's killer was Harley and she'd only been eleven years old.

'Oh my God, Harley. You are a master of your craft.' She glanced at Nyall's expressionless face. 'Christ! So you were right, big brother. The Gemini Gene does exist, after all.'

Before Renee could take a deep breath to calm herself, a voice from the doorway startled her. She glanced up to find it was Harley's, with a cold and demonic smile on her face.

'Yes, Dr Renee, the Gemini Gene does exist. And I believe you have a file that now belongs to me.'

Printed in Great Britain
by Amazon

42343580R00302